A Jacana book

A IS FOR ANCESTORS

A selection of works from
the Caine Prize
for African Writing

First published in 2004 by Jacana
5 St Peter Road
Bellevue
2198
South Africa

ISBN 1-770090-27-4

Cover design by Disturbance Design

Printed by Formeset Printers

See a complete list of Jacana titles at www.jacana.co.za

Table of Contents

Introduction 6

Caine Prize Stories 2003 Winner and Finalists

African Writers' Workshop Stories 2003

Introduction

"It Gives Me the Right to Write!"

On his return to Nairobi from winning the Caine Prize in 2002,
Binyavanga Wainaina promptly founded a literary magazine to help other
up-and-coming Kenyan writers to find an audience. *Kwani?* began as an
Internet magazine but within a year had been published in book form
(by Kwani Trust, Nairobi, 2003, with a grant from the Ford Foundation).
One of *Kwani?*'s first Internet stories was Yvonne Adhiambo Owuor's
Weight of Whispers, which Binyavanga submitted for the 2003 Caine
Prize. It won. Asked what winning the Prize meant for her, Yvonne,
proving herself a natural master of the unaffected soundbite, said, "It
gives me the right to write!"

The other shortlisted candidates in 2003 were Emmanuel Dongala
from Congo, George Makana Clarke from Zimbabwe and Rachelle
Greeff and Ken Barris from South Africa. Dongala and Clarke's stories
had been published in *Transition* (Issues 86 & 84, Duke University Press,
USA, 2000), and Greeff and Barris in the 2002 edition of *Modern South
African Short Stories* (ed. Stephen Gray, publ. Ad Donker, Cape Town).
Their stories and Yvonne's are gathered here alongside the product from
this year's Caine Prize Workshop for African Writers.

With the exception of Emmanuel Dongala, who could not escape his
teaching commitments, the 2003 shortlisted writers participated in the
2004 workshop, which also featured three other Kenyans – of whom two
have stories in *Kwani?* and the other is mentioned in its introduction –
plus four young South Africans and a young Ugandan. As in 2003, the
workshop was held at the Monkey Valley Resort, Noordhoek, near Cape
Town, with grant money from the Ford Foundation. Under the tutelage
– again – of Veronique Tadjo and Peter Merrington, each participant
produced in ten days a short story for publication in this volume. They
can thus be compared with the 2003 workshop product (see *Discovering
Home*, Jacana, Johannesburg, 2003).

Once again, bringing writers of different ages and from different
African countries to work together, writing and discussing their work
with one another in dedicated time and space, proved tremendously
valuable, both as a focus for concentrated effort away from distraction –

"For ten days you write and eat and sleep" – and as a collegiate forum for mutual encouragement and criticism – "I so rarely have the chance to discuss my work with other writers – and never with writers from elsewhere in Africa." Perhaps the most telling comments of all were about the breaking of isolation, "I'll always know I'm not alone," said Stanley Gazemba, who works as a gardener in Nairobi – echoed by Carol Fofo, a civil servant in Pretoria, "Now I know there are other people writing out there, young people."

Last year's workshop stories were all entered for this year's Caine Prize (as this year's will be for next year's). By the time this volume appears we shall know whether any of last year's made it to the shortlist. The Prize has generated workshops. The workshops generate entries. A winner produced *Kwani?*. *Kwani?* produced a winner. The Caine Prize multiplier gives us immense satisfaction. It means the Prize is truly encouraging the process of writing in Africa, not simply rewarding the product.

We hope it gives satisfaction to our sponsors, too. The Ernest Oppenheimer Memorial Fund and the Gatsby Charitable Foundation have already been keeping us going for three years now. The DAL Group from the Sudan have recently added their support, and the Ford Foundation provided most of the money for the workshops. We could not have done any of it without them.

Nick Elam
Administrator

Caine Prize Stories 2003
Winner and Finalists

Weight of Whispers
(Winner)

Yvonne Adhiambo-Owuor

The collection of teeth on the man's face is a splendid brown. I
have never seen such teeth before. Refusing all instruction, my
eyes focus on dental contours and craters. Denuded of any superficial
pretence – no braces, no fillings, no toothbrush – it is a place where
small scavengers thrive.

"Evidence!" The man giggles.

A flash of green and my US$50 disappears into his pocket. His
fingers prod: shirt, coat, trousers. He finds the worked snakeskin wallet.
No money in it, just a picture of Agnethe-mama, Lune and Chi-Chi,
elegant and unsmiling, diamonds in their ears, on their necks and wrists.
The man tilts the picture this way and that, returns the picture into the
wallet. The wallet disappears into another of his pockets. The man's
teeth gleam.

"Souvenir." Afterwards, a hiccupping "Greeeheeereeehee" not unlike
a National Geographic hyaena, complete with a chorus from the pack.

"Please…it's…my mother…all I have."

His eyes become thin slits, head tilts and the veins on his right eye
pulse. His nostrils flare, an indignant goat.

A thin sweat-trail runs down my spine, the backs of my knees tingle.
I look around at the faceless others in the dank room. His hand grabs my
goatee and twists. My eyes smart. I lift up my hand to wipe them. The
man sees the gold insignia ring, glinting on my index finger.

The ring of the royal household. One of only three. The second
belonged to my father. Agnethe-mama told me that when father appeared
to her in a dream to tell her he was dead, he was still wearing it. The
third…no-one has ever spoken about.

The policeman's grin broadens. He pounces. Long fingers. A girl
would cut her hair for fingers like his. He spits on my finger, and draws
out the ring with his teeth; the ring I have worn for 18 years - from the
day I was recognised by the priests as a man and a prince. It was
supposed to have been passed on to the son I do not have. The

9

policeman twists my hand this way and that, his tongue caught between his teeth; a study of concentrated avarice.

"Evidence!"

Gargoyles are petrified life-mockers, sentries at entry points, sentinels of sorrow, spitting at fate. I will try to protest.

"It is sacred ring...Please...please." To my shame, my voice breaks.

"Evidence!"

Cheek: nerve, gall, impertinence, brashness.

Cheek: the part of my face he chose to brand.

Later on, much later on, I will wonder what makes it possible for one man to hit another for no reason other than the fact that he can. But now, I lower my head. The sum total of what resides in a very tall man who used to be a prince in a land eviscerated.

* * *

Two presidents died when a missile launched from land forced their plane down. A man of note, a prince, had said on the first day that the perpetrators must be hunted down. That evil must be purged from lives. That is all the prince had meant. It seems someone heard something else. It emerges later on, when it is too late, that an old servant took his obligation too far, in the name of his prince.

We had heard rumour of a holocaust, of a land haemorrhaging to death. Everywhere, hoarse murmurs, eyes white and wide with an arcane fear. Is it possible that brothers would machete sisters-in-law to stew-meat size chunks in front of nephews and nieces?

It was on the fifth day after the presidents had disintegrated with their plane, that I saw that the zenith of existence cannot be human.

In the seasons of my European sojourn, Brussels, Paris, Rome, Amsterdam, rarely London, a city I could accommodate a loathing for, I wondered about the unsaid: hesitant signals and interminable reminders of 'What They Did'. Like a mnemonic device, the swastika would grace pages and/or screens, at least once a week, unto perpetuity. I wondered.

I remembered a conversation in Krakow with an academician, a man with primeval eyes. A pepper-coloured, quill beard obscured the man's mouth, and seemed to speak in its place. I was suddenly in the thrall of an irrational fear that the mobile barbs would shoot off his face and stab me.

I could not escape.

10

I had agreed to offer perspectives on his seminal work, a work in progress he called, 'A Mystagogy of Human Evil'. I had asked, meaning nothing, a prelude to commentary:

"Are you a Jew?"

So silently, the top of his face fell, flowed towards his jaw, his formidable moustache-beard lank, his shoulders shaking, his eyes flooded with tears. But not a sound emerged from his throat. Unable to tolerate the tears of another man, I walked away.

Another gathering, another conversation with another man. Mellowed by the well-being engendered by a goblet of Rémy Martin, I ventured an opinion about the sacrificial predilection of being; the necessity of oblation of men by men to men.

"War is the excuse," I said. I was playing with words, true, but oddly the exchange petered into mumbles of 'Never Again'.

A year later, at a balcony party, when I asked the American Consul in Luxembourg to suggest a book which probed the slaughter of Germans during World War II. She said:

"By whom?"

Before I could answer, she had spun away, turning her back on me as if I had asked "Cain, where is your brother?"

What had been Cain's response?

To my amusement, I was, of course, never invited to another informal diplomatic gathering. Though I would eventually relinquish my European postings - in order to harness, to my advantage, European predilection for African gems - over après-diner Drambuie, now and again, I pondered over what lay beneath the unstated.

Now, my world has tilted into a realm where other loaded silences lurk. And I can sense why some things must remain buried in silence, even if they resuscitate themselves at night in dreams where blood pours out of phantom mouths. In the empire of silence, the 'turning away' act is a vain exorcism of a familiar daemon which invades the citadels we ever change, we constantly fortify. Dragging us back through old routes of anguish, it suggests: "Alas, human, your nature relishes fratricidal blood."

But to be human is to be intrinsically, totally, resolutely good. Is it not?

Nothing entertains the devil as much as this protestation.

* * *

11

Roger, the major-domo had served in our home since before my birth thirty-seven years ago. He re-appeared at our door on the evening of the fifth day after the death of the two presidents. He had disappeared on the first day of the plane deaths. The day he resurfaced, we were celebrating the third anniversary of my engagement to Lune. I had thought a pungent whiff which entered the room with his presence was merely the Gorgonzola cheese Lune had been unwrapping.

Roger says:

"*J'ai terminé. Tout a été nettoyé.*" It is done. All has been cleaned.

"What Roger?"

"The dirt." He smiles.

The bottle of Dom Pérignon Millésimé in my hand, wavers. I observe that Roger is shirtless, his hair stands in nascent, accidental dreadlocks. The bottom half of his trousers are torn, and his shoeless left foot, swollen. His fist is black and caked with what I think is tar. And in his wake, the smell of smouldering matter. Roger searches the ground, hangs his head, his mouth tremulous:

"They are coming...Sir."

Then Roger stoops. He picks up the crumbs of *petits fours* from the carpet; he is fastidious about cleanliness. The Dom Pérignon Millésimé drops from my hand, it does not break, though its precious contents soak into the carpet. Roger frowns, his mouth pursed. He also disapproves of waste.

* * *

In our party clothes and jewellery, with what we had in our wallets, and two full medium-size Chanel cases, we abandoned our life at home. We counted the money we had between us: US$3723. In the bank account, of course, there was more. There was always more. As President of the *Banque Locale*, I was one of three who held keys to the vault, so to say. Two weeks before the presidents died, I sold my Paris apartment. The money was to be used to expand our bank into Zaïre. We got the last four of the last eight seats on the last flight out of our city. We assumed then, it was only right that it be so. We landed at the Jomo Kenyatta International Airport in Nairobi, Kenya at ten p.m.

I wondered about Kenya. I knew the country as a transit lounge and a stop-over base on my way to and out of Europe. It was only after we got a three-month visitor's pass that I realised that Kenya was an

Anglophone country. Fortunately, we were in transit. Soon, we would be in Europe, among friends.

I am Boniface Louis R. Kuseremane. It has been long since anyone called me by my full name. The 'R' name cannot be spoken aloud. In the bustle and noises of the airport, I glance at Agnethe-mama, regal, greying, her diamond earrings dance, her nose is slightly raised, her forehead unlined. My mother, Agnethe, is a princess in transit. She leans lightly against Lune, who stands, one foot's heel touching the toes of the other, one arm raised and then drooping over her shoulder.

I met Lune on the funeral day of both her parents, royal diplomats who had died in an unfortunate road crash. She was then, as she is now, not of Earth. Then, she seemed to be hovering atop her parents' grave, deciding whether to join them, fly away or stay. I asked her to leave the *corps ballet* in France, where she was studying, to stay with me, forever. She agreed and I gained a sibylline fiancée.

"*Chéri, que faisons-nous maintenant?*" What do we do now? Lune asks, clinging to my mother's hand. Her other arm curved into mine. Chi-Chi, my sister, looks up at me, expecting the right answer, her hand at her favourite spot, my waist band – a childhood affectation that has lingered into her twentieth year. Chi-Chi, in thought, still sucks on her two fingers.

"*Bu-bu,*" Chi-Chi always calls me Bu-Bu. "*Bu-Bu, dans quel pays sommes-nous?*"

"Kenya," I tell her.

Chi-Chi is an instinctive contemplative. I once found her weeping and laughing, awed, as it turns out, by the wings of a monarch butterfly.

Low voiced, almost a whisper, the hint of a melody, my mother's voice. "*Bonbon, je me sens très fatiguée, où dormons-nous cette nuit?*"

Agnethe-mama was used to things falling into place before her feet touched the ground. Now she was tired. Now she wanted her bed immediately. Without thinking about it, we checked into a suite of the Nairobi Hilton. We were, after all going to be in this country for just a few days.

* * *

"Mama, such ugliness of style!" Lune's summation of Kenyan fashion, of Kenyan hotel architecture. Mama, smiles and says nothing. She twists her sapphire bracelet, the signal that she agrees.

13

"Why do I see not see the soul of these people? Bonbon...are you sleeping?" Chi-Chi asks.

"Shh," I say.

Two days later, Agnethe-mama visited the jewellery shop downstairs. Not finding anything to suit her tastes, she concluded: "Their language and manner are not as sweet and gentle as ours."

She straightens her robes, eyes wide with the innocence of an unsubtle put down.

"Mama!' I scold. The women giggle as do females who have received affirmation of their particular and unassailable advantage over other women.

* * *

A week has passed already. In the beginning of the second one, I am awakened by the feeling I had when I found my country's embassy gates here locked and blocked. The feeling of a floor shifting beneath one's feet. There is no-one in authority. The ambassador is in exile. Only a guard. Who should I speak to? A blank stare. I need to arrange our papers to go to Europe. A blank stare. A flag flutters in the courtyard. I do not recognise it. Then I do. It is my country's flag, someone installed it upside down. It flies at half-mast. An inadvertent act, I believe. Shifting sands: I am lost in this sea of English, and I suspect that at five thousand Kenya shillings I have spent too much for a thirty-kilometre taxi ride. Old friends have not returned phone calls.

The lines here are not reliable.

* * *

Lune is watching me, her long neck propped up by her hands. Her hair covers half her face. It is always a temptation to sweep it away from her eyes, a warm silk. When the tips of my fingers stroke her hair, the palms of my hand skim her face. Lune becomes still, drinking, feeling and tasting the stroking.

Soon, we will leave.

But now, I need to borrow a little money: US$5000. It will be returned to the lender, of course, after things settle down. Agnethe, being a princess, knows that time solves all problems. Nevertheless she has ordered me to dispatch a telegram to sovereigns in exile, those who

14

would be familiar with our quandary and could be depended on for empathy, cash assistance and even accommodation. The gratitude felt would extend generation unto generation.

Eight days later, Agnethe-mama sighs; a hiss through the gap of her front teeth. She asks, her French rolling off her tongue like an old scroll, "When are we leaving, Bonbon?"

A mother's ambush. I know what she really wants to know.

"Soon." I reply.

"Incidentally," she adds, folding Lune's lace scarf, "What of the response of our friends in exile?…ah! Not yet…a matter of time," she says, answering herself.

"Agnethe-mama," I should have said, "We must leave this hotel…to save money."

It is simpler to be silent.

* * *

A guard with red-rimmed eyes in a dark-blue uniform watches me counting out fifteen 1000 Kenyan shilling notes. The eyes of the president on the notes blink with every sweep of my finger. The Indian lady in a pink sari with gold trim, the paint flaking off, leans over the counter, her eyes empty. My gold bracelet has already disappeared. Two days from this moment, while standing with Celeste on Kenyatta Avenue, where many of my people stand and seek news of home, or just stand and talk the language of home or hope that soon we will return home, I discover that fifteen-thousand Kenyan shillings is insufficient compensation for a 24-carat, customised gold and sapphire bracelet. Celeste knew of another jeweller who would pay me a hundred thousand for the bracelet.

I return to confront the Indian lady, she tells me to leave before I can speak.

She dials a number and shouts, high-voiced, clear: "Police". I do not want trouble so I leave the jewellery shop, unable to speak, but not before I see her smile. Not before I hear her scold the guard with the red-rimmed eyes.

"Why you let *takataka* to come in, *nee?*"

Outside the shop, my hands are shaking. I have to remind myself to take the next step and the next step and the next step. My knees are light. I am unable to look into the eyes of those on the streets. What is

my mind doing getting around the intricacies of a foreign currency?
I have to get out with my family.

Soon.

The newspaper on the streets, a vendor flywhisks dust fragments
away. A small headline reads: 'Refugees: Registration commences at the
UNHCR'.

The Kuseremanes are not refugees. They are visitors, tourists, people
in transit, universal citizens with an affinity…well…to Europe.

"Kuseremane, Kuseremane, Kuseremane"…unbeknown to me, one
whisper had started gathering other whispers around it.

* * *

The Netherlands, Belgium, the French, the British are processing
visa applications. They have been processing them for three, four,
five…nine days. At least they smile with their teeth as they process the
visa applications. They process them until I see that they will be
processed unto eternity, if only Agnethe, Chi-Chi, Lune and I could wait
that long. There are other countries in the world.

Chi-Chi's ramblings yield an array of useless trivia:

"In Nairobi, a woman can be called *Auntí* or *chilé*, a president called
Moi, pronounced *Moyi*, a national anthem that is a prayer and twenty
shillings is a *pao*."

"But Bu-Bu…So many faces…

"So many spirits gather here…"

We must leave soon.

* * *

The American embassy visa section woman has purple hair. Her
voice evokes the grumbling of a he-toad which once lived in the marsh
behind our family house in the country. One night, in the middle of its
anthem, I had said: "*Ça suffit!*" Enough!

Roger led the gardeners in the hunt which choked the croak out of
the toad. At dawn, Roger brought the severed head to me, encased in an
old, cigar case which he had wiped clean.

I cannot believe what this purple hair woman has asked of me.

"What?"

"Bank details…bank statement … how much money."

16

My eyes blink, lashes entangle. Could it be possible another human being can simply ask over the counter, casually and with certainty of response, for intimate details of another person's life?

I look around the room. Is it to someone else she addresses this question?

"And title deed. Proof of domicile in country of origin...And letter from employer."

Has she not looked at my passport in her hands?

"I'm not Kenyan."

She folds her papers, bangs them on the table and frowns as if I have wasted her time. She tosses my passport out of her little window into my hands that are outstretched, a supplication on an altar of disbelief.

"All applications made at source country...next!"

"Madame...my country...is..."

"Next!"

Woven into the seams of my exit are the faces in the line winding from the woman's desk, into the street. Children, women and men, faces lined with...hope? I must look at that woman again, that purveyor of hope. So I turn. I see a stately man, his beard grey. His face as dark as mine. He stoops over the desk – a posture of abnegation. So that is what I looked like to the people in the line. I want to shout to the woman: I am Boniface Kuseremane, a prince, a diplomat.

I stumble because it is here, in this embassy, that the fire-streaking spectre of the guns which brought down two presidents find their mark in my soul. Like the eminent-looking man in a pin-striped suit, I am now a beggar.

* * *

We have US$520 left. My head hurts. When night falls, my mind rolls and rings. I cannot sleep.

The pharmacist is appealing in her way, but wears an unfortunate weave that sits on her head like a mature thorn bush. Eeeh! The women of this land! I frown. The frown makes the girl jump when she sees me. She covers her mouth with both her hands and gasps. I smile. She recovers: "*Sema!*"

"Yes, sank you. I not sleep for sree nights and I feel..."

I plane my hands, rocking them against my head. She says nothing, turns around, counts out ten Piritons and seals the envelope: "Three,

17

twice a day, 200 shillings."

These Kenyans and their shillings!

It is possible that tonight I will sleep. The thought makes me laugh. A thin woman wearing a red and black choker glances up at me, half-smiling. I smile back.

I cannot sleep. I have taken five of the white pills. Lune, beside me in the large bed, is also awake.

"*Qu'est-ce que c'est?*" What is it?

"*Rien.*" Nothing.

Silence. Her voice, tiny. "I am afraid."

I turn away from her, to my side. I raise my feet, curling them beneath my body. I too am afraid. In the morning, the white Hilton pillow beneath my head is wet with tears. They cannot be mine.

The sun in Nairobi in May is brutal in its rising. A rude glory. My heart longs to be eased into life with the clarion call of an African rooster. Our gentle sunrises, rolling hills. Two months have passed. A month ago, we left the hotel. I am ashamed to say we did not pay our bill. All we had with us was transferred into and carried out in laundry bags. We left the hotel at intervals of three hours. We also packed the hotel towels and sheets. It was Lune's idea. We had not brought our own. We left our suitcases behind. They are good for at least US$1500. Agnethe-mama is sure the hotel will understand.

We moved into a single-roomed place with an outside toilet in River Road. I have told Agnethe-mama, Lune and Chi-Chi not to leave the rooms unless I am with them. Especially Chi-Chi.

"Bu-Bu, when are we leaving?"

Soon Agnethe-mama. Soon Lune. Soon Chi-Chi.

Chi-Chi has learned to say "*Tafadhali, naomba maji.*" She asks for water this way; there are shortages.

We must leave soon.

Every afternoon, a sudden wind runs up this street, lifting dust, and garbage and plastic bags and whispers.

Kuseremane, Kuseremane, Kuseremane.

I turn to see if anyone else hears my name.

Sometimes, I leave the room to walk the streets, for the sake of having a destination. I walk, therefore I am. I walk therefore I cannot see six expectant eyes waiting for me to pull out an aeroplane from my pocket.

Ah! But tonight! Tonight, Club Balafon. I am meeting a compatriot

18

and friend, René Katilibana. We met as I stood on the edge of Kenyatta Avenue, reading a newspaper I had rented from the vendor for five Kenyan shillings. Four years ago, René needed help with a sugar deal. I facilitated a meeting which proved lucrative for him. René made a million francs. He offered me fifty thousand in gratitude. I declined. I had enjoyed humouring a friend. I am wearing the Hugo Boss mauves and the Hervé handkerchief. I am hopeful, a good feeling to invoke.

"*Où vas-tu, chéri ?*" Where are you going? A ubiquitous question I live with.

I stretch out my arms, Lune flies into them as she always does. She wraps her arms around me. Her arms barely span my waist.

I tell her: "I am hopeful today. Very hopeful."

I still have not heard from the friends I have called. Every night, their silence whispers something my ears cannot take hold of. Deceptive murmurings. This country of leering masses – all eyes, hands and mouths, grasping and feeding off graciousness – invokes paranoia.

My friends will call as soon as they are able to. They will.

I realise this must be one of those places I have heard about; where international phone calls are intercepted and deals struck before the intended, initial recipient is reached.

* * *

A contact, Félicien, who always knows even what he does not know, tells me that a list of *génocidaires* has been compiled and it is possible a name has been included. Kuseremane. Spelled out by a demure man, an aide he had said he was.

Soon we will be gone. To Europe, where the wind's weight of whispers do not matter; where wind, and all its suggestions have been obliterated.

Even as she stays in the room, Chi-Chi leaves us more often than ever, a forefinger in her mouth. She has no filters. I worry that the soul of this place is soaking into her.

The city clock clicks above my head into the two a.m. position. Rain has seeped into my bones and become ice. My knees burn. The rainwater squelches in my feet. My Hugo Boss suit is ruined now, but I squeeze the water from the edges.

Club Balafon was a microcosm of home and the *Zaïroise* band was nostalgic and superior. The band slipped into a song called '*Chez*

19

Mama'. The hearth of home. The women were beautiful and our laughter loud. It was good to taste good French cognac served in proper glasses. We lamented the fact that Kenyans are on the whole, so unchic.

And then René asked me where I was and what I was doing. I told him I needed his help, a loan. US$5000, to be returned when things settle down back home. He listened and nodded and ordered for me a Kenyan beer named after an elephant. He turned to speak to Pierre who introduced him to Jean-Luc. I touched his shoulder to remind him of my request. He said in French: I will call you. He forgot to introduce me to Pierre and Jean-Luc. Two hours later, he said, in front of Pierre, Jean-Luc and Michel: "Refresh my memory, who are you?"

My heart threatens to pound a way out of my chest. Then the band dredges up an old anthem of anguish, which, once upon a time, had encapsulated all our desires. *Ingénues Francophones* in Paris, giddy with hope. This unexpected evocation of fragile, fleeting, longings, drives me into an abyss of remembering.

L'indépendance, ils l'ont obtenue / La table ronde, ils l'ont gagnée...
Indépendance Cha-cha, the voice of Joseph Kabasellé.

Then, we were, vicariously, members of Kabasellé's '*Les Grand Kalle*'. All of us, for we were bursting with dreams encapsulated in a song.

Now, at Balafon, the exiles were silent, to accommodate the ghosts of saints:

Bolikango...Kasavubu...Lumumba...Kalondji...Tshombe...

I remember heady days in Paris – hair parted, like the statement we had become, horn-rimmed glasses worn solely for aesthetic purposes, dark-suited, black-tied, dark-skinned radicals moving in a cloud of enigmatic French colognes. In our minds and footsteps, always the slow, slow, quick, quick slow, mambo to rumba, of Kabasellé's '*Indépendance Cha-cha*'.

L'indépendance, ils l'ont obtenu...
La table ronde, ils l'ont gagnée...

I dance at Club Balafon, my arms around a short girl who wears yellow braids. She is from Kenya and is of the opinion that 'Centro African' men are soooo good. And then the music stops. There can be no other footnote, so the band packs their musical tools, as quietly as we leave the small dance floor.

When I looked, René, Pierre, Jean-Luc, Michel and Emanuel were gone. Perhaps this was not their song.

"Which way did they go?" I ask the guard in black with red stripes on his shoulder. He shrugs. He says they entered into a blue Mercedes. Their driver had been waiting for them. He thinks they went to the Carnivore. It is raining as I walk back to River Road. Three fledglings are waiting for me, trusting that I shall return with regurgitated good news.

I am Boniface Kuseremane. Refresh my memory, who are you? There are places within, where a sigh can hide. It is cold and hard and smells of fear. In my throat something cries, "hrgghghg". I cannot breathe. And then I can. So I hum:

"Mhhhh…" *L'indépendance, ils l'ont obtenue…*

It is odd, the sounds that make a grown man weep.

* * *

I sleep and dream of whispers. They have crossed the borders and arrived in Nairobi. Like many passing snakes. Kuseremane. Kuseremane. Kuseremane. Kuseremane. Kuseremane.

But we left on the fifth day!

Now whenever I approach Kenyatta Avenue, they, my people, disperse. Or disappear into shops. Or avert their eyes. If I open a conversation, there is always a meeting that one is late for. Once on the street a woman started wailing like an old and tired train when she saw me. Her fingers extended, like the tip of a sure spear, finding its mark.

Kuseremane. Kuseremane. Kuseremane. Kuseremane. Kuseremane.

The whispers have found a human voice.

I can tell neither Agnethe-mama nor Chi-Chi nor Lune. I tell them to stay where they are; that the city is not safe.

Agnethe wants to know if the brother-monarchs-in-exile have sent their reply.

"Soon." I say.

One morning, in which the sun shone pink, I found that a certain sorrow had become a tenant of my body and weighed it down on the small blue safari bed, at the end of which my feet hang. The sun has come into the room, but it hovers above my body and cannot pierce the shadow covering my life. A loud knock on the door, so loud the door shakes. I do not move so Lune glides to the door.

"*Reo ni Reo, ni siku ya maripo*. Sixi hundred ant sevente shirrings."

21

Kenyans and their shillings! The proprietor scratches his distended belly. His fly is undone and the net briefs he wears peek through. I want to smile.

Lune floats to my side, looks down at me. I shut my eyes. From the door a strangely gentle, "I donti af all dey."

I open my eyes. Lune slips her hand into my coat pocket. How did she know where to look? She gives him the money, smiling as only she can. The proprietor thaws. He counts shillings. Then he smiles, a beatific grin.

I have shut my eyes again.

And then a hand – large, soft, warm – strokes my face, my forehead. Silence, except for the buzzing of a blue fly. Agnethe-Mama is humming '*Sur le Pont d'Avignon*'. I used to fall asleep wondering how it was possible to dance on the Avignon bridge. Soon, we will know. When we leave.

I slept so deeply that when I woke up I thought I was at home in my bed, and for a full minute I wondered why Roger had not come in with fresh orange juice, eggs and bacon, croissants and coffee. I wondered why mama was staring down at me, hands folded. Lune looks as if she has been crying. Her eyes are red-rimmed. She has become thin, the bones of her neck jut out. Her fingers are no longer manicured. There! Chi-Chi. Her face has disappeared into her eyes which are large and black and deep. I look back at Agnethe-mama and see then that her entire hair front is grey. When did this happen?

"We must register. As refugees. Tell UNHCR we are here."

Now I remember that we are in Kenya; we are leaving Kenya soon. Am I a refugee?

"You slept the sleep of the dead, *mon fils*." Agnethe said, lowering the veil from her head. If only she knew how prophetic her words were. Being a princess once married to her prince, she would have been more circumspect. I have woken up to find the world has shifted, moved, aged and I with it. Today I will try to obtain work. There cannot be too many here who have a PhD in Diplomacy or a Masters in Geophysics. The immigration offices will advise me. In four days we will have been here three and a half months.

The sun is gentle and warm. The rain has washed the ground. Kenyans are rushing in all directions. A street child accosts me. I frown. He runs away and pounces on an Indian lady. Everybody avoids the child and the lady, rushing to secret fates. Destiny. Who should I meet at the immigration office but Yves Fontaine, a former college mate. We had been at the Sorbonne together. He was studying art but dropped out in the third year. We were drawn together by one of life's ironies. He was so white, so short, and so high voiced. I was so tall, so black and deep voiced. We became acquainted rather than friendly because it was a popular event to have the two of us pose for photographs together. It did not bother me. It did not bother him.

"Yves!"

"Boni-papa." His name for me. Boni-papa. We kiss each other three times on either cheek.

"It is inevitable we meet again?"

"It is inevitable."

"What are you doing here?"

"A visa renewal…I am chief technician for the dam in the valley."

"Ah, you did engineering?"

Yves shrugs, "Pfff. *Non.* It is not necessary here."

The sound of a stamp hitting the desk unnecessarily hard. A voice.

"Whyves Fontana."

Yves changes his posture, his nose rises, he whose nose was always in the ground avoiding eyes so he would not be carried off by campus clowns.

"*Ouais?*" It is an arrogant *oui*. The type of *oui* Yves would never have tried at the Sorbonne.

"Your resident visa."

Yves grabs his passport, swivels on his feet and exits. But first he winks at me.

"Next!" The voice shouts. I am next.

* * *

From outside the window of a travel agency, on Kaunda Street, a poster proclaims:

'Welcome to your own private wilderness'.

At the bottom of the poster: 'Nature close at hand: Walking safaris available'. The picture in the foreground is that of a horse, a mountain and a tall, slender man wrapped in a red blanket, beads in his ears. It is all set within a watermark of the map of Kenya. I keep walking.

Beneath the steeple where the midday Angelus bells clang, I sit and watch the lunchtime prayer crowds dribble into the Minor Basilica. The

23

crowds shimmer and weave behind my eyelids.

The immigration officer demanded papers. He would not listen to me. I told him about my PhD and he laughed out loud. He said:

"*Ati PhD. PhD gani? Wewe refugee, bwana!*"

He whispers that he is compelled by Section 3(f) of the immigration charter to report my illegal presence. He cracks his knuckles. 'Creak'. 'Crack.' He smiles quickly. Fortunately, all things are possible. The cost of silence is US$500. I have 3000 shillings.

He took it all. But he returned 50 shillings for 'bus fare'.

"Eh, your family…where are they?"

"Gone." I say.

"*Si* I'll see you next week? Bring all your documents…eh. Write your address here." A black book. Under 'name' I write René Katilibana. Address, Club Balafon. He watches every stroke of my pen.

A resumption of knuckle cracking. His eyes deaden into a slant.

"To not return…is to ask for the police to find you." He turns his head away. He calls:

"Next!"

I have used 5 shillings to buy small, round, green sweets from a mute street vendor. Good green sweets which calm hunger grumbles. A few more days and we will be leaving. I have resolved not to bother compiling a curriculum vitae.

I join the flow into the church, sitting at the back. Rhythm of prayer, intonation of priests; I sleep sitting before the altar of a God whose name I do not know.

Chi-Chi says:

"They laugh at themselves…

"They are shy…they hide in noise…but they are shy."

"Who?"

"Kenya people."

We must leave soon.

* * *

We woke up early, Agnethe, Chi-Chi, Lune and I, and walked to Westlands, forty-five minutes' walk away from our room, just before River Road. We reached the gates of the UNHCR bureau at ten a.m. We were much too late because the lists of those who would be allowed entry that day had been compiled. The rest of us would have to return the next

24

day. We did, at seven a.m. We were still too late because the lists of those who would be allowed entry had already been compiled. We returned at four a.m. But at two p.m. we discovered we were too late because the lists of those who would be allowed in had already been compiled. I decided to ask the guard at the gate, with long, black hair and an earring, a genuine sapphire.

"How can list be compiled? We are here for sree days."

"New arrivals?" he asks.

"Yes."

"A facilitation fee is needed to help those who are compiling the list."

"Facilitation fee?"

"Yes. That's all."

"And what is zis facilitation fee?"

"US$200 per person."

"And if one…he does not have US$200?"

"Then unfortunately, the list is full."

"But the UN…Sir?"

He raises his brow.

I told Lune and Chi-Chi. They told Agnethe. Agnethe covered her face and wailed. It is fortunate she wailed when a television crew arrived. The guard saw the television crew and realised that the list was not full. Five UN staffers wearing large blue badges appeared from behind the gate and arranged us into orderly lines, shouting commands here and commands there. Three desks materialised at the head of the queue as did three people who transferred our names and addresses into a large black book. After stamping our wrists we were sent to another table to collect our Refugee Registration Numbers. Chi-Chi returned briefly from her spirit realm to say:

"Is it not magical how so full a list becomes so empty in so short a time?"

* * *

"*Toa Kitambulisho!*" I know this to be a request for identification. A policeman, one of three, grunted to me. I shivered. I was standing outside the hotel building watching street vendors fight over plastic casings left behind by an inebriated hawker. I was smoking my fifth Sportsman cigarette in two hours.

"*Sina.*" I don't have an identity card.

25

"*Aya! Toa kitu kidogo.*" I did not understand the code. Something small, what could it be? A cigarette. One each. It was a chilly evening. The cigarettes were slapped out of my hand. I placed my hand up and the second policeman said:

"Resisting arrest."

A fourth one appeared and the second policeman said:

"Illegal alien…resisting arrest."

They twisted my arm behind my back and holding me by my waistband, the trouser crotch cutting into me, I was frog-marched across town. Some people on the street laughed loudly, pointing at the tall man with his trouser lines stuck between the cracks of his bottom.

"Please…please chief…I'll walk quietly." My hand is raised, palm up. "Please."

Someone, the third one I think, swipes my head with a club. In a sibilant growl: "Attempted escape."

A litany of crimes.

"What's your name?"

"I…I…" Silence. Again, I try. "I…I…I…"

"Aaaaaaa…aaaaii…eee." It amuses them.

What is my name? I frown. What is my name?

I was once drinking a good espresso in a café in Breda, in the Netherlands, with three European business contacts. Gem dealers. We were sipping coffee at the end of a well-concluded deal. A squat African man wearing spectacles danced into the café. He wore a black suit, around his neck a grey scarf, in his hand a colourful and large bag, like a carpet bag. Outside it was cold. So easy to recall the feeling of well-being a hot espresso evokes in a small café, where the light is muted and the music a gentle jazz, and there is a knowing that outside it is cold and grey and windy.

The squat African man grinned like an ingratiating hound, twisting and distorting his face, raising his lips, and from his throat a thin, high sound would emerge:

"Heee heee heee, heh heh heh."

Most of the café turned back to their coffees and conversations. One man in a group of three put out his foot. The squat African man stumbled, grabbed his back to him. Rearranged himself and said to the man: "Heee heee heee, heh heh heh."

He flapped his arm up and down. I wondered why, and then it dawned on me. He was simulating a monkey. He flapped his way to

26

where I was, my acquaintances and I.

Sweat trickled down my spine. I think it was the heat in the café.

"What is your country of origin?" I ask him. Actually, I snarl the question at him, and I am surprised by the rage in my voice.

He mumbles, his face staring at the floor. He lowers his bag, unzips it and pulls out ladies' intimate apparel designed and coloured in the manner of various African animals. Zebra, leopard, giraffe and colobus. There is a crocodile skin belt designed for the pleasure of particular sado-masochists. At the bottom of the bag a stack of posters and sealed magazines. Nature magazines? I think I see a mountain on one. I put out my free hand for one. It is not a mountain, it is an impressive arrangement of an equally impressive array of black male genitalia. I let the magazine slide from my hand and he stoops to pick it up, wiping it against the sleeve of his black coat.

"Where are you from?" I ask in Dutch.

"Rotterdam."

"No, man...your origin?"

"Sierra Leone."

"Have you no shame?"

His head jerks up, his mouth opens and closes, his eyes meet mine for the first time. His eyes are wet. It is grating that a man should cry.

"Broda." he savours the word. "Broda...its fine to see de eyes of anoda man...it is fine to see de eyes."

Though his Dutch is crude, he read sociology in Leeds and mastered in it. He is quick to tell me this. He has six children. His wife, Gemma is a beautiful woman. On a good day he makes 200 guilders; it is enough to supplement the Dutch state income and it helps sustain the illusions of good living for remnants of his family back home. He refuses to be a janitor, he tells me. To wear a uniform to clean a European toilet? No way. This is why he is running his own enterprise.

"I be a Business Mon."

"Have you no shame?"

"Wha do ma childs go?"

"You have a master's degree from a good university. Use it!"

Business man picks up his bags. He is laughing, so deeply, so low, a different voice. He laughs until he cries. He wipes his eyes.

"Oh mah broda...tank you for de laughing...tank you...you know...Africans we be overeducated fools. Dem papers are for to wipe our bottom. No one sees your knowing when you has no feets to stand in."

27

He laughs again, patting his bag, smiling in reminiscence.

"My broda for real him also in Italy. Bone doctor. Specialist. Best in class. Wha he do now? Him bring Nigeria woman for de prostitute."

Business man chortles.

"Maybe he fix de bone when dem break."

I gave him 20 guilders.

"For the children."

It was when Joop van Vuuren, the gem dealer idly, conversationally asked me what the business man's name was that I remembered I had not asked and he had not told me.

In exile we lower our heads so that we do not see in the mirror of another's eyes, what we suspect: that our precarious existence rests entirely on the whim of another's tolerance of our presence. A phrase crawls into my mind: 'Psychic Oblation'. But what does it mean?

* * *

"What is your name?"

I can smell my name. It is the smell of salt and the musk of sweat. It is...surprise...surprise...remembered laughter and a woman calling me "*Chéri...*"

I want to say...I want to say Yves Fontaine. As Yves Fontaine I would not be a vagrant immigrant, a pariah. As Yves Fontaine I would be 'expatriate' and therefore desirable. As Yves Fontaine I do not need an identity card.

"I...I...My...I..." Silence.

The sibilant hoarseness of the Superintendent:

"Unco–oparatif. Prejudising infestigesons."

Agnethe-mama saw it happen. She had just raised her shawl to uncover her face so that she could shout at me to bring her some paracetamol for her headache. At first she thought she was reliving an old tale. Three men had arrived for her husband. She crawled up the stairs, lying low lest she be seen. Lune told me mama had sat on the bed rocking to and fro and moaning a song and whispering incantations she alone knew words to. In the four days I was away, making an unscheduled call on the Kenya Government, my mother's hair deepened from grey to white. We did not know that her blood pressure began its ascent that first day. Time, as she had always believed, would accomplish the rest.

28

It was at their station that the policemen found all manner of evidence in my pocket. All of which they liked and kept. After three days I was charged with 'loitering with intent'. At the crucial moment the proprietor turned up with my refugee registration card. My case was dismissed and I was charged to keep the peace.

Lune paid the Proprietor with her engagement ring. Whatever he had obtained from the sale of the ring caused him to put an arm around me, call me brother and drag me into a bar where he bought me three beers. He said, "*Pole.*" Sorry.

He said we did not need to pay rent for three months. He wanted to know if we had any more jewellery to sell. I said no. He bought me another beer. He slides a note into my pocket before he leaves. A thousand shillings.

The UNCHR are shifting people out of Kenya, resettlement in third countries. Soon, it will be us. Agnethe-mama now wakes up in the night, tiptoes to my bed. When she sees it is me, she whispers:

"*Mwami.*" My Lord.

Sunday is a day in which we breathe a little easier in this place. There are fewer policemen, and diffident laughter hiding in hearts surfaces. It is simpler on Sunday to find our kind, my people in an African exile. We visit churches. Agnethe, Chi-Chi always go in. Lune sometimes joins them and sometimes joins me. I am usually seating beneath a tree, on a stone bench, walking the perimeter wall, and if it is raining sitting at the back of the church, watching people struggling for words and rituals indicating allegiance to a God whose face they do not know. The hope peddlers become rich in a short while, singing, "Cheeeeessus!" Even the devastated destitute will tithe to commodified gods, sure that in the theatrics of frothing messengers, hope is being doled out. Investing in an eternal future? I do not have a coin to spare. Not now, maybe later, when all is quiet and normal, I will evaluate the idea of a Banker God created in the fearful image of man.

After church, to Agnethe's delight she found Maria. Maria and Agnethe used to shop in Paris together. Once they by-passed France and landed in Haiti. Maria's brother was an associate of Baby Doc's wife. They returned home unrepentant to their husbands and children; they treated their daring with the insouciance it deserved. It was fortunate Agnethe met Maria here because it was from Maria we learned that the Canadian government had opened its doors to those of us in Kenya.

Chi-Chi, emerged from her sanctuary to say "Bu-Bu…patterns of life…somewhere lines meet, *non?*"

A statement of fact. I am hopeful.

Maria was living well. Her brother had settled in Kenya years ago. His wife was from Kenya. Maria was with them.

"Is Alphonse with you?"

Agnethe, being a princess, had been unaware that after the two presidents had died, one never asked one's compatriots where so and so was. If one did not see so and so, one did not ask until the party spoken to volunteered the information of whereabouts. Alphonse was not with Maria. That was all Maria said. Even if Agnethe was a princess, because she was a princess in exile, she read nuances. She kept her mouth shut, and looked to the ground.

Maria's brother, Professor George, and his wife and his two children were going to the Nairobi Animal Orphanage. Did we want to visit animals with them?

"Oh yes. Unfortunately…as you imagine…money is…"

"Don't worry, it is my pleasure," Professor George said.

So we went to meet animals. We met Langata the leopard who did not want people staring at him while he slept. Langata felt the intimacy of sleep is sacred and should be recognised as such. Apparently, he told Chi-Chi this. So Chi-Chi told us. Professor George glared at her. Chi-Chi refused to look at the animals. Lune said animals lived behind fences to protect them from humans. Agnethe-mama was surprised to find that her dead prince did indeed look like a lion. She and Maria stared at Simba who stared back at them as if he knew he was being compared to a prince and the prince was increasingly found to be lacking.

"Why the name 'Professor George'?" I said to Professor George.

"They find it hard to say Georges Nsibiriwa."

'They' were his wife's people. I sensed the 'and' so I said: "And?"

Professor George walked quietly; he pointed out the difference between a Thomson's gazelle and a Grant's gazelle. Something about white posteriors. At a putrid pool, in which sluggish algae brewed a gross green soup, in between withered reeds and a hapless hyacinth, Professor George sighed and smiled. A dead branch, half-submerged, floated on the surface of the pool.

"Ah. Here we are…look…in the place you find yourself…in the time…camouflage!" A glorious pronouncement.

Surreptitious glance. Professor George then picks up a twig and

30

throws it into the pond. From within the depths, what had been the dead branch twisted up in a surge of power. Its jaws snapped the twig in two; a white underbelly displayed before transforming itself, once again into a dead branch, half-submerged, floating on the surface of the pool.

"Ah! See! Camouflage...place dictates form, *mon ami*. Always."

I start to tell him about the police.

Professor George nods; "Yes...yes...it is the time." And he asks if I have heard word from Augustine, a mutual friend who lives in Copenhagen.

"Augustine has changed address, it seems."

Professor George says: "Yes...it is the time."

I need to ask something. "You have heard about the list?" He looks up at me, his face a question.

"*Les génocidaires?*"

"Ah yes...but I pay no attention."

The relief of affirmation. A name's good can be invoked again. So I tell him, "Ah! It's difficult, *mon ami*, and...Agnethe-mama doesn't know."

"Know what?"

"Our name is on the list."

With the same agility that the crocodile used to become a log again, Professor George pulls away from the fence. He wipes his hand, the one I had shaken, against his shirt. He steps away, one step at a time, then he turns around and trots, like a donkey, shouting, looking over his shoulder at me:

"Maria! We leave...now!"

The first lesson of exile – camouflage. When is a log...not a log? When a name is not a name.

* * *

On Monday we were outside the UNHCR at four-thirty a.m. We hope that the list is not full. It is not. Instead there is a handwritten sign leading to an office of many windows which says 'Relocations, Resettlement.' At the front, behind the glass are three men and two women with blue badges that say UNHCR. They have papers in front of them. Behind them, four men, a distance away. They watch us all, their bodies still. I straighten my coat and stand a little taller.

31

We are divided into two groups, men and women. The women are at the front. They are divided into three groups: Young Girls, Young Women, Old Women.

At the desks, where there is a desk sign which says 'Records Clerk', they write out names and ages, previous occupation and country of origin and, of course, the RRN – refugee registration number. Those who do not have an RRN must leave, obtain one in room 2004 and return after two weeks.

Later, flash! And a little pop. Our faces are engraved on a piece of paper. Passport photograph. Movement signified, we are leaving.

"Next," the photographer says. Defiance of absence. Photographer, do you see us at all? Inarticulation as defence. Let it pass. Soon, we will be gone from this place.

The Young Women are commanded to hand over babies to the Old Women. Young Girls and Young Women are taken into another room. A medical examination we are informed. We are told to wait outside the office block, the gate. Perhaps we will be examined another day.

Agnethe-mama and I are sitting on a grassy patch opposite a petrol station. Agnethe, bites at her lips. Then she tugs my sleeve.

"Bonbon…do other monarchs-in-exile live in Canada?

"Perhaps."

Chi-Chi and Lune emerge, holding hands. It is two hours later and the sun is hovering, ready to sink into darkness. They do not look at either of us. We walk back, silently. Chi-Chi has hooked her hand into my waistband. Lune glides ahead of us all, her stride is high, the balance of her body undisturbed. A purple *matatu*, its music 'thump thumping' slows down and a tout points north with a hand gesture. I decline. It speeds off in a series of 'thump thumps'. Agnethe frowns. We walk in silence. Long after the *matatu* has gone, Agnethe says, her face serene again:

"The reason they are like that…these Kenyans…is because they do not know the cow dance."

* * *

When Lune dipped her hand into my coat pocket while I slept and took out eight hundred shillings, returning in an hour with a long mirror, I should have listened to the signal from the landscape.

Chi–Chi used Lune's mirror to cut her hair. She cut it as if she were hacking a dress. She stepped on and kicked her shorn locks. Agnethe-mama covered her mouth; she said nothing as if she understood something. For Lune, the mirror evokes memories of ballet technique. She executes all her movements with her legs rotated outward. Agnethe-mama looks to the mirror so she can turn away and not look.

Two weeks later, I kick the mirror down. I smash it with my fists. They bleed. Agnethe screamed once, covering her mouth. Silence enters our room. Silence smells of the Jevanjee Garden roasted Kenchic chicken; one pack feeds a frugal family of four for three days.

On the third day, I find Lune looking down at me.

"It was mine. It was mine." She smiles suddenly and I am afraid.

From across the room, Agnethe-mama: "Ah Bonbon…still…no word from the kings-in-exile?"

The anger with which the rain launches itself upon this land, the thunder which causes floors to creak sparks a strange foreboding in me. That night, while we were eating cold beans and maize dinner, Lune pushed her plate aside, looked at me, a gentle, graceful crane, her hands fluttering closed, a smile in her eyes.

"*Chéri*, we can leave soon, but it depends on a certain…co-operation."

"Co-operation?"

"A condition from the medical examination."

Agnethe looks away. Chi–Chi clutches her body, staving off in her way something she is afraid of.

"How do we co-operate?" I am afraid to know.

"By agreeing to be examined", she laughs, high, dry, cough-laugh, "…examined by the officials at their homes for a night."

"I see."

I don't. Silence. Agnethe is rocking herself to and fro. She is moaning a song. I know the tune. It is from the song new widows sing when the body of their dead spouse is laid on a bier.

Annals of war decree that conquest of landscapes is incomplete unless the vanquished's women are 'taken'. Where war is crudest, the women are discarded afterwards, for their men to find. Living etchings of emasculation. Lune has not finished yet. I sense I am being taunted for my ineffectuality by this woman who would be my wife.

"Now…it has been discussed with family, it is not a question of being forced."

33

A recitation. I lower my head. The incongruity of tears. A persistent mosquito buzzes near my ear. The food on my plate is old. Lune leaves the table; pushing back her chair, she places her feet in a parallel arrangement, one in front of the other, the heel of a foot in line with the toes of the other. Her right arm extends in front of her body, and the left is slightly bent and raised. She moves the weight of her body over the left foot and bends the left knee. She raises her right heel, pointing the toe. Her body is bent toward the extended knee. She holds the pose and says: "*Pointe tendue!*"

Conscious now, I read the gesture. She will perform as she must, on this stage. I can only watch.

"No."

Now Chi-Chi raises her head, like a beautiful cat. I know the look — tentative hope, tendrils reaching out and into life. Lune closes her feet, the heel of one now touching the toes of the other; she pushes up from the floor and jumps, her legs straight, feet together and pointed. She lands and bows before me. Then she cracks and cries, crumbling on the floor.

Outside, the window, the drone of traffic which never stops and the cackle of drunkards. Creeping up the window a man's voice singing:

"*Chupa na debe. Mbili kwa shilling tano. Chupa na debe.*"

Bottle and tin, two for five shillings, bottle and tin, Kenyans and their shillings.

* * *

I stood on the balcony staring at the traffic, counting every red car I could see. Nine so far. Behind me, Agnethe approached. In front of my face she dangled her wedding ring.

"Sell it."

"No."

She let it fall at my feet.

We used the money to leave the room on River Road. We went to a one-roomed cottage with a separate kitchen and an outside toilet. It was in Hurlingham, the property of a former Government secretary, Mr Wamathi, a drinking acquaintance of the proprietor. I observed that his gardening manners were undeveloped; he had subdivided his quarter-acre plot, cutting down old African olive trees and uprooting the largest bougainvillea I had ever seen, on the day we arrived. He was going to put up a block of flats. Mr Wamathi was delirious with glee about selling the trees to the 'City Canjo' for fifteen thousand shillings. His laughter was deep, rounded and certain with happiness.

He laughed and I felt hope joining us.

Agnethe started tending a small vegetable patch. Her eyes gleamed when the carrot tops showed. Lune made forays into a nearby mall, an eye-fest of possibilities satiating her heart, extending her wants. Chi-Chi, over the fence, befriended an Ethiopian resident who introduced her to his handsome brother, Matteo.

The day Chi-Chi met Matteo she slipped her hand into my waistband, looking up at me she said:

"He...can...see..."

Every day I tried to contact home, seeking cash for four air tickets on a refugee pass. Word appeared in dribs and drabs. Detail gleaned from conversations heard, strangers approached and newspapers slyly read.

The bank? Burned down. The money? Missing from the safes. And once, the sound of a name accused, accursed:

Kuseremane.

But hadn't we left on the fifth day?

The day flows on. I sit in different cafés, telling the waiters that I am waiting for a friend. Thirty minutes in some cafes. In the more confident ones, the ones which are sure of their identity, I can wait for a full hour before I make a face, glance at my non-existent watch, frown as if tardy friends are a source of annoyance and I exit.

Whispers had floated over the land of hills and nestled in valleys and refused to leave, had in fact given birth to volleys of sound. Now tales had been added of a most zealous servant instructed by an heir to sluice stains.

"Ah! Roger. *Mon oncle...*"

Excoriating women's wombs, crushing foetal skulls, following the instructions of a prince.

They said.

Today I woke up as early as the ones who walk to work, manoeuvring the shadows of dawn, crochet-covered radios against ears, in pockets, or tied to bicycle saddles. Sometimes music, rumba. And in the dawn dark I can forget where I am and let others' footsteps show me the way. I hear Franklin Bukaka's plea, pouring out of so many radios, tenderly carried in so many ways.

"Aye! Afrika, O! Afrika..."

I return from so many journeys like this and one day, I find Agnethe-mama lying on her back in her vegetable patch. At first I think she is soaking up the sun. Then I remember Agnethe-mama never let the sun touch her skin. An African princess, melanin management was an important event of toilette. I lean over her body. Then, head against her chest, I cannot hear a heartbeat.

I carry my mother and run along the road. The evening traffic courses past. Nairobi accommodates. Room for idiosyncrasies. So to those who pass by, it is not strange that a tall, tall man should carry a slender woman in his arms.

At the first hospital. "My mother…she is not heart beating…help."

"Kshs 12,000 deposit, Sir."

"But my mother…"

"Try Kenyatta."

At Kenyatta, they want a four-thousand shilling deposit, and I will still have to wait, one of about three hundred people waiting for two doctors to see them. I do not have four-thousand shillings.

"Where can I go?"

"*Enda* Coptic." Go to the Copts.

"*Tafadhali*…please, where are they?"

"Ngong Rd."

"How far?"

"Next!"

* * *

Agnethe sighs, opens her eyes and asks:

"Have the monarchs-in-exile sent our reply yet, Bonbon?"

"Soon…mama."

She has suffered a mild stroke.

I return to the cottage to pack a bag for mama. Exile blurs lines. So a son, such as I, can handle a mother's underwear. Agnethe-mama told Chi-Chi once, in my hearing, that all in a woman may fall apart, may become unmatched, but never her underwear. I pack sets of underwear for Agnethe: black, brown and lacy purple.

* * *

Kuseremane, Kuseremane, Kuseremane.

It seems that the whispers have infringed upon the place where my

36

tears hide. I cannot stop bawling, snivelling like a lost ghoul. My
shoulders bounce with a life of their own. Lune watches me, her eyes
veiled in a red, feral glow.

At six p.m. I rejoin a river of workers returning to so many homes. To
be one of many, is to be, anyway, if only for a moment. The sun is setting
and has seared into the sky a golden trail; it has the look of a machete
wound bleeding yellow light. It is an incongruous time to remember
Roger's blackened hands.

Agnethe has taken to sitting in the garden rocking her body, to and
fro, to and fro. She does not hum. But sometimes, in between the fro and
to, she asks:

"Have the brother sovereigns sent a letter?"

"Soon."

At night, Chi-Chi shakes me awake, again. My pillow is soaked, my
face wet. Not my tears.

The next morning, I left the cottage before sunrise. I have learned of
hidden places; covered spaces which the invisible inhabit. The Nairobi
Arboretum. The monkeys claim my attention as do the frenzied moaning
of emptied people calling out to frightened gods for succour. Now, it
starts to rain. I walk rapidly, then start to jog, the mud splattering my
already stained coat. The other hidden place is through the open doors
of a Catholic Church. Hard wooden benches, pews upon which a man
may kneel, cover his eyes and sleep or cry unheeded before the presence
that is also an absence.

* * *

My return coincides with Mr Wamathi's winding his way into the
house. He rocks on his feet:

"Habe new yearghh." 'Year' ends with a burp and belch.

"Happy New Year." It is July and cold, and time is relative.

Agnethe outside, uncovered. Rocking to and fro. She clutches thin
arms about herself, shivering.

"Aiiee, mama!" I lean down to lift her up.

"*Bonbon, il fait froid, oui?*' It is cold.

"Lune? Chi-Chi? Lune?" Why is mama sitting out in the night
alone?

"*Où est* Lune…Chi-Chi, mama?"

Agnethe stares up at the sky, from my arms.

37

"Bonbon…*il fait froid.*" Two anorexic streams glide down, past high cheekbones and nestle at the corner of her mouth. She looks up and into my eyes. The resolute eyes of an ancient crone. Now…now the cold's tendrils insinuate themselves, searing horror in my heart.

Chi-Chi returned first. She stumbled through the door, her body shuddering. She is wiping her hand up and down her body, ferociously, as if wiping away something foul only she can sense.

"Everything has a pattern…Bu-Bu, *non?*" She gives me the folded papers.

Three *laisses-passez.* Tickets to rapture. Let them pass. It favours Agnethe, Boniface and Chi-Chi Kuseremane.

I am not there.

I watch from afar, the ceiling I think, as the tall man tears the papers to shreds. I am curious about the weeping woman with shorn hair crawling on the ground gathering the fragments to her chest. I frown when I see the tall, dark man lift his hand up, right up and bring it crashing into the back of the girl who falls to the floor, lies flat on her belly and stops crying. She is staring into herself where no one else can reach her. A sound at the door. The tall, tall man walks up to his fiancée. Who bows low, the end of a performance. She too has a clutch of papers in her hand. The tall man sniffs the girl as if he were a dog and he bites her on the cheek, the one upon which another man's cologne lingers. Where the teeth mark are, the skin has broken. Drops of blood. Lune laughs.

"We can leave anytime now."

"*Putaine!*"

She giggles. "But I shall live, *Chéri*…we shall live…we shall live well."

Agnethe-mama heaves herself up from the bed and brushes her long white hair. I return to the body of the tall, black man whose arms are hanging against his side, his head bowed. He sees that Lune's feet are closed, the heel of one touching the toes of the other. She slowly raises hands over her head, paper clutched in the right, she rounds her arms slightly, *en couronne* – in a crown.

Paper fragments, a mosaic on the floor. I stoop, the better to stare at them. I pick up my sister. She is so still. But then she asks, eyes wide with wanting to know: "Bu-Bu…there's a pattern in everything. *Oui?*"

"*Oui*, Ché-Ché." A childhood name, slips easily out of my mouth. Now when she smiles, it reaches her eyes. She touches my face with her hand.

* * *

38

That night, or more accurately, the next morning, it was three a.m, Agnethe went to the bathroom outside. Returning to the room she had stepped into and slid in a puddle. She stepped out again to clean her feet and then she screamed and screamed and screamed.

"Ahh! Ahh! Ahhhee!"

She points at the rag upon which she has wiped her feet. It is covered in fresh blood. She points into the room, at the floor. I return to look. Lune is now awake. Lights in the main house are switched on and Mr Wamathi appears on the doorway, a knobkerrie in his hand.

"Where, where?" he shouts.

The neighbourhood dogs have started to howl. The sky is clear and lit up by a crescent moon. I remember all this because I looked up as I carried my bleeding sister, my Chi-Chi-Ché-Ché into Mr Wamathi's car, cushioned by towels and blankets while her blood poured out.

At the hospital emergency wing where we had been admitted quickly, a tribute to Mr Wamathi's threats, I watched the splayed legs of my sister, raised and stirruped. My sister, led to and stripped bare in the wilderness of lives altered when two presidents were shot to the ground from the sky. I remember a blow bestowed on a back by a defenceless brother-prince.

How can a blow be unswung?

A doctor and a nurse struggle to bring to premature birth a child we did not know existed. Chi-Chi's eyes are closed. Her face still. When she left us I felt a tug on my waistband as in days of life and her body lost its shimmer, as if a light within had gone off for good. She left with her baby.

The child's head was between her legs. A boy or girl, only the head was visible and one arm, small fists slightly open as if beckoning. Skin like cream coffee. The offspring of African exiles. An enigma solved. The Ethiopians had abruptly disappeared from the radar of our lives and Chi-Chi had said nothing. The dying child of African exiles in an African land. I stroked the baby's wet head. Did baby come to lure Chi-Chi away? A word shimmers into my heart: fratricide. I douse it with the coldness of my blood. I am shivering. A distant voice...mine.

"Leave them...leave the children." Keep them together...the way they are.

Landscape speaks. The gesture of an incomplete birth. Of what have we to be afraid? Metamorphoses of being. There must be another way to live.

39

"Is there a priest?" Even the faithless need a ritual to purge them of the unassailable scent of mystery.

"What shall we do with the body?"

A body...my sister. When did a pool of blood become this...absence? They let me cover her face after I have kissed her eyes shut.

Vain gesture.

Agnethe and Lune are outside, waiting. Islands in their hope. I open the door to let them in, gesturing with my hand. They step into the room and I step out. I let the door close behind me and try to block out the screams emanating from within. Staccato screams. Screams in a crescendo and then a crushing moan.

A nurse offers forms to be filled in.

"Nairobi City Mortuary."

It will cost eight thousand Kenyan shillings to rent space for Chi-Chi. I do not have eight thousand shillings. It's okay, the nurse says. I can pay it tomorrow at the mortuary.

Eeeh! Kenyans and their shillings.

Nurse turns; "*Pole.*" Sorry.

But Mr Wamathi makes an arrangement with his wives, and they find 35,000 shillings for Agnethe.

Is this it?

Later. After all the bluster of being...this? A body in a box, commended to the soil.

A brother's gesture: twelve torches alight in a sister's cheap coffin. Chi-Chi and her Nameless One will see in the dark.

* * *

It is a challenge to match paper fragments so that they match just right. It is fortunate there are words on the paper, it makes it easier. Three *laisses-passez*. Chi-Chi's is complete, almost new.

Lune returned to my bed. Agnethe's resumed her rocking which accelerated in both speed and volume. Her eyes are brown and a ceaseless rivulet of tears drips onto her open palm. But she smiles at us, Lune and I, and does not utter a word. Sometimes her eyes have a film of white over them as if she had become a medium, in constant communion with the dead. Sometimes I imagine that they look at me with reproach. I look to the ground; the quest for patterns.

I have lost the feeling of sleep. I will not touch Lune nor can I let her

touch me. It is the ghost of another man's cologne which lingers in my
dreams and haunts my heart. I am bleeding in new places. But we are
leaving.

"Bu-Bu, everything has a pattern, *non?*"

We will be leaving for Canada on Saturday night.

Agnethe shocked us by dying on Friday morning in my arms as I
entered the gates of the Coptic hospital. On the streets, as before, no-one
found it strange, the idea of a tall, tall man carrying a slender woman in
his arms. A pattern had been established, a specific madness
accommodated.

When Agnethe-mama left, the energy of her exit made me stumble.

"Ah! Bonbon! Ah!" she says.

At the Coptic gate, "*Mwami!*"

She leaves with such force, her head is thrown back against my arms.
Agnethe-mama.

The Copts cannot wrench her from my arms. They let me sit in their
office and rock my mother to and fro, to and fro. I am humming a song.
It is the melody of '*Sur le pont d'Avignon*' where we shall dance.

At the cottage, old bags with few belongings are packed. On the bed,
a manila bag with Agnethe's clothes, the bag she was packing when her
body crumbled to the ground.

"*Où est maman?*" Lune asks. Where is mama?

I stretch out my arms, and she lifts her hand to her long silk hair and
draws it away from her face. She rushes into my arms and burrows her
face into my shoulder.

"Forgive me."

We do what we can to live. Even the man whose cologne stayed on
her face. I have no absolution to give. So I tell her instead that Agnethe
has just died. And when Lune drops to the ground like a shattered rock,
I slap her awake, harder than necessary on the cheek upon which another
man's cologne had strayed and stayed. She does not move, but her eyes
are open. Arms above her head, hair over her face.

She smirks. "I'm leaving. I am living."

She grabs my arm, a woman haunted by the desire for tomorrow
where all good is possible. "I am leaving."

"*Ma mère...Lune-chérie.*"

Lune covers her ears, shuts her eyes.

For the most fleeting of moments, I enter into her choice. To slough
the skin of the past off. To become another life form. I look around the

room. Agnethe-mama's slippers by the bed. What traces have they left on the surface of the earth? The gossip of landscape. It is getting clear. I stoop low and kiss Lune on her forehead. In the pattern of things, there is a place in which the body of a princess may rest. Isn't there?

A Coptic priest, a Coptic doctor, Lune and I, Mr, Mrs and Mrs Wamathi – the sum total of those gathered around Agnethe-mama's. Lune's airplane bags are over her shoulders, her plane ticket in her purse. In four hour's time she will be in a plane taking her to the Canada of her dreams. We forgot grave-diggers must be paid, their spades attached to Kenya shillings. So I will cover my mother's grave myself, when the others are gone.

A plane departs from Nairobi. Kenya Airways to London. From London, Air Canada to Ottawa.

I have been laughing for an hour now. True, the laughter is interspersed with hot, sour, incessant streams of tears. Squatting on my mother's grave. The unseen now obvious.

Life peering out of lives. Life calling life to dance. Life, the voyeur. I will start dancing now.

L'indépendance, ils l'ont obtenue / La table ronde, ils l'ont gagnée...
"Mhhhh...Mhhhh...Mhh...Mhh...Mhhhh"
L'indépendance, ils l'ont obtenue...
Kabasellé laughs.

Who can allay the summon of life to life? The inexorable attraction for fire. The soul knows its keeper. Inexorable place, space and pace. I see. I see.

There!

Life aflame in a fire – gold sun. And dust restoring matter to ash. The ceaseless ardour for life now requited:
"Mhhhh...Mhhhh...Mhh...Mhh...Mhhhh."
L'indépendance, ils l'ont obtenue...
La table ronde, ils l'ont gagnée...
"Cha-cha-cha!"

Thus began the first day of my second life.

One day, a letter made its way to Kenya from Canada. Its first line is:
"*Cheri*, please let me know the date of your arrival."

A tall, tall man straightens the lapels of a fading Hugo Boss jacket. He cradles a shovel, listening to the sighing sentences of dust fragments filling a new grave. In his heart, an old phrase bubbles to the fore:
Soon.

Another week, another letter: "....when is your flight arriving?"

And another week after that, and the next, until a year has gone and then six months more.

I have joined the sentinels of the cemetery, an assorted collection of life's creatures, through which life gazes at life. Devoted dogs, gypsy cats, two birds which perch over certain graves, a hundred unobtrusive trees and of course spirits caught between worlds. Living gargoyles guarding entry points through which humans pass, dreaming in the day about shy, wise night shadows with which conversations broken off at dawn can resume.

The discovery of listening...

Catching landscape in its surreptitious gestures – patterns which point to meaning...

Waiting for the return of a name set ablaze when fire made dust out of two presidents' bodies...

I live in the silence-scope and perform the rituals of return, for life. Where I am, the bereaved know they will find, if they visit, that the reminder of their beloved's existence – the grave – is safe, that life watches and leaves signs on tombs; mostly flowers, sometimes trees.

I prefer trees.

Soon now, the wind-borne whispers will fall silent.

*

Yvonne Adhiambo-Owuor, a Kenyan, works as the Executive Director of ZIFF (Zanzibar International Film Festival), an East African arts and cultural resource centre and event producer. A closet writer, she was unmasked in 2003 when she won the Caine Prize for African Writing. When she is not being a bureaucrat, she tries to finish her first novel.

Clubfoot

Ken Barris

He watched his mother as she worked. Her hands were chapped, the flesh was pale. The light coming in through the window was stark, and bleached her face and arms almost the colour of milk. She was cleaning a galjoen, scraping off the scales with her old sharp knife. The scales sprang into the air, rasping off in silver-grey showers. The kitchen stank of fish blood.

He longed to talk to his mother. He knew she wouldn't answer. Her mouth was a healed gash. She was a creased milky body that breathed and moved and spoke only when necessary. He closed his eyes and tried to enter her flesh. He wanted to move her arms, see through her pale eyes. He wanted to live inside her where, perhaps, it was warmer. But she remained solid and distant, and he remained where he was on the kitchen chair, kicking his heels softly against its wooden legs. He could taste the whiteness; it was like eating chalk or sand.

The sounds coming from outside – the teasing wind, the screaming gulls, the sea – combined with the scraping of his mother's blade. They twisted together into lines of music, briefly caught, something he might sing; then they were sounds and noises. The scraping stopped altogether. The fish slapped onto the board, he heard the cold water tap running. He knew it was the cold tap because it sounded different to the hot one. Then came the paddling of her hands and the smell of Sunlight soap.

He opened his eyes again. To his surprise, his mother was watching him. As usual, he couldn't read the expression in her eyes. He looked away.

"It's cooler outside," she said. "Come, we'll walk down the beach."

Silently, he shifted off his chair and limped to the door. They stepped down onto the white sand, the scraggy grass. Light knifed into his eyes, and his foot hurt more than usual. He sat down on the step.

"I don't want to go," he said.

The flesh around her eyes seemed to soften. She said, "I'll carry you the first bit." She knelt down, turning her back to him. He climbed onto her back and wrapped his arms around her broad shoulders, his legs about her hips. With a grunt of pain or weariness, she straightened up

44

and walked down to the sea.

He pressed his face into the back of her neck. There was the jogging of her stride and the milky odour of her body. The breeze coming off the sea tugged at her hair; it brushed against the side of his face. Then his mother walked into the sea, and stood ankle-deep in the surging water. She let him down. The icy shock was a relief to his foot. They stood together looking at the horizon, holding hands.

"It's getting too cold," he said.

Reluctantly she turned away, and they began their walk down the beach. He crouched over a large stranded jellyfish – a pudding of flesh almost a metre across – and the mob of whelk boring into it.

"Is it dead?" he asked. "They're eating it."

"I don't think so," she replied. "I don't know."

"Can it feel?"

"I don't know. I don't think so."

He picked up one of the whelk by its conical shell. With nothing to attach itself to, the sucker squirmed about blindly. He put it back on the jellyfish and watched as it began to dig into smooth clear meat. He thought: it must have a mouth in its foot to do that. Then he straightened up and limped onwards. Pain curled through his foot and shot up the muscles of his lower leg. He turned back, and looked at his mother.

"Alright," she said, "we can go back."

But they stood still for a while. There was no-one else on the beach. They were alone with the white light, the noises of sea and wind, the long converging lines of the shore. Am I alive or dead, he wondered, Is my mother alive or dead? Can we feel? He heard his mother's voice say: I don't think so. I don't know.

* * *

It was a hot morning. He sat staring at the patch of light falling in through the open door. When he didn't blink for long enough, chimeric colours emerged from the rectangle of light and drifted across it. When he did close his eyes, their lids stung pleasantly. His mother was working in the kitchen and humming. It was a wordless song about being tired, and wanting things she didn't have, and about having things she didn't want.

He turned back to the rectangle of light. He could feel its heat on the

45

surfaces of his eyes. It was a dangerous desert, and he was flying safely in a boat above it.

He was distracted by the noise of an engine beating irregularly. It approached the cottage and pulled up with a rich squeaking of springs. His mother fell silent, and a door creaked open. They waited. Then, as the visitor's shadow fell across his patch of light, the reek of unwashed flesh entered the cottage.

It was hard to see the man who stood at the door, because of the glare behind him. He was tall and had long, wild hair. He cleared his throat and asked, "Would this be the home of Caitlin Turner?"

The boy scrambled to his feet. He looked around, to see his mother coming. She dropped the plate she was holding – it broke with a dull sound into two uneven pieces – and then she stood quite still.

"Caitlin," said the visitor, "Caitlin – it's been…" His voice tailed away, and he started again, almost pleading: "It's been a long time."

She bent down and picked up the pieces of the plate. She straightened up and said, "I suppose you'd better come in."

He came in then, his smell overpowering the small room. She looked at him in dismay. "God, Arthur, you're a mess," she said. "How on earth did this happen?"

He gestured lamely, let his hand fall. "I don't know," he replied. "One thing after another…I lost control, I suppose, quite badly."

As if driven by the same spring, their heads turned to the boy.

"Is he the one?" asked the old man.

She nodded: "His name is Luke."

The man and the boy studied each other. There was something wild about his face and eyes, his skin was brown with ancient dirt, his fingers were long and bony; they trembled when he raised his hand and scratched his chin. The boy was frightened.

"Luke," said his mother, "this is your grandfather, Arthur Turner. You can call him Arthur."

The old man grinned desperately, showing gaps in his teeth. His eyes were moist. He advanced on Luke, holding out his hand. Luke shrank back, and his grandfather stopped.

"I suppose not," he mumbled. The grin had vanished. "It's all too much for him."

Luke limped to his mother's side. Half his fear was her speech, her voice: usually when she spoke, it was as if she moved through deep water, or was caught dreaming in a heavy rain. Now it came out too smoothly and tasted sour. The old man had changed her into a different mother.

Her hand went down to his shoulder and stayed there. The grandfather filled the room with uncertainty. He seemed to be casting about, trying to find his bearings.

"Caitlin," he said, "I suppose people have told you that he is frighteningly beautiful."

"People around here don't talk. They don't talk to me. But I know that he is."

Her hand tightened on his shoulder to protect him from dangerous ideas. Again, there was a terrible silence. Then his mother said, "I suppose you'd like some tea."

"I don't suppose you have any brandy?"

"There is no alcohol," she said bluntly.

"Ah well. Tea then, thank you."

They moved into the kitchen, where there was a worn table and four chairs. Caitlin opened both windows as wide as possible, and the back door. She lit the gas and put the kettle on the ring.

"I'd forgotten," Arthur Turner said, "how charming this place is."

She made no reply, and kept her back turned as she gathered what she needed. He made no further attempt at conversation until the tea was ready. All the while, a mist of pain built up in the air. Luke knew that it wasn't his own, though he could feel it.

Caitlin poured for her father and her son, and then for herself. The old man took a sip and grimaced: "Rooibos tea," he said, "of course."

Caitlin watched him expressionlessly, and waited. He took another sip. "It's not bad, really," he said hastily. Still she said nothing.

He abandoned the attempt to communicate with her then, and his eyes roved about the room, picking out details aimlessly: the two–plate burner, the small paraffin fridge, the blue shelves, the patchy distemper, the stacks of chipped plates, the forlorn etching of Bird Rock in Port Elizabeth. He sipped his tea, and she sipped hers; perhaps a century passed in this way, while Luke studied the grain of the table surface, as he had many times before, the waves of dry brown colour that converged and then shook themselves free of each other and marched in endless ranks from horizon to horizon.

When he had finished his tea, Arthur put down his cup with a trembling hand. At last, he said, "No quarter given, Caitlin. I should have expected it. I'm sorry, I made a mistake. I was stupid to come back here."

Caitlin's shoulders hunched; she leaned forward and asked, "What was a mistake, Arthur? Coming here like this, or staying away for five years? I'd really like to know."

"I didn't come here to fight with you," he replied, rising, his lower lip trembling visibly. As he did so, his chair fell over backwards; they winced as it crashed. "I'm sorry," he repeated, bending over to pick up the chair. He straightened up, his face white under the grime. "I will leave you now. But please bear in mind that it was you – it was your decision – it was you who refused all contact, afterwards, after it happened."

His eyes strayed to the boy. It appeared that he wanted to say something to Luke, as a struggle of indecision passed over his features. Then he turned round and left the kitchen heavily.

Luke's mother remained hunched in her chair. "That is true," she mumbled, not to Luke; but she remained where she was.

The door of Arthur Turner's car slammed. Then there was a prolonged silence. The car door creaked open again.

"I think he's coming back," said Luke.

His mother looked at him mutely, her expression a mixture of dull anger and relief. Luke turned away.

Arthur returned. "It won't start," he said lugubriously. "I suppose it's the battery. Can I borrow your car? I'll try to get the damn thing out and take it in to Lamberts Bay. I'm sorry, you're stuck with me for at least a day. But I'll sleep in the combi."

"Don't be ridiculous," said his daughter. "You can sleep in here."

He stood where he was in the doorway, silent and proud.

"Providing," she added, "that you have a bath."

"Very well," he replied grumpily, and came in. "But there's no point in cleaning up until I've taken out the battery, is there?"

"I suppose not."

He sat down at the kitchen table, his ripe smell filling the room. The stink reminded Luke of rotting seaweed. He wondered if his grandfather came from under the sea too. There was a great deal of splashing, and a song. Arthur Turner had come back from town late that afternoon with a skinful of wine. He sang about 'jermin' officers crossing the 'rine'. Luke came to the blue-painted doorway – there was no door – and watched his grandfather labour to clean off his own filth. The soap didn't lather easily in this hard water.

Arthur stood up in the bathtub. He was painfully thin, except for a

48

sagging little belly. His skin was an ivory colour; his penis was darker, a thick blind earthworm the colour of cooked liver. His ribs stuck out, and there was a huge scar down his chest. The scar was shiny pink-brown skin, with florid stitch marks on either side. Luke wondered why he had been cut open, and what had been taken out. The water in the bath was brown.

"They drank the women and kissed the wine," sighed Arthur Turner, and staggered where he stood. "Careful," he said, "careful." Then he sat down, and eased himself back. "Oh God," he said. It sounded to Luke like a sob. Arthur rested his head against the back of the tub, breathing heavily, on the edge of snoring. Luke thought he might be asleep; but then he peered over the rim of the tub at Luke.

"You don't say much, do you?"

Luke looked down at the floor.

"You might find this hard to believe, boy, but I dreamt about you once. You had no face."

Luke raised his hand to his face. It was still there. There was a strange hissing sound, which frightened him; he realised that his grandfather was laughing.

"You can understand that missing face," said the old man. "Your mother kicked me out of her life before you were born. What do you think of that?" Old Turner splashed water about and snorted. "She's like that, you know," he said. "She can be obtuse. She becomes an obtuse mess in moments of great crisis. Mass, I should say, a doughy but unyielding mass of silence. It has an almost religious quality, you know, a religious mass. You can't really penetrate that, can you? It's baffling and tormenting, and of course utterly demoralising. To suffer in silence; to turn the other cheek – it's an abuse of power and a bloody lie, my boy, but I suppose you know that, better than most. Oh yes, you're an expert yourself."

Luke felt the weight and pressure of the words. He didn't know what they meant, but he liked 'obtuse' and 'tormenting' and 'bloody lie'.

"Obtuse or not, she kicked me out."

He looked up at his grandfather; Turner's eyes were focused on him now, glittering cruelly.

"I don't suppose you've met your father?"

Luke shook his head.

"Has she ever told you about him?"

"No," replied Luke, his first word to his grandfather.

"Of course she hasn't, with bloody good reason too." He lay back in the tub again, and muttered tiredly, "But she should have done something about your foot. She's let you down there, old son. Not my business, of course…"

Luke stood up and limped out of the bathroom.

Arthur called him back; he stood silently in the doorway.

"Has she ever told you?"

Luke shook his head, not knowing what question he answered. His grandfather rose messily out of the tub and seized a towel.

"She should have told you. She should have told you that you're good looking. No, you're more than that: you are an astonishingly beautiful child."

"She didn't tell me that," said Luke. He turned round and limped off to his room.

There was a tarnished mirror above his work table. He climbed onto his chair and knelt on it to look at his reflection. A solemn brown face stared back. He was slightly plump, with full lips, dark eyes and curly black hair. His grandfather was wrong. It was an ugly face; the image made him feel mildly sick. But he forced himself to look at it, and after a while the figure split off from himself and became a picture of someone else. He thought he could see that other person grow older, and become a dark, strong person, grow into a life that wasn't his own. He preferred then to look at the space behind and around the image. He peered in at the sides of the mirror, both sides, trying to see more. It was a clear world that he couldn't get into – everything in it was hard and clean and real. It was a better world.

* * *

Luke went out into the sun. The light was harsh and made him squint. He wandered round the side of the house to where his grandfather's car was parked, a decrepit Volkswagen bus, orange and white. He slid open the middle door and climbed in. He paused, stopped by the dangerous smell of human flesh, mildew, petrol, burnt oil. But he didn't mind the smell that much because it was steep and vertiginous – he could position himself in it, float at a certain level – and his curiosity drove him on.

It was brutally messy inside. Worn blankets, clothes, cooking utensils, a gas stove, jerrycans, food tins lay on the seats and on the floor. A pair of boots, a bloated pack of Vienna sausages, scores of books, sections of rubber tubing, an old portable typewriter. Luke didn't know what the latter was, though it interested him greatly. He pressed down on one of the buttons – marked E – and a grey arm rose up from the middle. He tried a different button, and the same thing happened. He lifted a small silver lever, and part of the device ratcheted noisily and swiftly to the side, giving him a great fright. He left the machine alone, consumed by anxiety that he might have broken it.

Under one of the middle seats, he found three yellowing typescripts, the paper blistered by exposure to moisture and sun; but then the world swam, revolved once and landed with a definite, inaudible thump. It was too hot in the bus, the stink had become unbearable.

Luke realised that this was Arthur Turner's house. It was a travelling house. He realised that his grandfather was a different kind of person to his mother and himself. He was a wild man who lived in a rich and violent mess, and didn't care about many of the things that his mother cared about so terribly much. At a level deeper than thought, Luke welded together composites: his grandfather was a type of man-animal, an everyday savage; he was turtle and hare at once.

He stumbled out of the bus head first, and fell onto the white sand and straggling seagrass, and somersaulted, and lay on his back. The earth and air outside were fresh, and he grew solid again, bit by bit.

He went back into the house. Arthur Turner sat at the kitchen table. He looked different, now that he was clean. His skin was pale, his limp grey hair fell across his forehead. Now his grey eyes were tired and shrewd. There was a cup of tea before him, and an untouched slice of toast.

"Do you want this?" he asked, pushing the plate towards Luke.

Luke silently took the toast and bit into it.

"Don't tell your mother," said Arthur. "She's trying to feed me up, but I don't eat breakfast."

Luke didn't reply; he was too busy with the toast.

"She thinks I'm too thin. I'm not too thin, I'm too old. In fact, in my view, your mother's too fat." He interrupted himself, quite irritably: "Don't you ever speak, child? You're depressingly like your mother. I wonder if you can speak at all."

Luke swallowed, and said, "I can speak."

Arthur raised an eyebrow and took a sip of tea, ignoring the boy's answer. At last he shook his head, dogmatically, and said, "I don't think so."

"I can speak," insisted Luke.

"I tell you what. If you finish that toast and pass the plate back here, and don't tell your mother you ate it, I'll confess that you speak all the time."

Luke dropped the remaining toast on the floor and stared imperiously at his grandfather.

Cruelty flickered in Turner's features, in his eyes. "I can see your father now. In your face, in your demeanour. But you don't know your father, do you?"

Luke was trapped. He didn't want to answer; but if he didn't, he would again be accused of being unable to talk.

"I know my father," he said. It wasn't true. He had never seen his father before.

"Of course you do," nodded Turner grimly. It was clear that he didn't believe Luke. "I know your father," he said. "I came to know him surprisingly well, despite our brief acquaintance. He gave me this."

He pulled his lank hair aside and leaned forward, to show Luke the tail-end of a livid scar on his scalp. Luke stared at it in confusion.

"It was a brick, boy. His instrument of choice. I tried to stop him, but I went down alright."

The old man straightened up, his mouth the same bitter gash that was his daughter's mouth, and let his hair fall.

"I was conscious, most of the time. I saw it, I saw most of your getting. But I couldn't move."

He smiled then, in horrible satisfaction. It was unbearable for Luke. The room had gone dark, and he didn't know why. He found it hard to breathe; he didn't understand his grandfather's words at all.

"That brick summed up everything," said the old dry voice. "It was his personality. You see things clearly when you're on the floor, broken and bleeding. The imprint of his personality, I should say. There is a relationship – in such moments – that surpasses explanation."

The old man shuddered, pulled himself back within his own skin. He glanced at Luke, apparently surprised to see him there. He looked down at his teacup.

"Perhaps," he said quietly, "that is why you have so little to say."

Luke's face had pulled into a rictus of weeping, but there were no tears. He limped out and disappeared back into the blinding white light.

* * *

52

Luke stood on the rocks and watched as a fisherman killed an octopus he had caught. He forced his gnarled brown thumbs into the bell of its head, hooking his fingers underneath, into the roots of the tentacles that struggled about his wrists; then he turned the creature inside out. It vibrated fiercely and went limp. Luke stared at the fisherman's hands, at the mangled animal hanging from them. Both were brown and mottled, iodine-stained. They were of the same world, shoreline monsters too ancient and violent to bargain with or to understand. A final convulsion ran down the tentacles.

His mother tugged at his arm and they picked their way through the series of rock pools, onto the beach. They walked some distance. The sky was calm now, this late in the afternoon. Acres of pale green light above the horizon, fading to mauve, long, silver sheets of light on the earth. They came to a halt and stood ankle deep in that mirror. The cold bit right down into the bones of his leg, but eased the duller, chronic ache of his joints.

"Is Grandfather a fisherman?" asked Luke suddenly.

"You should call him Arthur," replied his mother. "I would prefer that."

"I want to call him Grandfather."

His feet sucked into the sea mud as the water withdrew. His mother smiled angrily.

"But is he a fisherman?" insisted the boy.

"I don't think so. I doubt he's caught a fish in his life. What makes you ask?"

Luke thought of the octopus, and made no reply. Instead, he asked, "Why does Grandfather stink so much?"

"He doesn't anymore, Luke. He's had a hard time, I suppose. Things went wrong for him a long time ago, badly wrong."

Luke fell silent, wondering why things going wrong would make a person stink. Perhaps something had gone wrong with his bath; perhaps he couldn't find the soap.

"He used to be a professor," she said, more to herself than to Luke. "A professor of aerial perspective."

Luke glanced up at his mother. She smiled down at him and said, "He lost his own, you see, lost it entirely."

They waded out further. A particularly big hillock of waves rolled in, wetting Luke up to the middle of his thighs. He jumped, sucking in his stomach, shuddering.

"He taught people how to draw the sky, and the clouds, and the light in the clouds. He gave lectures on how to paint distance and light." Her eyes were moist. She said, "He gave lectures on many other things too. And he was a writer."

Luke understood none of it, but everything made sense: his grandfather was a mystery.

"He never thought he was good enough," she added. "Or perhaps he thought he was too good. I've never worked it out. In any event, he copied another writer, and so he got into trouble."

"Aren't you allowed to do that?"

"No, you're not. And then he started drinking more and more."

"He drank until he fell asleep," said Luke. "Like last night."

She smiled again and tousled his hair, and he jerked his head away.

"Perhaps we should go back," she said. "The tide's beginning to rise – I don't want you to walk too far on the soft sand."

She took his hand, and so they began the long slow walk back, the boy rolling as he limped.

"Grandfather saw my getting," said Luke.

Caitlin stopped, and looked down at him sharply.

"What does getting mean?"

She started walking again.

"What does getting mean?"

"Getting means where you come from," she replied, walking too fast for him now. He struggled after her. He still didn't understand, but knew his mother too well to push for a clear answer. Besides, he could feel the giant waves of silence that radiated from her stride, from the set of her back. There was something about his getting that upset her badly. Perhaps it was his grandfather's fault, perhaps it was his own: he knew he shouldn't have spoken about his getting. The light failed as they walked. His loneliness mounted up, until it battered at him like an onshore wind. He knew he would have to wait for her, perhaps several days. There could be no bargaining with her rage and fear. That was one of the most important rules of the world.

* * *

A southeaster gale built up, stacking up its violent energies in wearying succession, one upon the other. Gusts tugged at the roof and knocked the old sash windows, swirled without hindrance through the front and back doors. Fine drifts of sea sand built up on the floorboards and the mat, grit got into their food and ended up between their molars. It was a bullying, swaggering wind, a contemptuous wind. Luke hated every long minute of the storm.

The Turners sat at the kitchen table eating supper. The bare bulb seemed weaker than usual. The sound of the gale, its presence, dimmed the light. They ate snoek and brown bread and apricot jam. Arthur Turner chewed, his face a mask of distaste.

"If you call this fish a snoek," he said, "it acquires local colour. It becomes a regional delicacy." He took another forkful and chewed ostentatiously. "If you call it barracuda, it becomes a marine predator. Now that is an anomaly."

The word 'anomaly' pressed down on this small company of three generations: Luke felt its viscous weight pouring down over the table.

"Every kind of predator is forbidden as food, except marine predators. Do we eat eagles or butcher birds? Do we eat crocodiles? Do we eat leopards? But this is merely a snoek! – an incomprehensible word! – and therefore edible. Does that make sense to you, Caitlin?"

"Snoek is not barracuda," she replied. Then, with great articulation: "I don't know why you think they are the same."

"Christ, they look the same to me," said Arthur Turner. "Thin, pointy fish with big toothy mouths."

"All fish are predators," she said dully, and turned her attention to her plate.

"Well, exactly," he rejoined, but she ignored him.

Wind battered at the house, the light grew more dingy. Arthur Turner lifted his two–litre bottle of red wine with difficulty and poured himself another glass, his raised elbow trembling. He turned to Luke and said, "Would you like some wine, my boy?"

Luke shook his head. Caitlin looked up sharply, but again said nothing.

"A wise choice, Luke," said the old man. "This stuff is terrible."

Her silent rage filled the room. Arthur pushed his plate away, half the fish uneaten, and hunched over his glass of wine. Luke fiddled with his food, Caitlin chewed methodically. The wind blustered.

"The atmosphere in here is so thick," said Arthur querulously, "you could cut it with a knife."

His daughter ignored him.

"So damned awkward," he complained, as if to himself. "So damned difficult."

"And whose damned fault is that?" she snapped.

"Oh, mine undoubtedly. Everything here is my fault."

Her anger redoubled at his sarcasm, and burst loose: "You come here – I haven't seen you for *years!* – you practically *abandon* me and my child – you offer my son wine without consulting me – how do you know I approve of that? – and you expect, no, you virtually *demand* conversation when it suits you. Jesus, Arthur!"

Luke thought his grandfather would respond angrily, but Arthur seemed to fold over the wine, to shrink into his shabby jacket.

"I don't suppose it would help to remind you again," replied Arthur, his voice dry and calm, "that this was your decision. You've refused to see me for years. You know it perfectly well, Caitlin."

"I'm not going to discuss the matter further, not in front of Luke. God knows what it will lead to, or what you'll say in front of the boy. I certainly can't trust your discretion."

"Caitlin, you might hate me for saying this: but you will have to tell the boy one day where he comes from. These things always come out, and when this particular thing does come out – as inevitably it will – both of you will regret your silence. He will resent it to the day you die, and long after."

"That proves it," she retorted furiously. "I cannot trust your discretion at all – you've already said too much."

"Very well then, I shall have nothing further to say."

He hitched his chair around, with difficulty, so that he no longer faced her. He sat in crumpled dignity and glared at the corner of the room. Caitlin's fingers drummed on the table, then stopped. They flattened out. Luke wanted to laugh wildly, at the sight of his mother's pale, broad fingers spread out on the table.

Later in the night, Luke dreamt that his mother and grandfather still argued. Their voices raged through the thick wall, through the wind, almost merging with the wind. You've neglected the child horribly, said one voice. A clubfoot can be rectified these days. You can ignore the fact that it mars his beauty – but think of the pain of every step that he takes! It is shameful!

Christ, do you think I'm unaware of that? protested the other voice. I was broken at the time – I'm sorry, that's the only way I can describe it. I had no support, I still have no support; and I still am a broken personality, whatever you think of me. Besides, how dare you preach to me! If anything is shameful, it is you – practically telling Luke that he is the child of a rape.

The argument raged on, rising and falling. He thought he heard tears in his grandfather's voice, while his mother's was harder, grinding into the attack relentlessly. Arthur Turner's voice raised itself in a final wavering protest – an old man's helpless rage – and then, mercifully, Luke fell asleep.

* * *

He walked down the beach for a very long way. He didn't get tired as he usually did, and his foot didn't hurt. Sometimes he splashed his way along the icy water of the littoral, sometimes he pressed on through hot soft sand, above the tide line. It was a hot morning, but he felt comfortable. He was at home on this beach. He had walked along it and explored it ever since he could remember. Light seemed to spear through him, but not the heat; as he walked, he became a citizen of white light and salt air.

He saw a dark smudge in the water some distance away, obscured by the glare: a dark body lay in the wash of the tide, gently rocked by the action of the waves. Perhaps it was a human body. He thought at first that it might be his grandfather – it seemed to be a man in a shiny dark jacket – but as he drew closer, the illusion of human form fell away. He realised at last that it was a dead seal.

It had been gashed open, and its intestines and other organs were visible. Luke squatted down to study them. A cloud of flies buzzed around the exposed innards, whelk swarmed through them, their conical pink shells swirling rapidly as they dug into the guts, halting and reversing like small, startling mechanisms in a living clock. Luke studied this everted palette, astonished by the tubing, the sacs and bladders, the mixture of pastel colours and bitter gore. The eyes of the seal were open. They stared blindly up at the sky; the drying film over them reminded him of his grandfather's eyes. He questioned the seal: are you my grandfather? Do you know my father's name? Will you tell me that secret?

The seal's flippers were undamaged. They rested beside the cadaver like dull mechanisms of rubber, not animal parts at all.

He straightened up and walked further down the beach, much

further. The glare had grown more extreme, so it was difficult to make out details beyond the immediate shoreline. He stopped eventually and retraced his path. It was a very long walk. Perhaps because of the nature of the light, he missed the seal on his way back; perhaps it had been removed by the action of the tide.

There was no sign of his grandfather on his return. The bus had gone, his belongings too. Luke's mother was in a bad mood, clearly reluctant to talk about this departure or explain anything to him.

"Arthur left while you were asleep," she said. "I don't think we'll see him for a long time."

"Why did he go?"

"Why did he come?" she snapped, and that was her last word on the subject.

You made him go away, Luke thought dully. He will die soon and I will never know my father's name. He sat on the front step of the house for a long time, lifting handfuls of coarse white sand and letting it drift through his fingers.

* * *

Luke watched silently as his mother built a coffin on the sand in front of the cottage. Perhaps it was for his grandfather. She used materials that came from the sea: driftwood, shark egg pouches, oars of kelp, mussel shells, fish bones. She was an inept craftsman, and the coffin kept falling apart. Then she would leave it for days on end to spend her time hanging up fish to dry under the north-facing eaves of the cottage. They were called *harders*, silver fish about the size and shape of herring. As they dried, their silver skin grew bronzed, eventually turning a dull brown. Soon the whole north wall of the cottage was fringed with *harders*. For months on end, Luke and his mother ate nothing but salt fish.

She returned to the coffin, packing broken seashells into her weaving of kelp and driftwood. It was more like a basket than a coffin, a dry black tangle of organic matter. It smelt of salt, urine, rotting seaweed. As she worked on these two things, the coffin and dried fish, she began to change. Her pale skin gradually turned the colour of stained ivory; yet it retained a smooth texture, despite the wrinkles that grew around her eyes and mouth and under her chin. Her skin was badly-wrinkled silk. Luke knew that this change had something to do with the wind hunting

through the coffin, probing her sighs, the shuffling whisper of her
movements, the long speechless nights they shared. The wind dried her
out like the fish hanging from the eaves. There was a lesson for Luke in
this dream, one that lasted into his waking years. It demonstrated the
importance of skin: to whom it belonged, how smooth it was, its colour
and texture and how it breathed.

* * *

Early one evening, the man returned. It was his first visit that year.
He was a short, muscular man with a surly face and a scar on his
cheekbone that came from a knife fight. As usual, fear inflamed the
child, and he was unable to speak; it was wiser not to speak. His mother
also regarded the intruder silently. There was something prayerful in her
expression.

"I want meat," he said. "Meat and food."

She took sausage out of the fridge and began frying it. The man sat at
her table and waited for his meal. He knew she did not keep beer in the
house.

Luke kept very still, his eyes on the floor. Occasionally he would look
up and track his mother's movements. Ten minutes passed in silence,
except for the sound of fat hissing and bubbling. The rank smell crowded
the room, battering at Luke's senses. Then his mother scooped the
sausage into a plate and set it down before the man. She served him
bread and jam as well, with thick layers of margarine on the bread. She
made him tea, with four teaspoons of white sugar, then sat down before
him.

Her normally pale face was milky now; he chewed his food
vigorously, looking at her from time to time through his surly eyes. Luke
began to tremble. In the distance, faintly, he could feel rage and fear. Was
it his own? He didn't know; he didn't dare speak, or approach his
mother. He could only watch her, mutely drink in her presence. But she
was not there. Caitlin Turner was not his mother. She was a white sack of
nothing. The man at the table had sucked her away from inside and
hidden her.

Only once, he turned and stared at Luke, for a long time. The child
quailed. Then at last he turned away.

Presently he rose and stretched across the table, taking Caitlin's wrist
in his hand. Luke couldn't understand the expression on his face – was it

loathing? Was it anger, or desire? – he had a cold, dull, brutal face.

His mother rose meekly and followed the man into her bedroom. They left the door open, so Luke clearly heard his voice raised, though he couldn't understand the man's language. He heard the wet stinging slap of flesh on flesh. Then his mother said, "Wait," and she returned to close the door. After that, the sounds were muted but still audible: the nauseating percussion of his blows, the noise of their coupling, her mewling.

Luke huddled in his own room, his face turned to the wall. His body ached, his face burnt, he trembled with fever. The pain grew worse and worse. I am an octopus, he thought, thinking of the strong hands of the fisherman he had seen on the rocks, his brown thumbs.

The man was gone by the time Luke came out of his bedroom the next morning. His mother stayed in her room all that day. It didn't matter, as he knew she wouldn't talk, and he felt too sick to eat. She came out towards evening and limped to the table, older now than her own father. She sat down, unable to break the silence. Her lips were fat, overripe, split. There were new colours on the palette of her face, shades of indigo and yellow, crimson and taupe. Her silence deepened as colours bleached out of the light, making the colours on her face deepen too. I am here, said her silence. Nothing can be done. This is the cost of my life here, and of my motherhood. I make no choices: my life and death are indistinguishable.

This story originally appeared in *Modern South African Short Stories* edited by Stephen Gray (AD Donker, Cape Town, 2002).

*

Ken Barris lives in Cape Town and teaches at the Cape Technikon. He has published two novels, a collection of short stories, and a collection of poetry. Individual stories and poems have appeared in a number of journals and anthologies. A third novel, *Summer Grammar*, will appear in 2004. He has won the Ingrid Jonker Prize for poetry, the Vita Award for short fiction, and the M-Net Book Prize for his first novel, *The Jailer's Book*.

A is for Ancestors

George Makana Clark

R *is for Rain.* In *Fructman's Illustrated Dictionary for Little People*, a duck holds an umbrella against the slashing raindrops.

The rats had come with the rains. Nights, we heard them skitter inside the walls and beneath the floorboards of the bungalow, the scrabble of their tiny claws chasing us into our dreams. Mornings, sawdust fell through cracks in the beadboard ceiling and into our oatmeal as the rats gnawed at the beams, wearing down their long teeth. Afternoons, they slept in the stifle beneath the corrugated metal roof, and the house fell silent.

There was a burr in Mr Gordon's Rs, an affectation from his year in Scotland, where he had met Mrs Gordon. Perhaps he traveled to that country because he'd heard the women are so very fair. "Rrats," he'd say, looking down on the spoor that peppered his kitchen counters. He dredged it up from the back of his throat. "Bloody rrats."

In this, my twelfth rain season, the days played out by degrees, like the attic air that chilled with the advance of the mountain shadows. The season brought two types of rainfall: a deluge of heavy drops that beat on our heads until they throbbed, and a soft mizzle that crawled under our cuffs and collars and between the seams, weaving dampness into the fabric of our clothes. At dusk, when the vermin began to stir from their dreamless sleep, Mr Gordon would rise from his supper of bubble and squeak without excusing himself, and climb the ladder to the crawl space with a plate of fried meat to bait the spring traps. He also took a cold beer to drink as he stooped, breathing in the day's accumulated heat, and one of his enormous ledger books – the *coup de grâce*, I supposed, for any rat that might survive the snap of his traps. Perhaps he cherished this time away from me and Mrs Gordon, because he remained there until the air grew cold beneath the shrouded moon, reading aloud by torchlight from the massive ledger. His muffled, disembodied words drifted down on us with the sawdust a litany of receipts and expenditures, his own Book of Numbers.

On average, Mr Gordon filled one ledger book every three weeks with his cramped, backward-slanting scrawl. He pencilled all the transactions of his life into their ruled margins. Each ice-cream he bought for me on haircut day became an account receivable, and each time I completed a household chore he noted a reduction against my debt. Every full tank of gas in our British Ford was an asset to be amortised over the mountain roads he drove each day to and from his furniture store in Umtali. The brightly coloured scarves he bought for Mrs Gordon were entered as goodwill. Years earlier, Mr Gordon had ordered his carpenter, Sundayboy Moses, to construct a monolithic file cabinet for the ledgers: a wall of great drawers in the office above the furniture store, floor to ceiling, each as large as a steamer trunk. The joints in the cabinet were bevelled to appear nearly seamless, and the drawers glided on runners lined with stainless steel ball bearings taken from the wheels of derelict tractors that littered the Trustland. It was the last piece of furniture Sundayboy produced, his masterpiece, before he limped away northwest, toward the Unspeakable River where God resided.

Sundayboy's departure left Mr Gordon's store with four employees: Mr Tabori, a sales associate who had fled to Rhodesia after the fall of fascist Italy; two stockboys, Now Now and Pamwe, who worked for daily wages, unloading and uncrating furniture in the morning and running deliveries in the late afternoon; and the cleaning lady, Mrs Moses, who scrubbed Mr Gordon's toilets, emptied his waste bins, boiled and bleached his white shirts and underpants, polished his floors, and rubbed paste wax into the heavy wooden file drawers her husband had made. At home, Mr Gordon could not abide Africans, and so I was called upon to act as his servant. I fetched him his beer and jigger of scotch when he returned from the furniture store each night, massaged his knobbly feet, polished his ox-blood shoes, and lived on his property like a squatter.

Our house was a nine-room bungalow isolated in the mountains of Manicaland, outside of time and the world. My calendar was based upon the growth of my hair. Haircut days fell on the first and third Wednesday of each month, the only times I left the bungalow to join Mr Gordon on his daily commute into Umtali. He inspected my head before we set out, the pads of his fingers rooting through my bristles, "You have your mother's hair," he'd say, satisfied. I had to take his word for this. She kept her hair pinned tightly beneath a scarf, protection against the air-conditioning unit that blew full force, even during the raw nights that sometimes accompanied our dark Rhodesian winters. Scottish forebears hung on her dark walls, fixed and deathless in their sepia worlds – five grown sons standing around a seated patriarch, a small boy in pigtails and a kilt, a Royal Flying Corps pilot. They stared down on me with lithic eyes, folded hands, tight mouths. I only entered her room at dinner and supper, or when she summoned me with a bicycle horn. Mrs Gordon remained silent when I entered to place a tray of cold food over her knees and retreated with a sloshing bedpan.

Mr Gordon and I never spoke of passing. The matter of our ancestry was an understanding between father and son, something to keep from my mother. Our secret filled all the rooms of our house, up to the corners and crevices, leaving hardly enough room for the rats. We began our commute to the barbershop before the sun cleared the Vumba mountains and filtered its light through the rain clouds into the bungalow, though never into my mother's room, which faced west, its heavy curtains drawn shut. Mr Gordon hunched over the steering wheel as he piloted our British Ford through the mountain roads. Looking up through the windscreen that blurred and cleared with each pass of the wipers, he scanned the ridges above for snipers and saboteurs as we wound our way toward Umtali. Guerrilla soldiers sometimes infiltrated the eastern highlands to rev up an isolated farmhouse or waylay a motorist. We saw an ambush in every shadow as our British Ford lumbered along, and we braced for the deadly missile that would come speeding through our window. Once, a fallen tree blocked the road on a blind curve. The British Ford slewed on the wet pavement as Mr Gordon fought the skid, the massive ledger flying forward into the dash. We came to a stop amid the branches and leaves and watched as a dozen wild-eyed, unshaven Africans with glistening machetes emerged from the shadow to slit our scrags where we sat, hooked in our safety harnesses. But a week of heavy night frost had killed the tree, and the mountain winds had blown it over: these men were part of a road crew come to clear the debris. We watched them at work, lean muscles showing through yellow coveralls that left shoulders, knees, ankles, sometimes even genitals exposed to the *guti* weather. They sang their crazy song, *wari wari wari*, as they stripped the branches from the fallen tree and hoisted the sheared trunk off the road, down into the ravine. Then they trotted off in unison, still chanting the same two syllables in a sort of nonsensical invocation, perhaps to their God Mwari, the rainmaker. Their voices rose and fell with the wind, *wari wari wari*, as they disappeared into the long grass and the sheets of rain, leaving us to resume our journey and our tense waiting.

We went to the Shona barbers – Mr Gordon didn't fancy paying a pricey stylist for a crewcut, nor did he like the idea of a European inspecting our hair too closely. Because we were white skinned, we were seated immediately in adjacent chairs. While the barbers ran electric clippers over our skulls, I pretended to read the *Umtali Post*, turning the page at the same moment as Mr Gordon. On the day of the fallen tree, Mr Gordon handed me his newspaper and pointed to the lead story. There was a picture of an overturned motorcar, a Morris, on a mountain road. Bullet holes riddled the door panel. I gazed at it a moment, picturing myself inside.

".What's it say?" he asked, pointing to the article, "I forgot my glasses." The chair clippers buzzed in my ears.

"Well then, go on."

I shifted in my chair.

"Dammit boy, read it to me!" At this outburst, both of the Shona barbers ceased their clipping, unsure whether they should continue. I stared dumbly at the newspaper.

Mr Gordon knitted his brows. He pointed to the headline. "Read this then."

I shook my head.

"Bloody hell," he whispered, all harshness gone from his voice, "You don't know how."

I was still illiterate at twelve, a testament to Mr Gordon's devotion to the furniture store and his commitment to passing. Six years earlier, he and I had visited Saint Paul's School for Boys, where he'd hoped to board and educate me. We left abruptly after meeting with the headmaster. On our way home, Mr Gordon pulled up and shut off the engine. He stared through the windscreen, his hands still gripping the wheel, fighting the direction his life had taken. An admissions' application lay between us on the seat, along with a crumpled release form which, if signed by a parent, would allow the admissions board to conduct a background investigation into our family. A formality, but the very idea frightened him out of his senses, and I'd been allowed to stay at home with no more talk of school. We sat in our barber chairs in silence for several moments. "Of course you can't," he said softly. The Shona barbers resumed their clippings, and bits of hair fell about my neck. With a flourish that almost seemed choreographed, the barbers spun our chairs to face the mirrors, and together Mr Gordon and I absently nodded our approval.

"Come on, then," he said. I followed him as he pushed his way roughly through the queue of Shona men standing patiently for a free chair. Outside a hard rain pounded our shorn heads like drumming fingers, and the dank crept under our clothes against our skin.

We drove to a bookstore where I waited with the car, watching a team of policemen stop dark-skinned shoppers to inspect their radios, parcels, purses, and bags for shop bombs. A young Shona woman was asked to untuck her blouse and turn out the hem of her skirt. Clouds poured into the valley and rain fell, clearing the street of potential detainees. The police retreated beneath a news-stand. Fat drops beat against the roof of the British Ford, made in Rhodesia before the parts embargo, and the wind swirled ancestral spirits through the anti-draft window. The thunder that charged the air became the stamp of many feet in unison. I was asleep when my father emerged from the bookstore with a copy of *Fructman's Illustrated Dictionary for Little People*. The book's spine was black with gold pinstripes, reminding me of a suit Mr Gordon had bought and no longer wore, not since the day when an identically attired, especially dark Shona man knocked on the door of our house. It had been years since Mr Gordon invited anyone, servants or visitors, onto his property. Perhaps the man stood on our doorstep as a witness for one of the religious sects that had sprung up across Rhodesia in those troubled times. It had made a great impression on me, my father and his African *doppelganger* staring at one another from opposite sides of the barred door window that looked out on the veranda, each wearing the other's suit. It must have affected my father also, this mirror into a world that ran up against ours, because he withdrew to his study and left the man standing on the verandah. Wednesday was early closing day in Umtali, a relief for both of us, and Mr Gordon was not obliged to linger at the tuckshop where he would read the notices posted on the board over the cash register or inspect the polish on his shoes, or crack his lumpy knuckles while he waited for me to guttle my ice cream. We drove home, in our habitual silence, the slap of the windscreen wipers, the radio murmuring at sub-audible volume, traffic lights reflecting on the wet pavement that sucked at the tyres. "From now on you're coming into the store with me," he told me. "You'll learn to read like any other white man." The windscreen blurred and cleared with each pass of the wipers, and thus ended my aimless and unsupervised days at home.

* * *

S is for Store. In *Fructman's* a jolly, aproned man stands before a grocery with empty windows. Mr Gordon's furniture store was located

65

in the shopping district on palm-lined Main Street, where Africans
waited to make their purchases until all the Europeans had been served.
He hated that economic necessity forced him to deal with Africans at all,
and he vented his frustration on the shoe-blacks who tried to set up on
the pavement outside his shops. He kicked at their boxes, spilling rags
and tins of polish, before calling the police to move them along. That
first day, Mr Gordon brought me up to his office and seated me at the
unused half of a partner's desk built by Sundayboy Moses. As with the
great file cabinet, each piece of wood in the desk fit snugly into the whole
without glue or nails. Sundayboy had helped build Mr Gordon's
furniture store and, in its early days, produced much of the inventory.
This must have been a natural talent, because woodworking was almost
unknown among the people of the Unspeakable River. They made no
more than their carved boats would carry: spears, fishing nets, children.

Here at the partner's desk, I began my struggle with *Fructman's
Illustrated Dictionary for Little People*. The collection of ciphers that
corresponded to the picture of a ship started with the same letter as the
picture of a bumble bee. "Ship", I said aloud, pretending to read. I'd
studied the book for an hour and still not cracked the code.

"It's Boat," Mr Gordon pointed to the letter B and said, "Ba! Ba!"
He exhibited the same impatience with his stockboys – particularly Now
Now, who responded to all requests for work with "Yes, baas, I will do it
now now." Among the Shona now might mean two hours or two days.
'Now now' simply meant sooner than now. It was a source of constant
irritation to Mr Gordon that he had no means to express urgency to his
employees.

My assault on *Fructman's Illustrated Dictionary for Little People* was
interrupted when Now Now arrived late to the store. One of the crowded
lorries that brought workers in from the Trustland had broken down.
Now Now pulled at his white beard as he stood before his employer. Mr
Gordon put on his fatherly face. "I can't let you stroll in here at all
hours, Now Now. My furniture won't unload itself."

"Yes, big problem."

"You want to see me run out of business?"

"No, never, *baas*."

"Laziness and lack of discipline, that's what." Now Now had served
under Mr Gordon in the Rhodesian Rifles during the war. The Shona
stockboy was a decade his senior, but Mr Gordon spoke to him like a child.

"Yes, *baas*, very bad."

"I'm going to have to cut your pay."

"Yes, of course, *baas*."

"Now shift that lot into the showroom."

"Yes, now, now, *baas*." Now Now slumped against the wall and watched his employer storm away. He didn't blame Mr Gordon for his troubles. "It is my ancestors making mischief again," he said, and Pamwe nodded sympathetically.

"They do not stay well because I cannot afford to bring the meat and beer. The *bakkie* breaks down, my pay is cut, more bad luck."

Mr Gordon had packed sandwiches for our lunch that day. "Here's some meat for your ancestors' shrine," I offered, lifting the cold pork from between the slices of bread.

"No, no, little *baas*. No shrine, no statues," he said, accepting the gift. "I am no bleeding Pygmy or Portuguese Catholic. Ancestors never mind where they get their meat and beer. Any place does fine. Go well, little *baas*, I got to work now."

He settled back against the wall, staring at the greasy treasure in his hands, and I doubted the offering would make it to his ancestors. I ate the bread and returned to the partners' desk to stare at my book until the large block letters blurred on the page before me. I looked down through the window on Mrs Moses's little house, then studied the top of Mr Gordon's head for a while as he hunkered over the furniture store books on his desk. His reddish hair tended to kink noticeably next to his skull during the rain season, despite his monthly chemical process, and he'd taken to shaving a thin, pink part along the left side of his skull to maintain the fiction that he was a white man. We sat long and still, working until our backsides ached. Sometimes I would follow him out to the loading dock to watch him spit onto the gravel below. My father spat beautifully, another betrayal of his African heritage. He collected the saliva at the back of his throat, not ostentatiously like the red-faced Rhodies and Boers who farmed the valleys of Manicaland. Instead, he shaped it into an oyster with his tongue and sent it flying through the O of his lips in a graceful arc from mouth to target. He could imprison an ant inside a globule of spit at five paces. He also whistled perfectly, the dying art of his generation, and as he wrote in his ledgers he warbled strange and wondrous tunes that ignored conventional harmonics and stirred something deep inside me. He was always losing things – his service pin, a tie tack, a fountain pen – and I frequently found him turning out his pockets or searching beneath the desk on his hands and

knees. Each afternoon at three o' clock Mrs Moses would poke her head
into the office, her eyes searching Mr Gordon's face, and I wondered if I
were interrupting some duty she normally performed in my absence.
Before withdrawing, she shot me a cross look that should have explained
everything.

* * *

C is for Church. A family of little people holding hands at the
entrance beneath the steeple, elliptical halos floating above their heads.
The illustrator for *Fructman's* chose to leave them faceless. Sundayboy
acquired his Christian name because he took odd jobs from neighbouring
merchants on the Sabbath, when the furniture store was closed. Perhaps
Mrs Moses, returning from her church services, still looked for her
husband when she turned the corner into her yard: bent over a shop door
warped by humidity, the shavings curling up from the plane in his hand.
From his office, Mr Gordon looked down on Mrs Moses's house – a
windowless, one-room affair constructed of raw pine unmarred by nails,
each board joined tongue-and-groove. The Brothers of St. Augustine's
had given her husband his surname because he had come to the lonely
mission from the river, lying silent and bleeding in the bottom of a
shallow dugout, his wife standing over him as she poled the tiny craft
along the bank. Rainwater ran off the asphalt roof onto the unpaved
drive where Mr Gordon parked his British Ford. Though Sundayboy
had built the house himself, he never lived within its walls. He couldn't
sleep that first night inside, without stars, so he carried a blanket out into
the yard and lay down amid the lumber and sawhorses. Perhaps
Sundayboy pretended the shish of tyres on wet asphalt was the rush of a
strong current, and the soft rain on his face was the mist from the river,
the rumble of a diesel lorry the roar of a hippo. During thunderstorms
he would climb to the roof of the furniture store and stretch his hands
skyward. It was Now Now who told me the story about Sundayboy
standing there with arms lifted to God while lightning fell about him
and threw his shadow across the yard below. Now Now was sleeping on
the loading platform that night because Mr Gordon had docked his pay
and the old stockboy lacked car-fare to return to his wife and children in
the Trustland. Sundayboy refused to bring a child into this land so far
away from the Unspeakable River and the Begetter of All Things. He
continued to lie apart from his wife – he in the yard, she in the house –

until the cloudless evening when Mrs Moses went outside to where her husband slept, hiked up her nightgown, and lowered herself upon him, thus conceiving Ephat beneath the stars before Sundayboy was properly awake. This, too, Now Now had witnessed, for there were very few days when Mr Gordon sent him home with a full day's wages.

When Mrs Moses's son, Ephat, contracted the mumps, I was sent to sleep beside him in his sickbed. Mrs Moses's garden beds flanked the sole entrance to the house. Here she grew thrift, stonecrop, cast iron – a stunted, spiky show that grasped and irritated the ankles of visitors who strayed from the one true concrete path that led to her door. The interior of Mrs Moses's house was a reliquary of plaster saints and twisted crosses fashioned from bits of frond, collected over half a lifetime of Palm Sundays and nailed to the walls. The house smelled of ammonia and wood-oil soap and discontent. That night Ephat lay sweating and motionless beside me, bathed in the streetlight that shone through the sole window, his testicles swollen double. By midnight, when he'd kicked away all the bedclothes, his mother silently appeared. I watched Mrs Moses as she ran a cool washrag over his feverish body and sang a sort of medicine song, a yodeling chant whose meaning she'd probably forgotten. Her face was hexangular, lean and coffin-shaped in the streetlight from without. Mrs Moses noticed my open eyes and tried a smile. "Better to catch this now, before you become a man and you want children. You'll bring this disease home to your brothers and sisters, eh". She was unaware I was an only child. Mr Gordon never spoke of himself or his family to his employees. "I haven't got any," I told her. Mrs Moses digested this bit of information. "I don't want to be pushing, but is your mother a...sickly woman? A woman with only one child is almost sterile. Perhaps she could rub the oil from tsin beans between her legs for fertility."

Women from the Unspeakable River coveted children above all else, to replace the ones lost to disease and malnutrition and drowning and lightning, and fierce hippos. Mrs Moses leaned over me to kiss Ephat goodnight, and though he was my age, she sung to him as if he were an infant, "*sleep my little one, the night is wind and rain, drops fall in our meal, and the river floods its banks again.*" Inside her shirt, hanging on her neck from a chain, I saw a garnet cuff link, one Mr Gordon had been searching for in his office. Mr Gordon was the sort of employer who invited theft. Beaded lamps, bookends, throw pillows disappeared from the showroom, fountain pens and notepads from the office. Rather than lose face, he fixed the books to account for the shrinkage. I also stole from him – a shaving brush, a lapel pin that commemorated his service in a war he never spoke about, several liver pills from the pockets of trousers I laundered, nail clippers. Mrs Moses looked down on me where I lay beside her son, perhaps considering whether she should also kiss me goodnight. Instead she patted my cheek with a hand that smelled of oil soap and cooking fat, the same tacky mixture that covered all the surfaces of her house. Outside, rotting lumber creaked and shifted against the walls of the house, left untouched since the day Sundayboy stripped down to the dazzling underpants his wife had boiled in bleach and shambled away on his crooked leg, north toward the Zambezi, leaving her nearly sterile with only one child. He abandoned his carpenter's tools with his family; bevel saws and adzes and hand drills were now buried beneath the muddy gravel Mr Gordon had poured so he could park his British Ford and the delivery lorry within the security fences that surrounded Mrs Moses's yard. There was a sign attached to the fence, *Basopa lo Inja*, but the dog had followed his master north to the Unspeakable River, and there was nothing left to beware of in that yard. The house seemed to hold its breath, waiting for Sundayboy to return. That first night I had an incurable case of hiccoughs, and Ephat, sweating next to me, said it was a sign of my ancestors calling.

* * *

L is for Light. A naked bulb surrounded by a brilliant wash of yellow. This page of *Fructman's* is slightly warm to the touch. How many people remember clearly the moment they first began to read? I stared at the page in *Fructman's* facing the boat. A picture of a sparrow perched on a twig that floated on the page, and a wave of understanding flooded my brain. "Bird," I said proudly.

"Yes, that's it. Well done!" and he clamped me on the shoulder and anyone could see my father was proud of me. I took that moment and stored it away deep in my heart. This, then, was the first in a string of letters I would read during my lifetime; end on end, they would stretch long enough to circle the world many times. Elated, my father decided to take me to the tuckshop for an ice cream. I believe he would have bought this and not even written it into his ledger book as an account receivable, had our trip not been cut short when we stepped outside the store and he froze, his mouth working silently. I followed his gaze down to the

70

pavement where a shoeshine box lay unattended. He finally found his voice: "Bomb!"

My father hustled me back into the store and we scrambled through the narrow aisles of the showroom toward the back service door, bracing ourselves for the storm of fire and window glass. A customer swore as he stumbled over an accent table, knocking a ceramic vase to the floor. Mr Tabori shouldered me out of his path and I tore my trouser pocket on a drawer handle. A grandfather clock began chiming the hour. Out on the loading dock, Now Now, Pamwe and a delivery driver joined our stampede, and we raced down the alley several blocks before anyone thought to call the bomb squad. A false alarm, as it turned out – only an empty polish tin and a few scraps of soft rags. This, I later realised, was the shoe-blacks' revenge on Mr Gordon. When Ephat recovered from the mumps, Mr Gordon took me to the outskirts of Umtali to a clapboard doctor's office. Though patients overflowed from the crowded waiting room into the car park, Dr N'gono saw me immediately. Mr Gordon chose the Shona doctor for the same reasons he chose our Shona barbers. Dr N'gono felt my neck and scrotum for any signs of swelling and sighed, "Bad luck you didn't catch this now." He shone a light into my ear. "Your father had a bad case, just after you were born, nearly took him." As I dressed, I wondered if Mr Gordon would have risked more offspring if he hadn't caught the mumps in his maturity and left my mother nearly sterile with just one child.

I rejoined Mr Gordon on his daily commute along the shadowy mountain roads, returning each night to the bungalow to sleep beneath the rats, and though I continued to see Ephat every day after my reading sessions, he never invited me into the little house again. "It's the ancestors," he explained. "They don't stay well here."

Mrs Moses refused to speak of her forebears, much less provide them with offerings, and so Ephat knew of his ancestors only through dimly remembered stories his father had told – they were hippo hunters who took their name from the river from which they drank, a distal tributary that fed the Zambezi. Because it was forbidden for Sundayboy to give voice to this secret place where God resided, Ephat's ancestors remained nameless. Outside, neither of us knew how to conduct ourselves. We climbed stacks of lumber in silence, staring into the gray sky, or squatted in the yard to recover any of Sundayboy's ruined tools that had resurfaced with the rains. Our play took shape when Ephat suggested we become hippo hunters, and we fashioned thin spears from sharpened dowels,

71

wading through the deepest puddles in the yard to stalk sawhorse hippos, more dangerous even than crocodiles, especially in the water. But these unsatisfactory weapons bounced and shattered against our targets. We broke tradition and made slingshots from tree branches, carving and sanding and polishing them, as if they were the missiles themselves rather than the delivery system. I found surgical rubber in the first-aid kit Mr Gordon kept in the boot of the British Ford and we experimented with bits of gravel, marbles, and hard candy. Eventually Ephat discovered the ideal size, shape, and balance in the tractor-wheel ball bearings he extracted from the runners of the heavy wooden file cabinets. We held these perfect missiles between our thumbs and forefingers as we drew back the surgical rubber and released them with such force as could topple a sawhorse. One day, when my father went down to the sales floor to help Mr Tabori with the late afternoon rush of customers and Mrs Moses carried the dustbins downstairs to empty in the furnace, I saw Ephat enter my father's office with some meat in his hands. Curious, I followed, but found no one inside. I dropped to my knees and looked beneath the partners' desk, rose and went to the window and looked out into the yard below, but there was no sign of Ephat. It was as if he'd passed through a portal into the spirit world. Outside on the loading dock, Now Now unwrapped his lunch, expecting to find a sandwich made from the shank of a goat. The animal had wandered in front of a lorry that was taking him home to the Trustland, and the shank was Now Now's share for helping load its carcass quickly into the bed. He shook his head when he found only two grease-soaked slices of bread inside the butcher paper. "I swear on my beard, I'm going to beat my wife for this," he said. He stuffed one of the slices into his mouth and addressed me while he chewed. "I tell you, young *baas*, don't come home too late at night if you like meat for lunch."

I soon mastered *Fructman's*, and this time my father brought me with him into the bookstore and helped me choose: *Curious George, The Velveteen Rabbit, Goodnight Moon*. Each morning after the opening rush, it became his habit to leave the furniture store in the care of Mr Tabori. We sat at the same side of the partners' desk, his hand on one side of the book, mine on the other, while I read stories to him, shaping my mouth around the sounds of each letter until a word emerged. It was torturously slow going, and my father would provide me with the difficult words only after I'd stared at them for some time. We'd sit this way, me struggling, my father by turns encouraging and chastising, until midmorning, when we took our coffee out on the loading dock. I held the mug like my father, close to my nose without using the handle, letting the warmth soak through the ceramic into my fingers, drawing the steam into my damp lungs. We watched Mrs Moses work her stunted garden beds. She showed no signs of the chill and wet as she dug and pulled at the ground. Now Now said that river people are naturally cold and watery, because of the mist. One night when he had no money for the lorry to take him back to the Trustland, I saw him knock on Mrs Moses's door, but no one answered. "That is the way of it always," he said to me, smiling. "When you grow up, you'll weep."

After we took our coffee, my father would spread before me a daily balance sheet and income statement, identical to his own. Each time he paid an invoice, he subtracted the amount from the asset side of his balance sheet and added it to the expenses in his income statement. Then he handed me the bill to enter into the duplicate set of books I maintained as part of my education in mathematics and finance. From time to time my father looked across the desk at me as I worked, my spindly arms protruding from short sleeves, my spiky ginger hair, the heavy ledger before me, his own image in miniature. With both of us keeping books, the great cabinet began to fill at double its previous rate, and each time my father started a new drawer, the wood screeched and groaned from want of the ball bearings Ephat and I had pilfered for our slingshots. He would rub his forehead and sniff at the faint smell of meat. At home on a Sunday, I read Beatrix Potter to Mrs Gordon, raising my voice above the roar of the air conditioner: Once upon a time there was a woodmouse, and her name was Mrs Tittlemouse. Mrs Gordon ceased rocking her torso in the chair and listened, her venous hands no longer working at the armrests. She lived in a bank under a hedge. In the attic above, Mr Gordon stomped about, setting his traps, and sawdust floated down on us from the ceiling where the rats had gnawed at the beams. *Such a funny house!*

* * *

H is for History. On this page, the illustrator for *Fructman's* outdid himself. The people of the Unspeakable River lived in the weather with nothing to separate them from the wind and sky and storms and killing lightning and cold and floods, and any other disturbances the Begetter of All Things might fashion for his children. When Mrs Moses had brought her wounded husband to the priory, she must have wondered at the roof and walls that kept the missionaries apart from God: perhaps she thought

73

of all the children she could raise if she had such a place for herself. Perhaps it was she who persuaded the brothers to teach Sundayboy the secrets of their wood-building when he recovered from his wounds.

Ephat, convinced that his neglected ancestors had visited the mumps on him, moved out of his mother's house and began to sleep in the yard. I was released from my reading to join him there for an hour every afternoon. The rain fell over us out in the yard where Ephat now lived, and stories Sundayboy told long ago resurfaced in his son's memory like the rusting tools that sometimes rose up from the mud. I learned how the men immersed themselves in the torrent of the Unspeakable River at the height of the rains, armed only with their fists, voices, and teeth, to drive a hippo roaring and bellowing into the bush. There they forced it to kneel in the presence of a God the tormented beast could neither see nor understand. While the women fell to the ground and wailed for their drowned children, the men likewise prostrated themselves, panting and bloody, before the Father to petition Him to quiet the rain and return the turgid river to its peaceful level. As His shadow of light fell over them, they became lost in the rapture. Once, while the men beat the water about their waist to raise one of the creatures, a bull rose before Sundayboy. He wrapped his arms around the hippo's head, each hand gripping an ear while great, blunt teeth tore at him. Before the others could reach them, the hippo took him beneath the water, where such creatures are at their most dangerous. Mrs Moses poled the dugout containing the mutilated body of her husband from the headwaters of the Unspeakable River, into the Zambezi, and on to St. Augustine's. There, the brothers managed to save Sundayboy's leg and his reproductive organs, preserving Mrs Moses's hope that she might still have children. Sometimes Ephat talked about setting out north in search of his father, but I think he was afraid of what he'd find. One afternoon, when the time came for my father to send me out of the office, I went down to the loading dock to read *Babar* and listen to the rain. Now Now had settled into a sofa that he and Pamwe had unloaded, and I caught the tail end of their conversation.

"Not that I blame him, brother," Now Now said. "I'd fancy a go at her myself." Pamwe nodded his assent and glanced up at the office above the loading dock. "Heyya, what you listening for?" Now Now had noticed me with my book. "What's a go?" I asked him. Pamwe snorted. He was a few years older than me.

"You never mind, young *baas*," Now Now said. He rose from the sofa and called to Pamwe, "Come shift this lot inside before the rain comes."

74

And then to me, "Go find Ephat and play somewhere else." To Pamwe again, "Here, brother, take a side," and they carried the sofa through the swinging rubber doors and into the showroom.

I called for Ephat at the door of the little house, but there was no answer. Behind me, in Mr Gordon's office above the store, I could hear Mrs Moses, her voice caught between laughter and wailing. I wondered what a go with Mrs Moses entailed, and I shinnied up the beam that supported the roof tresses and crawled over the open loading dock and looked in through the office window.

It was a curious thing to see Mrs Moses naked below the waist in my father's lap, and though he trained his glassy stare in my direction he saw nothing. His fingers pulled at the brown flesh of her thighs as if he would have it for himself, and Mrs Moses wrapped her arms and legs around his waist pulling him deeper within.

My father's vision focused as he climaxed, and his roar caught in his throat as he met my eyes on the other side of the window. He pushed Mrs Moses from his lap, gathered his clothes, and went into the toilet without looking at the window, adding this incident to the list of things about which we would never speak. Mrs Moses sat on the chair where she had straddled my father moments earlier, rubbing the oil pressed from tsin beans between her legs to increase her fertility. Next she clamped them tightly together, twice crossed at the knees and ankles to hold in my father's arid semen. She remained in this position with her head bowed, praying I supposed, for some minutes before she left the room. I cannot say why I continued to look into that empty room, other than a queer feeling that this scene had not yet ended. The wind blew in from the mountains, pulling a thunderstorm behind it. Inside the office, the bottom drawer of my father's file cabinet glided open by itself, and Ephat climbed out. This was where he'd disappeared that day he'd stolen the goat meat from Now Now's lunch. Ephat made offerings to his progenitors from inside the last of the great empty drawers of the monolithic cabinet, surrounded on all sides by his father's craft. We stared at each other, and the window glass reflected the storm clouds that moved across the sky behind me, superimposing them on Ephat's face. His eyes smouldered with a hatred for me, who bore witness to his humiliation.

* * *

A is for Ancestors. Tear this page from your *Fructman's Illustrated Dictionary for Little People* and burn it. To look on it would bring death. The next morning, Ephat joined one of the repair crews that filled potholes and kept the mountain roads clear of scree and deadfall, and he slept that evening in the weather on the gravel bank of a highway that wound through the mountains like a river. As I waited in the office for my father to close the store, I looked down on Mrs Moses where she stood in the doorway of her childless house, flanked by stunted, nearly barren garden beds. The yard began to flood with rainwater, and she watched the derelict tools rise from the mud – a handless screwdriver, a rusty hacksaw blade, half a pair of pliers – and then sink again beneath the promised land where she had brought her family to prosper and multiply.

This would be the last day Mr Gordon ever brought me to the furniture store for reading sessions. Instead, he found me a place in The Springs of Living Water, House of Prayer and Boys' School. The headmaster, a charismatic man who called himself Brother Paul, was the African who had stood on our veranda in my father's suit, and the masters were all Ndebele from the south: muscular, fierce-eyed men. But they conducted no background inquiries into our family, and, as with our barbers, and our doctor, Mr Gordon found them less threatening than Europeans. Most of the students were Shona, except for me and three poor sons of a retired, alcoholic British soldier and his Indian servant. The brothers of The Springs of Living Water administered beatings when we spoke Shona words, or when I wrote with my left hand, or when I moved my mouth to read the Scriptures silently to myself, or scotched my sums, or pulled my hands away during group prayers, or remained silent when the brothers spoke in tongues. I welcomed the beatings that accompanied my immersion into the Springs of Living Water, because someone had to punish me for my secret ancestry.

With my enrolment, haircut days shifted to the Sabbath. Before daybreak, Mr Gordon rose from the narrow iron bed in his study. He cooked our porridge, noisily banging the spoon around the saucepan to send the rats scuttling into the walls before we sat down to eat.

The rains lasted beyond the season in the highlands, and dark cloud shrouded the mountains, revealing only a dozen or so metres of road before our British Ford and swallowing it up again behind us. Sometimes I heard the faint *wari wari wari* of a road crew singing, but though I strained to make out the great silhouettes through the cloud

76

and rain, I never saw Ephat again. My father and I had no conversation to distract us from the radio on the way into Umtali, and we listened to news of rebel activity, of motorists waylaid on lonely stretches of highway. We came to anticipate the attack so keenly that when the shot finally came through our windscreen, it brought on the satisfaction of an expectation fulfilled. It wasn't a bullet, but rather a perfectly smooth stainless steel ball bearing that punched a hole clean through the windscreen just below the rear view mirror, striking my breastbone before falling to the floor mat.

I lay in my seat, the breath knocked from me, my head below the dash, near the radio. The broadcaster spoke calmly and confidently into my ear as he read the standard procedure for motorists who find themselves under attack by terrorists: lie down on the seat or, if a barricade has made it impossible to continue or the vehicle is disabled, move away from the car, find cover, and wait for one of the regular army patrols.

I sat up in my seat and rubbed the spot over my heart where the ball bearing had struck me. My father and I had said so little to each over the course of our lives it seemed natural that we would not speak now. He settled back in his seat, whistling one of his odd tunes, as if there were no point in ducking to avoid an attack now that it had already come. We drove on toward our house, wipers flapping, the ball bearing rolling on the floorboard under my seat, the radio murmuring as if it were in the presence of the dead. By the time my father turned our British Ford, built in Rhodesia, into our drive and switched off the engine, the entire incident had never happened.

* * *

U is for the Unspeakable. There is no illustration for this on the final page of *Fructman's*, only that single, cryptic mark.

The comical bark of the bicycle horn summoned me to where Mrs Gordon sat in the boneless slump of an invalid. Her chair was turned to the air conditioner that roared full into her face, a windstorm from the highlands of Scotland that dried her eyes and rippled the scarf against her skull, the heather and green tartan of her clan flapping over her atrophied legs. It was Sunday, and I could feel more than hear my father's heavy footsteps above us as he baited his traps. Mr Gordon never brought the corpses of the killed rats down into the house. At times a

77

faint, sweetly sickening smell slipped through the cracks in the bead board along with the sawdust.

I lifted Mrs Gordon's hand from the armrest to massage it – poor circulation had turned her nails blue – and while I rubbed her fingertips, her knuckles, her palm, I recited a poem I'd read that day. *Alas! Alas! for Miss Mackay*, working oil with juniper into the cracked skin, *her knives and forks have run away*, and my mother squeezed my hand back. I dabbed at the milky substance that formed at the corners of her mouth and in the collups beneath her chin, *and when the cups and spoons are going*, and her features softened almost into a smile, *she's sure there is no way of knowing*. Perhaps it was this intimacy, or maybe I could no longer hold our secret any longer, and it spilled out of my mouth before I knew I had spoken: "Father and I are coloured".

Mrs Gordon's hands moved faster than my eyes could follow, and the blows stung both sides of my head at once. This was the first and only time she ever struck me, and by the time I realised she had boxed my ears, my mother had already swept me up and squeezed me against her. I stood dumb in the arms of this carline ghost come suddenly to life. Of course she would have felt the tight curls when she stroked the base of my father's neck in the early days of their courtship, the smell of his chemical process in her nostrils. She had been our accomplice all along, helping us keep our secret. "Don't talk rubbish," she said, softly into my ringing ears. The scent of juniper filled my nose almost to my eyes as my mother stroked my face, and this comforted me.

That night I had a dream:

An old African woman dressed in beadwork and wearing an elaborately piled turban stands at the door of my bed smoking a long-stemmed pipe. She beckons. I follow her up the ladder to the attic crawl space, where, from the darkness, hands grasp at my hair and touch my skin. They press close against me until I no longer know where they begin and I leave off, and we become almost seamless, like Sundayboy's furniture, pieced together with a bond much stronger than nails and glue. I smell meat and beer on their breath as they whisper their silent hunger in my ears.

I rose from this dream and climbed up to the attic crawl space, and the smell nearly knocked me back down the ladder. My father had left a torch at the edge of the opening, and I switched it on and shined it about – a pile of vinyl luggage, a streaked mirror, my mother's abandoned hope chest, my father's kit bag from World War II. There were no traps. The light played on the plate of meat my father had brought up earlier and left on a kitchen chair, now acrawl with rats. Of course it was his offerings, not the rain, that drew vermin to our bungalow in such great numbers. A ledger book open to that day's balance sheet had been propped against the back of the chair so our ancestors could see the worth of the furniture store to date. The chair and floor beneath smelt of spilt beer, wet fur, rodent faeces, and the residue of spoiled meat. The rats looked up from the remaining gobbets of flesh. They shrieked at the torchlight and sank their red teeth into one another in fright and confusion. I stared at this squirming, makeshift altar, my father's secret devotion to his ancestors now manifest. My legs dropped out from beneath me, and I found myself kneeling and bellowing, like a hippo bullied before the God of the Unspeakable River. A soft rain fell on the roof in strange rhythms, and the wind sounded beneath the eaves of the corrugated metal in notes identical to those my father whistled beneath his breath.

*

George Makana Clark grew up in Zimbabwe. He has published one collection of short stories, *The Small Bees' Honey* (White Pine Press), and his fiction, drama, and poetry have appeared in *Black Warrior Review, Chelsea, Georgia Review, Glimmer Train, The Massachusetts Review, The Southern Review, Transition, Zoetrope: All Story*, and elsewhere. He was the recipient of a 2002 National Endowment of the Arts Fellowship in Fiction Writing and a finalist for The Caine Prize for African Writing. He currently teaches fiction writing at The University of Wisconsin-Milwaukee.

Ouagadougou

Emmanuel Dongala

My father was nine years old, younger than I am today, when men
first walked on the moon. It may be hard to believe, but they say
when Papa was born, you couldn't follow the World Cup or the
Olympics on television. Coca-Cola had not yet introduced soft drinks to
our village; there were no music videos, no rap or ragamuffin – Michael
Jackson was not even a star. I wonder what people did all day long.

The white people who had occupied our country left in the year of
my father's birth. We got our independence and became a republic,
complete with a flag, an anthem, and ministers roving the laterite roads
in Mercedes.

Grandfather was decorated twice that year: first by the French on the
last Bastille Day they celebrated as chief rulers of our country, and then
a month later, on Independence Day, by the first president of our
liberated country. But Grandfather was doubly rejected in the dustbin of
history. Hero that he had been, he was a reactionary and a
collaborationist to the revolutionary Marxist-Leninist government that
held power when I was born. He had, after all, been decorated by both
the French and our 'neocolonial' first republic. He was one of the first
Africans to receive his certificate of Indigenous Studies and became a
schoolteacher. Public education, secular and republican, was an article of
faith for men of his breed: the future of the world was in education and
nothing else. Neither religion nor philosophy nor the ways of the
ancestors was to interfere.

One Sunday, passing in front of the school where he taught,
Grandfather noticed an unusual crowd. Upon closer inspection, he saw a
bearded white priest celebrating mass. (Back then, the priests still wore
long robes – soutanes – and spoke only Latin, even in the remotest
villages.) My grandfather flew into a rage at the sight of the intruder and
his faithful flock violating these grounds of secular, republican
education. He challenged the priest: "Monsieur, in the name of the
secular republic, I ask that you put an end to your show and leave these
premises, which are under my authority!" It seems that the word *show*,
used to describe his religious ceremony, was what angered the priest

most. Yet Grandfather didn't mean anything by it: he had learned the expression long before, when the Lemba high priests had permitted a colonial governor to participate in a non-secret part of a sacred ceremony that sustains the life, health, and harmony of the clan. At the end, the governor had put his white pith helmet back on and commented to the young schoolteacher who was accompanying him – my grandfather – "Not a bad show". And so, for Grandpa, any religious ceremony was a "show". But this priest took great offence at the word and declared that Grandfather was an agent of the devil. He then picked up the instruments of his office and left, followed out by the children of the choir. Now in those days there was a superstition prevailing in our country: if you had an argument with a priest, you should never let him leave your house without first pulling on the cord of his soutane. Otherwise he'd carry your soul away with him, and you would die right then and there, or you'd have the devil on your tail till the end of days. So as soon as my grandfather saw the black soutane heading for the door, swaying defiantly on the priest's waddling hips, he ran up and pulled with all his might and fury, ripping the cord clean off and tearing open the vestments. The priest responded by bringing his big cross down on Grandpa's skull. Grandpa screamed in pain and threw an uppercut at the aggressor's bearded chin. He narrowly missed his mark: fortunately, someone had managed to hold him back. The church filed a complaint. The white district commander, torn between justice (Grandfather was simply respecting the laws of the Republic, which called for public schools to remain secular) and racial solidarity with the compatriot, finally sided with the priest, who never again found the courage to come and say mass at the schoolhouse. You don't know Grandpa if you think he stopped there, though. He liked to brag about having a grandfather, real or imaginary, who had fought valiantly against the Portuguese on October 25, 1665, in the Battle of Mbwila. (Victorious, the Portuguese had beheaded the king of the Congo and looted his kingdom.) Grandpa wrote a letter of protest to the head of the school board, a white man who was in charge of all the religion's schoolteachers.

Unfortunately, the head of the school board was a friend of the district commander. He blamed Grandfather and threatened to fire him if he forgot his place again. This response had the opposite of the intended effect: Grandfather became furious and wrote an indignant letter to the school-board chief's superior, the school inspector for the whole French overseas territory, who in turn gave Grandfather hell for ignoring the chain of command and suspended his salary for six months. Everybody around Grandfather got scared, told him to calm down – not only because he couldn't possibly win a crusade against a priest and a white administrator, but also because he was risking his prestigious position as a schoolteacher.

Nothing doing! In a burst of arrogance, Grandfather added another name to the list of his ancestors: Kimpa Vita, better known as Dofia Beatriz of the Congo, a young heretic who had single-handedly raised an army against the Portuguese and restored the kingdom for a time. He took his finest quill, dipped it in a well of violet ink, and, hand on the blotter, wrote directly to the highest academic authority in French Equatorial Africa. Mr André Davesne, Inspector General. Davesne had written a book, *Tales of the Bush and the Forest*, which my father still piously kept, for, he told me, not only had he learned to read and write with this book, but Grandfather had saved his honour with it.

Grandfather wrote:

Monsieur Inspector General of Schools for French Equatorial Africa,

I, Tezzo dia Mayela, native teacher at the Béla school, appeal to your good will in the matter of an obvious injustice of which I have been the victim. This wrong is not worthy of our motherland in which justice is the natural complement of the triptych Liberty, Equality, Fraternity. For having defended the separation between our secular republican school system and the church by chasing away a bearded soutane-wearing papist who invaded the schoolgrounds to put on the show of a Sunday mass there, I have been thrice punished and reprimanded, and by an administrative authority no higher than the district commandant, the head of the school board, and the territorial school inspector. My faith has been shaken and I doubt that France, our motherland, can offer its indigenous citizens any protection whatsoever. Enclosed are the letters of reprimand sent to me.

I urge you to consider my case.

Yours bitterly and respectfully..."

He folded the letter and the enclosures, and slipped them into a thick paper envelope.

There was only one courier run a week, and back then this was carried out by a truck belonging to Mr Konate. Mr Konate had just moved to the region and started out as a trader; along with bunches of bananas, bags of manioc, chickens and pigs and mattresses, he hauled the village mailbag, free of charge. He had an old Dodge truck he'd bought from an American Jehovah's Witness for a pittance. (The French authorities had deported the missionary for preaching against patriotism, in particular against saluting the national flag.) For twenty weeks straight Grandfather showed up in front of the small post office, joining the crowd in front of the old Dodge, without receiving any answer to his letter of protest. Finally he grew weary, realising that an African will never get justice from a European. He began to sulk conspicuously during Bastille Day celebrations, and he refused to remove his hat whenever he saw the commander. His loathing for the bearded white priest who had invaded his school turned into a loathing for everything the priest and the church represented.

Years later, the matter was buried and virtually forgotten, but six months before our country's independence, the new (and last) white commander of our district sent his chauffeur to pick up Grandfather. This was quite an event, since, at this time when the parties were fighting to replace the white coloniser, Grandfather might be nominated district chief or even – why not? – commander. By the time he had found his tie, smoothed out the coat that he kept in a suitcase with sweet-smelling mothballs, dusted off his only pair of leather shoes and the felt hat he always wore, a crowd had gathered in front of the commander's office. The commander received Grandfather in person on the porch, shook his hand warmly before the crowd, and led him inside.

Grandfather was intrigued by this sudden consideration from the same administration that had wrongfully and shamelessly punished him, but for the crowd there was no doubt he was going to be the next territorial governor. After some solicitous remarks, the commander held out a letter from the *commissaire de la Republique francaise*, the representative of the President of the French Republic in Equatorial Africa. There was also a letter from Inspector General André Davesne, addressed 'Dear friend', indicating that Grandfather was the very type of African that France had always dreamed of, the perfection of its civilising mission – an independent, free-thinking man. Davesne praised him for defending the public school, and all blame was withdrawn from his record: Grandfather was to be promoted two ranks, his salary reinstated with back pay. As for the high commissioner, he observed to Grandfather that French justice was colourblind, that all French citizens were equal in the eyes of the law, and that, in view of his highly courageous act, an official acclamation would be included in his dossier.

By this time, Grandfather did not doubt that he was entering into legend, or at least the historical record. On the one hand, French officialdom proudly mentioned him in its speeches and official documents, cited him as a paradigm of benign colonisation, of the magnanimity and fairness of France in Africa; and so he was to be decorated on the final Bastille Day of French Equatorial Africa by the final high commissioner of the French Republic in the country. Meanwhile the new African leaders had obtained a bloodless independence: they needed heroic acts, and took Grandfather as the archetype of the obstinate and impassioned struggle of the African people against colonialism and obscurantism. So he was also decorated on the very day of independence, on the *Place des Héros*, by our new president.

In any case, less than ten years later, when a revolutionary regime was established by the army that had carried out the coup d'etat against the army that had overthrown our first president because he was a lackey of imperialism – by then, the events that made my grandfather a national hero were no longer heroic.

* * *

If my grandfather had been decorated by the French, they said, it was because he had been mentally colonised: he had internalised the culture of the masters, like a good nigger. And if Grandfather had been decorated by our first republic on Independence Day, that was because it was a neocolonial lying dog of a government in the service of imperialism, taking its orders from abroad.

* * *

I was almost ten years old when I met Grandfather for the first time. My papa and I spent a month in the mountain village where Grandfather had gone to retire. He was already very old, but he could still read through thick glasses. In his vast brick house, he had a study where he kept his most important memories. There were sculptures and carved masks, big books, old encyclopaedias, well-thumbed French mail-order catalogues from the fifties, especially *Manu-france* and *La Redoute*. I was immediately struck by the big cardboard map on the wall, which he must have used to teach the children of Papa's generation. The surface of the planet was cut out in a puzzle whose pieces formed a multi-coloured patchwork; a legend at the bottom attributed an empire to each colour.

And so there was a French Empire, a British Empire, a Spanish Empire, a Portuguese Empire, an Italian Empire, a Belgian Empire, a Dutch Empire, and Mandates of the League of Nations. I found my own country right away, bathed in blue – the same blue that covered much of central and western Africa. My country didn't exist as such; it was part of something called French Equatorial Africa. Another blue mass was called French West Africa. On this African map were many countries I had never heard of: Oubangui Chari, Anglo Egyptian Sudan, Upper Volta, the Gold Coast, Rhodesia, Tanganyika. I read names and places that sound strange and wonderful to my ears, rolling magnificently off the tongue: Rawalpindi, Chandannagar, Curacao, Sulawesi, Chittagong, Nizhni Novgorod. I savoured Timbouctou, Gaborone, Kalahari, Bahr-al-Ghazal, Kilimanjaro, and…Ouagadougou! What a fantastic name! Ouagadougou! I repeated the name twice, so loud that Papa heard, "Ah, Michel, you found your grandfather's old colonial map?"

"Yes, Papa. And was there also a Congolese Empire or a Senegalese Empire? Did we colonise Europe? France?"

He smiled. "No, my child, for reasons too long and too complicated to explain to you, colonisation happened in only one direction, north to south. But these countries have become independent, at least formally; many have changed their names to mark their break with the colonial past".

"Did they also change Ouagadougou?" I asked.

"Well, Upper Volta no longer exists, but Ouagadougou is still there".

"Ah," I was relieved. "Papa, I would like to go to Ouagadougou".

Papa laughed. "When you grow up," he said, "you can travel the world. You can go all the way to Ushuaia if you want. I see you're fascinated by this old map of the world. I shall give you a current map one of these days."

My grandfather was happy to meet me. He took me in his arms and put me on his knees. "So you're my little Matapari, whose birth is an enigma, eh?" He laughed. "But the world is full of enigmas, for nothing profound is revealed upon first sight. The universe is masked as it winds its course, and men, after eating, dancing, and making love, spend the rest of their time trying to decipher what is hidden behind the appearance of things. That is why they write books and why those who don't know how to write seek answers from forests, listen to animals, dig the earth, or watch the stars. You must know everything, my child, the books of man and the book of the universe. Learn, learn without pause

85

from the wise". I did not quite understand what he meant, so I stared into the eyes of my father, who nodded approvingly. They once asked me to accompany them on one of their peregrinations. They awakened me very late at night. While I was still staggering, rubbing my eyes, Grandfather said to me in a voice filled with mystery. "Come see the birth of a new day with us." The sky was still pitch-black, moonless, speckled with stars. Grandfather walked in front with a torch; I was in the middle; and Papa rounded off the procession. We were out about half an hour, I think, the sky paling little by little. It was only when we arrived that I realised we had reached the peak of the highest mountain outside the village. The climb had been rough; many times I slipped on the dew-wet grass, and many times Papa picked me back up with a firm hand while Grandfather teased me. But I was rewarded for my efforts: it was the first time in my short life I felt so close to the sky. I looked around me, and the vast plain spread out all the way to the great impassive river, slowly and majestically snaking its way to infinity. And then I saw it, like an eyelid opening on the world, preceded by golden rays. Little by little, as if wrenching itself out of the depths of the earth, we saw it, egg-yolk yellow at first, then brighter and brighter until it was blinding, the master of the world. The sun! That great organiser of our life, our seasons, our harvest. I saw him being born; now I knew where he came from. I had been initiated into one of the world's mysteries, the birth of a new day. I had deciphered a page of the universe.

* * *

I still remember the day I discovered another of life's mysteries. It was just a few years later; I shouldn't boast, but at thirteen, I was a tall fellow. I had become a great athlete, the one who would lead the school football team to the championship. That precious victory earned me something more precious still: a kiss from Aledia!

We were in the last minute of the game. I was playing left forward, as usual. Suddenly, I received a nice midfield pass from our sweeper. I jumped up, cushioned the ball with my chest, then blocked it with my right foot. I had barely gotten moving when two defenders were at me. I feinted to the right and pushed the ball to the left; the first defender fell away, and I slid the ball between the legs of the second one to find myself all alone, facing the goalie. I could read the panic in his eyes. But before I had time to lift my heel, I was tackled from behind. I collapsed nose-first on the grass. The referee whistled vigorously and took out a red card, calling for a penalty kick. Our fans were hysterical. Naturally, I was asked to convert the penalty kick. I took my place, savouring the goalie's anxiety for a moment, then kicked the ball to the right. He lurched left. Goal! Final whistle. I was smothered, picked up, and carried off on somebody's shoulders. I was Pelé, I was Maradona. We had won the cup!

The cup had been furnished by Aledia's father, Mr Hussein el Paisal Al Moustapha Husseini Morabitoune, one of the Lebanese who had settled here around the fourteenth anniversary of our revolution, when our little village briefly became an international city complete with airport, hotels, telephones, and fax, not to mention a multimedia conference centre. The energy of an entire nation was mobilised for three months straight for a ceremony that lasted but a few days, and once the party was over, the equatorial forest rushed to take back the land it had momentarily ceded. And so, out of all the folks who besieged our town, ambassadors, journalists, Zaïrean adventurers, West African merchants – only Mr Husseini El Faisal Al Moustapha Husseini Morabitoune had stayed behind. He had stores in the capital, and now enjoyed a monopoly over our little area, having pushed the competition into bankruptcy. Mr Konaté and his old Dodge truck were history; that brave Muslim had packed up and left for his native Senegal or Mali to live out the remainder of his days. But nothing had changed, as far as we were concerned, since the Lebanese man also had trucks that moved goods and since he continued to sell us Coca-Cola, videos, and canned foods that came from as far away as China or Korea.

The canned foods caused some controversy. Since they came from China or Korea, it was rumoured that they contained dog and cat meat. Mr Hussein El Faisal Al Moustapha Husseini Morabitoune smiled and organised a party where he had the labels read out loud by students picked at random: pork meat, corned beef, pilchards, sardines in oil, baked beans…No mention of dog.

It was said that in the 1950s there had lived in the capital of Belgian Congo a white man, a Portuguese with a magic flashlight. Each time he encountered a black man, he would shine the light in his eyes and the black man would start grunting and walking on all fours. All the white man had to do was catch him and fatten him up. Hair grew all over the poor captive's body; his skin became thick as hide. He became a pig! He ended up as sausages, blood, pudding, lard, and tinned pork.

The Portuguese merchants who used to run the stores in our villages had all gone home, but it was said that Mr Hussein El Faisal Al Moustapha husseini Morabitoune was nothing less than the reincarnation of the white man with the magic flashlight. His canned goods were actually the flesh of black people transformed into pork. Was it any surprise that he never ate this meat himself? Soon, people from Grandfather's and even Papa's generation confirmed the story about the white man who had ravaged Kinshasa. We became afraid to cross paths with the Lebanese at night for fear of his bewitched flashlight. In our country rumours run faster than a thief chased by a dog. When this news reached the capital, where Mr Hussein El Faisal Al Moustapha Husseini Morabitoune had stores as well, his business went into a tailspin. So the good man, who no longer smiled so much, seized the occasion of the National Culinary Fair to redeem his honour. They say that in Africa, particularly in our country, we produce nothing. We import almost all of our consumer products – cars, videos, Coca-Cola, and corn flour – though our country has great agricultural potential. To counter this ruinous trade imbalance, it was necessary to promote domestic products. That's why the minister of agriculture organised the culinary fair.

Papa and I visited the fair, and I was surprised to see that our country was so rich in fruits and vegetables; in the main exposition hall, mangoes, papayas, sour-sops, litchis, avocados, tangerines, safous, pineapples, guavas, tamarinds – and I'm leaving out a few – were laid out as far as the eye could see. Vegetables too. Who knew?

Mr Hussein El Faisal Al Moustapha Husseini Morabitoune, one of our country's most prominent businessmen, had been invited to inaugurate an agricultural competition for the occasion. He began his presentation by singing the praises of the chief of state for his far-sightedness and national spirit. He congratulated him for looking into local food production. But, as everyone knew and had been reminded by the Comrade Revolutionary Leader himself – Africa's problem was its deficiency in protein and vitamins. It was therefore vital that local recipes integrate the supplementary nutritional richness of the developed world by way of imported products. That was why he was inaugurating this "Competition of best local recipe made from canned meat."

Papa was incensed.

"Once again, someone minding only his pockets! Instead of encouraging the peasants to consume fresh products, he manipulates people with pseudo-science so that they will buy canned foods that have probably been sitting around for years. We have to shut him down, this merchant of illusions, this swindler, this creator of false needs. We're going to take part in this competition!"

No sooner said than done, Papa did a bit of research in the town's markets and then rented a spot at the exposition. A large sign was hung out front; it had green letters on a white background, magnificently traced with loops and upstrokes as only the teachers of Papa's generation knew how to do. The slogan read:

FOR PROTEIN, VITAMINS AND VIRILITY
EAT INSECTS!

Toward the back, a banner traced in revolutionary red with the same beautiful writing had the following injunction:

AVOID CANNED FOODS
EAT FRESH PRODUCE!

I must tell you, in my humble opinion, our exhibition was the most original. We had caterpillars (the two edible species found here): field crickets; cicadas gathered at the beginning of the rainy season; green grasshoppers; winged termites that lost their wings as soon as you touched them; fat, greasy, white palmiste worms; and others whose names I admit I do not know. Who needs frog's legs or *escargot*?

The agricultural minister and Mr Hussein el Faisal Al Moustapha Husseini Morabitoune nearly keeled over when they found themselves before our stand. Mr Hussein el Faisal Al Moustapha Husseini Morabitoune grimaced, then blushed as he read Papa's banner while Papa expounded, "You see, this is just a sample of the edible insects of our country; they are neglected sources of protein and vitamins, and they're delicious." He threw a fat grilled and salted palmiste worm in his mouth while I munched on a handful of caterpillars that had been boiled to a pulp in salty water. Delicious with fresh ginger drink!

"Taste some," Papa continued. "Try a grasshopper, Mr Minister, or perhaps our Lebanese friend would like a handful of termites?" (The Minister and the Lebanese contorted their faces in disgust.) "Beware of canned foods. First of all, it's expensive, and often the cans you buy are expired, and you risk botulism. Eat vegetables from your own fields, eat fruits of your native land – mangoes, papayas, tangerines, oranges. And you mustn't forget our edible insects, rich in nutrients." Papa went on and on, and the Lebanese blushed and blushed, until the minister of agriculture couldn't take it any longer.

"This is a provocation."

"Indeed," added another top party official, "this is a sabotage of our revolutionary activity."

Though the officials sulked, our exhibit won a true popular victory. People were glad to see the insects they knew so well – the very insects that some of their compatriots considered food for savages now that they ate *hachis parmentier*, sausages, camembert, and imported red wine – proven to be healthy and nutritious. We were victims of our own success. Few visitors could resist sneaking a handful of termites, two or three worms, maybe a caterpillar for a snack, so that our stand was empty and we had to close up shop before morning's end.

"Don't worry, Papa", I said. "It was awesome. We'll get first place!"

But we didn't place at all. That night, the television report about the exposition didn't even mention our stand. Instead, they showed the minister of agriculture next to a certain Mr Hussein el Faisal Al Moustapha Husseini Morabitoune, tasting a recipe consisting of *saka saka* – crushed manioc leaves – *au* canned corned beef, then a dish of crushed yam *au* canned pilchard, and finally red sorrel *au* canned sardines.

* * *

If I spared no detail tell you the story of this culinary fair, it was only to show you the importance of Mr Hussein el Faisal Al Moustapha Husseini Morabitoune, Aledia's father, the man who had provided this beautiful cup that was presented to my team. I climbed down off the shoulders of the crowd that had swept me off my feet after my magnificent, unstoppable penalty kick, and proudly took my position before the podium, with the rest of the players. The prefect was flanked by the Lebanese, the sponsor, and by Papa, the school principal. That was when I really saw Aledia for the first time.

She was supposed to hand the cup to the prefect so he could present it to me. She came forward in a magnificent flowered dress, so light that the wind would lift it up every now and then and she would try to push it back onto her thighs. Her long black hair tightened in a knot behind the nape of her neck before blooming again to hang loosely across the small of her back. She was smiling, and she was beautiful. She delivered

the cup to the prefect, who held it out to me as everyone cheered. I
shook the hand of the prefect. I shook the hand of Papa, who reminded
me of his credo '*mens sano in corpore sano*'. I shook the hand of the
Lebanese, who was still congratulating me, and just as I was about to get
down from the stand, the prefect who still had Aledia in front of him
asked her to kiss me. The crowd was yelling, "A kiss, a kiss!" She raised
her lips to my cheek and…kissed me! I quivered from the contact of her
lips as if a bolt of electricity had gone through my body. I was
submerged in a garden of fragrant orange trees and incense as the breeze
that blew through her hair and her face reached mine. I wanted to grab
Aledia, engulf her in my arms, and press my body against the breasts
that swelled beneath her dress. Aledia!

I missed the first step coming down from the stand and found myself
on the grass sooner than planned. I regained my footing without
dropping the cup, after a number of quick steps. Everybody laughed and
applauded, including Aledia. Afterward, I couldn't stop thinking about
her.

Aledia! At thirteen, I lived for her alone. Each time I was sent on an
errand, I made sure to pass in front of the Lebanese store, hoping to
catch a glimpse of my beloved. In fact, I had rummaged around in Papa's
thesaurus looking for words to call her: my doll, my chickadee, my
girlfriend, my love!

Finally one day I took action. Maman had given me nice jeans from
America, authentic Levi's. I was so proud of them that I decided to strut
over to see her and openly declare my love. I put on my nicest shirt, the
jeans, and my black Reeboks. I combed my hair and sprayed some of the
lavender cologne I had sneaked out of Papa's closet. I was well aware that
the pimples sprinkled all over my face could foil my powers of seduction
– Oh, how I hated those pimples! – but I decided to make my declaration
anyway.

This was really my day. Aledia was at the cash register by herself. A
heat wave flooded my face when I saw her smiling at the other end of the
counter. I swallowed hard, twice.

"One Coke please", I said while putting down two hundreds and a
fifty. She opened a big refrigerator, took out a can and…she recognised
me!

"Well, Matapari the champion, hello!"

I heard my heart knocking like a renegade tom-tom. There was her
hand, held out toward me. Her perfume invaded me, the same fragrance

from the stadium. I was drunk and knew not why, and instead of
speaking as I had intended and declaring my love, declaring that even
fresh water could not quench my burning throat and breast, I took her
hand and brought it to my lips as I had seen it done in a French movie.
And at that very moment, her father appeared!

"*Oukh roj!*" he shouted, "*I'th hab!*"

He was so red that I thought his face would explode. "Out, dirty
nigger! Get out and never set foot in here again!"

Then he went at Aledia in Arabic. I don't know how I got out of
there. Papa had told me many times that Einstein had shown that
nothing could move faster than light. I wonder if I didn't prove his
theory wrong that day, for no one has ever made such an escape. To this
day, Aledia's father, Mr Hussein el Faisal Al Moustapha Husseini
Morabitoune, still owes me the two hundred and fifty francs that I left
on his counter.

Some time afterward, he sent his daughter back to Lebanon. But I do
not despair; I know that Aledia loves me. Didn't she give me her hand to
kiss? I will find you one day, my beloved, and I will take you away, far,
far, away. We will go to a town whose name has long been in my dreams.
I've seen it in pictures, read books about it. It's on the border of Sabel;
there, no trees hide the immensity of the sky. I promise, Aledia, I will go
to Lebanon and snatch you from the claws of the Shiites, rescue you
from the Islamic Sharia. And we'll live happily ever after in
Ouagadougou.

*

Emmanuel Dongala is a writer from the Republic of Congo.
He now lives in the United States where he teaches chemistry and
Francophone African literature at Simon's Rock College of Bard and
at Bard College. He has received several distinctions including a
Guggenheim Fellowship and the Fonlon-Nichols Prize "for excellence
in creative writing and for human rights and freedom of expression"
in 2003.

Tell Him It is Never Too Late

Rachelle Greeff

Maria dos Ramos lived with the absence like one would with a disability. She suppressed her sadness. Buried her rebelliousness. Accepted it only in moments of spiritual clarity and arranged her life around the vacuum.

When she and Mario, her husband, retired to the home for the aged, Maria did not have to unpack and sort the fragments of a child's life. There were no boxes labelled in dusty, old-fashioned letters. No gloomy oak wardrobe reeking of mothballs. No outdated posters on the walls. Not one memory of a child who had already exchanged this musty bedroom for the world outside.

Still, the contents of their house crowded their new home, even though there were only two of them. It was a small semi-detached in a row of similar little houses. "It doesn't even have a back door," complained Mario, who insisted on referring to it as a flat. Maria preferred the word 'cottage'.

When Maria opened the fridge in the tiny kitchen she could move neither in nor out of the room. The rubbish bin was squeezed under the sink. And the first time she baked her Christmas cake it rose right up against the top of the dinky oven.

From the first day of their marriage fifty-seven years ago Maria and Mario did the dishes together at night. He washed, she dried. (A man, he declared, had a firmer grip for cleaner dishes. And why would she challenge him? He was a difficult man, he didn't like queries or criticism. Besides, she owed him so much.)

And when they washed the dishes they talked, but the new kitchen was too tight.

They were shattered, and their disappointment was as palpable as a guest in their new home, crowding in even more. Mario said nothing. Maria groped for words. They did not know how to talk about matters of importance or intimacy other than with his hands in foam and water and hers under the willing softness of the dishcloth.

That night, as always, Mario held her tight. His arm around her as if he owned her. Often Maria had difficulty falling asleep like this; even in love Mario was impossible.

In the dark Mario shrivelled up. He was so small in his dream, he recalled sadly to Maria as they lay in bed next morning, that she had had to carry him about in her thimble.

Her nocturnal fantasy was different and she gladly relived it: their new little roof had slipped open. They rustled their feathers, flew out on easy wings, circled into the limitless, breathtaking expanse, higher and even higher, until the people on the ground were merely black dots. In the flame-blue firmament they were weightless.

"Like the pigeons," Mario sighed, reminding her how they watched, always charmed, as their homing-pigeons dissolved, floating upward.

"They didn't disappear," Maria reminded him. "They merely went where we could not see. And they always returned."

Shortly afterwards, Mario left her.

As she walked into the bedroom with his coffee one morning, which she did every morning before they lay down again together, he looked at her in surprise. Something was terribly wrong, he said. He tried to prop himself up on one elbow and grumbled: "Christ Almighty, I still have to do the lawn edges which the boy didn't do, what ruddy bad timing."

With a small sigh he fell back on the pillow as she stood, stupidly, with his black, bitter coffee in her hand. The perfect death, like switching off a light – but this she only thought later as her mind replayed the moment like a stuck record.

Somehow she was expecting more, something more impressive. But there was nothing. Only Mario who stared right past her and a stillness, a quietness which seemed to listen to her.

So that was that.

It was as if Mario slipped away through the back door of his own eyes. She closed his eyelids, not registering that a blind had been drawn within her. He looked as if he was only sleeping. He might wake up any second.

She sat down beside him, quietly taking leave of him, her husband, lover, friend, object of her anger, her love, her life. She lingered, but compared to the exploration of a lifetime, it was fleeting. She paused at every mole and freckle. At the slight white growth in his ears. The lobes. With age his ears had grown into the tender framework of wings. His stomach was flat even now, only at the sides it prolapsed gently. The calloused soles of his feet. He had walked many miles in the *veld* with these feet. With these toes ever neatly kept. This strong bridge.

94

Only when she slipped her wedding band from his left hand, realising that the warmth of the ring was now fading fast and forever, did she collapse onto her knees beside the bed. Her tears were loud.

Eventually, at tea-time, she lifted the telephone to call the nursing sister in frail-care. Strange, she thought as she waited for her to pick up the ringing phone, the absence of protestation from Mario.

Hereafter Maria thought differently about death. It was not such an extraordinary event after all. It was merely another exit.

Now that she was one, rather than two, she had to leave the semi. The houses were only for married couples and she had to move to a room on the first floor of the main building.

The room was long enough for one single bed and armchair, wide enough for a wardrobe and a wastepaper basket. From the window she saw the home's washing-line with floral dresses and large flesh-coloured knickers flapping shapelessly in the south-easter like spectres struggling to quit. Behind this was another wing, and even further away she knew, though she could not see, were the bottle-green slopes of Kirstenbosch. This view she loved more than the front face of Table Mountain, the one on the postcards.

After only eighteen months of living in her space like a hamster, she was ordered to move downstairs into the room with Miss Watson. She was now considered not fit enough to be on her own, too far from the watchful eyes of the nursing staff. Miss Watson's roommate, Miss Ivy, had died. Management paired people of similar religion, and the same sex of course, once they got to the double-room stage. This was the first obvious move onto the conveyor belt which ended abruptly at the double wooden door. This unadorned door at the back of the frail-care section was not a trademan's entrance nor a soiled linen exit.

Within the first hour Maria understood why Miss Ivy had to move on.

Miss Watson, formerly headmistress of a well-known girls' school in the city, was an insufferable, raucous old crow. She scolded everyone who crossed the threshold: nurses, matron, doctor, the woman who did their feet, even Father Thomas. She ranted about everybody's "bad, bad manners just walking into my privacy".

The verbal abuse Maria could tolerate. More unbearable was the flatulence slipping from Miss Watson in successions of timid, but rancid emissions. Internally, thought Maria (a handkerchief sprinkled with wintergreen oil held to her nose), Miss Watson was already rotting.

Mario would not have put up with this. He would have summoned the
matron, or the manager, or both. He would have demanded something
be done at once about Miss Watson's slack anal sphincter.

She and Mario met in the autumn of 1938, when they used to stroll
at dusk from the boarding house to the dappled clump of bluegums
where he taught her magic. He could blow an angelic melody on a gum
leaf.

At first they were accompanied by a mutual friend, Harvey Thomas,
who was now her priest. Back then he was a student in theology. Though
they remained friends, Harvey withdrew from those intimate outings.
When he realised Maria had chosen Mario, he took up the cloth. He
projected his feelings to where he would never be rejected. Later he
thanked Maria. She had married him off to love eternal.

But spiritually Maria and Harvey remained close. Maria was always
fascinated by the angle, invisible to others, from which Harvey observed
the world. In her prayers she acknowledged how blessed she was to have
a companion of profound but simple divinity. One who was funny too.
Their cups of tea were regularly followed by uproarious laughter. Maria
never laughed that way with Mario.

But, strangely, Mario never seemed in the least jealous of this
friendship.

Because he was the one she grew to love more than herself. She often
wondered if love could be greater than this. People said maternal feeling
was stronger than conjugal love. Later, after a few years of marriage,
Maria began one of the first pre-schools in the Boland village where they
lived at the time, and she often gazed intently at the mothers and their
children. She endeavoured to weigh mother love, to compare it to her
marital love.

For many years she hoped she would know one day when she had her
own child. She visited doctor after doctor. Answering the same
questions, in the same position under the flimsy blanket on the
examination bed. Could they not please dim the terrible light? Was there
not a nurse who could do this?

However, no reason could be found as to why she should not be
impregnated. Her husband should come for a consultation.

But her husband refused. Bluntly replied it would be too humiliating.

Maria understood, and she did not blame him for not wanting to go.
For him it would be just too much.

As a girl, later as Mario's young bride, she dreamt of hearing the pitter-patter of toddler feet, of a little flock chirping sweetly about her. She had such a long and weighty name, it had to be balanced by a large family. She wanted enough offspring for all eight chairs around her heirloom table – one which had dwarfed her parents and her, an only child – and always another little one would be on the way, pushing her belly against the side of the table with its happy dinner-time pandemonium.

But it never happened.

Only much later, already in the single room upstairs, her stomach swelled. It continued, very slowly, under Miss Watson's gassing. How much Mario had wanted to see her like this, she thought self-consciously; her thoughts were so utterly inappropriate. She was decades beyond child-bearing age. Maybe she'd never even been fertile.

She did not want to draw attention to her rounded stomach and insisted on still washing herself.

Eventually the pain, not the swelling, compelled her to talk to the nursing sister. Three days later she lay under a nil-per-mouth sign and half a day after that she spat bile into a small kidney-shaped bowl. Harvey, ah, it's him, she recognised through the haze. He is holding my hand.

After seven more days and nights, Maria knew the tumour had been removed and that chemotherapy and radiation could help. They could try. The prognosis could be positive. She could have a few years more.

But, politely, thank you, she refused the offer.

Well, in that case nine months. At the most.

And Maria was satisfied. Because the longer Mario was away, the larger her loss grew. This was a growth which could not be cut out, and it hurt.

As long as the Almighty provided a large enough place for doing the dishes this time so that she and Mario could talk as in days gone by over two plates and two side-plates and two everything.

She had news for him too, a most wondrous announcement.

The surgeon who performed her operation was a young lad with a crown in the middle of his hair falling straight down his forehead. When he visited her the morning after the surgical procedure he had with him a small glass jar.

The neoplasm was hardly news to her, she'd been suspecting it for a long time. "And I do not care to see it," she thanked him as she motioned dismissively towards the jar still in his hand.

"No, no, Mrs dos Ramos," suddenly the young physician's clear

97

countenance glowed. He looked excited. "It's not what you think."

He held the jar high, like a schoolboy showing his trophy. "Look what we found in your abdomen!"

Behind the glass floated something which at first looked like slime, then, maybe, like a snippet of cartilage. It was creamy, the colour of bone. It was minuscule. It was a calcified foetus.

Maria listened intently to the medical explanation. Not once did she interrupt him.

"At some stage you were impregnated extra-uterinely, Mrs dos Ramos. And what then happens is that the embryo attaches itself to the membranes outside the uterus, where it literally stays. Lithopedion, that's what we call it. It's a rare phenomenon, one usually only reads about it."

When he left he wanted to take the jar with him to show his medical students.

Only then did Maria speak. "No, it stays, it's mine."

In the remaining months of her life in the frail-care section of the home for the aged, the glass jar with the tiny baby of stone stood next to her bed. The nurses and the cleaners busied themselves round it. They knew, primordially or practically, but they knew, all of them, about children. The life, the loss, the yearning.

Often Maria picked it up, nursing the jar against her bedjacket. She also lifted it from the formaldehyde. Closed her hand around the perfectly and minutely formed fingers, the ribs transparent like little fish bones, the large, amorphous head.

We do have a baby child, Mario, one which I carried inside me for all these years, hugged between you and me.

Then, one day, Maria asked the nurse to phone Father Thomas, who had not been to visit her that week. He must come for the last sacrament. And ask him, please, to also bring the water and the oil of the catechumen. Tell him it's never too late.

They pulled the curtain around her bed. Inside the cubicle of cream fabric there were only the two of them. She called him Harvey, as she always did when they were alone.

And he prepared his soulmate, Maria Teresa Jacquina dos Ramos, for her final death on earth. "The rites, Maria, will now carry you as they carried me all these years. As they will when you are not here."

For the second sacrament he lifted the small calcified child from the fluid and, cradling it in his hand, performed the rite of baptism. His voice faded to a whisper, "Give this child new life in abundance."

He kissed Maria on the lips, she closed her eyes.

She felt his tears on her eyelids, trickling down her temples, becoming one with her own. Far away she heard the rattling of food trolleys, the clanging of dishes. It must be twelve, time for lunch. Most were already seated. The others trailed behind, stiff, bent, shuffling. Tottering into the blessing like a phrase out of place.

Harvey took Maria's hand, his other hand still cupped her baby.

In her palm was delicate life. It was a dying bird faintly stirring, one last time, in remembered flight.

*

Rachelle Greeff was born in 1957 in Cape Town. 'Tell Him It is Never Too Late' is the first short story written by her in English. It was included in *The Torn Veil: Women's Short Stories from the Continent of Africa* (1998) and from there won her the Sanlam Literary Award for Short Fiction in 1999. She continues to publish stories in Afrikaans.

African Writers' Workshop Stories 2003

The Testimony of Terremoto

Yvonne Adhiambo-Owuor

The woman wraps her lilac scarf around her face to protect her nose from the wind's nipping. The movement exposes the lapels of her cream suit underneath her short red coat. She stares as the cold seagull trembles one-legged on a rock in the ocean against the wind-churned spray. It buries its head beneath its wings. The mad wind changes direction and now carries sand fragments into the land. Life has a way of getting on with its own destiny.

* * *

A specific witness, a man who had been jailed without trial, was being sought in all the nations of the world. The Tribunal looked for him because they hoped he would have plenty to say about his jailers.

It was an unusual gathering. An international tribunal of inquiry had been convened to deal with a strange demand: Colonel A. Smith sought from the world an uncommon justice, the restoration of his life to pre-war conditions. He sought compensation for the agonies he had undergone in executing orders to pacify populations while seeking weapons of mass destruction. He was haunted by the trauma of not finding these weapons and also felt he should be remunerated for the act of not finding them. Moreover, he thought he had not been sufficiently applauded for reducing 'collateral damage'. Only a third of the misguided missiles under his command found untargeted targets rather than his full arsenal. But mostly, Colonel A. Smith found it intolerable to live with his current self unless (a) restoration or (b) compensation occurred.

Regarding compensation, an exact sum had been arrived at with elaborate deliberation. It included conversations with existentialists. The sum of the value of Colonel A. Smith's life *(excluding VAT and legal fees)* had been written out, sealed in a blue envelope and presented to the tribunal's presiding judge. The package was safely hidden in the Judge's secret vault to which only the judge and the intelligence agents spying on the judge had access.

Colonel A. Smith's country was, to put it mildly, rabidly furious that he had rendered to naught their diligent work to ensure that their soldiers

101

would not be prosecuted for 'crimes of war'. This suit permitted unfriendly nations (assisted by the axis of evil) to set up this tribunal. The possibility that the people of Colonel Smith's country might be condemned to an eternal opprobrium similar to that heaped upon the German people for their ancestors' war deeds could be bad for foreign policies concocted from high moral grounds.

* * *

When Justice Ongwengo conspired to get included in the tribunal, he activated a labyrinth of promises and threats, seduction and plots. He was, however, bad-tempered about being unanimously elected presiding judge, a position he had specifically not sought. Someone whose soul he had torn bare in the course of his intrigues had found a puerile revenge in proposing his name for these arduous duties.

Now, he was vaunted as the Great-African-Example-to-The-World, his numerous credentials and achievements cited. He found he had become Honorary Citizen Extraordinaire of as many nations as there were in Africa. All his protestations were seen as the natural diffidence of a humble genius and ignored. His country, Kenya, had convened a special occasion to make him 'Elder of the Burning Spear'. Which meant that after his name, 'Justice Ongwengo' he could append the initials 'EBS'. It also transpired that after the manically popular Ethno hip-hop group, *Mujomba ya Homu*, he was the next most hip person in East Africa. The next month, after he shaved his head bald, he became the hippest African in the world.

* * *

The winds pranced down the mountains delicately carrying the scents of assorted mountain creatures. The aromas of life seeped into Justice Ongwengo's chambers. He sniffed the air and picked out a citrus-like scent. He wondered what it could be.

Justice Ongwengo, a compatriot of reality, was reflecting on the celestial magnitude of the tribunal's mandate, the machinations of the geo-politicians and Colonel A. Smith's quicksand case. He knew the odds of a purgative justice being achieved were negligible. What was certain was that Colonel A. Smith would be doing several talk shows, host a reality TV series, land a slot in Pop Idols and write numerous

'How To' books out of the experience.

The trial of the century, since the century was still very young, played itself out in Cape Town. The Hague, of course, was neither amused nor impressed. But since the Secretary General of the UN was African and three quarters of the world's valued resources were African, including clean water and Tanzanite, the Hague's chagrin remained in an elaborately bound blue and gold document filed under 'Noted' and kept in a vault in Geneva close to the one where the original documents of the Geneva Convention, the rules governing war games (Guantanamo Bay is not a signatory), had been safely stored.

Expediency, the flush of electoral success and populist parades caused the new government in Colonel A. Smith's country to humour the tribunal's demands and dispatch poster-size pictures of four respondents to the Cape. A former ally of Colonel A. Smith's country dispatched one. The posters would have to stand in for the accused persons and give the baying public something to gaze at and insult, especially since two of them used to be former emperors of the universe (or that is what sycophants buzzing about them used to say). They were respondents in this case because Colonel A. Smith named them, called them out and said, they were the ones who decree: "Let there be war". And there was war. They sent Colonel A. Smith to war where he lost his old life. The war had invested him with the facsimile of a life that he did not like at all.

"What do you seek?" Justice Ongwengo had asked Colonel Smith in a pre-tribunal first encounter.

"My life." The Colonel had answered.

Justice Ongwengo, his voice trembling with suppressed laughter studied Colonel A. Smith's eyes and said: "Do you think this tribunal will give you what you desire?"

The Colonel grabbed what was in Justice Ongwengo's eyes, trusting that it was a rope, not realising it was just a question mark, speaking to it he said, his voice dry: "It needs to." Simply that.

* * *

The couple walking along the beach that evening are startled by the poised and voluptuous grace of the woman standing on the edge of the cliff. Her short red coat against the yellow–orange–purple sky makes her look as if she is on fire. As if she senses their eyes on her, which she does –

103

she is sensitive that way – she turns. The heat shines out of her eyes and across her face glows a long, vivid scar. The woman hopes to shock.

Instead, the couple smile at her. She looks away, back at the cold Atlantic sea and soaks in the smell of the sea. It suffuses her soul. After they have passed, she glances after them. The evening sun has allowed a shaft of light to pierce through the clouds and point to the back of a large mountain. She stops, mesmerised. She wonders what the finger of the sun points to over and behind the mountain.

* * *

It was a windy day. The smog was, as usual, omnipresent and the sun shone a stilted red. Presiding Justice Ongwengo's concession for the tribunal was to shave his greying close crop off entirely. In hindsight, it was a bad move because it would later focus attention on the shape of his head and establish how really 'cool' he was. In his room, that morning, he had stared at his face in the mirror and observed that his mouth was set firmly. It looked disapproving, a touch distant. His spectacles were appropriately moon-rimmed and when he peered over them, he was wonderfully stern, like a judge, which he was. He smiled at his image then remembered that he had only wanted to immerse himself into the experience of the trial rather than preside over it. He frowned.

The sun had given up all pretences of heating the land and was skulking behind a grey cloud.

The hour before the trial began, Justice Ongwengo peered through the high chamber window on the third floor and glanced down into the courtroom. He lifted his glass of tangerine juice. He looked sideways at the tribunal's other members waiting for the official procession that would herald the commencement of the Tribunal of Inquiry. They were appropriately gender balanced in conformity with the demands of the International Women in Justice caucus: Lady Justice Skeens, Justice Pimenta, Justice Custodes and Lady Justice Sero. He hoped they did not hope that they would all become friends, comrades in a shared cause. He sighed, lowered his glass and glowered at the diminishing contents of his favourite juice.

* * *

The Third Millennium Extraordinary International Tribunal of Inquiry commenced. Justice Ongwengo's opening statement, on closer examination was similar to Justice Jackson's Nuremberg masterpiece of sixty years ago. Justice Ongwengo borrowed from these texts using a thesaurus to replace phrases such as 'war crimes' and 'apex of civilisation'.

He had started the Inquiry by saying: "This is not a military tribunal prosecuting war crimes."

Then he paid respect to the Nuremberg Tribunal precedent. He noticed the use of certain words caused a third of the seventy-five 'official observers' to flinch. These flinchers included his *Aide de camp* and seven men who were effectively blending in by sporting similar crew cuts and all season non-reflective sunglasses. Such words included 'concentration camp' and 'wholesale slaughter of populations'. He used the phrases often enough to cause the flinchers to stop taking notes and focus on sweating. He chortled. A low rumble that caused the table he leaned on to vibrate. How he relished the odour of fear; coupled with the whiff of guilt, it was a heady meal.

By the afternoon, like guided stealth missiles, rotten tomatoes, lemon pies and goat droppings had accumulated and a malodorous shrine rose before the posters of the five respondents. Two, with the large ears, had been singled out for special vitriol. Some anarchist had felt-penned satyr horns and Dali moustaches on them and on that of the female respondent. Justice Ongwengo said that the posters should be cordoned off for their safety, as if they were the Mona Lisa. A day later, from behind the shark-proof Plexiglas, the paper respondents glowered at Colonel A. Smith. As with all good pictures, whichever direction a watcher stood, the eyes on the posters looked back.

* * *

The woman walks along the shore, the sand between her toes. She walks until she can only feel and hear the sound of her walking and the wind and ocean flow into and through her. The smell of shredded seaweed shrouds the ocean. A sand plover veers madly off her path and she senses its microscopic panic. She would have walked on if she had not stumbled upon the wreck of a steamship, its hull buried in the sand. Had it lived, it would have been a beautiful ship. She crouches next to it and starts crying. But there are no tears, nor is her crying like anything that has been heard before. It is as if she coughs and coughs and nothing comes out. She huddles into her short red coat.

105

Justice Ongwengo lay on his bed, his hand beneath his head, his feet crossed, his shoes dangling at the edge of the bed. This was his seventy-first trial. His third commission of enquiry, even if it was not being called that. Long ago, he had tired of the incomplete justice of human beings.

"Vague ruminations of a dastardly species", he muttered to the fly on the ceiling.

Somebody had filled his room with marigolds and spider lilies. The flowers were depressed. They appeared shocked by the certainty of their demise whilst in full bloom.

"Heh, heh, heh," Justice Ongwengo chortled at the cut stems.

A few seconds later, they had drooped a little more.

Life was not just.

Long ago, he had watched, oddly detached, as a woman and her two barely born children were lowered into a grave. This truth had pierced his soul then. Life is not just. It was then and there that he had decided to pursue truth instead.

Justice Ongwengo was spending his life and position to serve his curiosity about the human soul, to provoke its face to show its pristine nakedness. A sublime moment was drinking in the face of an accused person for whom he spelled out a death sentence. It was not the decree that interested him as much as the sudden presence of a condemned soul pouring out urgent messages. One woman's eyes had literally popped out at his words: "You shall hang. You shall die."

A car-jacker, she had shot and killed her way to riches, with no scruples, for three years. When it was her turn to die, word lines appeared on her face, gesturing to the judge in vain. Justice Ongwengo had found her anguish to be honest and satisfying.

The more he discovered about the soul and its easy attraction to the lure of evil, the more he craved to immerse himself in its travails. What was true of being human?

Justice Ongwengo's acquaintance, Dr Yehuna Odongo, a forensic pathologist in Nairobi, let him imbibe of the different faces of death. Neither man exchanged words. Justice Ongwengo developed a fascination with the way of the human mouth at death.

He wondered, "Which truth seeks utterance?"

Once, after sketching the face of a prisoner who had apparently suffocated while 'trying to eat his socks' he told Dr Odongo:

"I suspect that evil though banal, is also a profound pleasure. As a judge with the power vested upon me by you…to determine death or life, I know within myself a willingness to administer suffering to another human being...not unlike this..."

Justice Ongwengo was curious about his own boundaries, the extent to which he would travel to meet with and consume life or desecrate it. Wherever he could encounter the darkest edges to which human beings walked with odd legitimacy, Justice Ongwengo sought to be. In this, he hoped to reconcile the tensions of justice and limit. The atrocities from the recent wars had never received a public airing before. This enquiry was the closest chance to illumine those dim depths.

In his private chambers the day before the tribunal opened, Justice Ongwengo drew stick men on a sheet of paper on which the Charter of the Third Millennium Extraordinary International Tribunal of Inquiry was detailed. The doodles stopped at Article 8 on the sheet. The Judge pursed his lips and moved them left, right suggesting yogic mouth exercises. Article 8 implied that responsibility for actions was vested in the individual and not in 'orders from above'. Justice Ongwengo thought of striking it out. He coloured in the 'a's' and 'o's' black with his doodle pen. The implications of Article 8 if applied to his life meant that he might one day be expected to render an account for each of the twenty-three people he had sent to the gallows. He was titillated by the idea of standing before the human race and proclaiming his officially sanctioned badness. He laughed long and loud as he rose from the chair, picked up his heavy coat and headed out.

* * *

The hole in the sand widens and shocked crabs dash out. She is scooping sand out, something for her hand to do while she thinks of nothing. After a while the sand hole is large enough to contain half her kneeling body. She fits herself into the hole and then compacts the sand. The wind plays with her hair. She does not look up because she knows that someone is not just watching her, but searching her soul. She looks up anyway and finds that a bald-headed, tall and large man with three lines across his forehead has stopped mid-walk and is staring at her as if he is furious with her. Still kneeling she looks back at him and unveils her rage. By then he has turned back and when she looks again, he is hurrying up the path, away from the beach. And the sea is creamy blue that day. She has never seen a creamy blue sea before.

* * *

Justice Ongwengo stuffed a soft-centred peppermint into his mouth.
He had distributed the contents of a whole packet among his various
pockets. He grimaced and turned his gaze to the courtroom crowd. He
grinned inwardly when he sensed the familiar palpable fear creeping into
the room. The faces avoiding his eyes were predictably similar, not in
their characteristics but in their expressions. He scanned the room again.
If the manners of the day permitted it, if he had not been forced into the
position of presiding judge, he would have bared his claws in
anticipation of the hunt. His heart raced in the knowledge of a primal
satisfaction to be had.

But then, his eyes faltered on the chiselled, scarred face of the woman
in the short, blood-red coat. His eyes stopped at her eyes, and then ran
down the jagged scar line that disappeared into her neck. When he had
stumbled upon her kneeling on the beach, she had evoked for him his
mother, Laja Maria, the *cantaora* Aurora Vargas, the great dirge singer
Selina Ojany, and another woman whose name he called in his heart, and
then, only in a whisper – all these women and then something more.
Fierce females, these women. They sang, danced, loved and hated
viscerally. They rolled their hips and pounded their breast, flaunted
rounded bellies and knew how to cry. From them, he discovered that
passion, fury, love, death and suffering were from the same wild, mad root.

Now, in his courtroom, the scarred woman turned her head and
looked back at him. She recognised him. She looked through him. He
abruptly ceased his musings and frowned.

* * *

"Name your enemy," Justice Ongwengo demanded.
"I have none," the Colonel replied.
"Why do you tremble, Colonel?"
Silence.
Then, slowly, licking his lips, low voiced, in a lisp the Colonel
answered: "I...am afraid...of who I am...that I will consume
myself...and like it."
On the doodle pad, the nib of Justice Ongwengo's pen broke with a
crack. So hard had he pushed it, diverting the energy of the guffaw in
him that would have certainly cleared the tribunal room.

* * *

108

Dr Hans Andre, Tribunal Counsel for Colonel A. Smith rose and called his first witness.

* * *

Eight months later into the inquiry, the ghastly face of the human soul had indeed been unmasked, its truth naked for all to read. Justice Ongwengo had guffawed at the performances of the prosecutors and watched the strident voices gradually get numbed in the face of evil so banal, so present and so entombed. He had sweated, enthralled, as Colonel A. Smith detailed his horror of the excitement he felt when he helped herd crying men and women into unventilated metal trucks in the desert.

Colonel A. Smith wept.

"…and when we opened the doors of the truck two days later, they were all dead."

The prosecuting attorney said:

"Were they all terrorists, Colonel?"

Silence.

"May have been."

"May? Just may?"

"They could have known where weapons of mass destruction were."

"Could, Colonel?"

The Colonel covered his face and whispered into his hand. "Their existence was a problem for…us…for me." Fortunately, no one heard him.

"Speak up, young man!" Lady Justice Sero spoke for the first and last time.

Justice Ongwengo chortled, and it was a rumble and the tribunal chamber rumbled with him. Even the Colonel smiled.

"How many human beings were sent to their deaths?"

Colonel A. Smith replied: "I dunno…a hundred and two?"

'You were responsible for this?'

Colonel A. Smith looked away.

Justice Ongwengo muttered, "The marriage of right and wrong."

"How can you be so sure of the numbers since you did not make notes?"

Colonel Smith said: "I hear each and every single one of their voices in my head."

The poster images still glowered at Colonel Smith. And the court was silent. The media observed that Justice Ongwengo had lowered and covered his face and his shoulders moved up and down, caught in the violent paroxysm of something.

Flashes from digital cameras and the whirr of film capturing light and form.

The next day, images of the presiding judge, under banners including 'Sorrow', 'Compassionate Justice', 'Via Dolorosa' and 'The Passion' were displayed worldwide in fifty-two different languages. Justice Ongwengo's brave public emotional display earned him the 'Pater Bernado's Dove Award for Humanity'. In his room the next night, Justice Ongwengo faced the mirror and groaned. He had not been crying. He had been laughing helplessly at the idea of the restless dead in Colonel A. Smith's head.

The next day, Dr Andre tried a new line of enquiry.

(Since the sun was to blame for shining on the truck and roasting people enclosed for their own safety within.)

Dr Andre asked:

"What job did you have from 2003 on?"

Colonel A. Smith said:

"I was in the holding facility at Guantanamo Bay where I became Colonel and was charged with the responsibility for the protective custody centre."

At midday Justice Ongwengo aroused himself from a catnap to ask a question that suddenly niggled at him.

"What does 'old life back' mean to you Colonel?"

"'Presence' your honour."

"What?"

"Presence…now there is only absence."

"Oh. I see." He shut his eyes again, preparing for another round of cat napping.

And so it went on.

Soon, it was eight months later and a witness from the cells under Colonel Smith's watch had been found.

* * *

The Trustees of the Pater Bernado's Dove Award for Humanity arrived en masse to present Justice Ongwengo with a bronze dove with doleful eyes. The Dove was without a cash complement. The Dove was handed over to Justice Ongwengo during a recess. Justice Ongwengo did not give a speech. This was thought to be in keeping with his ascetic and compassionate character. It was here, surrounded by an increasing troop of acolytes and assistants, it was here that Justice Ongwengo realised he was being driven insane.

In court, that afternoon he fixed his gaze on the scarred woman. His hands itched to tear away at the scar, its raw nakedness now a challenge. He peeled his eyes away from her face when he saw she was also feeding off his gaze.

Three hours later, he recessed court, addressing her directly. He closed his note pad and was dismayed to find that the doodles it contained were variations of the scarred woman's moods and faces and if stared at closely, each image led to another and unveiled a story. That night he dreamed of her and they were entwined around each other like two black mamba and they were biting each other to death, infusing venom into each other's souls. When he woke up, in the night, for the first time in thirty years he remembered what it was like to be afraid.

And he was surprised.

* * *

The witness had been found among a camel-trading, desert-living peripatetic race in the Chalbi desert of Kenya. The mounted police of the Anti Stock Theft Unit had located him. When he saw the horsemen, the man had wondered if perhaps these were the horsemen of the apocalypse he had heard about.

His desert companions had watched in silence.

They watched in silence as static crackled.

They were even more silent when a helicopter landed flinging dust into their camp.

They watched the man closely for a sign, any sign that he needed their help, that the daggers and spears they hid and held could be used if he wanted.

The man was tall, slender and dark like gold, if it had been the colour of the earth. His eyes were pale brown and lit from within. Strangely, or maybe not, he carried an *oud*. He wore the dress of the nomads, the uniform of the desert, but his face and head were unwrapped and burned.

It was what he projected that bothered the horsemen, a distinct soundless completion which kept him out of reach of even those who, holding his right arm, led him to the helicopter. He turned to the desert people and then dropped his *oud*, before boarding the helicopter. He would find them again, as long as they kept the music warm.

Then he was gone.

For the nomads, he had taught them another way of longing. They would include him in their yearnings. It was enough.

In Nairobi, they told him why he was sought and he laughed.

* * *

The sun wrestled with the Cape clouds. Table Mountain loomed superior and aloof. There were many moments in the evenings mostly, when Justice Ongwengo stopped at the foot of the mountain waiting for the step that would lead him up and over to another type of day.

The memory of the events of the *'annus horribilis'* as Counsel said, quoting the Queen of England, induced *'Poteshesh'* in Colonel A. Smith.

Justice Ongwengo asked: "Clarify Pitieshesh".

Prosecuting Counsel replied: "Posht Tramatic Shtress Shyndrom".

Justice Ongwengo said; "I shee".

'Jolly Judge', the media headlines squealed.

The Nouveaux People magazine, South Africa, had voted him the 'Sexiest Judge Alive'. Oprah wanted to interview him for her magazine, not the show. An investigative reporter had revealed that the Judge was single. But even as the gay community rushed to adopt him, another investigative reporter discovered that his wife, Sophia, died in his arms giving birth to twins, who also died. His *'Ahhhh'* factor augmented, Justice Ongwengo's trickle of offers for protection, nurturing and cohabitation from all manner of females and males now became a deluge. The African Governments had also assigned a squad from the African Union Preliminary Security Unit (AUPSU) to protect him. For every step he took, there were three and a half people taking the same step a second later. One evening Justice Ongwengo climbed on his bed, reached up to the ceiling and tested the boards for softness. The roof as an escape route had potential. He took to frowning insanely at his entourage when they fell into step with him. It helped to deter their zeal to serve him just a little.

In the eighth month of the trial it had been firmly established that Colonel Smith was still being assailed by ghostly shrieks that prevented his peaceful sleep. It was established that his wife (now ex-wife) had divorced him on grounds of desertion and cruelty and won. Finally, it was public knowledge that he had tried to commit suicide three times and once almost succeeded.

Justice Ongwengo was bored.

He much preferred to mull about what he could do to exorcise the scarred woman from his dreams. His doodles of her face were becoming too detailed for his own comfort. In three he had accurately depicted the serrated scar above her left eye. He tore the doodle pages off his note pad and crumpled them, smoothed the pages out again. He shred them into minute pieces that he tossed into the dustbin.

* * *

The key trial witness had been selected for the high drama potential that would help demonstrate the culpability of Colonel A. Smith's country. The Tribunal Counsel, Dr Hans Andre, had said, gesticulating like a rotund tenor on an opera stage: "He has been found".

"I am delighted for you, Counsel. Now…who is it that has been found?" Justice Ongwengo asked.

Dr Andre was on a roll.

"May it please the Tribunal, I wish to call as witness for the prosecution, Terremoto."

"Who?"

"Terremoto."

"What is a Terremoto?"

"The witness."

"Where is he?" The Judge asked.

"At this very moment on a plane over the Mozambique channel."

Before adjourning the proceedings, Justice Ongwengo stared at Dr Andre, his eyes reptilian. Despite himself, Dr Hans Andre shivered. In the courtroom, a scarred woman seeing the look wrapped her red coat closer to her body.

* * *

There was a time Terremoto had another name. And before that name he had had another name. He explained the name changes in this manner: "God gave birth to me again."

113

Being in Guantanamo Bay had effaced all names. When he had been blindfolded, bound and herded into a transport plane, in Afghanistan, he had been a *nay* player and dervish of the Syrian *Mawlawiyya* order seeking *The Teacher*.

From the hour he heard about *The Teacher*, he was possessed by a thirst to find him. It was said by the brotherhoods that *The Teacher*, during *sama* – the act of listening – would be visited by fire from the Divine heart and in this fire all those within his vicinity would be purged, in a painful ecstasy, of all their stains. It was also said that in his presence, as dervishes whirled they merged and became a white sphere of light. He had sought *The Teacher* with all his mind, soul, heart and strength.

Before Afghanistan, Terremoto had passed through Turkey. He came to Turkey from Damascus, his home for fifteen years. Before Damascus he had lived in Khartoum. Before Khartoum he had lived in Lamu. It was what he found in Lamu that led him to Khartoum. But before that he had been born in Zanzibar. His mother had come from Egypt and his father from Oman. When he was born he had a birthmark shaped like a star behind his knees. They had named him Suleiman Dalil Ali. Now he was simply Terremoto.

After Guantanamo Bay where he learned to dream of touch, he lost all his names. When his captors had permitted him to hear again, a stray melody had slipped into his cubicle. The melody beckoned, like *azan* – the call to prayer. The melody left. With all his names the melody left, but embedded in his life another quest in the very moment he discerned that he needed to quest no further.

So he sought the song.

When he found the melody again, in al-Andalus, he learned that it had a personality: *Siguirya*. An accompanist, *Paco de Antequera*. A name, *De Santiago y Santa Ana* and the one who evoked its essence, *Terremoto de Jerez*.

So he became Terremoto. On the day he found the song that had left with his name at Guantanamo Bay.

The day Terremoto entered the Tribunal chamber, the room was engulfed by a new and warm silence. Shuffling papers, Justice Ongwengo said, his voice soft:

"Terremoto…"

"Terremoto…" he repeated the name.

"Where were you born?"

114

Terremoto said: "Unguja, Zanziba."

"Tell me, Terremoto, do you know that man?" He pointed at Colonel
A. Smith.

Terremoto now turned to look at the Colonel who had slipped his
halo into a back pocket and was merely encircled by an aura of defiance,
and studied his shoes.

Terremoto bowed low, he said:

"Indeed."

The Judge noted the action and asked:

"Where did you meet?"

"*Khawsa.*"

The court murmured and Dr Andre glanced at his papers.

"Where is that?"

"It is a state, in Guantanamo Bay."

"A state?"

"Of retreat. Retreat."

Justice Ongwengo observed that Colonel A. Smith's head was also
lowered, but unlike Terremoto's bow, his was shifty. He grinned.

Then he looked at Terremoto, his eyes dark and stony.

"Do you know the meaning of 'oath'?"

Terremoto nodded once.

For the first time in a trial, Justice Ongwengo administered the oath.
He administered it as if it were a threat. His voice was as calm and clear
as a sure knife's edge. He kept his eyes on the witness peering at him
atop his glasses.

"Repeat this oath after me, '*I swear by God, Almighty and Omniscient,
that I will speak the pure truth and will withhold and add nothing*'."

The witness repeated the oath, staring back at the presiding Justice.
Not blinking.

Justice Ongwengo leaned back in his vast black chair. Almost swirling
it, he pursed his lips. He started, as if suddenly remembering something,
his eyes glinting behind the mildly tinted spectacles. He asked, almost a
whisper:

"Who is your God, the God for whom you take this oath?"

For three minutes, silence replaced the fear and thrill seeking. Three
minutes for the God the witness swore by to find a place in the room.
After three minutes the witness smiled as if he were the truth and for the
first time in the eight months of the trial, Justice Ongwengo beamed
back a smile.

The woman with the scarred face saw that the smile though dark, created a spark of light that touched the fire of Terremoto's body and unleashed something in her spirit that stretched its mouth and showed itself on her face as a frozen laugh.

* * *

The wind is quiet...like listening...what is it waiting for? The woman muses. She walks the Atlantic shallows. She asks the ocean: "If I kept walking and walking into you, would you keep me or throw me back?" The ocean waves whistle with the wind and seem to consider an answer. Sometimes, in the lowest part of her soul, she feels the roar of other oceans and their compelling invitation to dissolve. She has sought the portal for so long. He had smiled as if he had been fondled by truth.

* * *

From his balcony in the penthouse suite overlooking the peninsula, Justice Ongwengo watched the scarred woman hover in the shallows as if she were stuck between opposing push-pull forces. She and her snakes had stayed and played in his dreams. Where they were he was without strength. He was afraid of falling asleep now. There was a knock on his door. It was, without doubt one of his numerous, pointless aides.

Grabbing his black robe, he spun on his heels towards the door. He saw the Pater Bernado Dove staring at him with its hollowed eyes, wings stretched out. Chortling, he deliberately pushed it off the mantelpiece and it fell with a thud. Somewhat pleased, he picked it up and balanced it on the window sill trusting that the wind would take care of its future.

The knock on the door was louder, persistent and accompanied by a refined:

"Your Honour."

"Your ass," he muttered.

Justice Ongwengo contemplated the dove on the sill and wondered briefly if high was really that high. If he jumped from the sill, would he necessarily die if his intent was just escape? He imagined climbing over the mountain like the von Trapp family escaping to Switzerland. He finished draping himself with the robe, opened the door and found his entourage waiting for him. His bodyguards saluted. He groaned.

116

The morning gawkers had arrived a little earlier today. They waited to watch the magnificent procession of justice pass before their eyes. Justice Ongwengo was spotted and greeted with the rapturous applause usually reserved for drug-addicted film stars and hated dictators whose populace had been schooled in the art of 'welcoming the benign father (or mother)'. A thought crossed his mind and before he could think too much about it, he extended a wave that was a cross between the Pope's and Queen Elizabeth II's. A closer inspection of the palm up wave would have revealed that his second finger was isolated and pointed upward in the universally recognised sign for: "Have you lost your contact lenses?"

They entered the building and at the top of the stairs, he found the scarred woman waiting, one among the official crowd and watching him just as she did in his nightmares. He wanted to sweep past but instead halted briefly and the entourage halted briefly with him. He glared at her, pouring rage and anger through his pores, trusting it would seep into her. She glared back. She shoved his rage back into his face, adding more of her own. He faltered, as if he would stumble. He turned on his heels, doubly infuriated. But in his mind, he heard his voice whisper, "I am afraid."

* * *

Dr Andre, Tribunal Counsel for Colonel A. Smith said:
"Mr Terremoto, you are still bound by oath. Do you understand?"
Terremoto bowed low.
"For the record, what were you previously named?"
Terremoto shrugged.
Dr Andre referred the court to the exhibit 'J' which proved that Terremoto was born Suleiman Dalil Ali, had become Ahmed Saleh and then Ghassan al-Jamal. In Guantanamo Bay he became nothing.
Dr Andre said: "Can you explain the name discrepancies, Mr Terremoto?"
Terremoto said: "It is natural for the sojourner to seek his one true name."
"And as Terremoto, you have found it?"
Terremoto shrugged.
"Now, now, is it not true you were incarcerated on suspicions of perpetrating acts of terrorism?"
Terremoto bowed low.
"Are you a terrorist Mr Terremoto?"

117

Terremoto bowed low.

"Is that yes or no?"

Terremoto shrugged.

Dr Andre swung towards to Justice Ongwengo.

"Will you ask the witness to answer the question your honour?"

Justice Ongwengo said "No."

Dr Andre dropped all his papers. Justice Ongwengo smiled and placed his chin atop his hands waiting to see what would happen next.

Dr Andre tried again.

"Mr Terremoto, you were incarcerated under suspicion of terrorism. Are you a terrorist?"

"Perhaps. I know my *oud* and *nay* were taken…in Afghanistan …weapons of mass destruction…"

Justice Ongwengo laughed outright. A huge belly laugh that caused all suppressed titters to become a communal roar.

The poster pictures looked on, clueless.

After the court settled down, Dr Andre tried another line of questioning, one that could precipitate an attack on Colonel A. Smith. He realised they needed another witness soon.

"What do your remember of the events of the Bay, Mr Terremoto?"

Terremoto's mouth stretched in an ear-to-ear grin.

"The unmentionable."

Dr Andre clenched his fists in hope. "Yes?" he said, urging Terremoto on.

"The…the…silent everything and beautiful…oh the beautiful nothing."

He bit his lip, trying to find the purest and most still word.

"Dhikr'ulla." With his furthest eyes, he looked into and touched Dr Andre's eyes somehow and for a suspended moment, Dr Andre saw an old memory stir and he shuddered.

His voice now shaking, seeking present-tense reality, he shouted: "You hate my client, your captor, your jailer…Colonel A. Smith. Terremoto, do you hate your jailer?"

"You hate him…don't you?" He was pleading.

Slowly, Terremoto lifted up his head. Slowly. Now his face was chiselled with trails of horror. Justice Ongwengo scavenged on the pickings; his imagination supplied the narratives that would have caused the soul to be stretched to the extent it revealed it had been stretched. He leaned forward breathing shallow, aroused.

Terremoto said, his voice amused, as if with the next syllable he would laugh, at odds with the sculpted anguish of his face.

"I knew the depth and breadth of hatred, yes...but found that it is... limited." He paused, his eyes lifted to an unseen horizon, remembering. His voice did not change much except to deepen.

"The boundaries of hatred led...to dark...silence."

The room waited on his words.

"Then the stars within the spirit...appeared one by one and soon there was light...and the stars within...the stars had a song which became...one note."

The room waited.

"They said..." Terremoto stretched up his arm, palm up, gazing upward, he said, his voice lilting:

"...you who are enduring this...this which you sought...love!"

Terremoto smiled. He lowered his arm and glanced shyly at Colonel A. Smith.

"I remember him...as the one who taught me to hate...then pointed me to see silence."

"He...was guardian to a path I sought...where there is no vision...no dream...no memory...no thought...no movement...no change...*mhh*."

A gentle silence suffused the room, like a benign and loving presence.

"*The Teacher* is...without this Colonel...could I have learnt to let *The Teacher* find me? Perhaps not."

Colonel A. Smith slowly raised his head to look for the first time at Terremoto. Terremoto looked back at Colonel A. Smith.

Holding the look Terremoto added, speaking to the Colonel alone:

"The music of your radio...thank you."

The look helped something that was difficult and sad and hard and old to dissolve.

Dr Hans Andre and Justice Ongwengo lowered their heads. The scarred woman gazed at one and then the others and thought nothing. No one had the strength to ask who *The Teacher* was. In the presence of this silence, words were superfluous.

A minute later, Dr Hans Andre cleared his throat.

"Er...Mr er..Terremoto...er...we have reports here from the Red...er...Cross and eye-witness accounts...the torture...Colonel Smith himself has agreed to provide a detailed...er...Mr Terremoto what was it like wearing an orange suit which denied you the right to sense, to feel, to touch?"

Terremoto extended his palm upward, pursed his lips, seeking the right words. He frowned with the effort and listed his head as if repeating words that only he could hear.

"To not see...to not hear...to not taste...feel or touch...touch ...ah!" He swallowed.

"This lesson. Ah! Touch must be...the first language of the Divine."

He smiled, "...hearing is the other." He laughed like a rare warm brook stumbled upon in a desert. He laughed at a joke only he and his God understood.

Justice Ongwengo asked, his voice straining, as if the question were forced out of him.

"But-how-do-you-live-with-the-loss-of-all-meaning...the-loss-of-all-meaning?"

Terremoto gazed at Justice Ongwengo, speaking softly as if they were the only two in the room.

"Imagine when I have lost all I could lose...imagine now...the freedom of who I am?"

Silence.

"You love life?" Justice Ongwengo's voice was a whisper now.

Terremoto listened.

He said. " It was good...good to see the stars of the sky...and smell the growing grass...after darkness...to love the stars...it consumes completely but not as much as...to touch another's hand again...now...I live to taste touch...it consumes completely...touch you can only taste in love."

Silence.

"Still you had to find another name for yourself, Mr Terremoto?" Justice Ongwengo asked, his voice hard, eyebrows raised, eyes peering above his spectacle rims.

Terremoto laughed out loud, a laugh which tapered to a warm sigh.

"Oh no. It is not a name, Sir, it is a song."

The scarred woman's heart began to beat so hard it was softly audible to her ear.

A teardrop fell on Colonel A. Smith's shoes. Another followed. Then Colonel Smith covered his whole head with both arms. He said, once: "Aaaaarrrrrrrrhhh."

The silence purged the courtroom so completely that Justice Ongwengo in a deep, low, soft uneven voice recessed the court four hours earlier than he had previously done.

* * *

120

Justice Ongwengo had returned to his room, his heart weighed down and found that the wind had not only left the Pater Bernard Dove intact on the sill, but had managed to tilt it in such a way that its eyes were the first thing Justice Ongwengo saw when he entered the room.

"I am afraid," he said to no one.

But he did not know what he was afraid of. He lay on his bed, his robe and wig still on, placed his hand beneath his head and chose not to think.

* * *

She sits on the rocks on the edge of the sea and plays with the idea of sliding and slipping away with the next wave. An oystercatcher ducks while behind her a seagull caws. The outrage in the croak probably means that she has either sat on the bird's perch or the oystercatcher's successes offend the seagull. The harvest moon gleams in the night sky and she thinks about the day. And the silence of a man who is a song.

* * *

The oppressive presence in the room filled it with a subtly noxious miasma; its serpentine head nestled on the ceiling board and gazed down at Justice Ongwengo. Justice Ongwengo gazed back. Its ghost tongue flickered. Justice Ongwengo licked his own lips and thought he was thirsty. He shook off the dregs of sleep. He got up and found the Pater Bernard Dove still staring at him from the sill. He decided to put it out of its misery. So he pushed it off the ledge. Seven seconds later he heard a dull thud, and another and then nothing. He was sure he had been told that bronze could shatter if dropped from a high place.

The moon shone behind the mountain throwing Orion's starry belt into relief. The keening of approaching high winds amplified the lingering feeling of oppression. Justice Ongwengo scanned the beach, knowing why he did. Now, rejecting the knowledge. Five minutes later, he doffed his robes and wig that sat askew his head, threw on his heavy coat and left the room.

* * *

The woman notes the wind's sudden fury. But the lingering scent of the Presence, the silence of the courtroom, stays with her. She leans into it, pays no heed to the wind's attempts to goad her into the ocean. The wind quickly incites the ocean into a similar fury. She leans into the rock and is suddenly so cold. She lowers her head into her now damp red coat and waits for whatever will happen next. Sharing in her misery, the gull decides her company is better than no company at all, and nestles into her. Along the beach she hears the pounding of hooves.

A strange thing happens. In the wind-sprayed moonlight, a horse bursts through from behind the dunes. The wind howls, but the intensity of sound must be because many creatures scream then. The horse and its rider plow straight into the sea, propelled by a wind in a hurry.

The woman on the rock senses the intent of the malevolent wave before it appears. Higher than her rock, it surges in, throws itself at the beach, nets a catch of sand and other detritus and seeks her out — she would have gone if the rock had not wedged her into itself. The wave heaves itself engorged and disappointed, back into the ocean. It carries the horse and its rider away. The woman begins to cry. Something moves against her chest. She thinks her heart has finally broken free. She touches it and finds that a gull is depending on her to keep them both safe.

* * *

Justice Ongwengo laughed. Low and long, like a rumble. He roared and the furies gathered to use his voice. He saw the scarred woman was clinging to a rock; that she would be swept away. He watched and waited and wondered what her agony would taste of. So he poured himself out, stretching his spirit to flow around her and feel her fear. She felt it and grasped it and drank it and poured remembered dreams into it but then bit into it and infected it with her venomous pain. And on the beach Justice Ongwengo clutched his heart, grabbed his face and knelt clutching his stomach.

He was afraid. Because a scarred woman had penetrated walls of furtive dreams and refused to leave.

Because, at court that day, a song, not a man, had suggested that another way of seeing might exist.

Because, more than anything, he hungered to ask the woman if she thought this could be true. Then he remembered where he was and where she was and that he was waiting for her to die.

* * *

122

Eons later, the wind's rage had eased. It did threaten to return with renewed fervour. The man loomed into the periphery of her vision. She knew who it was before she saw him. She stood no chance against him, the wind and the sea. But she had a sure power now, that of choosing her way to the inevitable. She would deny him the taste of her fear. When his hand reached her shoulder she grimaced in her heart and kicked out at him, terrifying the gull that cringed in her coat. She strained cold, cramped muscles and sought to plunge into the sea.He held her back, his arm a vice. He pulled and she felt the skin of her arm peel and bleed. He dragged her to the shore, towards the dunes. She screamed.

He pulled her into himself, wrapped his arms around her and glared down at her. He could now trace the scar at will so he did. With the back of his hands he started at its tapering end at top of her right eyelid, down her face and slipped down her neck. His hands stopped.

"Where is its head?"

"At the place where my heart stops..."

The wind rushed to the rock she had recently perched on and found she had gone. It howled its disappointment and commenced a search among the shore and dunes, flinging sand in its wake.

She said: "A horse and rider plunged into the sea."

"Yes," he answered.

She told him, speaking into his left ear while the gull struggled in her damp coat: "There...where my heart ends...the snake's head."

In turn, he spoke into her ear: "Black mamba?"

She turned her head to stare at him, her eyes gleaming as if she were a black mamba. He returned her smile, his own eyes gleaming and he looked like a black mamba.

The wind found her, tried to draw them both into the ocean, covering them with sand and sprinkles of the sea. The gull squawked. The harvest moon struggled to maintain its optimism. Orion's belt was now obscured.

He asked. "That man Terremoto...is he true?"

She was silent.

"Not a lie."

"No."

"No," he said again.

The silence of the day inhabited them both. His fingers found the rest of the scar. He traced the line to the place where her heart ended. There he found and shaped the head of the snake.

"He is true," she thought.

* * *

The scar on her body was possession's headstone. Before she had died, she had been a performer of *Guedra* and *Raqs Sharqi* – belly dancing. A fine dagger-carrying camel trader turned oil-well proprietor had sought to own her, her songs and all her dances. She had allowed herself to be caught, tired as she was of dancing alone.

The dance fled her for her infidelity to its dreams. She felt the dance leave her body, flowing from her heart, leaking out of her womb.

She turned to the man, uncaring. And from the first night of the day of their marriage, he burned her. He left imperceptible scars.

By the second week of his possession of her, her husband had marked on her stomach, breasts, down her legs, the pin-prick signature of his dagger's tip. Her eyelids and her throat too.

In the private public parties, in the palace, they drank off the same chalice. Unlike other couples on that land, he kept his arms around her. She leaned into him as if she were always about to fall.

But she died the day she gave birth to a son.

She suckled her son and penetrated his life, this fragile one and swore to pull down stars to adorn his dreams. To rip the souls of leviathans to feed his whims, to claw the eyes out of that which dared offend him. She suckled her son and tasted him tasting her.

She was watched by the father of the son. He read these purest vows in her eyes. He tasted their light and he did not like the flavour.

He waited for her to fall asleep.

The next day, when she woke up, she had no son. They told her only after the pain of accumulating milk trickling from her swollen breasts caused her to moan for her son in a rhythmic litany of yearning. They told her she had no son.

She leapt upon the father. Entreated him to join the truth hunt and restore her son, her life. A shadow whispered across his face. She dismissed at once what it dared to hint at.

Later, a month later, locked into his body, her camel-trader husband told her, like so many dirty words poured into a whore's ear, he told her:

124

Of the sound a small neck, broken makes
And of a body, tiny, covered by the desert sands of ages
Of fragile hands grabbing, even then, for breath
Of aphrodisiac power given to a man who kills his son and kisses his
mouth before burying him.

He studied her face smiling as she slipped away, but he was waiting
for her and swallowed her in his loins before kissing her on the mouth,
just as he had kissed their son. Then he suckled her as if he was their
son.

He was aroused by the knowledge of her hatred. He fed it, filled it
and followed it. Her face and body oozed a sheen of a passion pristine
out of which her soul gazed at him with loathing. She craved morning so
she could discover fresh ways to hate and the night so she could immerse
herself in nightmares. Her revulsion bound her to him. She lusted to
consume him, but since he was her hate's meaning, beginning and end,
he satiated her.

He knew her. He searched her body for vials, using the time as a
crude prelude to a cruder mating. He would swap his plate of food with
hers. He watched her. He laughed out loud when she toyed with a bread
knife and glared at him, pouring out her rage into him. He took her rage
and cradled it in his heart, imbibing of it, playing with it, with her. He
laughed out loud.

"Ha, ha, ha, haaaaaaaaaa!"

Their devotion to each other was a legend; spoken about with sighing
smiles and often with unadulterated envy.

It is true, the spirit of dance had fled her long ago but the day she
kept her promise to her son, she adorned herself in her belly dancing
jewellery and waited for her husband to finish perfuming his beard.

The way of his death was simple.

It was public and it was in a poison vial, smaller than a tablet, hidden
in her mouth, between her teeth and upper lip. She dropped it into the
chalice they shared when it was her turn to drink. He sipped the cup
while speaking to the Minister of Trade, Technology and Industry, while
she lovingly stumbled against him.

It was a good poison that shocked his body quickly into a heart
attack. He crumbled to the jade marble floor and she fell over him. And
over the screams of others, while his voice curdled in his throat, she
drank in his death, flowing into the experience, feeling and tasting the
poison work its way through his blood, into his organs which closed

125

down one by one, and she smiled over him. He stared into her eyes and smiled back at her.

The sudden thought of another creature owning her held back his death. With his left hand he grasped his dagger. She had leaned over to sing curses into his ear, the better to urge him to hell. This was why he had the satisfaction of tasting her body's shock at being shredded by his dagger.

His last words were: "It is true. I love you."

The media, the public praised this worship – this raw consummation of an eternal love.

She hovered on the brink between space and time, and saw her son dancing her old songs. She realised the body is prison but chose to return. She was glad she did because she disappointed the media who had milked this tale of passion to a sour curd. She lied. She said her husband in paradise had beseeched her to return to earth.

Her husband had been buried. She sold his businesses and camels and used the money to dredge the depths of the world to find how dark deeds obscured human faces. Because he had been her husband and in the way of his life ensured that many were indebted to him unto death, when she asked, she was permitted to be 'official observer' at numerous conferences, seminars, trials and tribunals, any place where people gathered to excavate the meaning for madness.

"It is true. I love you." What is true? She needed to know this more than she needed her son.

* * *

Around the dunes, the wind had stopped whining for their lives. She remembered something again.

"A rider and a horse plunged into the sea."

Again he said, "Yes."

Silence.

He wrapped his arms around her. He remembered the dream of snakes entwined.

In the thrall of a stark truth there was no place or time for veils, she saw.

Justice Ongwengo thought; "Did someone imagine truth was light...that light was not dark?"

"Mhh," she said. As if she heard his thoughts.

126

He asked her: "Where will we go?" His voice was an almost-whisper.

She thought about the answer and the gull thought about it with her. It peered through her coat, saw that the wind was quiet and gently eased away, not even bothering to fly. They watched it shuffle away until it melded with the dark.

She said: "Over the mountain…what is there…over the mountain?"

"I don't know," he answered.

She suddenly leaned into him and caught the flesh of his neck between her teeth. She savoured the pulse of the carotid vein. He drew her closer, tightly to him and discovered he was no longer afraid.

The frozen laughter in her thawed and exploded out of her, throwing her body upward. She rose, still holding onto him. He got up, still holding onto her and, when she whirled, he whirled with her and it was as if they had melded into an ineffable light.

In a hotel a short distance from the beach, another man who had once whirled into light felt their dance and laughed. He left his room by way of an open window. But he left the peaceful silence behind.

Later, Justice Ongwengo winked at the moon. They were walking over dunes to the foot of the mountain. There, they started to climb. His back was turned, so he did not see the moon wink back.

* * *

Two weeks later The Third Millennium Extraordinary International Tribunal of Inquiry was disbanded following the mysterious disappearances of Justice Ongwengo and the witness, Terremoto. A court clerk observed that a scarred woman who wore a short red coat was also missing. But since no one sought her, the seekers forgot to look for her.

The authorities were waiting for bodies to turn up.

Twenty-three days later, Colonel A. Smith dropped his suit without bothering to inform his legal team. He also dropped out of sight and a Carthusian Monastery in France received a new member destined to find himself in silence. His disappearance was declared mysterious. Security was deployed to protect others associated with The Third Millennium Extraordinary International Tribunal of Inquiry. A tribunal of inquiry into these disappearances opened a year later. It was presided over by trial judge, Dr Hans Andre.

* * *

127

In a courtroom in Cape Town, behind a Plexiglas shield, poster size images of five would-be respondents crumble like so many dust particles on history's pages. Not even meriting a footnote.

*

Yvonne Adhiambo-Owuor, a Kenyan, works as the Executive Director of ZIFF (Zanzibar International Film Festival), an East African arts and cultural resource centre and event producer. A closet writer, she was unmasked in 2003 when she won the Caine Prize for African Writing. When she is not being a bureaucrat, she tries to finish her first novel.

The Scavengers

Ken Barris

Ptero·dac·tyl *noun* a flying dinosaur that lived millions of years
ago. From [Gr.] ptero: wing and dactyl: finger

– Fructman's Concise Illustrated Dictionary

Africa is a cosmopolitan city. It is crowded yet elegant, decayed and
yet full of promise. It perches on the rim of an old volcanic crater,
now a teeming, self-contained savannah. From their balconies in the
better suburbs, people look down on giant herds of antelope and giraffe,
zebra, buffalo and majestic elephant. The air is thick with sacred ibis,
heron and crows, pterodactyls, every kind of carrion bird and raptor
imaginable.

The sun rises blood-orange at this time of year. Every day I drive to
work past the library of Alexandria, the pyramid at Gizeh, turn off at the
old stone temple of Zimbabwe, the bloated marble palace of Mobutu
Sese Seko. Tourists crowd the walkways in African masks, buying hide
shields and *assegais*, eating the flesh of Gaboon viper butchered on the
street, or roasted tail of crocodile which is taken as a delicacy.

You can arrange war parties to hunt down Bushmen who live on the
fringe of the nearby desert. Slavers can be seen in the Arab quarter,
careful, suspicious men who smoke their narghiles. There are jazz clubs
and chat rooms, markets and theatres, marble-clad hotels and high-class
brothels. You can buy strong leather, cheap beadwork and copper, or dive
among the great white sharks basking in the marina. Of course, these are
tourist diversions; the locals only do these things when they entertain
visitors from overseas.

* * *

My own amusements are modest. I have a really good pair of Nikon
binoculars. When I bought them, I felt that boyhood flush of admiration,
of joy, that comes with a new bike or spear gun. They're older now,

129

scratched in places – none that matter – but they're still good. I sit on my roof garden in Waterkant Street and follow everything that goes by. Sometimes I watch the ships coming into Cape Town harbour, the tankers and oil rigs putting in for service, the container ships with their rusting multi-coloured stacks, the occasional luxury cruiser bringing rich German or British tourists. It's good for our economy. Sometimes I focus on the sex workers further down Waterkant Street, the way they dress and move, the way they flex their bodies as they slouch, exposing their thighs and torsos even in the coldest weather. I focus on the windows of the cars they get into – you usually can't see much after that – or concentrate on the lives I imagine they lead.

Sometimes I turn the other way, and watch the pterodactyls launching off the heights of Table Mountain, soaring lazily on the thermals that rise above the city bowl. They're pretty impressive, but can be a nuisance. Mostly they feed off rats and tear open garbage bags left out for collection, but occasionally they take a small dog or some kid's precious cat.

It exposes one of the fault lines of our society: a conservative stream of opinion wants to shoot or poison them, but the greens are too vociferous. The pterodactyls are indigenous animals, they argue, we have to live with them. But I say: wait till one of these scavengers takes a little child. So far, thank God, it hasn't happened.

The most troubling and impressive thing is when a drunken driver smashes into a pterodactyl feeding off road kill – the wrecked wings that aren't capable of folding properly in the first place, the contorted Satanic angles of the dead or injured beast, the driver's stupefaction.

* * *

Waterkant Street is narrow. You can only park on one side, and that leaves enough room to allow only one car through. Sometimes I sit on my front step – usually in the summer evenings, when the roof garden is still too hot to go near, with heat waves rising visibly off the green bitumen – and watch the inevitable result of this constriction. I watch what happens when two cars arrive outside my house, trying to go in opposite directions.

A one-way street like this brings out the worst in people. The question is: who is going to back off and reverse all the way down this narrow road? The answer depends on the nature of the adversaries.

Usually, the first one to threaten violence gets right of way. It doesn't work like that if the second driver is willing to respond with real violence, or if the second driver is stubborn enough to call the first driver's bluff. Then again, if the driver who first threatens violence meets his commitments, the results are unpredictable. It goes down to the balance of size and martial resolve.

Sometimes the more insistent party turns on me, as a displacement tactic. He might say, "What are you staring at, *doos?*" In which case I'll raise my beer to him in a friendly manner, smile placatingly, and say, "I'm staring at you, fuckhead."

Now he has to deal with my mixed signals, with the fact that he has multiplied his offensive objects, and with his moral responsibility to drive this mess to a satisfactory conclusion. Typically, his morale crumples, he backs off and then the victor by default and I exchange conspiratorial signs, as if some victory has been achieved when in fact it's just a failed narrative on the part of the aggressor.

When women are involved, however, the permutations become uncontrollably rich, depending specially on whether one or both parties are women. In either case the violence becomes more verbal and yet more damaging, as women have bigger speech centres in their brains than men.

The point I really want to make is that down here I don't need my binoculars. The carnivores and scavengers are present on the street, prowling about so restless and inflamed.

It gets extremely hot in February. I hate living here at this time. You wake up exhausted, and even at seven-thirty in the morning, you resent putting on your shirt. When you come home from work, you're covered in grime. Your clothes are stiff with static, and spark when they come off. At night when you dream, you can see the souls of men and women rising to treetop level, sulking in the heat, merging sometimes, blitzing off the electricity supply cables, getting tangled in each other's nightmares, unable to rise further. And the tortured psychic mechanisms of street children flow up into the air too, from further east in the city, from the hard pavements of Darling Street and the steps of the City Hall, wrapped in the souls of their sleeping dogs, tasting of hessian and newspaper.

One such night – I mention this only because it is typical – I was obliged to wrestle with an angel in my sleep, who promised to leave my memory of the night intact if I could pin him down two out of three.

He beat me; yet I still recall in a fragmentary way his towering staircase, which somehow was not distinct from his wings, and how it led directly to the flat pinnacle of Table Mountain. Perhaps this great monad eluded me by slipping into a cheap structure such as metaphor, which we often mistake for the phlogiston of their real personalities. I do know that he was a seraph from the River Zambezi, travelling further south for reasons of his own. In any event, I believe there are more suicides and road deaths in February than any other time, except Christmas, and people become unreasonable.

* * *

One Sunday in late February, the heat in Waterkant Street became unbearable. I had a cold shower and took my car down to the Waterfront, hoping it would be cooler in that giant air-conditioned space. It was only marginally cooler inside, and terribly crowded. There was no hurrying about. I had to drift slowly through the wide concourses, taking my place in the damp and overheated procession of passers-by, shoppers, refugees, time-killers like myself.

On certain holidays you find silver men and golden women at various places in the Waterfront, dropped off at strategic places, confluences of traffic and so on. They wear period costume, typically an exaggerated image of the thirties, or sometimes the bizarre dress of an era which never existed, theatrical rather than historical constructs. I stopped idly before one of these, a golden-skinned woman wearing a leather aviator's cap, zebra skin doublet and jodhpurs. A luxuriant blond ponytail escaped from her cap, suggesting wildness tightly constrained. I stopped because I found her particularly beautiful under the golden pigment.

The heat must have affected me worse than I realised, because I wasn't sure if she were actually human, or some kind of artefact programmed for limited arcs of movement. She kept quite still, arrested in an attitude of listening, left hand raised in mid-gesture. Then, as if she sensed the pressure of my attention, she moved towards completing the gesture, lurching to a halt before the point of completion. I wondered if she were animated by public attention. Could it be a photovoltaic element in her painted skin, galvanised by the sensitive ocular probe of the observer? Yet she showed a sly, calculating intelligence in her eye when she imagined I wasn't watching, which inclined me to the belief that she was in fact human.

The golden woman settled my inner debate with shocking clarity. She vacated her poise altogether, melting down in a fluid, graceless slackening of tissue, of cheeks, of arms and breasts. Her head bounced on the tiling. Her eyes opened wide and as she looked briefly into mine, transferring to me her surprise and helpless protest, her dread. Then they slowly went dull, closed, and she lay still.

I was astonished by this collapse. I was even more bewildered by the fact that no-one else seemed to notice. I looked around indignantly, but people walked by as if nothing had happened. The golden woman lay on the floor, her legs twisted to the side, her arms outstretched. Perhaps they thought that this was a normal operation of the mechanism, and so the appalling responsibility of doing something about it fell to me.

"Who are you?" I wanted to ask her. "What makes you move and breathe? Do you have thoughts that are different to mine? Are you really a human being?"

Instead, I reached out and placed two fingers against the side of her neck. Her golden skin was strangely cold, greasy to the touch, and yet metallic beneath. There was no pulse at first, but after shifting my fingers around and applying more urgent pressure, I discovered the steady beat of her heart. Relieved that she was alive, I began to withdraw my hand. She stirred then, and opened her eyes. They were blank, as if the content of her mind had been erased by her fall.

It presented a dreadful window of opportunity. I could say to her or do anything I liked. She was in my power, as long as no-one else noticed or cared. She was stripped of self-knowledge, and therefore helpless. A quick glance confirmed what I desired, and feared even more. The crowd streamed about us, chatting, arguing, staring vacantly, eating ice cream. We were alone in a cell of indifference.

The moment passed. Nothing happened. It was a moment of recognition only. Slowly, with great uncertainty, she placed her hand on her own neck, where I had touched her.

"What have you done?" she asked.

"Are you alright? I think it must be the heat…you seemed to faint. I was watching you."

She sat up, struggling to take off her doublet. I wanted to assist her, but felt that I had no right to touch her, now that she was conscious. Could I talk to her? She did thank me, but studied me ruefully, obviously hoping that I would go away. And so I did, realising only much later that the tips of my middle and index finger were daubed with the gold that covered her skin.

* * *

I had a pounding headache. I sat on my front step, nursing a beer, watching the light fade in Waterkant Street. I had little else to do. A Mini with a hole in its exhaust came growling up the street, making a ridiculous din for such a little car. It stuttered violently and died opposite my house, steam pouring through the grille. The driver made a number of ill-judged attempts to restart it, but eventually gave up.

A wiry young woman in jeans and a black shoe-string top climbed out, clearly in a rage, and slammed the door.

"What do I do now?" she called out to me. "I'm stuck."

I shrugged my shoulders, too apathetic to think about helping her.

"Jesus," she said more softly, shaking her head. "What do I do now?"

I stood up reluctantly and approached her. The Mini stank of burnt oil.

"I don't know much about cars," I said. "But I think it's just overheated. Wait till it cools down and I'll give you some water."

"Thanks. I don't have any choice. Do you know how to put water in this thing?"

"I'm sure I can work it out."

We sat down on my front step. She glanced at me covertly, trying to gauge whether I could be trusted. I reacted with discomfort. Perhaps my headache obscured my vision, as I had trouble seeing her clearly; yet I felt her presence keenly enough, a tangible unsettling warmth.

"Would you like a beer?" I asked, trying to bridge the pain of this moment. I wanted her to leave me alone, but knew that she couldn't. I grudgingly understood that I wanted to touch her.

"How long will it take the car to cool down? How long do you think?"

"I don't know. Twenty minutes, maybe half an hour."

"I might as well then. Thanks."

I rose to fetch the beer, almost resenting her calculation of my hospitality against the available time. But resentment died away. It wasn't worth the energy in this heat, in this headache of a city.

A hooter blared in the street as I was about to return with the beers, the usual gorged battle cry of arrogance. I went outside, cursing under my breath. A blue BMW squatted before the Mini, its driver hooting even now in manic indignation. The woman stood, crouching slightly, hands on her hips. The window of the BMW slid down.

"I'm stuck, you moron," she blazed at him. "Can't you see that fucking steam? The fucking car's on fire!"

The steam had mostly abated, though a lazy tendril or two still curled out from under the bonnet.

He stuck his head out the window, a man of about fifty with glittering spectacles. He was red-faced and self-important, used to getting his way.

"Do you need to use that filthy language?" he replied in measured, righteous tones. "Is that necessary?"

I intervened, my pulse beginning to quicken: "Is it necessary to hoot like that? Are you crazy? She's not trying to park her car there! Can't you see that she's stuck?"

His aggression suddenly deepened in response: "Then get the bloody thing off the road!"

"We can't," she snarled back. "You're in the bloody way!"

She was right. For once there was a parking space open, about ten metres behind the BMW.

"There," she said, pointing. "It's behind you, moron. Look. Use your eyes."

He swivelled his head further out and saw the parking space. His beefy colour deepened to beetroot. Not in embarrassment, but because he was obliged to reverse; which meant that he was about to lose the battle of Waterkant Street, and even worse, lose face.

Tyres squealed as the powerful car shot backwards, nearly slamming into an entire string of parked cars. He slowed abruptly, inching back until the front of his car lined up precisely with the furthest point of the opening.

She grinned at me suddenly: "Do you think we should sit down and drink the beer first?"

I smiled, and said, "Maybe not."

She got into her Mini, I pushed it into safe harbour, and the BMW roared off.

Our conversation was easier after that. My headache lifted slightly. She stayed long enough to have a second beer. We filled her radiator and the car started. Perhaps she liked me – in any event, she

135

accepted my business card – but it was obvious that I'd never see her again.

* * *

Nights were unpleasant. I slept badly. I dreamt one night that I found a wounded angel on my lawn. Its left wing was broken and dragged clumsily behind. There was an amused horror on its face, probably reflecting an impossible thought: I am a dying immortal.

This was a bitter cold Sunday. It could only be a spirit from one of the hot planets, blown by fierce solar winds entirely off its orbit. Now it was wrecked and helpless in my garden.

My dog saw the exile and bristled. As he sensed its brokenness, the need to kill the angel surged in him like lava. The dog attacked, the angel scuttled through the bars of my pool fence. It went too far and tipped wildly into the water. It didn't sink immediately, but floated amongst the oak leaves, its buoyancy quite alien, visibly wrong. It wore an aspect of ghastly patience.

I fished it out with the leaf net. It rose out of the water tangled in last summer's blue nylon netting, with the corpses of those large black and yellow beetles that feed on rose petals, and the drowned snails hanging out of their shells, extended and lifeless as the organs of hanged men.

I didn't know what to do. Perhaps, I thought, I should quickly break its neck. When I was a child, I had seen chickens killed this way, head and neck grasped firmly between ring and index finger and flicked hard, the kind of sure action a child could only admire – the birds were then flung high over the stone wall of the pig pen as they were diseased, while the sows fought each other, snuffling and grunting after such bloody largesse – but I lacked the moral fibre to put the angel out of its misery. I did have a gun in this dream, an old .38 special with a two–inch barrel, and found the thought of shooting the angel easier to contemplate. But even that was grotesque; I found the idea embarrassing. The angel took advantage of my confusion and disappeared into the bushes behind the pool. I didn't think it would survive the night, wet as it was, shocked and so badly injured.

I left it to die.

Scouting around just before dusk, I found the angel's mask, discarded in the long grass on the fringes of the shrubbery. It was cut from half a walnut shell and seemed sturdy enough. But by morning

136

there was only an oval of dust on my desk, understated silver matter like the scales of a moth's wing. It gave off a reproachful scent reminiscent of patchouli, or when sunlight fell on it, a metal tang of bergamot.

* * *

My phone rang at work. Someone I didn't know – her name was Nadima April – wanted to speak to me. She turned out to be the woman in the overheated Mini. Her voice was surprisingly practised, more formal than it had been on our first encounter. I supposed that she was phoning from her own workplace, and this was her professional voice. I covered my embarrassment, my pleasure, and agreed to meet her for a drink in a couple of days' time.

We met at the Waterfront, at a restaurant overlooking the Victoria Basin. This time there were no gilded men or women haunting our space. Yet the water was silver in the evening light, the boats resting on it doubled in silver. The light gilded Nadima too, touching her with a beauty greater than her own.

Nadima drank white wine, I drank red. As she lifted her glass I noted a sculpted quality in her hand. It was finely modelled, made of bronze, perhaps, of warm dark stone. Sculpture can be more interesting than any human original. Some particular emotion is singled out and made evident. Her face, for example, was mobile and alert. Humour and warmth, intensity and hostility, puzzlement and wit appeared there, vanishing as easily as they came. Her hand by contrast spoke only of pleasure. It grew unbearable that she was model and carving united in one shape. I needed to touch that hand. I needed to trace its hollows and knuckles, read its lesson, absorb its silent warmth.

I was allowed to read the topography of her body later on, the grain and algorithm of her sex. I lay with her on my rumpled bed, forming a prototype alphabet from which all possible letters could be derived. But as we slowly moved together, my mind began to roam. I found myself dreaming of a golden woman who once had stained my own hand gold. I imagined long dialogues in which she confessed the shames of her childhood and I forgave her these, explaining who she was. In another endless cycle we married and fought to the point of mutual destruction. Eventually we betrayed each other and suffered a painful divorce. A third troubled picture gave her cancer. I sat at her bedside as she lay dying, a broken man, and not only in the turmoil of fantasy.

137

I tried hard at first to pay attention to my partner in flesh – for a while I struggled to remember her name – but slowly desire waned and my interest fell away. In the end it was I who became stone, a grey friable rock that could only absorb light and radiate nothing. The woman walked out in a fury in the middle of the night, and hasn't contacted me since.

* * *

The sun continued to beat down fiercely; the air was stifling. I continued to sleep badly. But February gave way to March and the heat finally broke. Sheets of rain slanted across the city, relieving our thirst, our boredom. It's pleasant to sit on my roof garden now, at least when it isn't raining, and watch the sea traffic through my fine Nikon binoculars.

More recently, it's been raining 'dactyls. They come crashing down on the pavement or directly onto cars, often causing damage and setting off the alarms. It's not uncommon to see one caught up in the branches of a tree, its wings wrecked and bleeding, torn by the boughs that hold it captive. They're incapable of sound, other than a defiant hissing noise, and of course the desperate leathery beat of their wings. At first they hiss like kettles, then the sound grows weaker; their eyes grow weak and dim, the struggle gives over. It's a wrenching experience, to witness this burgeoning failure of robust life.

No-one is sure what has caused this plague among the pterodactyls, but scientists speculate that a virus originally human – perhaps even the common cold – has mutated, and become deadly to the ancient saurians. The breeding colony on Lion's Head, and the larger one on the buttress above Skeleton Gorge, are both under duress. I understand that if they fall below a critical number, it's likely that the species will die out. You only find them in this part of Africa, the Cape Peninsula. I don't think it matters much to the common citizen, though we do take a dim-witted, insular pride in them – almost as if we owned them, which of course is absurd.

My view is that they were here long before human beings evolved. They're part of our heritage, almost as old as Table Mountain itself. However, many would dispute that. Some contend that they only took up their station on the mountain with the advent of white settlers, having emigrated on the jet stream from a harsher climate, perhaps the cliffs of Tierra del Fuego. Others argue that they originated in the Greater Rift

Valley. No-one is certain, though most people get dogmatic on the subject (should they ever think about it at all) and argue heatedly. It's rather as if the pterodactyls bring out the worst in us Africans, which is odd. We're normally quite a placid community. But they are dying out now, leaving us unsure of who we are, and what we mean to say.

*

Ken Barris lives in Cape Town and teaches at the Cape Technikon. He has published two novels, a collection of short stories, and a collection of poetry. Individual stories and poems have appeared in a number of journals and anthologies. A third novel, *Summer Grammar*, will appear in 2004. He has won the Ingrid Jonker Prize for poetry, the Vita Award for short fiction, and the M-Net Book Prize for his first novel, *The Jailer's Book*.

Mantracker

George Makana Clark

A head, five pillars of greasy smoke rose to support the gloaming. Below us, a blur of denuded land strung with Christmas tree lights. A flare arced over the Zambezi River, reflecting on its surface. The Alouette made its descent and the Christmas tree lights became strings of small ground fires.

Bongi dangled his legs out of the open door of the helicopter, ignoring me as he pretended to read *Being and Nothingness*, not even looking up when the pilot made a steep banking turn to throw a scare into us. Bongi held his cigarette between his middle and index fingers, palm covering his mouth, the way Sartre smoked in the photo on the dust jacket.

We used to smoke Kingsgate cigarettes together, but Bongi switched to Madisons. By changing brands, he hoped to distance himself from me and my blood reading. I spat out into the sky in an attempt at nonchalance. The ground rushed up at us. There were no waves of grass beneath the beating blades, only seared earth.

Takeoffs and landings in this sector were touch and go, and the Alouette was already rising before our feet touched the ground. The concussive din of rotor, turbine, and wind faded away to a faint drone.

We'd been delivered, Bongi and I, along with this story, into a *kraal* on the edge of a burning village. Smoke poured from the window of a wattle and daub hut that formed one side of the enclosure. Charred cattle and goats occupied the *kraal* in various attitudes of agony. Their stomachs heaved and sighed as they released their grassy gasses. Some had died standing, others writhing, hooves in the air. With the helicopter well away, a mob of ibises returned to feed on the fleshy tongues, eyeballs, anuses, and udders.

The police had already rounded up the villagers and loaded them onto buses to be shipped off to a keep, where they would live out the war encircled by razor wire, dogs, and guards.

Bongi stowed *Being and Nothingness* away in his rucksack. The book had belonged to Weatherhead, the third member of our tracking team, newly deceased. I slung my FN rifle and stared across the river into

Zambia where the enemy lay hidden somewhere in the tall grass, the thornbush, the mopani trees that stood in silhouette against the darkening sky. I felt their gaze wash over me, as palpable as the smoke and heat.

A bulldozer rumbled toward the *kraal*. I reckoned the village had been singled out for destruction because its inhabitants provided meat and information to the terrs. Or they had participated in an all-night unity celebration. Or some of the young people were observed using the triple handshake that identified them, in the troubled times of this story, as supporters of the guerilla movement. The bulldozer peeled back the earth like a scab.

I watched a stick of police reservists bash up for the night behind a Leopard armored car, the only cover going in the hammered landscape. Their sergeant trained his field glasses on the far bank, searching for snipers. Some combat engineers smoked in silence around a concrete mixer. Two scouts erected an eight-sided tent.

Earlier, Vampires had descended on the village, each jet armed with a 50-gallon drop tank filled with frantan, Rhodesian napalm made from polystyrene and jet fuel. One tank could incinerate a compound, a mealie patch, a grain storage shed, or a *kraal* filled with livestock. The smoke deadened all sound and stank of burnt animal fat, petrol, and plastic.

Bongi and I squatted on our haunches and waited for someone to come along and tell us what to do. Leaflets littered the village. One read: *Your ancestral spirits are very angry with you. As a result of this, there will be great famine. Only the government can help you.*

The two scouts had finished putting up the tent and were now lifting something flat and heavy. As they carried it into the tent, the surface of the object flashed grey-blue, the same color of the twilight sky. It was a full-length dressing mirror.

I examined the ground in the failing light. The bombers and the earth mover had thrown up a lot of dust, which would complicate things in the morning. Already it was settling over the spoor. There were women's footprints, smallish with splayed toes. The men of the village had gone north across the Zambezi to find work in the copper mines, or to join the guerillas. The rest of the prints were made by children. The people who lived in this forgotten corner of Rhodesia considered it an obligation to produce as many offspring as possible so there would be enough of the living to honour all their ancestors. The prints were partial, balls of feet and toes only, sometimes sliding and skidding. The people of this village had been running blind.

One of them had trod on a bowl and left blood on the shards. I glanced sideways into the dried blood – the edges of the vision are better suited for this sort of thing – and an image superimposed itself on the stain: *The air is laden with humidity, the breathless shrieking of fighter jets, dread. As the drop tanks fall from beneath the Vampires' wings, the owner of the blood cannot help but to stare upward, motionless, to watch what comes down on her from the sky. A searing splash, the melting away of flesh and consciousness, the exposure of bone and agony.*

I closed my eyes to the blood, and the image disappeared.

Bongi's voice came from behind. "Haven't you brought us enough bad luck with your blood reading?" he said.

I spat onto the shards and stood. "Weatherhead made his own luck," I said.

A lorry backed up to the *kraal* and a pair of light infantrymen tumbled out of the cab. I watched them pull several asphyxiated newborn goats out from beneath their nannies. The kids' flesh was relatively untouched by the chemical fire. The infantrymen heaved the carcasses onto the bed of the lorry and drove away with meat enough to feed their entire commando.

An unbroken egg lay just outside the kraal. Bongi followed as I stepped through the scatter of fence sticks. It wasn't an egg after all, but rather a golf ball.

A curious parade moved toward us across the wasteland, Major Sowers at the lead. The major was dressed entirely in red from boot to beret. A soldier followed, shouldering a bag of golf clubs. A parrot hopped after them, swearing in Spanish.

Major Sowers carried a patch of artificial grass. I recognised him from the photo in *The Umtali Times*. The headline ran: 'Actor Finds New Role Fighting Terrs'. According to the article, Major Sowers had played Pontius Pilate in a production of *Jesus Christ, Superstar* that ran for two years at the Rep Theatre in Salisbury.

"You're standing in my fairway," Major Sowers said, ignoring my salute.

The caddy wore no rank on his fatigue jacket. Like Bongi and me, he sported a tan beret. He was graying at the temples, a bit old for the Scouts. I read the name sewn above his breast pocket: *Foote.*

Foote signaled to the bulldozer driver to switch off his engine. Major Sowers placed the artificial turf beneath the golf ball. Foote selected a two iron and offered the club, handle foremost, to Sowers. Major Sowers accepted the club and addressed the ball.

I'd never been to the theatre, but there was a sort of ritual between Major Sowers and Foote that I imagine must exist among actors on a stage.

"*Chupa mi pinga,*" the parrot said, providing the chorus.

Major Sowers sent his ball sailing toward a distant pennant that fluttered near the riverbank. Foote waved at the bulldozer and the machine roared back to life, fuming.

The major squinted into the twilight and spoke peevishly to his caddy. "Can't see a bloody thing."

"I'll have someone pour some petrol onto the river," Foote said. He handed me the golf bag and stamped off toward the concrete mixer to bully the combat engineers into firing up the Zambezi.

Major Sowers turned his attention on me. "You're the blood reader, then," he said. Bongi shuddered at this casual utterance of my birthgift. Major Sowers strode toward his golf ball, his red clothes now purple in the dusk. Bongi followed, then the parrot. I slogged after them beneath the weight of the clubs, dragooned into the rag-tag procession. Behind us, the bulldozer pushed the burnt livestock into the pit.

Major Sowers looked over his shoulder at Bongi and me. "There's only two of you. I ask for a tracking team, I expect to see four trackers."

"We lost a man last week," I said, immediately regretting my choice of words. Bongi shot me a look as I lined up my excuses: our team was already a man short; Weatherhead had been reading when he should have been paying attention; the man we were tracking possessed the ability to appear and vanish at will; my blood reading had brought bad luck down on us.

But Major Sowers didn't ask me how or why Weatherhead was lost. Instead, he turned to Foote. "Ah, these are the chaps who were tracking that Zorro character."

"Comrade Zorro," Foote said. My heart jumped at the sound of it.

Sowers harrumphed. "A ridiculous name."

"The terr snipers name themselves after comic book and movie heroes," Foote explained patiently. "Comrade Tarzan, Comrade James Bond, Comrade Batman, and so on."

"Just so," Sowers said, losing interest. He ordered Bongi to run ahead to the flag that marked the cup. "Your man reliable?" he asked me when the right flanker was out of earshot.

143

I shrugged.

The major pushed back the scarlet beret and mopped his brow with his sleeve. "If you don't know, you can't trust him." We continued our march toward the ball. "Foote'll have to go with you," Major Sowers said. "He knows the basics of tracking. Good man, Foote. I'm sure we can scare up somebody to round out the foursome."

"Who're we after?" I asked, afraid of the answer. "Comrade Zorro?"

The major looked at me like I was simple. "Foote'll brief you once you're underway."

As if summoned by the third incantation of his name, Foote appeared out of the darkness at my shoulder. Ahead, Bongi hunched beside the flag in the light of the burning river, waiting to be struck by a sniper's bullet or the major's golf ball. Major Sowers chipped onto a patch of hardpan that had been designated as the green, then two–putted into the cup.

"*Cago en tu leche*," the parrot squawked.

Major Sowers kicked at the bird with his red boots. The parrot clacked its beak at him. "*Jou ma se poes*," it said, switching to Afrikaans.

"The bugger'll outlive me," Major Sowers grumbled. "Belonged to my father, and his father before, damn him. Bought it from a whorehouse in Cape Town." He made a show of sighing. "Curtain time, Foote. It's getting too dark for the terrs to see me."

Major Sowers looked out across the burning river into the darkness. "There's drama in combat," he said, addressing his unseen audience. "The terrs understand this. That's why they'll probably win."

We watched the major stride toward the octagonal tent that served as his dressing room, the parrot hopping after him, swearing now in German.

"Silly old git," Foote said.

"Why's he dressed all in red?" I asked.

"Throws the terrs into a muddle. Blood scares the piss out of their spirit mediums. They can't even look at the colour." Foote took the golf bag from me, rummaged a flask of Scotch from the zippered pouch and passed it round. Bongi refused to drink with us.

"Ever hear of the Zambezi hippo hunters?" Foote asked.

"Dunno," I lied. It was a story to scare children. Bongi shifted uneasily.

Foote watched me take a pull on the flask. "They say round here that God made the hippo hunters from the mud of the Unspeakable River, wherever that is. I've heard they can stay beneath the river surface for extraordinary lengths of time, rising from the mud only to dispatch their enemies." Foote took another swallow before returning the flask to the pouch. "Imagine what kind of scouts those bastards would make."

Pinpoints of light shone in the trees across the Zambezi. Strains of music floated above the far bank, finger piano and voices. "The terrs are truly switched on, young corporal," Foote said in a fair imitation of the major. "They'll be at it all night. Hope you're a heavy sleeper. We'll be underway at daybreak while the tracks are still fresh."

"Whose tracks?" I asked.

Foote narrowed his eyes at me. "I hear your last mission was a proper balls-up," he said. "Last chance, Corporal. Just don't bitch it." He strolled away, leaving Bongi and I alone beneath the yellowed toenail clipping of a moon. There were no lights on our side of the river; full darkness brought out the snipers. I could no longer see the hippo snouts that dotted the river, though intermittent tuba-bellows confirmed their presence.

We sat cross-legged on the hardpan green, Bongi and I, each with our own packet of cigarettes, empty Coke can, and lighter. I flicked the lighter, taking in the smell of butane, savouring it. The trick to smoking at night is to keep the burning end in an empty can. A sniper will shoot you in the mouth if you show a lighted cigarette.

I smoked out the pack and started another, watching the quarter moon until it had risen midway in the night, a time when the women and children of this village would have gathered around cooking fires to tell stories. I wondered how many ancestors around here would go forgotten, now that the living were so thin on the ground. A landmine exploded on the periphery of the village and we were flat on our stomachs, rifles in hand, sighting on nothing. A porcupine, probably, looking to chew on fresh bones.

The air was smothering, the ground still hot from the napalm, so we returned to the *kraal* to lie down on the cool turned earth. There were other, closer patches of disturbed earth in the village, but I thought I might sleep better if I knew what was buried beneath.

I turned my back on Bongi, closed my eyes, and dreamed the same dream I'd had six nights running:

We're on our first mission. Bongi is on my right flank, Weatherhead on my left. Weatherhead walks with his head in his book. With a three-man team, I have to function as both lead tracker and tracker control. We're hunting Comrade Zorro, a sniper credited with eleven kills.

As the trail grows colder, Bongi and I break training and walk close enough to speak. Rumours of Comrade Zorro swarm like bees in our conversation.

"They say Comrade Zorro can summon the river mist to hide his approach."

"Before the war, Comrade Zorro made his living as a strangler who procured human organs for sorcerers."

"I heard that Comrade Zorro's ancestors direct his bullets."

We're like children, scaring each other into laughter.

The spoor is old, time has eroded Comrade Zorro's footprints, and so I don't bother telling Weatherhead to put away his book and pay attention. A mist rises from the river.

The dream ends, as do all my dreams since that day, with Weatherhead alive, Bongi still my friend, Comrade Zorro's rifle yet unfired, three of us walking toward another who's waiting to step out from the mist.

* * *

There was a barracks story going around a while ago. It was about a commando leader who conducted a sweep of a remote tributary of the Zambezi. His scouts came across numerous bare footprints, though by the third night, they had still not seen another human being. The commando leader sent out a night patrol to capture someone for him to interrogate, and they returned with a slight, naked man, clad only in river mud. The pressure lamp had failed, making it impossible to see the prisoner's features. The commando leader wrapped his fist in his belt and ordered the tent cleared.

No-one witnessed what was said or done inside the tent, but the soldier who stood guard at the flap said later he heard the soft thump of leather against ribs, coughing, and finally the unmistakable gurgling a man makes when he's choking on his own blood. When the guard, still fresh from training camp, found he could no longer stomach this, he burst into the tent where his commanding officer stood breathing heavily over the still prisoner.

The guard heard the bellow of hippos, and shots rang out on the perimeter of the camp. The hippos, inexplicably, were lumbering out of the river to charge the sentries. The bulls roared as the sentries' bullets struck them in the face and chest, but still they came on, until the river smelled of cordite, blood, and faeces, and the living hippos could no longer climb over the pile of carcasses that lined the bank.

"Throw the prisoner into the river," the commando leader ordered, clearly rattled. "Let the bloody hippos have him."

Afterward, the commando leader could not be persuaded to return to the bush, even under threat of military discipline. He accepted a reduction in rank and was sent down to our unit to serve as adjutant officer amid a cloud of disgrace and rumour. The ex-commando only left his desk to use the latrine. The light in his office was never extinguished. It was said he never slept.

On the evening of Weatherhead's death, Bongi marched up to the adjutant officer's desk, a camp table covered with invoices, memos, written orders, and carbon paper. Bongi saluted smartly and requested a transfer to another tracking team. The reason, Bongi said, was that his team leader was a sorcerer with unnatural powers. Our previous A.O. would have dismissed this claim as superstitious rot and Bongi would have drawn extra duty after a good dressing down. Instead, the ex-commando leader leaned forward in his chair.

Bongi hesitated for a moment. "He read Weatherman's blood, Sir. He told me he saw death there, pouring out of the river."

The adjutant officer dismissed Bongi and summoned me from where I stood eavesdropping outside the tent.

"Your flanker says you're a blood reader."

"Sir," I said.

The adjutant officer picked up the bayonet he used as a letter opener and cut his finger lengthwise, laying open the fine bones and joints. A stain spread across the forms, memos, orders, files, and carbon paper. There was deep fatigue in his eyes. "Tell me, Corporal, what do you see?"

I looked aslant at the ruined finger, the liquid. The light bulb overhead reflected white on the fresh blood. I read aloud what was written there: *"I see you as a teenager standing over the still form of your mother. There's guava juice spilled on the kitchen floor. Your father pushes you aside, kneels, and places his head to her heart. He begins pounding her chest."*

The adjutant officer slapped his hand in his own blood, breaking the image apart. "No, no, I don't care about that!"

When I told him that I could only read what was written in the blood, he cut open another finger, and I witnessed another image from

147

his life, this time from his early childhood. Distressed, the adjutant officer sliced open third finger, pad to knuckle. But he had been brought up against the limitation of my birthgift. Blood yielded only random, disconnected images, a string of crystalline moments from the bleeder's life, or that of his mother, or her mother, or any one of a succession of ancestors stretching back to a time when there was no time. Or it revealed uncertain snatches of the bleeder's future. Sometimes I glimpsed the present, though this consisted only of murky secrets.

The adjutant officer buried his face in his hands. When at last he looked up, his fingers had left five stripes of blood that ran from the left side of his forehead to his cheek.

I took a chance. "Is this about the prisoner you interrogated?" You never know how an officer will react to a personal question.

The adjutant officer tried to wipe his face, but this only made matters worse. His fingers had swelled to the size of sausages. "He claimed he wasn't a terr."

"Who was he then?"

The adjutant officer continued to stare at the blood-sodden orders, the files, the blotter, his ruined fingers. "He said he was the Weaver of the Universe, the Shaper of the World. He said he was God of the Hippo Hunters."

The ex-commando leader started on the right hand, the bayonet slipping in his damaged fingers. "Let's try again," he said.

I turned my head until the image fell in the periphery of my vision. *"I see you in a schoolyard, reaching into the pocket of a younger student. You're taking money from him, I think."*

The adjutant officer groaned audibly.

"What do you want me to tell you?" I asked, raising my voice.

"I want to know…" He took a moment to consider what it was that he wanted to learn from his blood. "I want to know if it's true. What the prisoner told me."

The adjutant officer kept me standing over his camp table into the small hours, until the blotter could no longer contain all his blood and his essence ran down the folding legs and pooled at his feet. He dismissed me only when he had run out of fingers.

This all happened two days earlier, before the Vampires descended on the village and consumed it with fire.

* * *

I woke to the beating of helicopter blades. I saw Foote wave the machine down, a figure jumped onto the ground, and they disappeared into Major Sowers' tent.

Looking out over the desolation, I wondered if the survivors had arrived at the keep, if they would search the sky as they debussed, looking for omens of rain even though they no longer had crops that needed water.

Bongi was turning the pages of *Being and Nothingness* in the new light, reminding me of Weatherhead. It was bad luck to read from a dead man's book. Suspended halfway between sleep and wakefulness, I knew that Bongi would cop it on this mission, sure as fate. "You don't even know how to read," I told him. It was the cruelest thing I could think to say.

"You don't need to know the words to understand what's inside this book," he said.

Bongi stared at the pages and ate powdered milk straight from the packet. As a civilian, he'd been a chef for the servants at the Portuguese Club. Bongi couldn't read recipes and so he cooked by his nose, sniffing the air to know when the dish was done. Even in the field he took pride from his cooking – at first – beating and marinating the questionable meat Weatherhead brought back from his bush hunts. But his nose had become useless from huffing too much butane, and when he sniffed over the camp stove it was to keep mucus from running into his sauce. All his dishes tasted like thrice-heated leftovers. He quit cooking.

In the early dawn, I could make out the bleached and gnawed bones of animals scattered across the minefield on the outskirts of the flattened village, the ball of quills that had been the porcupine, the Zambezi beyond flowing sluggishly under a layer of mist.

The combat engineers were pouring concrete over the filled pits to ensure the dead remained buried. I watched the police reservists scramble into a five-ton lorry where they sat on sandbags to protect their genitals from landmines.

After the lorry drove away, a young woman wandered into the village; the police always missed someone. She fell to her knees beside the wet concrete.

"I'd like to have a go at that myself," a voice said from behind me. It was Foote. "The trick to shagging a local is don't put anything in their mouths you want to keep." He traced his bottom lip with his tongue while he watched the woman. "Come on," he said, finally. "There's someone I want you to meet."

149

Foote led Bongi and me into Major Sowers' dressing tent. It smelled like mildew, though there'd been no rain for months. Another man sat on his haunches in the corner, staring at the knotted cords in his muscular hands. He was barefoot, his fatigue trousers tied above his ankles with boot laces. Three pairs of combat boots hung around his neck. Some terrs changed boots to confuse trackers by leaving different prints. A rifle with a sniper scope was slung across his back. The parrot paced the length the tent. "*Poephol*," it said.

"Morning, young corporal," Major Sowers said. He stood before the dressing mirror, watching me in the reflection. The major had traded his red outfit for tailored and pressed fatigues. His cheeks had a ruddy glow, making me wondering if he'd applied makeup. Major Sowers introduced the stranger with a flourish. "Meet your new left flanker, Comrade Zorro."

"*Encouler de Poulet*," the parrot swore.

Bongi moved near, close enough for me to smell his powdered milk breath. "*Takafakare*," he whispered, forgetting his English. We're all dead.

Foote gave Major Sowers a look. "Haven't you got things to do?" There was something in the way Foote said this, and in the way Sowers complied, that made me realise the orderly outranked the major.

"Yes of course," the major said, softly. He bustled out of the tent, starched uniform rustling, the parrot squalling obscenities at his heels. I wondered if Foote kept him around as a decoy for snipers.

"We captured Zorro not long after he shot your flanker," Foote said, once Major Sowers had left. "He's going to guide us to the Unspeakable River."

Comrade Zorro continued to stare at his strangler's hands. It wasn't unusual to turn a captured terr. But to have him replace the flanker he shot – it was a monstrous idea.

"Why us?" I asked in a voice no longer my own.

"You're the bloody psychic. You tell me."

I looked out through the tent flaps to where the village woman sat on her knees beside the newly-poured concrete, singing to the mass grave. I wanted to bury this story in the dead village, walk away from it.

"Pack up your kit, boyos," Foote said brightly. "We're off to recruit some hippo hunters for the Rhodesian Security Forces."

* * *

One of the terrs was a woman. The close proximity of the footprints to the urine-spattered sand made this plain. Toes and pads, no heels – the imprint of a squatter. We'd picked up the trail outside the razed village.

Foote stood beside me. I could hear Major Sowers puffing under the weight of the radio as he tried to catch up. Bongi was on my distant right flank. Comrade Zorro, on my left, was nearer, because the tracks ran parallel to the Zambezi, perhaps a hundred metres from its bank.

There was a man with the woman. They had urinated together, side by side. Intimates. The man's urine was dark. "Kidney damage," I said. "I've seen it before in men with malaria."

"Or he's taken a bad beating," Foote said.

"*Chupe mantequilla de mi culo,*" the parrot said. The parrot's owner stood away from us, sulking. Foote had ordered Major Sowers to carry the radio.

Fishermen drifted past us with their dugouts and lollipop-shaped paddles, looking for fish trapped in the isolated shallows of the low river. The hippos had come up on the floodplain to graze. They stopped eating as we passed, raised their heavy heads, stared at us.

I carried only my rifle, two canteens, salt tablets, glucose tablets, vitamins, cigarettes, empty Coke can, Zippo, and a can of butane lighter fluid. This was our first day.

The wind came up from the east each afternoon but provided no relief from the heat.

The land is poor, fit only for producing mealie, thorns and flies. Egrets waded the shallows. A bask of crocodiles sunned themselves on the bank. Bee-eaters, fish eagles, and whitebacks perched motionless in the trees. We passed a relay radio station. The operators ignored us, busy setting up their equipment, but one of the guards raised his FN rifle and playfully sighted on me.

* * *

The two flankers bracketed us, moving away in open terrain, drawing nearer when the undergrowth thickened, always maintaining sight-distance.

We followed the spoor north and east, the footprints closer together now. The right outstep was deeper on the man.

"He's leaning on her," I said. "Are you going to tell me who we're tracking?"

151

Foote ignored my question.

"You need to keep me informed," I said. "I might see something important and not know it."

Foote thought for a moment, smiled. "We're hunting the God of the Hippo Hunters. His celestial highness got caught up in a sweep by one of our commandos a while ago. The interrogator was a bit too keen, thought he'd killed his prisoner. Tossed the body in the river. Next thing, the god surfaces upriver, on the far bank, doing his routine for the terrs."

"His routine?"

"He goes into this sort of trance, says he's God of the Hippo Hunters, Weaver of the Cosmos, so on. The terrs laugh at him, think he's a nutter. Nobody believes him, save this one sniper, a woman, who helps him escape."

"How do you know all this?" I said.

"Comrade Zorro told us at his debriefing." Foote barked out a laugh. "Turns out the woman's his wife."

The distance between the prints shortened. They were getting tired. We found berries and roots in their stools.

We scuffled as we walked, our feet leaden with the heat that came up through the ground and into our boots. We saw an enormous bull shark that had swum upriver from the Indian Ocean and now thrashed in two feet of water. I could hardly stick the sight of it.

At nightfall we came to a village and Foote spoke to their headman, a woman whose limpid eyes filled the thick lenses of his glasses to the edges of their frame, giving her a lost look. I looked into the blood that shot through the whites of her eyes: *Her optic nerve has wasted away. The eyes still see, but the images no longer reach her brain.*

We bivouacked that night in the village of blind women. They prepared us a chop of round beans, monkey nuts, and mealie meal. The few children slapped at moths over the cooking fire until their palms were covered with dusty guts. Wet, cheesy patches of white surrounded their corneas. "Bitot's spots," Foote said. "From eating too much corn and not a lot else." They wore mealie sacks as overcoats. After we ate, the children swarmed over Foote, covering his knees and lap. He laughed as he opened his rucksack and passed out tins of bully beef.

I stood first watch. In the distance, a group of mercenaries had set up camp, mostly Americans who'd served in Vietnam, a few Portuguese chased out of Angola, French paras from Algeria, anybody who would answer the advertisements placed overseas for 'Safari Guides with military experience.' Rhodesia was a choice place to relive lost battles. They set cooking fires and fired full clips into the bush at the slightest noise, a sorry lot to have about.

There's a trick to standing guard without falling asleep. Dig your nails into your palms until there are little divots of flesh beneath them. Bite your thumb until you taste blood. Smoke into a tin.

The thing about soldiering, the part they leave out of all the stories, is the slowness, the stillness, the crawl of it all. It's not quick reflexes, or keen marksmanship, or skill in hand-to-hand combat that makes a good soldier. Rather, it's the ability to switch off. I opened my tin of lighter fluid and inhaled deeply, waiting for the heaviness, the roar in my ears. We'd taken up smoking when we joined the scouts, Bongi and I, then huffing butane. Something to do when you're switched off.

I heard a noise and sighted my rifle on the darkness. I could hear the Zambezi current. The voices of the mercenaries. I strained my eyes to see into the void.

"The harder one looks at a thing, the less he sees of it." It was Comrade Zorro come to relieve me at guard.

"What sort of things?" I must have asked. Often, when I've been huffing, I hear only the words spoken to me, seldom my own.

"Who can say? Shapes. Lights. Movement. Things too quick for the eye. Long ago things. Secret things that don't belong in this world." He looked at me.

That night I had a butane dream. *I'm kneeling over Weatherhead, trying to tape an empty cigarette packet over the bullet hole in his chest in hopes that the plastic wrapper might staunch the wound and keep his breath inside his body. When I tell him I'm sorry, he looks up at me and says it doesn't matter.*

* * *

There's vomit on the ground in front of the woman's footprints. I rub some between my fingers, smell it. She'd been taking a decoction of foxglove and rue to help settle her weak stomach. "I think she's pregnant," I said to Foote.

Comrade Zorro had abandoned our left flank and was standing over me.

Major Sowers stepped up to the sniper, hand extended. "Congratulations, old sausage!" he said. "You're going to be a father."

Comrade Zorro refused the major's hand. "I haven't seen my wife since the rains," he said. He withdrew again to take up his flank position.

At midday we heard laughter and splashing paddles. Three orange rafts filled with revellers floated toward us. There were large white letters on the sides of the crafts: *Canada Adventure Tours*. The rafters took our photos, waved, shouted out the names of their home towns, and disappeared downriver.

Ancient, twisted baobabs dotted the floodplain. The sun was fierce.

"Could we break for lunch?" Major Sowers asked. "This radio's damned heavy."

"No time," Foote replied, kneeling. The sides of the prints were uneroded. "We're nearly on them."

We came to a branch in the river and followed the spoor south, along the tributary. "Come see," Comrade Zorro said. "Here is the mouth of the Unspeakable River. It is said this is the place where Arab slavers were drowned in their own shackles by the Hippo Hunters. Put your hand in the water. It's colder here." I refused.

By midday, Major Sowers was grumbling audibly. The parrot, silent now, rode atop the radio on the actor's back. Foote tried to jolly Major Sowers out of his mood. "Think of the story this'll make. Maybe they'll let you play yourself in the movie. It's the role of a lifetime." Major Sowers seemed to brighten, so Foote continued, "Smile for the cameras!"

Major Sowers was smiling when the sniper shot him. He'd turned to face Foote, so the bullet came from a right angle, shattering his front teeth and incisors but otherwise leaving him untouched.

Comrade Zorro returned fire and I heard a wounded cry off in the tall grass. Bongi swept around and we closed in to find a naked man, covered in dried mud, his head cradled in a woman's lap. A rifle and single shell casing lay beside them.

The mud man looked up at us, blue eyes glittering. "I am the Weaver of the Universe," he said through his teeth, "the Shaper of the World. Tremble before me. I am God of the Hippo Hunters, Speaker of All Languages, Teller of All Stories, Origin of All Words." The mud on his belly was dark and wet.

"Quick," Foote said, grasping my wrist and pulling me over to the wounded man. "Read his blood."

154

I kneeled and turned my head aslant. *I see a missionary, a brother of the order of Saint Augustine, struggling along the banks of the forbidden river. He makes slow progress. His porters have all abandoned him. At the end of a day, he sleeps with his head on his bible.*

One night an unnatural silence falls over the bank and the monk sits up. Shapes rise from the river, seize him and pull him roughly down the bank and beneath the water's surface until he's flailing against the muddy bed.

The monk wakes, face up, beneath a canopy of ancient mopani. Half starved, body ridden with parasites, in the grip of a malarial fever, he stands in the presence of a being both terrible and ineffably sad. A deity more tangible, more immediate than the God of his bible.

The monk prostrates himself before the God of the Hippo Hunters and asks in a tremulous voice: "How may I serve you, Lord?"

I stared into the blood and mud. "He's not the God of the Hippo Hunters," I said to Foote. "He's the praise poet for the God of the Hippo Hunters."

* * *

At sunset, an Allouette brought a camp dentist who repaired Major Sowers' mouth without novacaine, grinding down what was left of the teeth and crowning them with a grey resin. There was a rancid smell in that screaming pain – nerves and enamel burning with friction from the spinning drill.

We loaded the wounded monk into the helicopter which rose and banked toward the half-sun on the horizon, bearing him out of this story.

Foote had wanted to keep Comrade Zorro's wife so he could debrief her himself. She sat against a tree, expressionless, hands and feet bound. Comrade Zorro sat facing her. Foote was nowhere in sight.

Her name was Comrade Wonder Woman. She was a sniper in the war of liberation. She was the wife of Comrade Zorro. These three pieces of information were all Foote had been able to learn after two hours of interrogation. Comrade Zorro insisted on being present during the interview to ensure his pregnant wife was not beaten.

The snipers spoke softly together after the interrogation, but it was a quiet night and one develops a keen ear in the bush.

"Is the baby keeping well?" The voice was Comrade Zorro's.

Silence.

155

"Why didn't you shoot me?" Comrade Zorro asked. "It was an easier shot."

"Wasn't it you who taught me to shoot officers first?" There was humour in her voice.

"You were my best student, Comrade Wonder Woman."

"But my final shot missed," she said.

"You hit his teeth," Comrade Zorro chuckled. "There are things besides wind and sun and cover that can spoil a shot." There was a pause before he continued. "The last man I killed, just before I fired, I saw his soul rising up from his body."

More silence.

"Is this to be our life's work?" Comrade Wonder Woman asked.

"You would rather sleep with a lunatic?"

"He said he was a voice in the wilderness, making a path for his Lord. They beat him and laughed at him, but still he believed."

The two snipers fell into silence.

Major Sowers sat apart, whimpering softly, until Foote told him to shut his gob. We have no patience with our wounded; we show them no sympathy. It was Bongi who finally went over and placed a hand on Major Sowers's shoulder. "You know why the bullet missed?" he said. "God is saving you for something else."

"*Doos*," the parrot said.

I huffed from my tin of butane and lay back, listening to the nightjars. I thought of Weatherhead's soul rising above his body just before Comrade Zorro pulled the trigger. Images flashed before my closed eyes, but malevolent spirits rose from the river and snatched them away before they could fully take shape. What is this story showing me? I'm afraid to look at what it is showing me.

* * *

I woke the next morning surrounded by a mist. Comrade Zorro and Comrade Wonder Woman were gone, their sniper rifles and uniforms discarded on the river bank.

We followed the Unspeakable River south. As we tracked, Foote tried to make Sowers laugh, but the major refused to show his ravaged smile. Days earlier, a leopard had travelled this way, its prints now barely visible. Because they live in forests and hunt near the river, leopards are regarded as mediators between heaven and earth.

156

The tracking team entered an empty village where we found a cooking fire still burning beneath a vat. The inhabitants had been brewing beer. We walked past overturned bowls, open doors, our rifles held at the ready. A few chickens scattered at our approach. There were muddy footprints coming up from the water. Dry prints as well, running away from the river. I examined the kicked dirt where the villagers were brought up short and dragged back into the Unspeakable River.

"Remarkable," Foote said, piecing it all together. "Imagine if these blokes were on our side." I'd heard of men like Foote, shadowy figures who combed the empty places of our nation to find new recruits for this widening war.

A few hours' walk brought us up against a vast canopy of misshapen mopani trees. Foote turned to me. "Wait on that rise with the radio, corporal. If we don't come out by morning, get on the horn and rain hell down on them."

"*Je m'en branle*," the parrot said. Major Sowers adjusted his beret to a cocky angle, picked up his obscene little bird, and followed Foote and Bongi out onto that liminal stage. Perhaps this was what God had been saving him for. I watched from a small height as they disappeared into the riverine canopy. It was the last time I would see any of them.

I needed to switch off, so I huffed some butane and settled back into an uneasy dream.

Thousands of hippo hunters surge from the coppery water, eyes glittering behind mud masks. I see their god rising from the current, urging, inciting. A flood of violence bursts the banks, and death pours out of the Unspeakable River. I'd seen this all before, in the blood from Weatherhead's sucking chest wound.

I roused myself from my butane stupor. The tracking team had not been gone long, maybe a half an hour. Below, in the Unspeakable River, I saw thousands of dark shapes moving against the muddy current toward the canopy.

I raised the relay station on the radio and gave them the co-ordinates for the air strike.

* * *

Green, bat-like shapes appeared on the horizon. Egrets took flight amid the din of the Goblin engines. It was a squadron of Vampires with

157

full bomb racks and rocket rails. I could see the glint of the fifty-gallon aluminium drop tanks. The underside of each wing sported a green roundel encircling a lion that brandished an ivory tusk. The Vampires released their cargo of explosives and pyrotechnics, concussing the earth and forcing the Unspeakable River to flow backward and flood its banks. Napalm fire consumed the forest canopy like a plague.

I huffed from my tin and waited for the butane roar to replace the roar of the flames. Enervated, I fell back and let the heat from the fire wash over me.

The butane brought no comfort, sleep, nor dreams. I sat up and stared at the burnt matchstick trees. The river brought a parade of human and hippo corpses past me. I am the story, not the man who did this thing.

I looked for signs of the tracking team among the bodies, but all I saw was the tiny carcass of the parrot and the dust jacket of *Being and Nothingness* floating together in the current. The afternoon hours hung over me, suspended in the still, humid air.

* * *

I woke from a butane dream with a raging headache, unsure of where I was. I had lost all sense of time in the days since the bombing. I stood, unsteady, and resumed tracking the spoor along the corpse-lined banks of the Unspeakable River, stopping only to huff. Butane dulled the hunger pangs, and I'd eaten nothing since we left the village of blind women. The butane had nearly all evaporated, most of it up my nose.

The trick to walking among bloated corpses is to cover your face with your sleeve, to avert your eyes from the images written on their blood. You can do anything in the bush if you know the trick of it.

I tried to switch off as I walked, but pieces of the story kept surfacing in my thoughts. The parts I remember seem filled with coincidence. But coincidence is inevitable. And if our stories are filled with inevitabilities, blame it on the Weaver of the Universe, the Teller of All Stories, His penchant for pattern.

The Unspeakable River was completely still. The spoor was kenspeckle, the trail easy to follow. I no longer existed outside this story. These words don't leave an imprint on the mud. Each morning I set out alone to track the person responsible for murdering the tracking team,

for obliterating an entire people. Each night the footprints would bring
me back to where I began.

*

George Makana Clark grew up in Zimbabwe. He has published
one collection of short stories, *The Small Bees' Honey* (White Pine
Press), and his fiction, drama, and poetry have appeared in *Black Warrior
Review, Chelsea, Georgia Review, Glimmer Train, The Massachusetts
Review, The Southern Review, Transition, Zoetrope: All Story,* and
elsewhere. He was the recipient of a 2002 National Endowment of the
Arts Fellowship in Fiction Writing and a finalist for The Caine Prize for
African Writing. He currently teaches fiction writing at The University
of Wisconsin-Milwaukee.

Senti's Diamond Tear

Carol Fofo

Smog was beginning to cover the skies and workers were returning from town. Little Pappie was among the workers. He carried his large school bag on the right shoulder, steadying it up as he went along and in his left hand he tightly held his violin case. Kapo and his entourage were passing by Zone Two in order to get to Zone One. They had initially agreed to drive through Van Onselen road but decided to walk, cutting through Moemise. As Pappie entered the street he sensed that there was something wrong. The street was empty. There was no laughter of children playing. Dogs barked. The dice players were also not there. A curtain would shift and a face would briefly pop out. The workers he was walking with had also taken different routes. All of Moemise was forewarned that Kapo would be passing by. Pappie's home was not far off so he continued to walk. A long powerful whistle! "*Tjo vi tjooo! Vi tjo tjo tjo tjo tjo…*" He recognised the sound and tried to run but they were already there. You could tell that they had washed but their armpits told a different story. Pappie stood there with his bottom lip shivering.

Kapo pointed at the violin case and one of his boys took it. The boy opened the case, showed Kapo its contents and shut it again. The clicking sound was the last that Pappie heard. They left without saying a word to him. A gust of air entered his eye causing a flood of tears. The violin was school property. Losing a musical instrument was punishable by expulsion from the orchestra. Pappie did not like playing and he feared that his parents would think that he lost the violin deliberately.

"I'm tired. Driving has spoilt me." Upon reaching his backroom, Kapo held the violin in his scrawny hands to inspect it. He put it on top of the wardrobe and pondered its future. He wondered whether it was a wise move to steal something he couldn't use. Besides, if he returned it they would think that he was getting soft. He was skinny and people said he was too old for his body. At twenty-two he looked thirty. He hardly ever smiled and they said he killed many people, although it was never proven. He had a girlfriend who stayed with him in his room. He got tired of sending her back home after weekends of hard orgies

and commanded her to stay. There were other girls but Senti was
the queen. She and Kapo were always impeccably dressed and
people say he tipped well at the salon. She never wore the same outfit
twice. Her brothers had many times tried to take her away but Kapo
fought them off. The last attempt was when Kapo nearly killed one of
them. He threw a couple of notes at them and said it was her *bogadi*
(bride price).

From then on Kapo referred to Senti as his wife and instructed
everyone to do so. Senti never liked Kapo. She endured months of living
in that hell hole because her brothers took the money that Kapo had
thrown at them. He was jealous and possessive. Each day he would take
her to school, bring her lunch and fetch her after school. She was not
allowed to visit any of her friends or to have contact with her family.

Senti could not understand why the violin remained in the house.
Kapo was a smart man who dealt in things of value. Why would he steal
a useless thing like that? What did the violin mean to Kapo? He would
take it out, let it screech, put it back in its case and place it back on top
of the wardrobe. Yet he found himself not wanting to sell it. He couldn't
think of anyone who would buy it; besides, what could the street value of
a violin be? There was a time, far away, when Brook Benton, Beethoven,
Billy Holiday, Belafonte, Makeba, Mbuli and Margaret Singana were
members of his family. It was a time of Motlake hunched over his piano.
A time of the penny-whistle and marimba. A time as far away as the
aeroplane could take his father. Kapo grew up bragging to his friends
about his great musician of a father and how he would someday come
and take him to America. Masekela and Makeba came back but his father
never did.

The things Senti saw on television, in the novels and magazines she
read brought certain ideas to her – ideas of sandy beaches and open
spaces, of high seas and deep valleys, of countries far away. She was
intelligent and articulate. Her parents had high hopes for her. They
were of good standing in the community and wanted her to have a
sound education. It was difficult for them to accept that her fate was in
the hands of Kapo. The abduction was a marriage contract. Night after
night she endured the painful thrusts he subjected her to. She knew
better than to resist, especially when his day did not turn out as planned.
She harboured a deep hatred for him. Ideas of *ga le phirime* (rat poison)
and long sharp knives crossed her mind but she was too afraid to
entertain them.

161

One day Senti risked a beating and mockingly said, "Kapo, why don't you take violin lessons? I can see that you want to play but are too stubborn to admit it to yourself." Kapo kept quiet but thought hard about it. "I can't use it for any other thing," he thought; "the more I see it, the more I wish I could play." He couldn't tell Senti but the sounds from his childhood visited him in his sleep. When he woke up, he would look at old pictures of his father and listen to his old records.

His BMW would be seen outside Bapedi Hall. Bapedi Hall was a cultural centre where one could do ballroom dancing, body-building, play tennis, volley ball and other sports. They offered music lessons as well. He inquired inside and the management decided to take him. "Everyone deserves a chance in life", they said. At first the thought of learning and being subjected to authority did not appeal to him.

On his first day his music teacher asked him where he had acquired his violin. "It was a gift from my grandfather." The teacher, Mrs Hatfield took on the challenge of turning him into a musical genius. An arduous task! Cellphones and wallets were reported missing. When staff members complained to Mrs Hatfield about her young protégé, she just said: "Oh dear! We can't deprive him of tutelage. Who knows, he could be the next Menuhin." They had to put up signs that there will be no peeing outside the toilets. Smoking and drinking were strictly prohibited and anyone caught with dagga would be expelled. As Mrs Hatfield suspected, Kapo proved to be gifted. He played so well that she arranged special classes for him in time for the spring concert the following year. Senti was able to sneak out to visit her parents during lunch. Peace reigned and many people in other zones thought Kapo was either in prison or had died.

She discovered a vulnerable side to him. He would cuddle the violin and play for hours on end. He would cuddle her too. The beatings subsided. It made her uncomfortable as she could no longer predict his moods which were now governed by music as much as by his *tsotsi* desires.

* * *

The orchestra was preparing for the concert. They were going to perform before the cream of Soweto. The donors of the Bapedi Project were also going to be present. Cars filled the Vista parking lot while taxis dropped other people at the gate. The conductor, Richard Cox greeted people in the foyer. He wore his famous Dashiki. *Imilonji ka Ntu* lined the stage. They have an aura of superiority, these musicians. Their chins jutting out and their lips slightly curved downwards watching us crows with disdain. I think their gowns are rather dull, Senti thought. At the bottom of the stage sat the orchestra. Senti had dressed Kapo in the finest tux. She insisted on him shaving his head to get rid of his tight knots. She had someone make her a long red dress that she had seen in *Fair Lady* magazine. Little faux diamonds further accentuated the spaghetti straps. Her hairstyle was perfect. One could not tell her real hair from the weave. Her sandals were the same velvety material of the dress. She floated into the hall and took her position in the front row where she could monitor Kapo. She was aware of the stares and gloried in the attention.

On her left sat a scholarly type with spectacles. An Aramis man in navy microfibre pants, a light orange shirt and a fawn linen blazer.

"So, whose girlfriend are you?" he asked.

"What do you mean?"

"Come on. You can't be here by yourself."

"Of course I can."

"Or are you with your friends?"

"Well…" She stopped mid-sentence recollecting that her private life was nobody's concern.

"If you are alone, can I take you out to dinner then?" he asked without hesitation.

Senti kept quiet but pondered the man's invitation: "Dinner! I wish I could drive to town, eat at a pavement bistro, sip wine and go home to my mansion."

He looked familiar. She had heard that gentle voice a thousand times telling her how much he loved her, had felt those gentle arms around her and had walked between masses and masses of flowers to be met by him at the altar. It was another world where Kapo did not exist.

Richard Cox raised his baton and the music filled the arena. A soprano missed a high note and the audience gasped. Sacrilege! Kapo was doing fine but Senti's mind was not on him. She stood up to go to the ladies'. The man followed from a few paces. When she emerged from the bathroom, a polished set of teeth met her. A gentle touch on her shoulder which she could not resist, a warm breath, the perfume stronger and more inviting… Senti was transported deeper into the woods of her imagination. The soft music playing from the hall seeped through the door. The player! The player of the music was Kapo - Kapo

163

the brute! She jumped and like a kitten scurried back into the hall. Fortunately for her Kapo played with his eyes closed. The music stopped; he opened his eyes; beamed at her. She clapped and forced a smile.

She was allowed inside the VIP lounge for lunch with the musicians and their partners. Kapo ate like a lactating lioness and embarrassed Senti. She moved towards the balcony. Kapo grabbed her by her hand causing her plate to fall. She leaned down to pick up the food. He also bent down, gave her his infamous glare reminding her of who he was. The Aramis man witnessed the whole scene. He moved towards them. "Don't worry about the food. The cleaners will pick it up," he said. They both stood up. "*Ntate*, you are a genius. I wish I could play like that. You know, Puccini can be difficult but you handled him so well. Oh! Sorry, I'm, I'm Victor." He was a board member of the Bapedi Project. He extended his hand waiting for Kapo to return the pleasantries. "Sure," he said and turned to leave. Senti stared at Victor like a springbok caught in bright lights. It was a plea for redemption. He shook his head and watched as they walked away.

For the first time in his life Kapo had done something legitimate and did it to the best of his ability. On the way home he couldn't stop talking about how nervous he had been at the beginning and how exciting the whole thing turned out to be. It was in that same moment that he remembered how he had acquired the violin. He became quiet. She too kept silent.

The media reports were kind. The Bapedi Project had a bright future. They were particularly interested in the violinist who played with his eyes closed. Victor was also interested in him. His excuse was that he had to get the chance to meet his beneficiaries, to be more involved in the project. And thus started the trips to Bapedi Hall to see the musicians practise and be with the beautiful Senti. Sometimes he brought along his son, Little Pappie. Because Pappie did not continue with his lessons after that fateful day, he would spend time playing with the other children outside.

Senti came as usual. At first it was a look, a nod and a half smile. Next it was the exchange of cell numbers followed by rapture during lunch breaks. In the evenings during practice sessions, they pretended not to know each other.

* * *

"We'll need to search every bag! No one leaves the building until the thief is caught!" Bro Oupa, the caretaker was livid.

"What's going on?" Victor asked.

"Someone lost his wallet. Five hundred rands, gone! We are tired of this thief. Today is his day. He must pay. Sisi, call the police!" All the men went into one room and the women into another. "The children must also be searched. We are not taking any chances," Oupa continued.

Each one took turns to frisk the other. Their cases and instruments were laid bare before them. When Victor got to Kapo, he took out his violin and recognised the inscription: P. M. which stood for Paul Molefe, his son. Victor's eyes lingered on the inscription. Kapo realised that the inscription was not just the manufacturer's tag but meant something to Victor. Victor spoke calmly, trying to nab him: "Where did you get this violin from?"

"From my grandfather, Pontsho Motlake," Kapo sounded confident.

Sensing the tension, Bro Oupa called them into his office. Kapo sat on a chair while the two older men stood leaning against the table. Ms Hatfield and Senti both sat on a bench near the window. Bro Oupa was the first to speak: "Kapo, we are not fools. We know all about you. Give back the money you stole and return the violin to Bro Victor. If you don't, we will have no choice but to hand you over to the police." Kapo answered in a tone of arrogant defiance: "If you want to send me to jail, go ahead." Victor was trying hard to control his temper. His hand moved vigorously on his head as if buffing it. His teeth kept flashing in a menacing way as his face contorted in different expressions. Senti and Ms Hatfield were quiet the whole time.

"Sisi, are the police here yet?"

"No, Bro Oupa. They said they can't waste their time with petty issues like a missing five rands," Kapo smiled.

Bro Oupa dismissed the others.

Pappie came into the room to look for his father and then saw Kapo. "Papa, papa, it's him! He's the one who took my violin!"

"You are lying!" Kapo said.

"My son never lies."

As they were arguing, Victor's cell phone rang. He took it out of his pocket and handed it to Pappie while he dealt with Kapo.

"It is mama," Pappie said.

"*Ijoo!*" a shocked Senti whimpered as she leaned forward towards Victor. Her eyebrows met and her nostrils flared. Victor's composure

165

collapsed. He wanted to say something to Senti. Kapo made a quick arithmetic and his jealousy came to the fore. He launched at Victor. Some shiny object resembling an *oukapi* missed Victor's heart and seared his arm instead. Bro Oupa was quick in his separation tactic. Kapo cried in agony as Oupa's knee dug into his ribs. Victor's kicks were mainly targeted at the head.

Mrs Hatfield ran screaming with the boy to Sisi's office. Senti followed them crying: "How could he do that to me! They are all the same. Kapo's going to kill me now that he knows! *Ijoo mmawee!*" All this time the cell phone was on and Pappie's mother could hear the commotion from the other side. Mrs Hatfield took the phone and tried to reassure her that everything was fine.

The two men carried an unconscious Kapo to Bro Oupa's car. The clinic was not far from the hall. The nurses took over. "The doctor will see him tomorrow at seven," one said. Bro Oupa grudgingly filled in the forms for Kapo and they went back to the hall.

"Senti I'll take you home. Kapo's car will stay overnight here. Bro Oupa, thanks. You saved my life," Victor said and they parted.

Pappie insisted on sitting at the front creating an awkward silence in the car. It seemed strange to him that his father never asked for directions and that Senti never navigated. But he kept quiet. The dice players were sitting by a tyre-fire singing. Victor wanted to follow Senti to the main house to explain to them where Kapo was. "That is a stupid idea. Do you want them to know who and what you are?" Senti angrily asked, still sobbing. Victor tried to touch her but she pushed him away. "*S'ka ntshwara! Se'o k'wena!*" she screamed at him declaring an end to their liaison. The figures from the fire approached the couple. Victor knew that they could kill him and the boy. He quickly got into the car and drove away.

As he was tucked into bed, Pappie related the evening's drama to his mother. The proper thing to do was to lower their voices so that Pappie could not hear. Victor's version was that of a Kapo panicking under pressure and attacking him. "You can't believe everything he says. You know how kids are!" Victor said. There was crying, pleading, swearing and bags zipping as the angry footsteps of a wife were heard leaving the man who paraded his adultery before her son.

The black refuse bag seemed too small for Senti's belongings. The maxi taxi hooted and she hurried out. The dawn will meet her elsewhere.

166

*

This story hopes to become a voice of the silent abducted women and all women who will never know the joy of marriage. When they are seen in beautiful clothes and having lots of money to spend, people assume that they are happy. When they don't press charges, people assume that they are content. When people don't see their bruises, they assume that they are well cared for by their partners.

To these women:
"Lift up thine eyes to the hills from whence cometh thy help.
Thy help cometh from the Lord which made heaven and earth."

*

Carol Fofo was born in the winter of 1968. Her mother is a schoolteacher who passed on to her the love of books. She is married to Joel, a pastor who is in platinum mining. They have a son, Tumelo. She majored in English at Vista University and did an Honours in publishing at Wits. Apart from odd temp jobs, she runs a printing business from home.

The IOU

Stanley Gazemba

The labourer coughed and turned over onto his side, causing the creaky narrow bed to squeak in protest. He was covered with sweat from head to toe, and the beddings were soaked, emitting a sharp pungent smell. And still the sweat poured from his skin.

Last night he had broken into violent spasms, his body trembling so much with fever his wife had had no option but to go and knock at the master's house and beg that the man be taken back to hospital. Now the fever had subsided a bit. Only occasionally would he clasp his arms over his chest and, for that brief moment, the wooden bed would go *trrrrr…!*

The room was not much, six or so square feet of salvaged bits of cardboard nailed onto a low wooden frame, the rusty zinc roof hanging low so an average man had to bend to avoid grazing his scalp. The owners had made an effort to shield their modesty by pasting old newspapers all over the walls with glue made of *chapati* flour and water. And now the newsprint was slowly turning yellow in the weather, punctured by bites made by the giant roaches living in the rotting boards, looking to get at the dried bits of flour.

There was a small table that had been fashioned out of old tomato crates beside the bed, next to it a stool on which the labourer's medication was placed beside a half-full tub of water: a few aspirin and paracetamol tablets wrapped up in old newspaper.

On the other side of the table was a folding chair for the occasional guest. That was about all the furniture there was.

Everything else was stacked in large carton boxes on the hardpan floor underneath the bed.

In the far corner was a cheap Chinese stove that prepared the family's meals, on top of which were stacked a handful of well-scrubbed *sufurias* and worn plastic plates.

Yet again the labourer turned over and this time he attempted to rise to his elbow. His lips and throat were parched; he urgently needed a drink of the water in the tub. But then, as he tried to reach for the tub his strength failed him, and he fell back on the hard stuffed mattress with a groan. He wished his family were here to attend to him. But he realised they had to go out and work.

A fresh bout of spasms came all of a sudden and his whole body shook violently, his torso thrust off the bed, clenched teeth chattering. Giant beads of sweat popped up on his forehead and the thin, patched blanket slid to the floor.

Then it passed and he stayed on his back, panting softly as he regained his breath, arms stiff as ramrods by his side. His eyes were giant yellow balls that protruded from his skull, turning slowly above the jutting cheekbones, surveying the room.

He watched a giant fly zap in and out of a column of light running down from a hole in the roof to a spot on the beaten floor. It seemed to enjoy its game because it disappeared for a while, and then reappeared to start all over again. The labourer wished he had just an *ounce* of that strength the fly was wasting on its purposeless game; just enough to get up and reach for the tub of water.

As midday approached the fever got worse. His body temperature was alarmingly high, and his lips were dry and scaly, jaws locked together. The headache hammered on, threatening to split his head in two. He was very weak, but he knew that he must summon up strength and reach for the water. In a moment of fright he forced his gummy lips open and gave a cry for help. A croaky whisper escaped his lips, but went no further than the cardboard walls. A scary silence surrounded him. The only respondent was a little gecko that lived behind the old newspapers on the walls above the stove, which now came out of hiding and stayed there, staring at him with glassy amphibian eyes, scimitar tongue darting in and out of his mouth.

With an immense force of will the labourer heaved and rose to his elbow, edging towards the water. He teetered a while on the point of his elbow, the room swirling round and round before his eyes, panting harshly. The bedside stool swam in and out of his vision like a mirage on the brink of harsh wasteland, the newspaper that contained the aspirin close, and yet far, unreachable, like a dim light at the end of a winding tunnel. He was weak, almost to the point of death, but yet again he summoned up strength and reached for the water, tipping over to the edge of the bed. As his hands clawed towards the dancing white tub he felt an enormous wave of dizziness come over him.

He rolled over and fell to the hardpan floor.

They found him later in the evening, arm folded and trapped underneath him, head resting on one side, slimy yellow saliva drooling

169

from his half-open mouth. There was a pained expression of stubborn resoluteness on his face, which had turned a pale ashen colour in death.

* * *

It was a cold, drizzly Sunday morning after the burial. The labourer's wife sat on the bare wooden bed contemplating. The old stuffed mattress was rolled up and tied with sisal string into a handy bundle, resting on the floor beside the carton boxes that contained all their possessions. The lone chair was folded and stacked on one of the cartons. The stool had been turned upside down and in the narrow space between the legs she stuffed their well-folded clothes and the patched blanket, a sisal string tied in a loose X over the bulging sides in a manner that would be easy to carry with one hand.

The children could be heard playing in the little grassless yard outside, already bathed and dressed in their best clothes. Now all that remained was for the store-keeper, Juma, who had been her late husband's best friend, to arrive, and then they would be going on their way. They needed to start early because, while Kiambu was only an hour's walk from the farm, it would be much further with loads on their heads in the hot overhead sun.

They were going to her cousin's place, a little wooden shack in the outskirts of the town that she had agreed to share with them until they found work on the flower farms and a new place of their own.

Now that *Baba* Ndonga was no longer here, the woman knew that it would be virtually impossible to make ends meet from what her and the children earned on the farm. The only option was to try her hand at the flower farms, where it was said they paid better for a day's work.

It was better while *Baba* Ndonga was still able to work because, on top of his daily wage after milking and feeding the farm-owner's cattle, he was allowed a pint of milk and groceries from the farm-owner's kitchen, which helped a lot to sustain them. Sometimes, after harvesting the maize and cabbages and the rich man's wife saw that the yield was good, she would give Juma and him a whole sack of grain to split between them. This was a most welcome treat that, if used well, could see them through a couple or so months. In this way they were able to deposit some money in the savings account they operated at the Post Office in Kiambu. But now all that was no more.

At long last the familiar whistle of the storekeeper sounded outside.

170

The children ran up to greet him and, holding onto his hands, ushered him into the house.

"Sorry I am late, *Mama* Ndonga. The service took forever to come to an end," he said apologetically, brushing water from his raincoat. "And on top of that, as usual, the Gachie bus just wouldn't come on time!"

"It is okay, Juma. It's still early," she said with a smile, which still couldn't clothe the pain in her heart. She started readying everything so that they could leave.

The storekeeper took the stool and the metal trunk, while she carried the mattress and carton box. Ndonga took up the stove while his sister, Mukami, carried a little bundle of clothes tied up in an old headscarf.

The drizzle kept up as the little party made their way through the maize field, ducking underneath tall maize stalks that leaned into the way. For some reason, a silence had fallen over them. Even little Ndonga, who usually liked to make fun of Juma whenever he came visiting, seemed to know that they were onto something clandestine, and clammed up. Indeed he had wanted to ask his mother just where it was they were going, and if at all they would be coming to visit. But then, somehow, he knew that it was not a time for asking questions. And so he followed silently at the end of the trail, hoping that wherever it was they were going would be more fun, and that there would be more interesting lads to play with than the drab lot at the farm.

At the fringe of the maize field, however, just before they got into the line of trees that ran all the way to the main gate, the woman stopped to glance back one last time at the place she had called home for the last thirteen years. She looked towards the tiny zinc and timber shack, leaning at an angle against the landscape, standing forlornly at the end of the field. There wasn't even a single tree to keep it company. Her eyes followed the narrow winding path that ran from it through the maize field up to the cattle *boma*, and then on to the main house, which, from where they stood, was partly hidden behind a grove of giant banana trees. This path that had been beaten by her husband, springing out of bed in the middle of the night and racing to the cattle *boma* to deliver a calf, or just dashing off to some emergency at the main house.

Ndonga had stopped too, and was following his mother's gaze. He knew what she was thinking…She was thinking about his father. She had been doing that a lot lately.

Well, he missed him too. It had been fun with Dad around, there was no doubt. He remembered him walking with them through the maize

171

fields on Sunday afternoons during the sunny months towards Christmas. Usually Mukami would be sitting astraddle his shoulders while Ndonga ran alongside, chewing a piece of sugarcane he had brought them from their aunt's place in Banana. Right then, when the late afternoon sun shone through the tall cypresses on the fringe of the field in countless parallel shafts, the maize would be dark and green, just preparing to bring out their crowns, succulent stems fat like sugarcane, leaves swaying gently in the breeze. On the pleasant afternoon breeze would be the perfume of coffee flowers, for the coffee trees in the plantation that started at the end of the maize field would be in full bloom, the scent drawing many insects that buzzed around the bushes like bees.

Ndonga looked towards the spot by the house where his father's grave was slowly being overgrown by grass. He could see it clearly from where they were standing. It was a spot he liked to avoid the way one would a poisonous snake coiled on a bush.

At that moment his mother nudged him and they walked on into the trees after the other two.

* * *

J.P. King'ong'o, or simply JP to his cronies, was not in the best of moods for a Sunday morning. He had had a quarrel with his wife over the milk money just before she had left for church. On top of that the newspaper boy had not delivered the paper, meaning he could not update himself on what had transpired at the Party's general meeting, which he had failed to attend. And it was just too drizzly to take a walk in the garden. There seemed to be little to do in this weather, and it appeared as if he would be hitting the bottle early today.

As he strolled onto the rooftop terrace that jutted over the western wing of the sprawling house he thought he saw movement at the edge of the maize field. He looked more closely and discerned the foursome making their way into the trees.

Of course it was a Sunday, the day the farmhands took off work to go to church or to visit their relations. But then the bundles the four were carrying and the route they had taken was what arrested his attention.

It must be Mbugua's widow and the children, thought JP as he climbed down to the hall, where the green phone that was linked to another in the guardroom was.

172

"Sempei!" called JP into the phone, which he had yanked off the hook.

"*Epa!*" said the Maasai guard at the other end, obviously startled out of a doze by the charcoal brazier in the hut.

"Go out to the trees towards the cattle *boma* at once and see who those four are, leaving the farm by the lower entrance...*haraka!* Stop them until I get there!" said JP with a ring of authority in his whining voice.

"*Epa!* Right away, Sir!"

JP slammed down the phone and heaved himself up the stairs to get his shoes and a coat. Shortly, he reappeared, dangling the car keys, a felt hat slouched at an angle over his shiny bald head. He walked through the connecting door and as he climbed into his Range Rover, he thumbed the button on the wall that operated the electric garage door. The door wound upwards with a whine, the corrugated steel sheet coiling up inside its housing. Shifting gears, JP sent the Range Rover roaring into the slanting drizzle.

* * *

The path wound through a clump of wattle and ended at a low wooden gate that was nailed shut with crossbeams. The farmhands had cut a narrow passage in the rusty barbed wire by the gate, which opened onto the road on the other side of the fence.

They crept through the *panya* opening and onto the muddy road, just before JP's Range Rover swept round the bend and screeched to a stop a yard from where they were.

* * *

"Good morning! Rather late for the Sunday service the four of you, aren't you?" said the smiling farm-owner, leaning out of the open window. His fat jowled face was resting on a beefy forearm, shifty little eyes scrutinising the startled farmhands with a mixture of suspicion and amusement. "Or were you headed somewhere else?" he said, eyebrows rising slightly as his gaze roved slowly over the loads they were carrying. "Huh? Seems to me like that might be the case...Eh?...Juma... is it?" he said at length, switching off the motor and climbing out of the car.

173

And as JP got out of the car a rustle was heard in the trees behind them. The bushes shifted to reveal the Maasai guards standing there, spread out in a semi-circle, leaning on their long sticks, watching silently.

"Juma!" called JP, his calf-leather shoes squelching in the mud as he approached.

"*Eee*, Boss!" said Juma, lowering his load to the wet grass and snapping to attention.

JP approached, stopping in front of his storekeeper. His gaze was still fixed on the woman and the children. The drizzle pattered on his leather coat and slid down in tiny rivulets. His patent leather shoes, clearly not made for the conditions, were rimmed with red mud, the shiny leather beaded with tiny droplets of water.

"Where are you going?" he said at length, his shifting gaze finally resting on the dumbstruck storekeeper. "*You* are not taking off with the widow, are you? At least not this early, before the grave is overgrown with grass?" His thin smile widened an inch at his own bland humour.

"Er…Boss…sh…she asked me to help her carry her belongings to her cousin's place…"

"Is she leaving already? Tired of working on the farm?" The last question was directed at the woman.

"I'd like to try my hand at something else," supplied *Mama* Ndonga, seeing Juma was at a loss. "I don't think I will be able to raise the children single-handedly if I keep working on the farm."

"I see," said JP, stepping back and pushing his left hand into his pocket. The other hung by his side, dangling the car keys, more the way a child might do a rattle. "You are tired of the place…it is understandable." He took a swallow of phlegm, taking another step back, before continuing, " But then, one would expect, lady, that you would let your employer know you were leaving?" he spun around suddenly, an icy steeliness in his eyes, that were fixed squarely on the woman. "Why the silent sneaking out, *Mama* Ndonga…eh? Why take this unusual route?"

"Er…Aah…" the woman, her throat gone dry, struggled with the words. Beside her the clearly uncomfortable storekeeper was wringing his hands, gaze trained on the muddy ground.

"…You didn't want to bother the *tajiri* this early in the morning, is understandable," quipped JP with an understanding nod. And then he raised his head, and this time a foxy look had crept into his shifty little eyes. "Or perhaps you *deliberately* didn't have to bother the *tajiri*…is it? Eh? That you were running away from something…?"

Now the woman started fidgeting, the confidence she had exuded earlier waning. What did he mean 'deliberately'? She looked at the children, still clutching their loads, looking uncertainly at their employer and back at their mother, sensing the latter's mounting fear.

"Eh? You had something to hide, *Mama* Ndonga?" repeated the employer, drawing closer.

"Err...I don't understand, Sir," said the woman, licking her lips nervously.

"Aha! You don't understand. Well, I will remind you." JP's gaze shifted casually from the farmhands to the posse of silent Maasai guards in the trees, as if to reassure himself that they were still there. "Indeed I will, *Mama* Ndonga." He gave a low cough to clear his throat and moved an inch closer.

"Of course you remember your husband's illness, given it was only the other day. It is very sad that Mbugua had to pass on. He was one of my most faithful employees all the years he worked on this farm." A look of commiseration passed over the wealthy man's face, but then it was only cursory, for shortly the foxy look returned. "You will remember too, *Mama* Ndonga, that you came to me for help to take him to hospital?" continued JP, a steely edge creeping into his voice.

"Yes," nodded the woman, her toes digging stiffly inside her worn canvas shoes.

"Aha!" JP nodded, the way a prizefighter preparing to charge a foe he has painstakingly coaxed into a corner would do. "Yet again it is with a lot of sadness that we had to lose the services of a good man. But then, even as we buried him on the farm, there was a little issue that we hadn't discussed, my lady...and with reason too. For it would have been most improper at the time, saddled with the funeral as you were."

Now the cold steeliness was all too obvious in the wealthy man's probing eyes.

"This little matter, *Mama* Ndonga, is the hospital bill your husband accumulated, and which, in my responsibility as employer, I shouldered for him. However," finally the wealthy man locked stares with the woman, "and, seeing he obviously didn't inform you, it was not for free. The arrangement with your husband was that he was to repay it later from his wages."

The pronouncement settled with a sinking finality, the way a struggling bull might lower slowly to the ground at the abattoir after the last breath-gushing throe.

175

"Now, *Mama* Ndonga, I would appreciate it if we could discuss this little matter at my house before you leave."

And with that the wealthy farm-owner turned and walked off to the parked Range Rover, his expensive shoes squelching in the red mud.

Just as he reached for the door handle he turned around and said, "And I hope you don't mind the guards helping you with the luggage, seeing it is quite heavy. You could certainly do with a helping hand in this weather."

And as JP shook the rainwater off his coat and climbed into the car, the Maasai guards emerged from the trees and approached the stunned foursome, reaching for their bundles. They were hardly smiling.

There was nothing left to do as the Range Rover ploughed a U-turn in the rut-marked road and roared off with a spray of mud. *Mama* Ndonga took the children by the hands and followed the lanky guards into the trees back the way they had come.

* * *

Ndonga lay on his back and gazed into the liquid darkness, which swam with hundreds of formless night creatures. He was unable to go to sleep because of the itching all over his neck and arms where the nappier grass blades had sliced his skin. There was a raspiness at the back of his throat that refused to go away, and which occasionally induced a dry cough that left him gasping for breath. He didn't know it, but it was the fine felt hairs on the leaves and stems of the nappier that he had inhaled all through the day, and which had settled there at the back of his throat. It was most uncomfortable.

Beside him on the mat they shared, his little sister Mukami slept peacefully, her snoring soft and regular; angelic. Their mother was also fast asleep on the bed, as her deep steady breathing indicated.

Only Ndonga was awake, kept company by the scurrying of the rats and the scaly rasp of cockroaches on the cooking utensils in the corner.

It was nine months since they had returned to the farm, and it was getting even more unbearable by the day. Ndonga's mother said that they had only one more month to go, and then they would complete repaying the money his father had accrued in illness. But even that one month seemed like a year. That was because things had changed. Now they had to work under supervision. Where Ndonga had had a fairly easy time picking coffee berries with the other children on the estate, now he had to cut nappier and alfalfa for the cattle and ensure they were well fed and watered. On top of that he still had to scrape the dung in their pens and push it on a wheelbarrow to the manure pit. Usually, that had been his father's work on the farm, but now that he was no longer here, and his debts needed to be paid, the boy had to take over.

It is at the manure pit where his mother's turn began. She turned the composting manure and wheeled it on to the cabbage and maize fields. That is, after she was done with washing in the kitchen yard and scraping the giant urns in the kitchen where the farmhands' porridge was prepared.

It was tough work, pushing the heavy wheelbarrow laden with dung, but then it had to be done. And all the while there was always someone hovering in the vicinity, if not the farm-owner or his wife, then it was one of the Maasai guards.

Sometimes Juma came by from overseeing work at the coffee estate and helped push the wheelbarrow, but then he had to be careful because it was clear he was not expected to help in the cattle yard. His work was in the fields. The cattle *boma* had been under the charge of Mbugua.

Only Mukami had a fairly easy time, working on the coffee farm as she had before. But still she now had to attain a set measure of berries a day, and so she couldn't afford to kid around. Indeed, often she had to set out earlier and stay later than the other children.

But now Mother said that there was only one month to go. A measure of relief came over Ndonga at the prospect. He wished the day would come sooner when they would take their possessions and leave the farm. It was no longer the same as it had been when Father was around.

As these thoughts coursed through Ndonga's mind, he raised his hand to brush at a whining mosquito. The callused palm brushed his cheek, grazing a tender itchy cut that was inflaming into a welt. He winced and forced his hand to stay down. Scratching would only make the cuts worse.

It was as he lay thus that Ndonga heard noises outside, sounds like someone...no, some *people*...moving about stealthily in the night. The movements, although measured, were different from the usual night sounds. Someone was stealing about the house.

Ndonga stiffened, his ears cocked. Beside him, his little sister turned over and engaged into deeper breathing.

As his alarm grew, Ndonga thought he heard the sound of something pouring – like water coming out of a jerrycan. Shortly the smell of fuel came clearly to his nostrils. It was a familiar smell, the distinct smell of the fuel Juma often poured into the generator housed in the little hut beside the cattle *boma* whenever there was power failure at the farm. Ndonga listened, greatly perplexed, certain that it was not his imagination because his eyes were dry as day.

That is before the night suddenly exploded in a bright orange flower that rose up skywards, enveloping the corner of the hut farthest from where they were sleeping.

The enormous light flooded the room through the chinks where the rotting boards in the wall had separated.

"*Fire! Mama! Fire!*" screamed Ndonga as he sprang to his feet, shaking his little sister with urgency, at the same time as he leapt onto the narrow wooden bed where their mother slept.

The guards and other farmhands who lived on the farm rushed to the forlorn little hut by the cattle *boma*, roused from sleep by the yelling. They fought the fire, dousing it with water that they drew from the drinking trough in the cattle shed.

As for the cattle, they gazed from the darkness of their pens with fright in their glassy unblinking eyes, startled by the bright flames that had suddenly lit up the night, ready to bolt.

People ran helter-skelter, their terrified cries adding to the confusion. But it was all in vain.

The fire, aided by the explosion of the Chinese cooking stove, defied all their efforts and engulfed the little hut in a deadly embrace, the hungry flames finding welcome tinder in the timber and cardboard walls.

Soon the first zinc sheet curled up in the heat and exploded from the harnessing nails with a soft pop. It flew into the night, wafting on the warm current created by the fire, and landed with a fiendish slowness in the nearby maize field.

In no time the little hut was reduced to charred rubble and smoldering embers.

* * *

Mama Ndonga heaved on the wheelbarrow and felt a muscle in her back rip. The barrow wouldn't move. It was stuck in a rut in the muddy path, the dark mud thick and unyielding. "*Ngai!*" she lamented, wiping sweat from her brow. She gave another heave, putting in more effort, and the barrow tilted to the side, careening out of her grip, spilling the load of dung in the mud. She felt the earth come up to meet her, the hot afternoon sun burning the back of her scalp. She let go of the barrow handle and sunk to her knees by the path-side.

Visions of the farm-owner played in her mind like a stuck record, the words he had kept reminding her as the *fundi* built the little lean-to by the chicken-house where they would now have to live on borrowed items and time, refusing to go away.

"…You burnt down my house with your stupid stove, woman! *My* house! That house cost money to build…iron sheets, timber… all burnt…*gone!* How senseless of you! You are given housing, for which you don't have to pay a cent in rent, and yet you turn around and burn down the very house! God knows what would have happened had the cattle *boma* caught fire…but thanks to the quick action of my guards it didn't. We would be speaking thousands of shillings here, woman, *millions* of shillings lost! Thank God it was only your house, you stupid woman!"

"But it was not my fault…I didn't start the fire…" she had tried to defend herself. To which the farm-owner had thundered. " Shut up! *Nyamaza!* You wouldn't know half the measure of loss we would be talking now, you hear? You don't know, so just shut up!

"And now you will have to pay for the damage…yes, you will pay for all my iron-sheets and timber you destroyed, you ungrateful woman…!"

As the picture of the irate farm-owner replayed in her mind, *Mama* Ndonga, resting on her haunches in the dirt, leaned forward and buried her face in her calloused hands, tears of frustration welling in her eyes at the prospect of another six months' work on the farm to pay for the damage; and the humiliation of having to beg for even the clothes she wore.

And as she thought about these things, the pounding headache that had been her unwelcome companion lately started again, threatening to split her skull right in two.

That was until she felt the clammy little palm of her son, now looking more like an eighteen-year-old street ruffian for the life he had had to adjust to, resting on her shoulder.

"*Mama…Mama!* Are you alright?"

Ndonga, having waited for his mother to return the wheelbarrow in vain, had got worried. He decided to come and investigate, because lately, she had appeared rather ill, even though she insisted she was fine. She was growing even more gaunt of appearance, her brow lined with constant worry.

179

"*Mama!* Here…let me help you…you must go and rest," he breathed close to her ear as he struggled to get her to her feet. She recognised the bony frame of her son, and willed herself to rise to her feet and help him get her out of the mud. She had to lean on him though, for she was very weak. But still, even in her distress, she had to smile at the strength of her son, who had been just a wee bit of a boy the other day. For a twelve-year-old, it amazed her sometimes what an ox of a lad he had transformed into…so strong, this Ndonga of hers…

As son led his mother staggering step by step to the little lean-to at the back of the chicken house where they lived, a pair of eyes was watching. Juma had been on his way to the store to collect a piece of hose to fix a burst section of the spraying network that spanned the coffee estate when he came upon the scene. As the two limped slowly round the corner, Juma turned and went into the tool store, troubled by thoughts.

He pitied the widow, and at the same time he felt anger. He wanted to help, and yet he realised – with a tinge of shame – that there wasn't much he could do to help. What if JP conceded to their leaving the farm, just where would they go next? Were they assured of finding work elsewhere? Or would they turn into street beggars like those who sit at street corners in Kiambu town, singing church hymns and rattling chipped enamel bowls at passersby? Could he, Juma, offer them any support?

Now, that was one tough option. All these years he had been working on the farm, and yet he didn't even have a house of his own in his home village in western Kenya. Let alone that, he didn't have any savings! The little money he had put together had been blown away treating a chest infection the previous year that the doctors had said had been caused by the spraying chemicals he inhaled on the farm. Indeed the situation might have turned fatal had he insisted on hanging onto his savings.

Indeed, afterwards, the doctors had warned him to stop working with chemicals, something he had found rather absurd because, how then, did they expect him to feed himself?

Still, he couldn't help wondering what had become of JP.

Well, while the man had never been known to be the most generous of employers, Juma had never known him to go to such lengths to recover a debt. It made one wonder just how much money he had lent Mbugua…or *had* he?

As he pondered over this new thought, Juma realised that there had been no one to witness the man give Mbugua money as he claimed. In other words, as it stood now, it was a pact made with the dead who

180

was not there to speak for himself. And if so, was it right to seek redress from the dead?

Even as Juma mulled over this matter, he realised that the burning of the house had compounded it further. Now, *that* complicated matters. For some reason, nevertheless, too much seemed to have happened too soon. Somehow it didn't add up. The Mbuguas had been living all this while in that little house and there had never been a fire. Why now?

And that was just the tinder to spark a volatile situation. The rest of the farmhands, forgetting for a while their everyday complaints about working conditions on the farm, were beginning to talk about the matter. Juma could hear them whisper among themselves in discreet little gatherings. It was apparent they were unhappy about the treatment JP was subjecting Mbugua's widow to.

They all watched her little girl clamber up coffee trees, popping berries into her tin from daybreak to sundown, and were in agreement that the family were being unfairly harassed. Juma feared that there might be trouble; for only a worker understands best another worker's plight. Weren't they cast out of the same mould?

As Juma slung the piece of hose over his shoulder and locked the store, he decided to pass by the little lean-to and check on the woman. She had appeared to be in a particularly bad state as her son had assisted her to her feet.

What Juma didn't know, even as he went to see after the health of the widow, was that that was but the beginning of her misfortunes.

* * *

Having seen that the mother was safely put to bed, Juma was preparing to leave when he saw the door of the little lean-to push inwards. It swung in an inch and the well-polished calf-leather toe of JP's unmistakable shoe stepped over the threshold. Juma looked up slowly and locked eyes with the cold stare of the farm-owner, who all this while had been watching the movements of his store-keeper from the rooftop terrace, where he had just had lunch.

"And the coffee picking is going on just fine while you take time off to visit your mistress, is it, Juma?" JP's voice, just like his stare, was icy, knife-like. "*Ehe?* Is this all the work you people do for the afternoon when I am not around?"

181

"Er, *Mama* Ndonga has been taken ill, Sir. And I came by to check on her."

JP's eyes now looked beyond the startled storekeeper into the dark hut. He took in the woman, white-eyed, lying stiffly on the bed, her son standing fidgeting nervously beside her.

"Ndonga! Out!" he suddenly bellowed, sweeping into the room like an elephant into a cage of twigs. "I am not going to pay you people for lazing around doing nothing on the farm, hear? I am fed up with this nonsense about illness every other day. Get out, you *chokora*...go back to your work!"

Ndonga, who had been searching for an opening in the crowded doorway, slipped past the rotund farm-owner and out back to his work.

"Stupid boy!" added JP after him, taking a swing at his backside but missing.

"As for you," he turned to Juma, who was standing stiffly in the middle of the room, the coiled hose held awkwardly over his shoulder. "Who told you your responsibility was overseeing the health of the workers? Eh? Who gave you the mandate to decide who works and who doesn't...tell me!" JP was really worked up.

As Juma retreated, at a loss for words by which to defend himself, he knew it would only take a single utterance to turn the confrontation physical. "Get out, you dog! I pay you to ensure the coffee is harvested, and not to mind if some hapless widow is well or not, hear? Get out...*Ngui!*"

The thoroughly humiliated Juma bowed out of the hut and hastened down the path that led through the maize fields. And it was just as good he had not answered back for, hovering outside the hut within hearing distance, pretending to patrol the chicken yard was one of the Maasai guards. Somehow, they were always within the vicinity of their employer, ready to do his bidding.

Mama Ndonga, now that she was alone in the hut with her worked-up employer, drew back on the narrow bed and started to rise, frightened all of a sudden.

After the others had taken leave the hut had become too still, the air charged.

"He-he-heeee..." JP's manic laugh suddenly exploded in the electric silence. "Unwell, eh? Woman?" he moved around the bed, inspecting her. "There is a way to find out, you know..."

His tone, now that they were alone, had changed, a huskiness

182

replacing the sharpness that had been in it. All of a sudden the fear became real. Mama Ndonga, her illness forgotten, suddenly wished she had left the hut while she still could. She could hardly see him in the gloom in the hut because he had kicked at the door, cutting out the light. But she could feel his mind turn all the same.

JP walked towards the bed, a nervous smile playing on his face. He reached out and touched her shoulder, but she cringed back and slapped at his hand, baring her teeth in a warning manner.

"Hey…hey, you know it doesn't have to be this way," said JP more softly, sitting on the bed. "You really don't have to fight me at all, *Mama* Ndonga. We can be good to each other, you know…what do you say?"

The woman cringed further back against the wall, gazing steadily into his little eyes, recalling the stories she had heard said about the man. For a moment her gaze shifted, searching the bed for something with which to defend herself.

"Hey, hey, my dear, you know you are truly a beautiful woman and, like I told you earlier, I can make you even more beautiful! You don't really have to work in the fields. I can make your life comfortable. I, JP, have got all the money in the world, you know. *You* only have to say the word. Come on, think about it. This needs to be only between me and you, we can forget the past, my dear *murata*."

Seeing that the woman was still, JP took it for an invitation and reached to touch her, aiming for her breast.

But *Mama* Ndonga's arm shot up suddenly and she struck him hard on the wrist. *"Go away!"* she snarled, fear rending her voice into a charged whisper. "I am still a married woman, and will never be your mistress, hear? *Don't* you touch me!"

JP, a little surprised, drew backwards and massaged his wrist. And then something snapped inside him and he remembered who he was, JP, the feared political operator and top businessman in Kiambu, whose path no-one in their right senses dared cross.

"*Mama* Ndonga, are you going to be difficult still?" he snarled, climbing onto the bed. "I thought time had taught you a few lessons, eh? Remember this?" he fumed, whipping around his left wrist, which he bared.

Mama Ndonga opened her mouth to scream, visions of a rainy evening many years back inside her now-burnt hut replaying in her mind with a surprisingly fresh vividness. A vision of JP crowding in on her, sprawled on the bed, resting from the afternoon's work while Mbugua and the children sheltered in the cattle *boma* where they had accompanied him to feed a newly-born calf. It was an incident she hadn't dared share even with her husband because of the dire consequences he had threatened her with. And all this when she had thought it over, forgotten. But how wrong she had been.

"Yes, you remember, do you?" said JP, his face close to hers in the semi-dark, shiny little eyes piercing into hers. He stuck the wrist closer to her face so that she could see the scar that was still embedded in his skin, and which had been inflicted by her teeth as she fought him off. That is before her husband's whistling had sounded outside as he returned from the emergency in the cattle shed, interrupting them. Her husband, naïve Mbugua, had never suspected a thing.

"Aha! There you are! I told you I would be back, didn't I? Now the day has come."

Such fear as she had never known took hold of her at this sudden change in his manner, constricting her throat like a vice. Yet again she opened her mouth to scream.

"Don't you dare!" he warned her, fumbling with the buckle of his snakeskin belt. "I have two guards out there with instructions to deal ruthlessly with anyone who approaches this house. No way, you are all mine now, woman, *to do with you as I please*. He-he-heeee!" He finished with a soft laugh that echoed within the narrow confines of the little cardboard hut.

The manic glint in his eye was frightening as he crowded over her on the bed, grabbing for the front of her bodice, pinning her back with a heavy forearm that was thrown across her chest. She gasped and drew back against the timber walls, causing the fabric to tear, leaving her breasts exposed, bared to his absorbing scrutiny. "No one escapes JP, woman, *you* should know by now," he whispered, reaching for her left breast, his breath smoldering her face, slobbery lips wetting her cheek. "*I* can be very patient, you know."

* * *

Ndonga heaved on the laden wheelbarrow one last time, and as it rolled to a stop beside the chaff-cutter, he let out his breath in a tortured gasp. It had been hard enough cutting and gathering the nappier in the hot afternoon sun, but getting it up to the cattle shed on the heavy barrow was simply torture.

And as he regained his breath, dark face moist with the effort, he remembered the encounter with his boss just a while back, and hastened to flick on the switch that operated the electric chaff-cutter.

In the sheds beside, the cattle started lowing softly in anticipation of the feed.

As the machine hummed on, Ndonga lifted a bunch of nappier and placed it on the jutting spout, feeding it into the belly of the machine slowly like he had seen his father do countless times. He watched the huge wheels in the belly of the machine turn slowly, drawing in the nappier inch by inch, shredding it to little pieces that it ejected at the other end into the large wooden trough. It was amazing how the machine could reduce a whole barrow-full of fodder to just a tiny hill of chopped feed in such a short while.

As Ndonga fed the insatiable machine, his thoughts wandered back to his mother, lying there in their little house. He wondered how she was, and if the rest had made her feel better.

He dreaded to think that the illness had got worse. It scared him, thinking of her writhing helplessly in the bed all alone, just like Father had been in his last days. Somehow he was glad that his little sister had not been with them at the time. It was good that she was working in the coffee estate; otherwise there would have been two cases to worry about. Still, he worried about little Mukami. He hoped that the work over at the coffee estate was not as tiring as tending the cattle was.

Meanwhile, as the boy's thoughts wandered, the machine ate up the fodder inch by inch, the turning steel gears drawing in the leaf ends sticking out into the feeding spout, and onto which the boy was still holding. That is until Ndonga felt a tightening pull on the ends of his fingers. The next minute a searing heat was traveling up his hand.

Jerked back to the here and now, Ndonga's gaze dropped to the machine, only to see his hand disappear into the narrow opening.

Panicking, he gave a tug, at the same time as he piped a piercing scream, just as the numbing pain jolted up his arm.

* * *

Juma had just got to the coffee estate when he realised that he had forgotten to fetch a length of PVC piping that he would need to join the pieces of rubber hose. And so he turned and made his way back to the store, making a detour through the maize field because he didn't want another encounter with the boss after what had happened at Mama Ndonga's house.

It was as he was passing behind the cattle shed to approach the tool shed from the back that he heard the scream.

He ran round to the yard in front of the cattle pens, dropping the coiled hose he had still been carrying.

When he saw the boy struggling with the whining machine, Juma dashed to the master switch and shut it off.

* * *

They crowded around the still boy resting in the shade, horrified at the messy pulp that his hand had been reduced to, and which he cradled in his lap. Everyone was craning to see the injury, crowding him, cutting out the air that he needed most. There were the Maasai guards, who had got there first, and also the other farmhands from the adjoining kitchen yard. There was also the boy's shocked mother, who looked pale and distraught, together with the farm-owner who had appeared from the direction of the chicken-house.

JP, a look of confusion on his moist face, called the guards aside and asked them to ensure everyone returned to their workplaces while he went to fetch the car.

The Range Rover came around shortly and they carried the numb boy inside, placing him on plastic sheeting that had been hastily spread on the back seat to avoid soiling the fabric.

Juma climbed in after the boy while his mother, who had gone into a faint after viewing her son's injury, was carried back into her little lean-to by the chicken-house.

As the Range Rover swung out of the yard, churning up dirt, the Maasai guards moved menacingly towards the gathered workers, and reluctantly they dispersed.

* * *

Miss Julia Nyokabi, partner and co-founder of Nyokabi & K'Opiyo Co. Advocates, was a fairly successful Nairobi criminal lawyer. The number of clients she had successfully represented in court rolled off the tongue like the who's who of the large cosmopolitan city. And, just like her partner in the firm, she was fairly rich too. However, while her partner flashed his success about, you would hardly say the same of Miss Nyokabi if you met her.

Her neighbours along Kiambu Road hardly knew what she did for a living, for she chose to live a quiet humble life, hardly the party girl. She didn't accompany them to the races on Sundays, nor did she play golf.

She lived alone in her three-bedroomed house, save for the Christmas months when her nieces came visiting from her married sister who worked as a structural engineer in Botswana. There weren't that many relations because there had been only the two of them in the family, and when their folks passed on, she stayed on in their house, and had lived thus since.

Every morning she left her residence promptly at six thirty and joined the crawling traffic, her seven-year-old Toyota Corolla fairly unnoticeable amongst the flashy SUVs that people in the neighbourhood drove to work.

One such day she was sitting in her car, stuck behind a smoke-belching construction truck waiting for the traffic to ease on. She was trying not to glance at the morning paper because she knew it was a bad habit while driving. She had decided to go via Wangige along the Kikuyu route on to town because she wanted to pass by a client who worked in Kikuyu town. Her eyes were glued to the misty window on her side, and it was only after a while that she realised what it was that had captured her attention.

The donkey that was harnessed to the cart was old and bony, its ribs sticking out through its leathery skin. A large festering sore covered its flank, attracting a swarm of blue flies even this early in the morning. It stood by the roadside, large ears moving slowly back and forth, waiting for the car that had blocked its way to move on into the line of traffic. The little cart was laden with freshly cut nappier grass, and sitting atop it was a shabbily dressed young man...or was it a boy? It was difficult to tell because he wore an old cloth cap slouched over his face. However, it was not that, nor the donkey's condition that attracted the lawyer's attention.

The boy was engaged in some play with a huge glove he wore over his right hand that was shaped like a mitt – or a wicket keeper's glove– and which was made of some thick, tough plastic material. He was taking off the glove and putting it back on, and in that brief moment that it was off, Miss Nyokabi thought she missed seeing the hand it was supposed to cover...otherwise her eyes were playing tricks with her.

With the curiosity that can only be aroused in a lawyer of long practice, she wrung on the wheel and pulled over sharply onto the shoulder.

The boy, who was in the process of removing the glove, pushed it hurriedly back into place. He picked up the rubber whip atop the mound of fodder and prepared to lash the donkey.

"Hello!" said Miss Nyokabi in a pleasant way as her profession had coached her.

But the boy had already lashed at the donkey and it was moving forward. Miss Nyokabi ran alongside the cart and persisted, made even more curious by the boy's strange reaction, determined to climb onto the cart if need be.

Seeing that the lady was reaching for his hand the boy slithered off the cart and hopped onto the ground, breaking into a run. But then Miss Nyokabi had not been the athletics champion at Kenya High for nothing. Kicking off her pointed office shoes, she hitched up her skirt and gave chase. Curious motorists stared after them, wondering what the smartly dressed lady could be chasing the urchin for. Perhaps he had stolen her purse.

By the time the lawyer grabbed the boy's coat and swung him around, she was out of breath, for it had been a long chase.

"*Ehe?* Why are you running?" said the lawyer, looking at the gloved hand. "Something the matter with your hand there?"

Now that he had lost the chase the boy stood nervously by, quite fidgety and ill at ease. He looked left and right, searching for an opportunity to escape.

But obviously the lawyer wasn't going to allow that. She covered him well, like a hunting dog might a cornered rabbit.

"What is your name?"

The boy glanced nervously left and right, and she had to apply pressure to his wrist before he piped, "Ndonga."

"Good. Is that your donkey?"

"Uh-uh! It belongs to JP. I was sent to fetch fodder. I…I d-didn't steal it, Madam," he added, begging to be believed.

"You didn't go to school today?" said the lawyer, peering into his shifty eyes.

For answer the boy averted his gaze and shook his head. The lawyer thought she saw a sad look cross his face, but shortly the impertinence returned.

"Why?"

A mute silence met the question.

"So, why were you running away?" said the lawyer, changing tact. "Here, let me see your hand."

The boy gave a frightened struggle, tensing up all of a sudden. But the lawyer was prepared for it, and she grabbed his wrist in her vice-like grip. With the other hand she loosened the strange glove that was strapped in place with Velcro strips. A faint odour rose from the open glove, like that which a dried carcass might give off.

With a mounting sense of mystery, the lawyer went on to pull it right off.

"What...?" she said. But the question died on her lips as she gaped in shock at the mangled stump of hard bone and twisted tissue that was hidden behind the glove.

"JP said never to take it off, especially around strangers," mumbled the boy, his words punctuated by pitiful sobs.

* * *

Miss Nyokabi parked the car by the rough road and switched off the engine. Beside her was the officer from the labour office, together with another officer from the ILO office. They were here to confirm what the woman had told her, and to gather evidence.

"So, do you think we will nail him?" said the ILO man.

"Sure, why not?" said the lawyer with a thoughtful frown. "If we can find solid evidence, I think our friend will be facing a charge sheet a mile long. Other than the labour-related offences, a rape charge makes it even stickier. He *definitely* won't crawl out of it," said the lawyer with conviction.

"Rape? You mean the man raped the poor woman on top of it all?" said the labour man, astounded.

"You don't know half the pain I felt listening to that woman's account," said the lawyer, her gaze focused on the rut-marked stretch of road ahead. "You know what? This is one case I *must* win," she stated softly. "There is just no way I can lose it."

"You are right, Miss Nyokabi," acquiesced the ILO man. "Some cases you just *must* win."

"Well, there comes the woman," said the lawyer at length, pointing through the windshield. Standing in the tall grasses, a patched, tattered shawl tightly wrapped about her thin shoulders, was the boy's mother, who had just emerged from the narrow opening in the hedge, and who was beckoning to them.

They climbed out of the car and embarked on the dangerous mission.

* * *

It was during the second week, as they were driving slowly along the rutted road on their way from serving the wealthy farm-owner with the court order, when the lawyer looked in the driving mirror and saw the olive-green Range Rover following them. It was the same car they had seen parked in front of the palatial house on the farm. It was being driven at speed, and was coming right at them.

"Seems like we've got company," said the labour man in the back, twisting around so he could have a good look at the driver of the car.

"Our friend JP is definitely not out on a leisurely drive through the farmlands," said the ILO man, reaching for his cell phone. He hurriedly placed a call to an unmarked police car that, as prearranged, was patrolling the area.

A strong companionship had grown between the three of them during the two weeks they had been working on the case, a sense of purpose that could only be satisfied by the successful completion of the case.

The Range Rover beared down on them, headlights flashing. Miss Nyokabi swung the little Toyota to the roadside as she caught a mean look on the face of the driver of the Range Rover, JP King'ong'o, clearly reflected in her rear-view mirror. The Toyota banged into a rut as the Range Rover drew level and JP leaned out, a venomous look on his moist face.

"You are dead people!" he snarled as he swerved the wheel suddenly and the Range Rover slammed sideways into the smaller Toyota, forcing it off the road.

On the other side, beyond the thin hedge, the ground dropped into a deep gorge, a fall of about sixty feet to the tree-covered valley.

Miss Nyokabi slammed on the brakes and the Range Rover eased off, swerving to the far end.

But it was only for a while. Soon it swung back into the road, coming in for another assault. This time the iron bull-bar caught the little car in the ribs and sent it shooting into the hedgerows.

That is before a white Peugeot wagon appeared further down the road and, as it swung across and screeched to a stop yards from the scene, four police officers leapt out, their guns drawn.

"It's over now, JP," said the senior officer, his revolver leveled at the window of the Range Rover. "You've had your fun for long enough."

* * *

The last of the construction workers finished their lunch and ambled out of the kiosk back to their work at the new site on Mombasa Road. And as they left, the proprietor of the kiosk took stock of their entries in the little 'credit' book that she kept locked away in a drawer in the inner room. In the yard outside, her two helping hands were busy washing the dishes in the huge tubs filled with warm soapy water. The sales had been good today.

A pick-up truck drew up to a stop outside and the driver leapt out, calling to one of the girls to bring his lunch of *githeri* and *chapati* as he was hungry. He had done a long run of deliveries today, and still he had to make two more trips to Gikomba market. Juma was always complaining, but he wasn't unhappy with the job. In any case his health had improved a lot since he had left the farm and come to work here. He was much happier.

In the inner room the baby announced her waking with a piercing cry and Mama Ndonga had to break from her work to go and attend to it. The baby was a healthy feeder who did not ask, but demanded. Happy Nyokabi, she had named it, after the courageous lawyer who had changed their lives. And such was the brightness she had brought into their lives her siblings could hardly wait to come home from school to hold and play with her.

And as the woman stood outside the kiosk suckling her baby, watching the shadow of the overhanging acacia bough play on her cherubic cheeks, she felt a wave of immeasurable joy flood through her. Her husband Mbugua might not be here to witness all that they had achieved, but, certainly, now there was something to hope for. It felt good to be alive.

*

Stanley A Gazemba was born in 1974 in a tiny village called Inyali in Vihiga District, Western Kenya, to teacher parents. He was schooled at Mumias Boys' and Kakamega High School and is currently a final year student of journalism at Kenya Polytechnic in Nairobi. He works as a gardener in a Nairobi suburb. He has published the novel *The Stone Hills of Maragoli* and won the Jomo Kenyatta Prize for Literature in 2003. He is married to a beautiful countrywoman, Joy, and they have a son, Kidula, who is one and a half years old.

Just a Cat

Rachelle Greeff

Thoughts scurry through Leo's mind like mice. They carry pests and germs between their tiny spiky teeth and their nails grate against the inside of her skull.

She needs to fumigate her cerebral pests. Alcohol, she discovers, stops the scraping only for a little while. Anti-depressants make her dull. So she starts yoga classes. In the beginning the greatest challenge of the classes is not the postures, but the silencing of the mind mice. It's hard for long. But she's a good student. She listens intently. She absorbs meaning from spaces between words.

Leo has listened to her yoga teacher's voice for months. When he says her name, Leonora, it's clear water over old rock in a shady place. She's a language teacher, so she knows it's a corny image – but so what, she has no intention of sharing it. After a year or so the teacher's water voice is a constant and Leo takes its memory home.

Here the dog barks, her two boys and their friends clash, crossing shouts like swords, bombing graphic cities on the computer, stomping on their cooldrink cans until the tins crunch and die. The African Grey mimics every sound, but his small brain fails to return it harmoniously. The acoustics of Leo's old house with the high ceilings are explosive.

With the help of her yoga teacher Leo manages to create pockets of inner stillness. Max, her husband, destroys these developing pockets of peace not deliberately, but easily. When Max is at home he takes the boys on hikes, teaches them to surf and build kites. They love him for that. But like Leo they are disturbed by the dark cloud that sometimes shadows him.

* * *

"Quieten your minds," the yoga teacher says. "A quiet mind finds balancing easier. Start in *Tadasana*, find your balance. Root your left leg, make your right leg light. Then slowly lift the right leg and place the

193

right foot as high as you can, flat against the inside of your left thigh. *Vrksasana*. The tree balance."

There are moments when the yoga students banter with one another and laugh and dispel all notions of stillness, especially when they battle to master a posture and fall out of it clumsily. But towards the end of a class, after an hour and an half, as they move straps and blocks and bolsters away from their mats, they have earned their tranquil focus. They settle on their backs, close their eyes, relax their legs, letting the knees fall out, spreading their arms. The teacher walks among them, placing little silk cushions filled with linseed on their eyes.

"As your body grows still, observe the state of your mind. It should be at peace. Once you have mastered the posture, quietness can be called upon at will." The teacher is careful not to step on their mats as he weaves in and out before he retreats to his own mat in the front. Here he sits upright, his bare legs crossed simply. "Allow your body to sink into the ground. Be dead to the world outside. *Savasana*, the corpse pose."

The simple, strong postures increasingly sustain Leo. Help her focus on the task at hand. Lower her blood pressure. She observes her cats at home. It seems as if they've been doing yoga for a long time.

The longer she carries the yoga teacher's voice, the less she yells at Max. It is not that she dislikes him. It is something in him. She's terrified of this thing. It can rip her out of his life.

When Leo first got to know Max she tried to call this thing by clever names. It became a game of chess, pushing psychologically amateurish words round like pieces. In the end Max didn't capture her; he simply wasn't playing. He was neither aggressive nor depressed, didn't have a problem with alcohol or with his parents to whom he never talked and whom he refused to see.

She couldn't find another name for it and Max didn't help her. This is why she calls it a thing.

Before getting rid of her own rodents, she often yelled at Max: "You're petrified of the waste in your brain."

Having grown up in a home cemented by silences, she knew no other way to communicate disappointment and hurt. You can save a forest of trees, she accused Max, but you're not able to save one little life. Your own little life.

After seeing a counsellor she applied remote control therapy at home. Max threatened to abandon her. So she stopped seeing the

194

counsellor. (It was a relief; the counsellor yawned often.) She stopped counselling Max.

You can dress a man, but you can't hold his hand.

* * *

As her stillness increases, she grows distant. She closes her car window to the stabbing decibels of the taxis. Tells her boys and their crew of semi-men from the neighourhood, not unkindly, to please close her bedroom door and leave her alone for an hour or so. Sometimes she naps. Sometimes she simply lies still, breathing evenly.

The two marmalade cats, Tinktinkie and Poplap, are stretched out sleekly with her on the bed. They purr in the afternoon sun. Poplap diesels away, her whiskers trembling. Tinktinkie, who was named after a petite local finch, makes a sound so tiny, to hear you have to put your ear to her fur. From time to time the cats yawn, showing bright pink mucosa. Or they extend a simple, rounded paw. She admires the way the cats preserve their energy, how they will their ochre eyes to possess you.

Leo still rolls on the mat with her younger son. Strokes his older brother. Strikes like a surly old lioness. Wrestles free from her household, with such slow movement, you hardly notice.

But distancing herself from the thing in Max is different. His shadows trap her too.

Max is an environmental barrister. Nothing is ever a problem, of course, he'll do it. Not to panic, he'll sort it out chop-chop. His phone rings continuously. He talks to "another green fucking fascist". Or declares loudly that "developers should be shot at dawn with flame-throwers".

He doesn't call people that to their face, of course not. He brings it home to Leo. Like the cats bring their *goggas* and lizards and broken birds.

People steal Max's energy. He has many invitations.

* * *

By the time Leo and Max are married for twelve years they decide, out of nowhere, to mate their dog, a bitch, with a dog of similar high pedigree. The bitch is actually too old for that. But not that old, they argue. Strange, why hadn't they thought of it before? They fall into it passionately. Read about mating and whelping and training. Bring each

195

other bits of information the way they came with small gifts in the beginning of their relationship.

Finding the correct mate takes forever, but they know it's him when they see him: stout chest, wide hindlegs. Their bitch is smaller, with longer legs. They'll make good puppies. The owners decide courting will take place away from either of the dogs' homes. The obvious place, halfway in between, is a field of arum lilies. It takes three days, in drizzling rain. Neither of the dogs has mated before and they struggle. Max holds the dog while the dog's owner directs his penis. So, it's a graceless affair all-round, Leo thinks as she crouches in front of the bitch, holding her head, stroking her ears. She's disappointed, she thought at least animals were more or less always spot-on. The bitch whimpers as the dog locks inside her. Then he turns on the axis of his own organ, his back to her. Glued together they stand like this for ten, fifteen minutes, looking in opposite directions.

*　*　*

Leo and Max look forward to the birth, it will bring new life to their home. As for the boys, they're always happy for new distractions.

The wendyhouse in the backyard is turned into a labour ward. Max makes a huge square bed with low sides. The first of eight puppies arrive at sunset. Two more follow an hour apart. Instead of licking and eating the amnio-sacs, the mother devours the puppies. Leo, who is making supper in the kitchen, walks in as the last of the three puppies wriggle like a baby rat inside its sac before it disappears behind its mother's teeth. She crunches easily through the newly born bone. She hardly needs to chew her child. At four in the morning the vet works his gloved hand into the birth canal. Milk fever, he grunts. Calcium withdrawal from the brain, whole lot goes to the milk. Also see it in Jerseys. He pulls out the ones the mother cannot, or will not, push out.

They take the puppies away from her. The vet sedates the bitch and after the medication has kicked in they bring the surviving puppies back to her. Maybe she'll feed them now. But her back stiffens and she snarls. Max lies on the floor beside her. He strokes her with one hand, lightly holding her jaw with the other, making soothing sounds, while Leo tries to latch the puppies onto the teats. Gradually the bitch relaxes, it seems. Leo and Max are exhausted and badly need to sleep.

196

When they get back to the mother dog a few hours later she has ripped off a puppy's ear. A shard of bone sticks through the hindleg of another. Leo takes them to the vet on a hot water bottle and Max rescues the last three. The injured puppies die seconds after the vet pricks their skin. Leo returns home with the puppies dead and the hot water bottle still warm.

Let's bury them under the new podocarpus, Max suggests. His voice is flat, it conveys nothing.

"You mean the yellow wood?" Leo cries a bit at the grave. Max hugs her with the gentleness usually reserved for the boys and the puppies.

In her wrought-up madness the bitch refuses to suckle the surviving three. Leo and Max raise them by hand.

Max is a good father for their boys, he's also good with the puppies. He takes paternity leave and sits on the floor in the middle of the night, using strong fingers gently to urge the tiny jaws open. From a syringe he drips two millilitres of a calcium-rich veterinary concoction onto their weak strawberry tongues. He repeats the procedure hourly, then two hourly. He potty trains them. He circles the anus with a finger tip, the stimulus needed for their bowels. While he cleans their bums with wads of cotton wool dabbed in liquid paraffin their eyes close and they fall asleep, drops of milky potion around the snouts. Feeding slows down to only three times a day and when the puppies feed themselves, Max and Leo crack a bottle of Pongracz.

The puppies soon bounce after the cats who run off at leisurely pace, leap onto the garden wall where they wash, not casting even a glimpse at the dogs yapping for action far below.

The dogs fall mostly under Max's care. He buys their food, takes them for walks, gets them injected. Leo sees that his relationship with them is uneven. The bitch is a disappointment to him. He accuses her of growing fat and deaf.

"But eight children, Max, surely she's forgiven?"

"Maybe." Still, he usually ignores her. The puppies are grown by now. Max favours the coal-black male, Adam.

From the safety of their truck the rubbish-removal guys taunt the pack of dogs. "Blood-suckers," they tease laughingly. "Check the blood-suckers."

* * *

The smallest of the young bitches is the first to corner a cat in the backyard as Leo is hanging out the washing. Her shrill barking brings her brother, Adam, crashing through the pet door, dashing to the corner where the cat is hissing with her back arched high, as in yoga, but with too much anxiety to open the lungs. Leo shoos the dogs away, coos into the cat's ear as she lifts her into the fig tree. It is Tinktinkie, the tinier of the two cats. They love this tree. Thick, non-slip branches, huge green leaves against Africa's summer sun.

As Adam charges, Leo notices his gleaming testicles. He spreads his groin when he runs, making space for his dangling manliness. Figs, she thinks, ripe figs.

That night she suggests they have the bitches spayed and the dog neutered.

"We don't want to go through all that again, do we?"

He doesn't reply.

She persists: "What's more, we simply can't afford it."

"Nope, I'm not cutting off Adam's balls."

As she bends to wash her face in their bathroom, he moves up against her from behind. Under her hands the ceramic basin is smooth and solid. Max's force – all puppy fondling gone – turns her on terribly.

* * *

Leo continues hanging the washing, feeding the pets and the boys, giving extra Afrikaans lessons to school children in the afternoon, doing yoga at night. The yoga teacher says they must not underestimate the power of backbends. It makes one honest, makes you say things you've suppressed, he says as he walks with naked feet among the mats. From where Leo lies on her back the high arch of his foot is feminine.

"*Ardhava Dhanurasana,*" he breathes without straining his voice as he curves his trunk back and lightly falls onto the palms of his hands behind his ankles, his crumpled sex exposed to the universe. Leo smiles as she tries to imitate him. She's a stick insect. She does not arch or glide back, she snaps.

* * *

Max turns forty. He talks of headaches. Doesn't have wine with supper anymore. Doesn't initiate talk. He looks trapped, but turns his back on Leo at night. It prevents her from helping him with his turmoil. Besides, it's the thing in him. Previously his moods affected her more. Now she simply continues.

Then, over many gentle autumn weeks, he thaws. This has also happened before. But he still rants against either the minister of environmental affairs or the German magnate planning a health farm in the middle of a wetland. They are 'cunts', these people, or plain *kak*. Leo believes he does not carry on like this outside. He still gets numerous phone calls.

"Absolutely, no problem," he laughs into the receiver.

When Leo alerts Max to his limited vocabulary and specifically to his predominant use of the word cunt as opposed to prick he says: "It's just a fucking word."

The arteries in his necks are bruised lashes, but no need to hide them like a teenager his love bites. He flies off on his motorbike, a thunderous hard thing of swollen size, the straps of his crash helmet beating the air.

And he comes back. Max always comes back. Into the house, into their bed. He opens her like a much-loved book.

Or he crouches in the garden pulling out what he calls invasive aliens without cursing them, or, if he does, he curses them silently. He washes and polishes his Moto Guzzi, touches it as he did the puppies and before that their babies in the bath. Leo will never forget his biker's palm cupped around a baby's head. Or he wears an apron in the kitchen and works his fingers into the dough of the sunflower rusks – his speciality – adding crushed wheat and molasses. Hums Chet Baker off tune. Bakes Uncle Jim's honey pudding until first the kitchen and then the entire house are wrapped in the flowery comfort of sweet starch.

"Max, you should have Adam looked after," Leo mentions lightly, in passing. "He's becoming aggressive. I'm not concerned about the boys, of course not, but about their friends. He jumped up against one, the other day, and the child's screaming spurred him on. Luckily, I was there."

"Please, Leonora, Adam is not aggressive."

"Yes, I know he's not aggressive. It's the way people react to his barking and his jumping up. It makes him nervous or excites him or whatever; he acts instinctively. That's all I'm saying. The cats more or less live upstairs now."

"God, you're always so anxious, wasn't the yoga supposed to make you better? Anyway, I still see the cats around the garden."

Leo says nothing. She also loves Adam. Testosterone teddy, she calls him. He lies dreaming and farting at her feet when she teaches Afrikaans, he invites her to put her feet on him. She could probably sit on him with all her weight and he wouldn't bulge. He is a solid clod of muscle, of stubborn habit. The bull part of his name unfairly belies the sleek black coat, his strong, long nose and intelligent terrier ears.

A few days later a friend visits. She feels unsafe around Adam, she says. Eye contact with him, she complains, is as hard as eye contact with a shark. Leo is surprised at her own response: she feels hurt.

But she doesn't tell Max this. She doesn't want him to go off again.

The cats now entirely avoid the downstairs part of the house and the garden. The landing on the stairs has a gate: the cats live above, the dogs below. Apartheid. Leo installs a sand box in the bathroom and permanently leaves open one upstairs window, leading onto a flat roof to an adjacent garden with squirrels and oak trees. The cats eye the squirrels, crouch as if to pounce. But they're too lazy, or too urban. They catch nothing except geckos, which they offer, purring proudly, to Leo in her bed. Now see, says Max, even your sacred idols act on instinct. But they still linger with Leo on her bed facing the setting sun. They continue their conversation of eyes and fingers. Talking to the cats helps bridge the gap between yoga and home.

"Slowly and in your own time rub your palms together, cup them over your eyes. It softens the eye," says the yoga teacher. "Roll over onto your right side and slowly, slowly let the world in again."

They sit with legs crossed. Place their palms together in *Namasté* and bow their heads. "Thank the Divine within."

Leo rolls down her car window when she drives home. It is spring. She invites the frangrances of the jasmines and honeysuckles into her car. She breathes deeply, observing her breath. *Pranayama*. Your breath tells you where you are.

When she parks the car the dogs do not run to meet her, barking and smiling. When she walks into the house it is silent. The absence of sound roars. Before her in the entrance hall is her beloved grandmother's jug and basin. It's what she always sees first on entering her home. It's the object of her belonging. Tonight it has no words of welcome. It spells it simply: I'm dead, I cannot save you.

* * *

It is the younger son who steps out of the kitchen. His brother and Max appear wordlessly from other rooms as if on cue.

The heart of dread is a slow place.

The young one speaks and he cries, because he is little and aching: *Mamma*, Adam trapped Tinktinkie in the basil, *mamma*.

Spattering it with blood. Mostly hers. Her scratches on his nose were deep, but dry. He shook her in his jaws, flung her in the air, spraying her blood spectacularly over the other herbs: the parsley, the origanum, the peppermint. The boys watched, screamed for Max, who was on the phone, to do something. The sound they heard from the cat was new to them. They didn't ever want to hear it again.

Max fumbled. Then dragged Adam, with the cat locked in his jaws, to the hose. He opened the water on him. It washed away the blood, but still Adam did not let go. He was drenched, so was the dead cat. He let go only when Max grabbed him by the balls.

* * *

Leo goes alone to the outside bathroom where Max has wrapped Tinktinkie in one of the boys' old baby towels, only her face peeking out. He has placed her in the basin to hug her till Leo comes. He has neatly brushed her damp and ruffled hair. She lifts her dead baby from the basin. She closes the round eyes which are now black marbles. She whispers into the deaf dead ear.

It is good, says the teacher as the pads of his feet caress the tiles, there is a time to weep.

But, remember, Leo, it's just a cat.

*

Rachelle Greeff is a freelance journalist. She has published three collections of short stories, two novels, three childrens' picture books and a collection of humorous essays. She has won the CNA Prize, the Sanlam Prize for Fiction and the RAU Prize for Creative Writing. She lives in Rosebank, Cape Town.

Drones

Parselelo Kantai

Drone (noun)
A male bee that has no sting, does not gather pollen, and exists only to mate with the queen bee.
Drone (verb)
To make a continuous low humming sound.

I owe Muhindi money. Six weeks' worth of *nyama* fry and *chapatti* lunches, incurred in March and April. I did the arithmetic last night. At Ksh 80 per lunch, that comes to about half my May salary. Muhindi likes to boast that nobody in the Industrial Area fries meat like his wife, with the green peppers, garlic, *dhania* and a "secret ingredient, *Wanjohi-bhai*, straight from my home town Alighar in India, no less". True, perhaps, but it's been two weeks since Charles, his Luo cook, left when Muhindi refused to give him a raise. Now, there are angry murmurs from dissatisfied customers. Clearly, something is missing from Muhindi's food. Even Muslim, my boss and editor of *The Traveller*, who is considered a legend in his own lunchtime, was muttering darkly post-lunch yesterday that he was going to start carrying packed lunches if the food didn't improve. And that's saying something considering the quality of Muslim's wife cooking. Besides, she's always forcing him to go on a diet. Muslim mumbles to her over the phone that if one takes her cooking into account – dead salads, boiled beans, burnt rice, no meat, never any meat – he has been on one for the last thirty years. My stomach growls, makes demands I cannot meet.

This *matatu* reeks of the water shortage, of unwashed passengers whose systems have to metabolise cabbage and *sukuma* nourished on sewage, and the meat of truant city goats that feed on it. I probably smell the same way, of things that are about to go bad. I disembark at the Lusaka Road bus-stop. After I pay, I have enough for two cigarette sticks of Sweet Menthol. They'll take me through the morning. Muslim will, grumbling and criticising, finance my afternoon indulgence. At five-thirty p.m. or thereabouts, Oluoch, the accountant will call my name on the payroll, and I'll have enough for beers later.

I cross the narrow pipe that acts as a bridge over the Nairobi river, the shortcut to Chepsabet Road, where the office is. In the beginning, I couldn't take the stench. The sight, the memory of the river at odd moments – smoking a cigarette while taking a shit, between a round of beers, right after sex – would make me retch. Now it's not so bad. Like most crises that stay unresolved for long enough, it has become bearable, part of the general mess. I don't even notice it anymore. When I first started working for *The Traveller* as chief photographer (don't be impressed, there's only one photographer at the magazine, but the title looks good on the masthead), I spent a morning talking and taking photographs of the street kids that live on its banks. It has acted as a form of insurance ever since; unlike most people, I have no fear of being attacked, robbed or raped by them. That was years ago. I can't remember whether we actually published the pictures. I wave at one of them, with his bag of other people's garbage slung over his back, pissing into the river. He manages to wave back.

The three *mkambas*, three crows in old brown suits and safari boots, are at their usual perch of old tyres outside the Green Sun Tea Kiosk on the river bank, deep in conversation. It is only recently that I discovered that they are not on Chepsabet Road just for the scenery, the dust-and-oil ambience, that they do fairly brisk business selling those old tyres to the garages on this street. There's Man-Sammy, washing his plastic plates and tin-cups by the standpipe next to the line of river-kiosks, where most of the labourers eat. He hides his dreadlocks under a cap, now that he is, very loosely speaking, a chef. He would probably be making more money from the kiosk if he wasn't so high all the time. It would, at the very least, reduce the short-term memory loss.

"I'm busy," he says. "Take your cigarettes and leave the money on the counter." He looks up as I'm leaving: "What's wrong with your face?" He shakes his head, returns to his dishes.

The other day, as we were smoking a joint, it suddenly occurred to me that there was something wrong with the name of his kiosk: What the hell is a Green Sun? I suddenly asked him. It's the other name for Nairobi, he replied, carefully, a little proudly. It took a lot of convincing on my part for him to finally accept that Nairobi is not called the 'Green Sun' but the 'Green City in the Sun'. Funny that.

There's Muhindi now, leaning out of the upstairs window of The Placid Rendezvous, contemplating the half-deserted street, the second-hand spares shop, the scrap yard of dead cars next to it, Anne's Express

Boys, where all the courier delivery people are slightly disabled (chronic limps, left-hand paralysis, extreme myopia); that operation, I suspect, is a front. No way can she be making a living off this. Then there's Mr Johnson's Garage (est. 1967), directly across the dusty and potholed road from The Placid, shut down for probably the last time two weeks back when the bank said no more overdrafts. There's old oil trickling from beneath its closed gate, blood from the head wound of the corpse. Next to it, the bright and blue banner above the small, lighted window announcing the offices of *The Traveller*.

Muhindi's cheek is swollen with morning *paan*. His *shalwaar kameez* is taut across his belly. He sees me before I can duck. He waves, smiles, an alarming thing, all red teeth and bulbous eyes.

"*Wewe, Wanjohi-bhai,*" He calls from upstairs. Lazy, fat man's voice. "*Usinisahau leo, bhenchod.*" Don't forget, you mother-fucker. Punjabis, I learned during my student days in India, are rude. They can't help it. Muhindi is pleasant enough. He knows I won't pay today, but he'll get his money somehow (a quiet word to Muslim when things have gone a little too far, who will then rant and rail at me, invoke the big themes, how honouring one's debts is the decent thing to do, realise he is getting nowhere, sigh, talk to me about his personal embarrassment in this matter, reach into his pocket. I'll use the money as a down-payment of sorts, become a regular customer again, run up a new tab…and so it goes).

Business for Muhindi is usually middling to bad. He made the mistake of offering credit so that he could compete with the cheaper kiosks on the river bank. Now he is afraid to antagonise his debtors just in case they abandon him. He treats his staff like most on this street, with a casual cruelty: low pay, no medical cover, no leave, the usual, but they can take home the leftovers at the end of the day. Like most employers around here, he would be shocked and hurt if his workers ever went on strike. He was genuinely indignant when Charles asked him for the raise.

"Look, *bhai*," Muhindi calls. "You grown so thin, like a Somali watchman." He laughs at his own joke. "And your face, punch-drunk only!" I give him the finger. *Chutye.* He aims and spits straight into a puddle just in front of me. It stirs a little, turns red, glimmers with old engine waste, and I get a brief, distorted reflection of myself. Apart from the usual everyday bumps and dips, two boils have appeared on either side of my face, bruising my cheek-bones. The boils are not painful.

They ache a little. They are not pretty. I try to snatch some fragments of the tune idling in my head as I walk towards the office. It's like grabbing at a fly, irritating.

I recognise one or two of the mechanics from Mr Johnson's Garage among the quiet horde around the entrance to the office. Look at them, occasionally reaching out for dying conversations, waiting for the door to open and someone, foreman, no-bullshit imprinted on his face will emerge and start pointing, picking out you, you and you, not you, look at them hoping for work, any work. I creak open the main door to *The Traveller Magazine, Printers and Publishers since 1975.*

I shouldn't have bothered. The reception is empty anyway, unless you count the woman on the visitor's couch, her face buried in an old copy of *The Traveller.* I go past the clocking machine. She has nice thighs, brown, unblemished, one crossed over the other, boardroom style, the black power-skirt riding so high up that you get a flash of the white panties buried deep within. The word for them, I mean the thighs, is assertive. They say, unsmilingly: "We are empowered. We know what we want. We have an MBA. We won't let you in until we've had a bottle of wine and dinner at Lord Errol's." Jesus, what's this hangover doing to me? Did she just know instinctively that I was checking her out, that I would because I am that type? Because there was definitely an element of pissed-offness when our eyes met, hers behind the blue, square-rimmed glasses, mine no doubt flailing guiltily in a sea of red, of broken capillaries, hangover tears. Whatever. I head towards the tea counter.

It's nine forty-five a.m. *She* usually arrives around ten a.m., so maybe I'm lucky today. I've escaped the public tongue-lashing. I hate clocking in, and not just because I am not a morning person and therefore always late. It is degrading. I dislike that somebody owns my time and can do with it what *she* likes, especially her, Mrs Knight, the old colonial who inherited a printing press and magazine from her father, and for whom time stopped during that age when things were done properly, people knew their place and pompadours, short skirts and stockings, worn regardless of the weather, were fashionable. Muslim, always so accommodating, says that Mrs Knight isn't racist, but she's not colour-blind either. Clocking in, running the card through the jerky time-code machine, you and fifty jostling others, confirming, legitimising that all you are is a cog in the wheel for eight hours, five days a week and sometimes on Saturdays, it reeks of indentured servitude. I may be a slave, but I don't like being reminded of the fact. To avoid it, I pay

Francis (janitor, 'tea-editor' as Muslim once christened him, first one in, last one out), a small sum at the end of the month to clock in for me.

I bump into Francis coming downstairs, wearing that reverential look that always indicates that he has just delivered Mrs Knight's briefcase from her old Land Rover to her office upstairs. Too bad. Too bad for me. Seeing me always gets Francis going. He has this notion that whatever depths he may sink to, there's always me below, scraping the bottom of the barrel, the rocky pavement outside a seedy bar on Accra Road, the public verbal hiding from Mrs Knight, debt. She took him on as her odd-job 'boy' many years ago, sweeping her compound, straightening her suburban lawn. His job as janitor is a promotion beyond his wildest expectations, a new lease of life in middle-age without, of course, a commensurate salary raise. He is grateful and loyal. He named his last daughter after her, misspelt it: Night.

He smiles.

"*Ubaya wako, Njohi,*" he begins. I know where this is going. He clears the counter of its cups, prepares me some tea. His moods are faithful to Mrs Knight's temperament. You can judge what mood she's in from him. On a bad day, he will deny you tea. He has long since abbreviated my name to Njohi, alcohol in my language. "The trouble with you, Njohi, is that you can't hide what you were doing last night. It always shows up on your face. Why not just stick to drinking over the weekend?" He chuckles, shaking his head. I am the source of most of his private amusement. He serves me a cup of tea from behind the counter, still smiling: "*Mama yuko. Kimbiya.* She's in. Run upstairs. She has been shouting for you for the last ten minutes. I told her you had gone to buy cigarettes."

I refuse to be rushed. "*Habari ya Night?*" How is Night, I ask, sipping the proffered cup of strong tea, my hangover medicine. How is Night: The daily question that is my private amusement at his expense. He never gets the irony – he is not supposed to, not really – naming his daughter after that woman, whose darkness he so happily inhabits. She is childless. Her bloodline will be extended by him. By gratitude.

Francis's face clouds over. "She's sick again. I need to take her to the clinic. It's a good thing we're getting paid today. I can take her tomorrow." I remember her first toothache. She was in agony. Francis told her – Night was three then – that if she went to sleep it would go away. Our salaries had been delayed again. Mrs Knight was being especially democratic when he went to ask her for an emergency loan.

206

She said she did not want to hear tales of dead uncles, sick relatives. Nobody was getting paid, not even her. By the time he could organise some hospital money the infection had spread to her gums. She's a little older now, and has taken to covering her mouth when she smiles, to hide her stunted, black teeth. Francis is always talking about her. He says she's a happy child. I wonder how that works, with her laughter stolen from her.

His face brightens, the chuckle rises in his throat: "*Kimbiya*, bwana. Mama wants everybody on best behaviour. *Watu wa bank wanaingia leo*." The bank people are coming in today. I finish my tea. He takes my cup, refills it. Mrs Knight must be feeling quite confident about this deal. She thinks it's a secret but Oluoch can't shut his mouth, so that by the time the second batch of potential investors was being shown around the premises, we all knew they weren't just 'guests'. Oluoch was telling us the other day that there's enough in the account for another two months or so. If new money doesn't come in, we'll join Mr Johnson's boys in the unemployment queue.

The printing press is here in this long, cavernous room on the ground floor. I am laughing a little to myself as I go upstairs, at the sight of binders and cutters, inkers, machine operators suddenly transformed into painters. Everybody has a brush and a tin of paint. Everybody is diligently going over the ancient machines, painting over the rust, the age. I can hear Owino's voice at the other end, urging them on, these loyal workhorses. It's hilarious, the lengths she has to go to impress the bank. In the old days, Muslim was saying, all it took for new funds was a call to one of her mates at the bank, white of course, and part of the Karen crowd. Now the banks have become more careful. The white boys have been replaced by black ones, with MBAs and American accents. They didn't know old Mr Johnson or his long and intimate history with the bank. They told him no more overdrafts, no more unsecured loans. They don't know Mrs Knight.

The last incident with an investor will go down in the annals of *Traveller* history as the funniest event ever. He was fifty-something, money made in a series of dubious operations on Kirinyaga Road, his suit one size too small, the complicated smell of stale sweat blending with yesterday's *nyama choma*, roast goat from Kiamaiko, trailing him like a swarm of flies. He had short, thick fingers, black nails. The way he twirled his pinky finger with the elongated nail – twirled it, that is, when he wasn't using it to pick his nose – you would think he thought it was a sex object. Mrs Knight wore a forced smile throughout, was even chatty as she took him around. Later, her secretary said, she was literally holding her serviette to her mouth trying not to puke as he chomped open-mouthed on the biscuits, downed the dainty cup of tea in one gulp, then sat back and let out a long, satisfied burp. After careful consideration, said the letter dictated immediately after he'd left and posted two days later, I do not think we can do business together. Thank you for your interest, etc., etc. Yours Sincerely. She abandoned the idea of new investors, went to the bank on bended knee. She'd rather starve than endure *that*. Irony of ironies, he bought a printing press on Enterprise Road. It's thriving. Oluoch reports that she's mortgaged her Karen house, the one she was born in and her father died in, for this deal. I climb the stairs. Midway up, I get a glimpse of Mrs Knight, her thick legs in their stockings, her pumps, the corner of her skirt, walking into our office. All trace of humour dies.

She is in the inner office, Muslim's office, with a guest. I go to my desk, busy myself, my back towards them, tensed.

She is saying: "...This is Mary Hunter-Lewis. A dear, dear friend of mine. Mary's just taken up gardening and would very much like to contribute to the magazine. A column, perhaps? I don't know. I'll leave you to handle the intricacies, Muslim. Mary, this is Muslim Omari, our editor. He's quite a special, erm, Kenyan, you know, he was in university at Oxford." Mrs Knight never made it to university. When Muslim was at Oxford, she was raising horses, on a ranch by the lake in Naivasha.

"A pleasure to meet you, although I believe we've met." Muslim is putting on his most affected accent, simpering.

"Not that I can remember," says the woman firmly.

"At the country club, in Karen."

"Really?" This is said with more than a little scepticism.

"I'm a member myself. We met about a month ago, I was with my wife, Christine, the captain of the ladies' golf team."

There's a brief silence, then a gasp.

Then the rally: "Of course, you're Christine's husband! I'm so sorry...but of course we *have* met. I didn't realise...Oh dear, I wouldn't have...It's just so unexpected...Perhaps you've lost some weight?...So unexpected." Her voice trails off.

Mrs Knight is on another subject: "Muslim, do you have any idea where Wanjohi is?" One-Joey: all these years of yelling at me and she still can't get my name right. I find the contact sheet I've been looking for.

Nobody notices me walking into Muslim's office. Muslim is seated in front of his typewriter, his head twisted towards Mary Hunter-Lewis, a tall, middle-aged woman in shorts and running shoes.

"Here they are. The staff pictures." I panic, briefly. My hands sometimes betray me, especially on the morning after a night's drinking. Mercifully, they remain steady as I hand over the contact sheet to Mrs Knight.

She suppresses her irritation in deference to the guest. There will be no shouting for now. She crinkles her nose at me, more at the alcohol seeping through my pores than anything else. Her sense of smell is sharp, ageing predator, all leathery dewlaps and sunburnt jowls. Her mouth is a red gash, her eyes hooded by bushy eyebrows. Her greying pompadour sits like a mane on her head.

Muslim, sensing her discomfort, scrambles to his feet, opens the window, a small, round man in tweeds and a bowtie, white socks sinking into the fading, red carpet, a luxury from an earlier time, when the magazine was turning away advertisers.

"It's so stuffy in here. I can never remember to open the windows," he apologises, cover-up artist. His accent reaches across the seas for a street in London. He went to Oxford. He studied English. He married a white woman. He pays for all of it, his obsession to belong, in ways he no longer notices, little humiliations. He's been working here ten years, ever since he 'retired' from a petroleum multinational, where he was MD. Rumour has it the board was forced to dismiss him, because employees were threatening to go on strike. They said he was worse than the white boss he'd replaced during the heady days of Africanisation. But he walked away with full benefits, invested in a petrol station, got robbed blind. A friend of Mrs Knight's, an expatriate Englishman he grew friendly with at the club, had a word with her. It was as good as any letter of recommendation. She was looking for a 'Kenyan face', for PR purposes. He was hired in a week. He knows nothing about magazines, but is good with the staff, in Mrs Knight's opinion. Harry, Mrs Knight's long-time lover, comes in thrice a week, to edit. There are framed certificates on the dusty walls, awards won four, five years ago, longer. There are files everywhere. Muslim is, of course, wary of computers. Mrs Knight is loathe to invest in them. She makes our excuses. We leave Muslim with Mary, telling her an Oxford story, the one about him on a Saturday night in "'68, or was it '69, I can barely remember now", when he was broke and badly needed a drink, and hit on the idea of passing himself off as a visiting scholar from Harvard and ended up getting free whiskies all night.

"They only discovered when I stood on the counter and began to sing songs in Pokomo. But you really should hear my impersonation of an American accent. Christine was so impressed, she married me!" Mary twitters, charmed.

When we are out of sight, Mrs Knight grabs me by the collar. She slams my back against the wall. "I want those photos, you alcoholic little shit!" she hisses. "In the next two hours. Developed and *displayed* before the bank arrives, do you understand?" I can smell her, incipient halitosis, perfume, white person's smell. I can see the faint moustache. "You will get the frames from Kamau, hang up the photos along the staircase, and then you will go to Oluoch for your money and leave the premises for good, do you understand me? I'm fed up with your bullshit. Fed up, One-Joey." She releases me, stands back panting slightly, looks at me as if I am a gob of phlegm. "And do something about your face." She marches off.

I sit down at my desk. I've just been fired for probably the tenth time this year. It's always like this when there's a big event. These sessions, these confrontations, they excite her. In the evening when everybody's left and it's just me and her, there will be little overtures. Come to my office and have a cuppa tea and let's unwind, I've been so tense, One-Joey. God, then she'll close the door, slither up to me on the couch and then she'll take my hand, playfully, draw it to her breast and then I'll be touching her exposed flesh, white and sagging, my hands rolling down her stomach, over undulating hills, unexpected *kopjes*, pastoral savannahs, lower, my hand inside her skirt, lower, lower, into ancient nooks, hitherto unknown crannies, oh that feels so good, One-Joey, right there, into the familiar, dry gulley now flooding, ooh yes, right there, Oh God, don't stop, don't stop, don't stop. Why do I do it? WHY DO I DO IT?! WHY. DO. I. DO IT??!! Fuck. Why am I trembling and I know it's all a charade? She knows me. She knows I can always do with a little extra money, the thousand bob, sometimes two. After. I hate her. I need to calm down, otherwise. Otherwise what? What will I do? What do I ever do? Fuck. It's a good thing I stole a joint from Man-Sammy's. I can smoke it in the dark room while I develop the photos.

In here, in this dark chamber downstairs just off the printing room, I am king. The sign at the door says DARK ROOM. STRICTLY NO ENTRY. Nobody enters, except me. I am the only one with keys to this place. I switch on the safe light. Now the room is red and strange. The match glows briefly, like the flash of my Nikon in the dark. The marijuana smoke burns down my gullet, taking no prisoners. I choke, I always choke. Why am I reaching for my face? It feels alien, a floating thing on its own, wet with tears. It must be the joint. It must be. Would it be possible to unscrew my head, replace it with someone else's? My mind wanders a little. Time is a rubber band, stretching slowly, expanding, twanging abruptly. Mice scurry along the floors of memory. I can see so clearly how I got here, from there, the train station in Delhi, the first gnawing signs of desperation, the worship of a little money, how far it can take you. The night at the train station with Tsitsi, Tsitsi from Zimbabwe, when we had no money but had to get back to college in Bombay.

What happened to that old man? Where was he going, with all that luggage sitting around him? But he deserved it, that old man, drooling like that, his saliva an earth wire from his half-open mouth to the floor between his legs, his head dancing jerkily in sleep. I laugh out loud, then I stop suddenly, listening. Did somebody hear me? Can she smell the joint? Shit, maybe the fumes are travelling straight to her office. So what? What's the worst she can do to me? Fire me? That's funny. And Tsistsi had started sobbing, the silent tears streaming over her fingers, down the back of her hand, when I saw our deliverance, the wad of rupees in the old Indian's shirt pocket. I hear myself chuckling, a gurgle from a disembodied head. The station in Delhi now seems washed in red light, a twilight zone memory. We would have been lynched, both of us, if anybody had seen me. The crucial question, however, is this: would they have deported our charred remains, or would the Indian authorities have ordered a cremation? I'm laughing again, halfway down the burning joint. They definitely wouldn't have appreciated the talent, the way I made the old man lean against me, the dexterity of my desperate fingers reaching across his shoulders, into his pocket as I looked the other way, soothing Tsitsi. They wouldn't have appreciated the act of love. We still missed the train, after all that. Tsitsi, always so decent, never asked how we were able to get first-class tickets, and I never told her. We were so drunk when we boarded the next day, drunk more on exhilaration than on that cheap, awful Indian booze. On the train, falling asleep after making love on the narrow bunker, there was a whisper from somewhere deep and dark and far, that my real ability was hide and sneak. My ability was survival, inhabiting anonymous spaces, not a degree course in

211

literature or photography. Survival. My mother wept when I landed back in Kenya, high and vague, smiling sheepishly, photography diploma in my hand luggage, diploma but no degree.

My tongue is thick, my teeth feel alive, mobile, loose. What's that in there, in between the molars? I worry it loose. Gristle? No, I don't think so. Can't remember the last time I ate. Paper, it turns out. Why do I have paper in my mouth? The rubber band twangs, the mice scurry. The floors of memory dissolve into a scene from last night. At the counter of the new bar at the Hilton. What was I doing there? It's coming back now. It was happy hour. The advert had said that beer was at half-price. I know I arrived a few minutes before Happy Hour. I remember looking at my watch, drumming impatiently against the varnished wooden counter top, observed people coming in through the mirror behind the barman. Then...then everybody was laughing. The barman began to get nasty. I was being dragged off my stool by a bouncer. Now I'm being held down, bad dog. My mouth is being forced open, by which time nothing matters. The humiliation is complete. I let them discover the bill, even though I could very easily have swallowed it. Ah, now that song returns, a flash flood of memory, the hypnotic thud of bass and drums. Reggae. Reggae at the Hilton? Maybe later, in the *matatu*. But somehow, I can hear it playing over the hoots and taunts of the patrons, their eyes squinting with laughter, with warning. Don't go where you don't belong. The lyrics and the music I remember, not the title...

"And when you play a bad card /
And when you play a bad card..."

It's an old Bob Marley and the Wailers tune. Anyway, luckily the barman was able to retrieve most of the bill, although they seem to have left a fragment of it behind. When they had forced out the half-chewed bill, did they have to dry it, then file it away, for tax purposes? I hope so. That's the last time they'll enjoy my custom. Fuckers.

Okay, time to work. Now where do we begin? Steady hands, steady, steady. Insert film in reel tank. Add developer solution. Lid it. I don't mind the waiting so much. I can hear the printing machines, starting up, stopping. They must be testing them, just in case they break down during the bankers' tour. Put film in stop bath. Pour out stop bath, rinse and add fixer. I can hear Mrs Knight's voice. She must have come to direct operations herself, imperious general. Open tank and look at negatives. She's going to have a little shock when she sees these, developed and displayed. She wanted staff pictures. She'll get them. Put negatives in wetting agent solution. Dry negatives. Place Kodak paper in developer tray under enlarger. Put negatives in enlarger and focus. The test looks okay. Jesus, look at the time! Have I been here that long? I'll only develop five. That should do the job.

In the printing press, everybody is standing at attention, watching paint dry. I find the frames on my desk. Should I show these prints to Muslim, for a second opinion? He considers himself, despite overwhelming evidence to the contrary, a connoisseur of the arts. These prints, I believe, are art – they take full advantage of the fading evening light, bathing beautifully Mrs Knight's office in oranges and browns. Posed action shots, profiles, even a still life, all perceptively taken, brilliantly rendered. There's Simon, the press supervisor, with Mrs Knight, and there's another of Oluoch, again with Mrs Knight, his averted face a study in concentration, then there's another of Mrs Knight alone, unaware of the camera. I hear her voice downstairs, an unusual sound for her, fawning almost, echoing in the printing press. The bank people must be here. I need to work fast.

"We insist on the highest standards at *Traveller* magazine," she is saying. I hang up the last photograph at the bottom of the stairs.

I can hear Muslim, sonorous: "The market at the moment is saturated with all kinds of travel magazines, mostly for the domestic market, although why anybody would want to sell travel magazines to Africans is beyond me!" Titters. There's the sound of a machine starting up, coughing, choking. Then a moment of silence.

"Simon, what's wrong with this machine? We got them just the other day. Call Pradesh and tell him about it, immediately!" She should have been an actress. Those machines are at least 25 years old.

"As I was saying," Muslim soldiers on manfully, "*Traveller* still manages to reach the right audience. We are proud to list among our subscribers the likes of Lord Stevenson. Thank God he retired in Mombasa a few years ago. It's saved us so much in postage! International postage rates are ridiculous!" Three sets of laughing voices, the third female. "Also the likes of Mrs Wainwright, the widow of the late inventor, Sir Wainwright. She's been coming to Kenya for the past 40 years. Unbelievable, if you ask me. Every year without fail, and she takes all her travel advice from *The Traveller*." There is the expected smugness at the end of that sentence.

"Perhaps you'd like to see our photograph collection before we get down to business," Mrs Knight smoothly suggests. They are coming this way. I scurry upstairs, hide and peep. The scene at the bottom of the stairs, it's like from something out of a movie, although what's interesting for me is that 'The Bank' is Ms MBA thighs from earlier on. She's holding her hand to her mouth, in a classic – posed you may say – expression of shock. Muslim is collapsing in slow motion. Francis, who will pick up, like the rest of us, his last salary from Oluoch in the evening when everything has settled down a little, is rushing to save Muslim from injuring himself. Mrs Knight is, of course, transfixed by the images of herself with a number of her employees, unwinding after a long day.

*

Parselelo Kantai is a writer masquerading as an investigative journalist. He lives and works in Nairobi where he is the editor of *ECO Magazine*, an environmental quarterly. *Drones* is his second short story. He plans on turning it into a novel.

A Turn in the West

Andiah Kisia

Charlie and I have one of those friendships that arise out of crisis and is strengthened by a continued production of the same, so that when I found him sitting outside my door step that July morning, I knew there was trouble brewing. Knowing Charlie, it had probably percolated and was ready to serve. We've had nothing but bad times together, Charlie and I, and it's as good a foundation for a lasting friendship as any I know. Better than most in fact because trust is at its very essence. You can get real close to the guy who hides you from the cops and gives you the fare to get out of town. And when you start off like that, you can't go back to small talk and niceties and bullshit. So it was with Charlie and I: conducted in the space between mild disturbance and catastrophe, it was the only real friendship I had.

It might be accurate to say even that it is the only friendship I have left, the only one I haven't shed along with my innocence, the only one that has survived the accretions of cynicism and the knowledge that no longer allowed us to excuse the divergences between what we wanted in our lives and how far short the people we knew were falling from that or flat out opposing it. It became impossible to make excuses for the people in our lives, their inadequacies and the accumulation of little cruelties we'd inflicted on each other over the years. Perhaps my only friend since I discovered the nest I had gotten so cosy in was full of vipers and other unsavoury things.

He smiles when he sees me, eyes shadowed behind dark glasses, gives me the treatment, turns on the smile. Smiles out loud. Like floodlights coming on.

"Mato!"

It's the nicest thing about him, a sudden, unexpected softness in a handsome but hard face. It has a quality in it of childish glee, unfettered and vital. It confers on him a vulnerability that is quite out of keeping with the man I know. That man has nothing left in him of innocence or of softness.

Charlie has an abiding contempt for people. He looks at them as providers of things only. When he first meets someone, he evaluates

215

them, what they're made of, how much of that he might want and what he can have. He makes his mind up quickly and his conclusions are rarely complimentary. But then he smiles, hiding contempt behind the flash of teeth and the infectious chuckle. Then they laugh with him, with the same infectious glee. Laugh with him laughing at them. That smile has gotten Charlie into and out of more shit than a longdrop. Has left women spreadeagled in its tracks, people feeling slightly taken for a ride, scratching their heads and thinking that really, they should have known better.

I first met Charlie four years ago; a good-looking man lying shirtless on the couch in a mutual friend's house, smoking weed and playing video games. He was between deals again and homeless. Charlie has seen more couches than most furniture salesmen ever will. Between deals and homeless is his usual state of affairs. When he isn't working, he plays video games and smokes spliff. What Charlie calls work is of great interest to law enforcement officers in several states. They've been trying to catch him for years. Charlie reserves his deepest contempt for the police.

He has the easy charm that shysters have as a matter of course. Shysters and criminals and gigolos and other likeable rogues. He knew that I had seen what so many other people failed to and he smiled that smile at me, genuinely amused. We hit it off immediately.

* * *

I'm not happy to see him exactly. I love Charlie but I need more trouble in my life like I need a hole in the head. I slow down, smile back while the wheels turn and turn in my head. He sees my indecision and his lip curls slightly. He doesn't believe I have it in me to send him away, and he's right, because I bend to pick his bag up off the top step and reach into my pocket for my keys.

"How'd you find me?" I ask him opening my front door.

"Grapevine," he says and smiles again.

I laugh. "No shit."

"Were you hiding?" he asks me.

"What do you think?"

He laughs out loud at that, bending over and slapping his thigh. He knows what I'm hiding from. And he knows as well as I do that it's a waste of time playing peekaboo with yourself. You always know where to look.

216

"You?"

"Always," he agrees, still grinning. "Always."

* * *

The bag is Louis Vuitton, the relic of an older, more prosperous time. Last winter to be precise. That winter of content brought also a camel-coloured Jones of New York trench coat, two suits made to measure at the Polo store on Walnut Street and five pairs of Allen Edmonds shoes. The guys at the Polo store were a little surprised to see us. They were even more surprised to be paid in cash. They examined it as if it were a souvenir of a far off and rather quaint age. I think he must have looked pretty stupid lugging that bag around on the Greyhound. But then Charlie's things, the good things in life, are indispensable as distractions from the squalor he's made for himself. And he never denies himself anything he wants, even if someone else has to pay for it.

Inside my apartment, he unpacks his Playstation Two and plugs it in. That too is from last winter.

"What? No couch?" he says jokingly and settles down happily enough on the cushions strewn around the floor and begins to play.

"So dude," I ask. "What do you want to do?"

It's a rhetorical question. Other than the weed, Charlie only ever wants to do one thing. I break out the beer. It's bad.

"Skanked," he says disgusted after a hefty sip.

"Skanky."

I shrug. "I like skanky better," I tell him. It's like, an active property. Beer with attitude."

"Yeah well, we can't fucking drink it, now can we?"

So I take it back to the bar where I'd bought it.

"There's nothing wrong with it," the owner tells me.

"Easy for you to say."

"There's nothing wrong with it."

"Taste it then."

"I don't drink beer in the morning."

"Fucking superior bastard," I think. "Well I do," I tell him. "Well I *was*. And I can't drink this beer I just paid for because it's bad. So either you give me my money back or you change the beer."

"There's nothing wrong with it."

"You already said that motherfucker."

217

He's unflappable and adamant.

I've made a lot of enemies the last couple of years, and this asshole is way up on a very long list of names. But I'm thinking he doesn't deserve such a central place in my thoughts, not even my murderous thoughts or my merely malicious ones. Unfortunately, as the local purveyor of alcohol, he wields a certain amount of power, and that with utter enjoyment and no irony. I leave the six pack on the bar and slam the door behind me on my way out.

Outside, the heat hits me, heavy and wet and close on, all the sights and sounds of our growing African ghetto: the Blue Nile restaurant, the White Nile restaurant, rinky-dink little stores alive with smells of alien condiments and food.

The high-pitched guitar of some Congolese band provides the soundtrack for the groups of idling men and the slow unfolding of lives without purpose. I look at the street with the old distaste now softened by intimations of escape. I'm out of here, beyond the gnarled grip of this poisonous place, beyond its myriad predations and its cloying pettiness. And I'm not coming within spitting distance of it again.

Charlie is hunkered down among the cushions on the floor and I can see that I'm losing him already. He looks up when I come in and makes a sweeping gesture with his hand.

"I approve," he says.

"Fuck. So do I man." Another round of slightly hysterical laughter. There's nothing in my apartment except the cushions on the floor and a few mismatched plates and cups I got at the flea market. But we've been through worse Charlie and I. We laugh a long time.

Laughter and cruelty, staying the sly thing that was skirting slowly around us.

* * *

When my friend had thrown Harry off her couch, and out of her apartment, he'd asked if he could crash on mine. The house I was living in then was the worst one yet. Even Harry who had learned to remove himself from the mostly unpleasant circumstances in which he found himself was shocked. It was a mess. Not just untidy, but so dirty that the dirt had become somehow integral to the house itself.

Things got worse every day. On a really bad day, the decline was hourly. Strange stains appeared on the wall. A draught came in through another broken window. The wooden floor outside the bathroom was always wet and began to rot.

I had allowed Abdoul, a Malian friend of mine to move into a three-bedroomed house I'd found. Big mistake. There are four official tenants on the lease and between ten and fifteen actual ones. That's how these West Africans are. They take extended family to its logical, disastrous extreme. I had welcomed the company at first after the isolation of my last place, enjoyed the easy chatter, the freestyling and the guitar playing and the endless cups of green tea. By late night, they'd all be gone and I'd have my peace again.

But then the traffic began to get out of hand. The visitors stayed later and later until they'd dispensed with leaving altogether. I'd find someone crashed on a mattress in the living room, then two, then three, and they'd still be there in the morning or in the afternoon when I came in from school. They came in earlier and earlier. They were there in time for breakfast and stayed for dinner. At all hours of the day, the house was alive with the rapid-fire chatter of Bambara.

The neighbours are up-in-arms. When the landlord shows up to do a body count one morning, people disappear into closets with practised alacrity.

Four people remain in view, only two of whom he recognises. He looks around mildly then addresses one at random. "Hello," he says. "It's Abdoul, isn't it?" he asks, reading from the lease. The man nods and smiles. He doesn't speak a word of English. He got off the boat only last week and he hasn't learned to negotiate dry land.

I discover that Bambara culture has no concept of personal property. I find some idiot wearing my dry-clean-only winter jacket after putting it through the wash. It is barely recognisable. I wonder why he took it in the first place in the middle of summer.

"Who gave you that?" I ask him.

He tells me he found it upstairs. I pull it off him roughly and drag him into the living room.

"Where's Abdoul?" I ask the mob lolling about the on the couch and on the floor.

"He went to work," someone volunteers.

"And you are?" I ask.

"Maktar," he says, smiling.

"All right Maktar. Get the fuck out of my house." He doesn't understand. Maktar is used to preamble and dissembling and the practised use of proverb and metaphor and beating eloquently about the bush and approaching the matter at hand from as oblique an angle as possible.

I'm sick of translating my English into Bambara hand signals. I haul him out by the collar along with the clothes thief. A chorus of protest erupts. I come back and haul another guy out. Maktar, smiling bemusedly, is making his way back in. I stretch out a leg and catch him with a vicious kick. He yelps in surprise, but understanding is beginning to dawn. I go back for the others but they're already collecting their things and clearing out. I lock the door behind them and wait for Abdoul.

I tell him that I never want to see any of that mob in here again. He is apologetic, almost obsequious, promising to sort things out. The vermin stays away for a week before the first little critter skitters in again. We settle into a comfortable pattern of forceful eviction and gradual recolonisation. I have to do this alone because Charlie has retreated into a mist of weed and Lara Croft. Finally I resign myself to my fate. The neighbours continue to complain and the landlord continues to drop in unexpectedly. But these guys have out manoeuvred immigration authorities across Europe. They've given the INS the slip. He never catches them.

One summer morning I wake up to find an odd little group ranged along the couch; three young men and an old woman, the Sahelian dust still clinging to them. It is a band just arrived from Mali for a series of concerts in the North East, Abdoul's latest money-making scheme. Needless to say, they will be staying with us.

Abdoul has disappeared.

I give them the finger as I walk by and they smile at me and nod.

I make another discovery. Bambara culture has no understanding of rudeness. The visitors smile uncomprehendingly at my most transparent insolences. I try every one I know. I invent a few.

The band practises into the night, singing their plaintive praise songs till the sun comes in at my window and I get up bleary-eyed and with an edge on my anger that never blunts.

These visitors attract a trail of admirers and hangers-on in larger numbers than before. They cook vile-smelling dishes and eat together from a communal plate, spilling rice and pungent stews all over the floor, talking all the while.

I think that this is what it must have been like at the court of Mansa Musa or Sundiata Keita. *Boubou'd* men with sauces dribbling out of corners of their mouths, oral histories bellowed around mouthfuls of *yassa*, audible mastication, slurping and eructation. Where I'd once imagined majestic households, peopled by elegant men, haughty men who ruled by divine right and wore privilege easily, like a favourite trinket, now I just saw two dudes with bad table manners and whose hands you probably didn't want to shake.

One afternoon I walk in to find the woman sitting on the couch wearing a bolt of cloth loose around her waist and nothing else. I stare in horror. I am speechless, indignant. I sign my disapproval to her. She stares placidly back. I demand an explanation.

"She feel very hot," someone tells me. I lose it. I throw everyone out again. The woman's breasts flop about as she runs. The refugees mill about outside the door. The cops come. I'm incoherent with rage. I tell them that I don't know who these people are. The Malians cover the woman up and cart her away.

Abdoul reappears looking sheepish. He tells me that my mother called last night.

I complain about the noise, the noxious cuisine. I insist that any half-naked women on my couch must look good with their clothes off.

Abdoul is genuinely puzzled by my lack of courtesy, but he's too polite to get angry.

My mother writes me a hysterical letter. I wonder how she found my address. The strange accent on the phone has convinced her that I have fallen in with Nigerians. She warned me about Nigerians before I left home. The implications are ominous. "Are you selling drugs? Are you robbing and plundering?" She calls again and prays for me for half an hour over the phone. I wonder how she got my number.

The band finally disappears.

At the end of the summer, I tell Charlie that Pan Africanism is an obscenity. The sound of a *kora* striking up revolts me.

"These people are animals," I tell him. "I have more in common with Jesse Helms."

I've had it with their feudal manners and their chivalry and their decorum except when it really matters. Like what the fuck did they eat that their shit floated like that and required three flushes as a matter of course? And when did eating with a fork ever hurt anyone? And why should I have to convince anybody that I used toilet paper before I came to America?

"You're frothing at the mouth," Charlie laughs. "Have a beer."

My patience has run out and I stare down the possibility of moving

221

in with my brother. But it is already too late. The whole block is up-in-arms. I find the eviction notice when I get back home. Charlie fucks off to Marietta.

I grit my teeth and submit to my brother's self-righteous ministrations, his room and board. I begin to keep a diary. It's full of self-pity and a barely controlled hysteria. I think that one day, years from now, I might find all this amusing.

* * *

I drag Charlie out of the house and we walk down to another African bar. We're more than spoiled for choice these days.

Charlie is in a bad mood. He grimaces, "I can't believe I'm back here. In fucking Philadelphia." He hates the place. "It's hideous."

I tell him that it's just his suburbia withdrawal speaking. "I hate the burbs and the block upon block of organised unimagination."

"Like this is any better." He snarls his dislike through uneven breaths.

"Got a little bigger?"

"Shut up."

"How does a poor guy get so fat?"

He wants to go back home to Marietta. Back home is actually Kinshasa, Congo, but after all these years, that's like another country. He can't go back to Marietta because he's broke and he's broke because the last deal didn't work out. When a deal didn't work out, there was always the added possibility that the ink wasn't quite dry on another warrant for his arrest. Then he'd come to pay me one of his increasingly infrequent visits. The logic of our lives, a vicious little circle.

We turn into a side street and the world changes back to the University City I love: the three-storey Victorian houses and the immaculate lawns. It lasts only three blocks. The grit and grime of Walnut Street loom ahead. I wonder how I never noticed how ugly this place can be, and why I'm still here so long after I did.

Took Charlie to do it. Took Charlie to do a whole lot of things.

* * *

The bar is empty when we get there except for Papa the owner taking stock and cleaning up. In the evening it will be a warm and fuzzy caucus

222

of cabbies, dishwashers, toilet cleaners and burger flippers. Africa's huddled masses in the flesh.

Only last year, this was a Mexican restaurant. No one can remember when the last Mexican left. Now the bartender is Rwandese, the cook is Indian and the waiter is Jamaican. The food is inscrutable. It's close enough to Penn that a lot of students still come here. It's an odd mix, the inheritors of the earth and its wretched mingling with little acrimony, the "one day, you'll work for us if you don't already", subtext underpinning the interaction.

Papa's not surprised to see me so early in the day. He has served me beer first thing in the morning and last thing at night. If he has any opinions about my drinking, he keeps them to himself. Which means we get along like a house on fire, or as famously as anyone can with Papa. He's the sphinx of West Philly. Says little, laughs less, but obviously has a handle on things. While African businesses are folding all over the place, he's still making money.

"No credit today," Papa says in an approximation of humour.

Not a problem. I'm flush. In one pocket I have a Visa card with a starter credit line of eight hundred dollars. In the other I have five hundred dollars worth of cleaning dirty dishes and tidying up after incontinent arseholes. Until just now, it had assumed and maintained an immutable identity as Mr Dugan's money. Rent. Not any more. I absently reconfigure and reallocate my resources. Rent will be late again this month.

Papa remembers Charlie from the last time. Charlie's a hard man to forget, and when he's set his mind to convincing you, a hard man to dislike. Papa is obviously convinced. He gives us our beer, "on the house" and smiles a half regretful smile as he says it. I've only once seen Papa to give a beer away and the guy had to lose his mother first, and even then sympathy stretched only to two Bud Lights.

"How do you do it?" I ask him, shaking my head.

He smiles. That's how.

A man walks in, pool cue in hand. His name is Berhanu and he's handsome in a pinched, ferret like way. Too much beer and too little food, most of it cadged. He has two upper teeth missing where someone punched them out. I met him two years ago when misery was in active pursuit of company. I must have been pretty damn miserable to put up with him as long as I did. He must have pissed someone off again to have to come in here. The Ethiopians drink in their own bars.

223

Berhanu has an explanation for all the happenings on Baltimore Avenue and America in general. His theory stretches to include much of Sub-saharan Africa, with the exception of South Africa and Ethiopia. Eritrea is included. One day he shares it with me, leaning conspiratorially close to my ear. "Ze darker zey get," he tells me, "ze dumber zey get." The result of a lengthy introspection. I tell him to fuck off.

* * *

Papa owns three bars and a club, the only African club in town. It's a pretty shite place, dark, smoky and with an indestructible smell of fish lurking in the carpets on the floor and on the walls. But it's the only club Africans have to go and listen to African music and to meet other Africans. Pretty much everyone comes there, as well as West Indians and more and more African Americans. It's also a place of business. Where African men meet African American women to marry. For a fee sometimes, but often enough, from a heart-warming desperation. When thirty percent of your own men are in jail, it's hard enough to just find a black guy to be with. Africans have the added advantage of a non-felonious culture and an appreciation for hard work. The Mbira, the club, is Papa's cash cow.

For such a shrewd businessman, Papa is pretty damn naïve where his family is concerned. His nephew Bob runs the bar, although it would be more accurate to say that he runs it into the ground. Bob always manages to be drunker at closing time than the drunkest customer, and that's saying something. Papa just turns a blind eye and keeps him on, though the nightly receipts must tell a story of steady incompetence and occasionally of wilful transgression. He doesn't ask the questions he doesn't want the answers to. He doesn't look too closely at the sins he doesn't want to see. He just bends over and takes his shafting like a man. For God and for family.

Another nephew just arrived from Malawi last week and is learning American. He's already learned to say "Y'all ain't gotta go home, but you've got to get the fuck out of here," at closing time.

The two o'clock closing time takes some getting used to. Other than a hand-me-down constitution, a virulent inferiority complex and an enduring awe of London, drinking hard is the only thing the British left us when the checked out in 63. Last call is like a personal affront. Every

night a fight breaks out between the bartender and a bunch of Kenyans
who don't want to leave. That's where Kevin comes in. No one wants to
argue with a 6' 4", 250 pound guy. They drink up and leave, complaining
and hurling insults as they stagger out the door vowing never to come
back again. But of course they do. Every day.

It's only midday and I figure that I'll be only slightly late for work. I
drink too-sweet Coke and watch football.

At one I call the restaurant and tell them that I'll be half an hour late.
At two I call to say that I'll be at least an hour late. Car trouble doesn't
seem to be getting fixed. I think about calling again at four but abandon
the idea. I remember my laundry in the washer. I start to drink beer.

I'm still there at five when the first of the wretched begin to trickle
in.

Papa, and I'm sure he knows it, is like a coffin maker or an embalmer.
He makes his living off the misery of others. There's a whole lot of it
thinly camouflaged around these parts. Any night of the week, Tijuana
would make the folks at the United Negro College Fund weep. There's a
whole slew of degrees going to waste here. There are PhDs working at
Wawa and 7 Eleven selling hot dogs and Rough Rider condoms, MBAs
driving cabs, good engineering degrees guarding parking lots and
pharmacists mopping the aisles at the dollar store. And every evening
they came in, sloughed off their miserable realities and stepped into a
few brief hours or normalcy and humanity.

Here they could be simply themselves. No need to translate who they
were and what they had been into a non-metric quantity, a sentence, a
two-sentence education. Here they were more than the sum of their
paltry weekly paychecks. They were what they had been, what they had
set out to be, what they still thought they could be. Not only the cab
parked outside or the lingering smell of mustard and relish. Everyone
had worthy antecedents.

Here we skirted around the lingering bitterness and confusion and
talked of better things.

This was perhaps what lay at the bottom of the disproportionately
bitter exchanges at closing time. No one wanted to go out into the
darkness outside. Into the cold and the anonymity. Just another Zulu.

And every week, every beginning of semester, a new bunch of faces
stepped off Sabena at JFK and made their disparate ways to a cousin's in
Minneapolis or DFW or Norristown, just until they could get on their
feet.

225

About nine, Bob walks in with some girl. Experience gives her the once over. It hits me then how long I've been here that I felt only weariness at some other bright-eyed youngster at the starting blocks.

I was exhausted just thinking of what things she had to learn, what battles she'd have to fight, the depths to which she might sink.

No doubt the others saw it too. Eagerness thwarted and then quickly perked up at a fresh bit of pussy. I ordered a triple of bourbon and drank it down.

There were things I had set aside to think about, one day in quietness that I was still so far from. Mysteries that America had revealed to me. There was a theme running through this room. A lack of volition that I had never been able to understand.

As if the surround sound, turn-the-knob-all-the-way-up volume at which the world outside conducted itself froze one into inaction. It was too much for those, such as us, used to sylvan peace. As if an inability or a failure to translate oneself, to augment oneself to the same ear-splitting decibels meant that one became the moral of the story being told along the length of the bar counter and at the wobbly tables in the back. Inagency. Failure.

Distance from reality, the postponement of life which we lived here every day, allowed one to tell oneself the tallest tales, to cultivate and protect all sorts of outrageous half truths and to believe them. And then, when someone pointed out the discordances, to defend it, and that often viciously.

Since that happened often, since men were called upon to defend the fibs, their life-sustaining fibs, and themselves on a daily basis, a fight was bound to break out every day. A fight of such viciousness, all sharp teeth and claws, it was frightening.

Tonight it was Driss who had blundered into an unpleasant reality. His dearly cherished mirage was politics. He talked about it every day. How much he had always loved politics. How he was going to be in government, how well he had prepared himself for this inevitability by taking a first in political science and then an MBA just to be sure. Second in his class. He said it as if the reality of eight years of driving a cab was not a fatal impediment to that eventuality. As if he had a one-way ticket to Togo in his safe at home. As if he hadn't sickened from involition. As if he wasn't fated to always dream of better things he could never have. When the subject turned to Togolese politics, Driss was in his element. He knew the whys, the wherefores. The minutiae. Someone

226

interrupted him and was shot down. That someone tried again with the same bloody results. Then he got angry.

"My brother," he said, "It doesn't matter how many degrees you have, or whether I never went to school. Your cab doesn't know your degree and mine doesn't know I don't have one."

Don't fuck with a man's illusions.

Driss put his Heineken down on the bar and rolled his sleeves up neatly while the other man watched these preparations with a wry smile on his face. He knew what he had done. And he knew the consequence. He went down heavily under the force of eight years of misery distilled and delivered to his jaw. All the venom he would have unleashed on life had life had the temerity to dare him to dance.

Kevin ambled over smirking and pulled Driss away easily enough. "Fighting outside." Driss walked out and drove away.

Charlie groans in disappointment at having his entertainment so summarily truncated. The feeling in Driss is too close to something I am consciously trying to suppress for me to derive any pleasure from it. I need to leave. There are more than enough bars in University City to get trashed in.

* * *

We get home at three. My phone blinks, pregnant with messages. We sleep the sleep of the damned.

The discourteous explosion of the phone by my ear jars me awake. In the haze of uncertainty, I feel only fear. I do not know what I have done, only that there will be hell to pay. I let it ring until the answering machine kicks in.

It's Ed. He asks me to call him back. I am 20 hours late for work. I begin to count excuses like sheep.

The phone wakes me up again. I am now 24 hours late for Ed. But it's Joanna on the line. She lays it on business-like and thick as hell.

"Martin?" she says, "This is Joanna calling," as if I wouldn't know that voice from hell anywhere. "I haven't seen you today and I'm wondering what's going on. I must say this is very unprofessional of you and thoroughly irresponsible. I must say I am very, very surprised."

Yeah right.

"As you can imagine, John is very upset and so am I. I took a chance

227

on you giving you this job, and I am very much looking forward to your explanation."

Guilt trip. Very nice. Might have worked on a lesser soul.

"You have my number. Call me."

Fat chance.

John is the guy who got me the job. No doubt he's pissed. I'm making him look bad. I have done from the beginning. He's one of those Kenyans who came here with their eyes on a prize and are working their four jobs to get there. Plus school. Hats off to them boys. I wasn't interested. Until now.

It's something of a humiliation for me to have to ask him for a favour. He knows it too and plays it for all it's worth.

"I don't know," he says, looking pensive. "There aren't that many openings right now."

I'm not in the mood to play. "Just get me a damn job, okay?" I tell him. He laughs.

John is the hooker-upper for a certain type of Kenyan arriving in America every month. He knows every restaurant kitchen, gas station and care home for miles around.

We hadn't exchanged more than a few words in all the years we've known each other. We have nothing in common but our passports, and that isn't basis enough for any interaction. At this point, I'm way beyond expedient alliances. Nostalgic unions. I think I'm doing him a favour even by asking him for a favour. Maybe I'm still caught up in my Haverford snobbery. Those other guys are more Delaware County Community College types. The closest a lot of those guys will ever come to Haverford is driving along the Main Line. Or maybe they'll get jobs cleaning the dorms or mowing the lawns.

When I show up at the restaurant, the others, and there are many others, aren't too happy to see me. They're unhappy with newcomers muscling in on their floor scrubbing, adult diaper changing niches. Especially newcomers like me, looking down my nose at everyone. Some are only too happy to see me and give me 'how the mighty have fallen' smirks. We barely tolerate each other, say as little as necessary and keep out of each other's way.

I remember when there were twenty Africans in West Philly. I could weep just thinking about it. There was just me and Charlie and Charlene and Papa and his three nephews and one or two other guys who kept themselves to themselves and didn't bother us too much.

228

I'm not sure when or how it changed, but one day walking down Baltimore Avenue, I look around me and do a triple take. It feels like fucking Addis Ababa or Ouagadougou or some shit. I mean, I remembered when we couldn't get a bag of maize meal for any amount of money, but now you could have *ogbono* and enough okra to make you green, and people at the grocery store stayed right with you when you asked for couscous or plantain. At Oscar's deli there was even a Nigerian sub on the menu and the owner was fucking Greek.

It astonishes me the disparate realities that can inhabit even such a small space as this. The immiscible universes lying cheek by jowl, even in a neighbourhood this small. The professors of classics in the apartment above the Aba market woman who had got lucky in the green card lottery.

Now I could count my white neighbours on one hand. The fucking neigbourhood was gone to hell in a hand basket.

Now there was a fucking grapevine stretching from the fucking motherland and spread all around North America and parts of the Caribbean. You couldn't do fuck all these days without your third cousin six times removed hearing about it in Winnipeg and calling you in a panic.

The afternoon brings back sharp reminders of all the cisterns I have known. I puke and flush, puke and flush for an hour then go back to sleep.

I wake up again at six and lie on my mattress, prostrated by this latest manifestation of my own stupidity. I'm impaled on my mattress by the shaft of a brutal massing of pain between my eyes.

I manage to call Ed and tell him that I'm sick. It's not far from the truth. I tell him that I'll be in next week. No doubt Joanna has fired me by now. Ed, I think, will keep my job for me. I'm almost sure of it. He'll just give me a tongue lashing and be dramatically disappointed like only a queen can be. He'll ask me to think about whether or not I really want this job. Like, *really*, *really* want it, as if I give a shit, then he'll sigh and put me back to work. I'm the best darned grease pulveriser he's ever had. And I was employee of the month just last month. And if he doesn't, there's plenty more dead-end jobs where that one came from.

When I finally get up, I walk to the laundromat and switch my still damp clothes from washer to dryer then go and get some take out. We eat in silence. Eight o'clock finds us back on Papa's bar stools.

We come back every day for a week. By the next Sunday I'm broke.

229

I negotiate a credit line with Papa and we drink steadily for another week. Then even Papa begins to make unpleasant noises. With great difficulty, I negotiate another credit line at one of the Ethiopian bars, mostly so we have some place to go in the evenings. Charlie in my apartment all day is starting to get on my nerves.

I see it less and less as my apartment now, and more and more as Mr Dugan's seriously underperforming investment. My rent is a week late by now. Mr Dugan's secretary has already left two messages on my phone informing me of her concern about the chronic lateness of my payment. It will take three weeks of my three paychecks to recoup the money I've spent on booze. Trouble is, I only have one job now. I think.

My mortal fear of the mailman returns. I scan his face with trepidation as if he's read my mail and knows what horrors are contained within it: what bad tidings, what summons, what final notices. I have panic attacks at the thought that my mother might have found me again and that I'd find one of the cheap brown envelopes with my name described in her painstaking hand. The pain and the worry incorporated in each laboured capital. Today, however, the mailman just waves as he walks by.

Before Charlie showed up again, I had ordered my life into a semblance of order. Ditched the drinking and taken up a variety of new habits, the most novel of which was my new found industry. Every morning I would buy one cup of coffee at $1.25, one pack of Marlboro Medium at $3.25 and one copy of the New York Times at $1.50, each little ritual perpetuating the fiction of purpose. Forty-two dollars a week. Bare bones, bare minimum.

Then I'd walk across the Schuylkill to the Houlihan's on Rittenhouse Square where I was a productive member of the American labour force. My day consisted of steaming hot water, a hose and pulverising the accretions of our continental menu from an assembly line of plates. Two evenings a week, I took the train to South Jersey to the care home where I was in charge of three patients for the night. Three evenings a week, I dozed off in the guard's booth at a parking lot off South Street. What money I made went to rent. All of it. Memories of the flop house still haunted me. It was the beginning of what I thought would be a relatively brief process of reconstructing my life. Now that plan is shot to hell.

We've run out of ideas Charlie and I. Nothing to do, nothing to be done. Charlie is innocent of the unfolding drama. He never mentions it at any rate, and he doesn't lift a finger to help. And he never gets off his ass. When I run out of money, he stops leaving the house altogether. He spends

230

the days on his back with Lara. I think it's a miracle he hasn't got bedsores.

"Hey man," he says to no-one in particular. "I'm hungry."

"What the fuck do you want me to do about it?" I ask him. "I'm not your mother."

He's surprised and hurt, but I'm in no mood to be charitable. Between terror of my mother and Mr Dugan, I think my blood pressure must be about to burst my capillaries and that I'll die in a haemorrhaging mess on the floor. The strain is killing me.

But this is the first verbalisation of the problem I have only suspected. Charlie wanting. I know all about his legendary taste, and even though he hasn't asked for anything before this, I feel that I'm somehow falling short, that I'm not giving him all the good things he should have. Unable to fulfil my obligations to myself, I resent these mostly unarticulated obligations to another.

I go to the ATM for my last twenty bucks. After a worrying period of inaction and silence, I am informed in whirring machine speak that the twenty dollars has ceased to exist. I can look forward to a maximum of seven dollars and thirty-five cents.

There is only one machine in West Philly that dispenses money in denominations less than ten dollars and it's ten blocks away. The ATM at the Thriftway supermarket, the last machine in this neighbourhood that gave out five dollars, just upped their minimum. Screw this, I think. Screw the credit union and its hidden charges and screw the University of Pennsylvania and its affluent student body and its gentrification of University City.

I begin the unpleasant walk to the Penn Hospital ATM. I am having an angry conversation with the contriver of all things, including irritations like these. If I'm going to walk all this way, I tell him, I'd better be able to get that five dollars out of my account or I'm going to be very angry, and who knows what I'll do then? I insert my card with trembling hands. The old whirring and I'm in luck. Five dollars comes sliding out. It's already budgeted for.

I need cigarettes. I promise myself I'll quit as soon as this is over. My suspicions that I am terminally ill are healthy enough without the additive of proven carcinogens. With the rest of the money, I buy a week's supply of Ramen noodles for Charlie. I don't doubt that he'll be vocally ungrateful. Charlie dreams of medium rare rib-eye steaks at Shula's. In his book, Ramen noodles do not qualify as food.

Charlie eats them all, complaining all the while, in one fell swoop. The steaming, watery, unappetising mess disappears down his throat and we're back to square one.

We're about to get thrown out onto the street and I'm spending my time like some cave woman, foraging for an adult male. "Dude," I tell Charlie, "if I get thrown out, so do you. What do you plan to do about it?"

"I'm working on it," he tells me, sinking slowly into somnolence. "Give me time."

"Maybe Charlene can help." I say out loud.

Charlie sneers. But Charlene is up to her brand new prosthetic balls in her own crisis. She's changed her name to Charles.

"Charlie my ass," Charlie says when I tell him.

"Actually it's Charles."

"Charlie, Charles, whatever. All she needs is a good screw. Or a shrink. Not a dick."

* * *

There's only one other person on my money hit list. It is important that I maintain an element of surprise. I decide to catch him at home as soon as possible.

When I come out of my room, my coat is gone and so is Charlie. His coat is hanging on the hook on the door. Nothing in my wardrobe goes with camel and I know I'll look like an impostor in that coat. But there's nothing to be done. Half an hour of abject begging yields forty dollars. The rank taste of humiliation sets my teeth on edge. I think that begging doesn't become me. It pisses me off that the cracks are beginning to show. I never had to share my misery with anyone before. Before I could always find my ingenious way around it. Alone.

I hear footsteps behind me and start to turn, but it's too late. It's the guy I passed five blocks away and he's right up to me. He throws an arm around my shoulders and pulls his shirt up a little to show me the butt of what looks like a Glock in his waist band. "This is a stick up," he tells me, as if I hadn't already guessed.

I want to tell him that that's a hell of a corny line. What does he think this is? *Boyz N the Hood*? *New Jack City*?

It's the fucking camel Jones of New York trench coat. A Market Street, Liberty Place, Society Hill coat. Fucking Charlie, man, and his fucking impeccable taste. The man's arm is still around me. We keep walking down the street, so happy together. We look like brothers or best friends or black queers. Him Tarzan, me Jane. It's the fucking coat, man.

I give him my wallet and he takes his arm from my shoulders. He's pissed when he finds only forty dollars in it. He looks at the jacket and back at the wallet.

"This it?"

I nod.

The dynamic of this relationship irks me.

Like how he's just reached his grubby hand down into the guts of my privacy.

"No credit cards, nothing?" He says it as if I've committed a terrible *faux pas*.

I shake my head.

"What fool?"

Like how he can call me stupid and get away with it.

"I ain't got no credit cards," I say in American, saving him the effort of translation.

"Well, why the fuck not?"

Like how he has the temerity to ask why I don't have more shit for him to take off me. I stop walking and so does he. "'Cos I got bad credit. Like you, no doubt."

He looks up and down the deserted street then reaches for the gun in his waistband. "You'se a smart motherfucker huh? You think you smart don't you? Huh?"

The momentary bravado has already abandoned me. I shake my head dumbly then underline my point. "That's it man. All I've got." I pull my pocket liners out of my pants. "That's it."

He drops his shirt back over the butt of the gun and puts my wallet in his pocket. He nods at me and turns to go. Then he stops and pats my ass.

I think about that for a minute. I hear that in South Africa, robberies are thorough. Man or woman, they take everything you have. Even if you're a guy, they just flip you over and bang the hell out of you. I see him a block ahead running easily, springy and no doubt feeling quite pleased with himself. He hears the footsteps coming up behind him but it's too late. When he turns, I'm waiting. The blow catches him in his windpipe and he crashes to the ground.

"What the…"

"What was that?" I ask him. "What the fuck was that?" He just clutches at his throat and gasps. "You queer?" I ask him. "You a fucking fairy?" He's in too much pain to answer me or to pose any danger at all, but I hit him again to make sure, then frisk him and take my wallet back. I take his wallet too and the gun. He has way more money than I did.

"Fuck you," I tell him before walking away.

By the time Charlie comes in, my anger has surpassed expression by speech. I jump on him as he closes the door and we grapple with each other for a bit. Charlie is strong and it's good of him to merely push me away.

"What?" he asks, when I stop struggling. "What's wrong with you?"

I point.

"What?"

"Give me my fucking jacket back."

"You're that pissed over a stupid jacket?"

I make inarticulate gurgles of anger and he takes if off and tosses it to me. Then he tosses a hundred dollars after it. A few days later, when I have recovered my good humour, I tell him about the mugger.

"No wonder you were pissed," he laughs. He tells me to be careful when I walk around at night. "It's curtains if he sees you again. You better believe it."

I pay Dugan off next day but the month's already half gone and rent is due in two weeks. I'm first in at Tijuana again. I'm well and truly plastered by the time my brother walks in. My stomach drops.

He doesn't know where I live. This is the third bar he's been in tonight looking for me. As usual, a group of my countrymen comes in with him. I think he is terrified of his own company, that maybe he'll put himself to sleep and crash his Acura into a lamp post.

I'm certain it's not my company he's after. There must be a problem of appreciable dimensions to send him dredging the less-fashionable Philadelphia watering holes.

His friends hang back nervously and stare at me like I'm a circus act or something. They ask after my health with an inordinate interest. I ignore them.

Memories of the fatherland itch like a scab I refuse to scratch.

* * *

234

That is no country for hypochondriacs; phlegm-filled and vaporous. With its tubercular proletariat who had turned the streets into a microbular spittoon, haggard mothers toting babies with appalled thrushy mouths. The lice-ridden madmen, singing filthy songs on the corner of the 680, the obscenely misshapen beggars: a wantonly misplaced hip here, dugs outthrust on an outpointed chest, torqued hips swivelling between crutches, making a lewd, disease-mangled progress down the street, the stink of the native quarter and its welter of small lives, each one brutish and short.

And the men are simply insidious, corrosive like acid eating away at the base metals of my mind. Distance and discourtesy is my prophylactic against these living reminders of what I left behind.

* * *

I wonder how it came to this, an unpleasant premonition in a decaying Mexican-African dive. It had begun with such promise.

It was less than a week after I got to America that a panhandler told me he'd suck my dick for 70 cents, and I almost came in my pants from the sheer joy of it. Here, I thought, was life outdoing fantasy, the dream fading into a paltry knick knack and the reality looming like some exotic bird in hand. There was a whole bunch of excited immigrants who had come here on the slim pretence of a student visa. Charlene who wanted to take a dildo to the shit that had screwed with her in Kenya and a bunch of other guys all with stars in their eyes. A whole bunch of us middle-class exiles from real life. Tara and all the other daddy's girls who lost their heads and did things that would have sent their parents to their graves. One mad summer we had an unspoken competition to see who would have the most notched-up bedpost by the time we were done. Each night her screams of conspicuous copulation would put my respectful screwing to shame and each morning there was a new motherfucker shaking the piss from his dick in the bathroom or having breakfast downstairs. My eggs and my bread and butter. And all that time, the indestructible certainty that we would have what we wanted. That we would have our hearts' desire.

What we didn't know then is that we were just strapping up at the top of a run for a free fall like nothing we'd ever known.

235

I'm at the bottom now.

"Mum called," my brother tells me. "She wants to talk to you. She's going to call again at eight tomorrow." He pauses briefly and then very quietly adds, "You'd better be there." I know it's taken some courage for him to tell me what to do, and so I know that this must be important.

My interview with my brother leaves me abraded. Charlie is gone when I get home. There is a depression in the cushions that I think may be permanent, but that is all. The Play Station is gone, the camel jacket is not behind the door and the Louis Vuitton bag is not in the closet where he kept it.

Dugan's secretary has left a message on my phone. She wants me to come in tomorrow. Urgently. Stress on the urgently. "I'll see you then," she says sweetly and hangs up.

*

Andiah Kisia is a dissolute and mostly impecunious writer. She inhabits a garret in one of the more colourful neighbourhoods of Nairobi where she occasionally stains paper with ink and indulges a by now unhealthy obsession with Virginia Woolf.

A Man Among Men

Siphiwo Mahala

A man can never be a man in the eyes of other men if he does not
believe in himself. I always believed that I was a born leader; only as
time went by, I learnt that many people shared the same sentiments
about me. Mine is the voice that pierces through the ever-deaf ears of
the residents of Sekunjalo. Even the most conservative elders in the
community listen when I talk. Only highly reputable leaders receive that
kind of esteem in Sekunjalo.

My first attendance at a community meeting was not, however,
in the interest of assuming leadership. Nor was it in entrusting that
responsibility to certain individuals. It was never in my nature to poke
my nose into the affairs of the community. I was only there to
express my fury at what the people of Sekunjalo were doing to me.
Sekunjalo is an informal settlement erected across the road from
Section D in Joza Township, where my house is located. In terms of
political grouping, Section D and Sekunjalo fall under Zone Six
because of the geographical proximity between the two settlements.
It is difficult to say the settlement is the legacy of apartheid, as it
emerged in 1993, a year before the first democratic elections in
South Africa. That was the time when the leaders of the
movement told people not to pay rent to the apartheid government.
It was apparently one of the fighting strategies to dismantle
the regime.

During the campaign for elections politicians promised to build
people houses with running water, proper sanitation and electricity.
We expected these things to happen immediately after elections.
More people migrated from the rural areas with the hope of finding
jobs and better accommodation in the cities. The number of homeless
civilians rose rapidly. More squatter camps emerged in the whole of
Grahamstown and, apparently, in most cities across South Africa.
Sekunjalo is a product of this movement. Since the squatter camp
emerged it became a microcosm of a cross-section of characters found
in the South African society. I have grown to become part of this
community.

237

Survival in Sekunjalo takes its own form. There are certain unwritten rules that every resident must adhere to. If you dare disobey these rules you will suffer the consequences. Those rules include being friendly to every soul that you come across and making sure that you are known in the entire community. I unconsciously disobeyed one of these rules and the scar at the back of my head bears testimony to that. It was in 1991 and I had just come back from the university for winter vacation. I was walking home with my wife, Thuli, who was my girlfriend at the time. I passed a group of young men playing dice under a street light at the corner of Nompondo and Ncame Streets. I had heard about a notorious group of gangsters called Mongroes, who were famous for their proficiency in using knives with the skill of a butcher. One of them called out to us.

"*Heyi, yizan' apha!*"

Thuli wanted to stop but I tightened my hand on her and took a pace forward. The man called out again.

"*Ndithi yiman' apho!*" telling us to stop.

I turned to look and saw the tormentor holding what I thought was a glittering blade in the dark. I made an about turn to the left and took to my heels. Something hit me on the back of my head. I stumbled and fell, but I promptly got up and ran like I never had during my sprinting days, with stones flying behind me. It was only when I got home that I felt the sharp pain and the blood on the back of my head. Now I was worried about Thuli. The gang was also known for cogently making their way into women's 'under-waists', irrespective of their age. For girls, according to the creed of the Mongroes, salvation lay in acquiring a companion within the group.

Thuli later arrived in the house without a scratch. She told me that nothing had happened to her because her brother was in the group.

"Themba, why did you run away?" she asked.

"I wasn't running away. I was just going home to get my stick."

In the olden days having a scar on the back of your head was a sign of cowardice. That's because in those days men carried sticks wherever they went. As a modern man I did not carry a stick all over the place. There was no shame in running home to fetch it. I realised that salvation for me relied on making friends with Thuli's brother together with his companions. I developed friendly relationships with the fiercest thugs in the settlement as insurance for the safety of my family. Of course, I had to pay a protection fee in the way of buying them beer whenever they asked for it, which was every time I bumped into them.

A more positive factor that connected me with Sekunjalo was that my parents lived and died in the settlement. I had moved to live with my aunt in Grahamstown while my parents lived and worked on a farm. When the proprietor expelled them, they became some of the first residents in Sekunjalo. My parents were very popular in the community and are remembered as some of the pioneers in the settlement. It was the people of Sekunjalo who informed me about the fire that cut short my parents' contract on earth. I can still remember that morning; I walked like a lunatic possessed by demons, hurrying to see if my parents survived the flames that had engulfed the squatter camp. The stench of burnt objects assailed me from a distance. I was later to learn that part of the smell came from the charred remains of my parents. My parents' remains are now part of the soil of Sekunjalo. The settlement became part of me. An eternal bond sprung between me and the settlement.

My relationship with the residents of Sekunjalo became a mixture of compassion and respect. They treated me with the affection of a son, and with the esteem of a school principal. Such is the admiration you get when you are a good man in the community. I later realised that respect comes with responsibilities, as I found myself obliged to carry out duties that I never imagined I could do. I found myself having to be the Messiah of the settlement. Every man and his wife came to me with whatever trouble they had, adamant that I would do something to help. This started in a way that utterly hid its potential harm from me. First, old man Jongilanga and his wife came to visit after I had my first child. I was so proud that I told them not to hesitate to ask for anything.

Now I understand that was the moment I set a trap for myself. By opening the door to the couple I later realised that I had opened it for the whole of Sekunjalo. The man would come with another neighbour, who would tell me what good neighbours they had been with my parents. Then they would complain about their living conditions at Sekunjalo. The next day they would come and ask for some water, as they did not have running water in the settlement. I would allow the two men to help themselves, only to find out there were four others waiting with their twenty-litre containers outside. Once I allowed the two, the other four did not need to ask for my permission. They followed the 'give one, give all policy' at my expense. At first I pretended not to notice the trick they were playing until the numbers grew even larger.

239

I called old man Jongilanga and told him about my anxiety. He promised to relate my apprehension to the rest of his neighbours. The numbers of people coming to my yard decreased, indeed, but the number of containers fetching water never did. Jongilanga would come driving a donkey cart with a friend. They'd be carrying twelve or fifteen twenty-litre containers in the cart. I had to be much firmer in telling him that I was not prepared to support the whole of Sekunjalo. That was not the end of my problems.

The next thing was that I would hear footsteps in my yard followed by the pouring of water into a container in the middle of the night. I got tired of talking to residents who would always turn a deaf ear to my complaints so I bought a brand new padlock to lock my gate. When I woke up the next morning I discovered that the padlock, together with the gate, was gone. I felt that these offenses were enough even for the most charitable philanthropist to harden his heart. When I got the notice for a community meeting I saw it as a chance for me to give the residents of Sekunjalo a piece of my mind.

* * *

Our people have no business with time management. As far as I understood, I was thirty minutes late for the meeting but still, I found people standing in small groups along the corridor. I was raving with anger so I chose not to speak to anyone, lest I unleashed the fury on the wrong person. I sat right at the back in the middle row to make it possible for me to observe others. The chairperson of the meeting was Skade, the regional Youth League leader and, according to him, a former commander of a section in the Congress' military wing. He began the meeting by welcoming the attendants, especially the 'first timers', as he put it. I knew the specific mention of first timers was directed to me.

I had not been seeing eye-to-eye with Skade, and his juvenile remarks were meant to humiliate me in front of the residents. They did not embarrass me at all because I knew that at the end of the meeting my mission would have been accomplished. One cannot believe that even though our relationship was now that of a frog and a snake, Skade and I were once as close as a man and his shadow. We grew up and attended school together. We used to play marbles together and later played for the same soccer team. We had shared almost everything.

240

Skade's involvement in active politics is what sparked the differences between the two of us. How he got involved in politics is a story that still puzzles me up to this day. The fellow got arrested in 1985 for a mere public indecency offense. At the time black people were not allowed to use the same public toilets as white people. Skade was caught emptying his bladder against a tree and sent behind bars for six months. It was in prison that he met political detainees who recruited him to the movement. When he was finally released he emerged as a hero who had defied the apartheid laws by urinating in public.

Shortly after his release, Skade went to join the military wing in exile. He came back in 1991, after the apartheid government lifted the ban on political organisations. I was already at university, training to be a teacher at the time. He felt that I was not fully committed to the struggle. He had a tendency of using every possible opportunity to remind people about his prowess as a liberation movement cadre. If he had done something right, it was because he had been trained in Lusaka. If things did not go according to his wishes, it was because people were jealous of him because he had been a freedom fighter.

Skade read out the agenda, which was composed of issues that did not affect me and thus I had no interest in them. I was determined to stay until we got to the stage of AOB, where attendants would be allowed to discuss Any Other Business. The first item on the agenda was the nomination of our Zone's representatives in the Makana City Council. Since I was there in the meeting, I had to vote and I was prepared to vote for anybody, as long as it was not Skade.

The first man to be given the floor to nominate a candidate was old man Jongilanga. He was my father's 'age mate' and whenever he spoke he never forgot to make mention of that. He was the walking encyclopedia of the history of our people and a potential biographer of my father. As a young boy I used to visit his house and sometimes spent the night. The family was highly religious and they prayed every night before going to bed with the old man conducting the sermon. By the time he finished his wife often had to wake the children who had long fallen asleep during the lengthy prayer. His speeches were not different either. I could not understand why Skade had to give him the floor first. Old man Jongilanga rose to his feet leaning on his walking stick, which had seen so many years.

241

"I beg to nominate that son of Gwebani sitting over there," he said pointing with his stick in my direction. I was visibly stunned, as I did not expect him to get to the point that soon, let alone nominating me as their representative.

"Gwebani was my age mate," he continued, "We were circumcised together…"

"Old man Jongilanga, your circumcision has nothing to do with the current situation. Please…" Skade said with annoyance.

"Young man, don't you dare tell me how to speak. Did you forget to bring your respect with you when you came back from the forest?" the old man had raised his voice. "What I am saying is that, this young man's father was a great man, a man of integrity. He is buried in this soil of Sekunjalo."

"Old man Jongilanga, all I'm asking you is to please talk about the man in front of us and not about his father. If you have nothing to say about Themba you can sit down and give other residents a chance to nominate."

"That's what I'm getting at. You see, that son of Gwebani sitting over there is now a teacher. He is the head teacher of the biggest school in our area. Gwebani's son knows poverty, as much as he knows wealth. He knows our ways; he also knows the ways of the white man. He has a very humble background, and yet, he is such a progressive man. If we want a good leader, we should look for someone who knows how to get his head above the depressing conditions of the township and stand tall as a shining star. Gwebani's son is such a man. I am seated."

For a moment the room was filled with uneasy stillness. It was clear that Jongilanga's words had pierced into everybody's heart. It is amazing that as you walk around living your life people are actually observing, analysing you and documenting your actions and behaviour in their minds. I was deeply overwhelmed by the old man's words. Skade himself was astonished.

"Thank you, thank you old man," Skade said with agitation and then continued, "Now, does anybody agree with what the old man has said? Does anybody want Themba, the man living in the big house across the street, to represent the poor people from the shacks?"

I could hear in his tone that he had regained his iron resolve to annihilate my image. I saw several hands immediately dropping like giraffes bending for twigs on a short tree.

"Comrades," he continued, "remember that in this meeting we want someone who will represent our needs. We want someone who will stand as our voice in expressing concerns of the poor and not those of the rich. Now, I say it again, does anybody, other than old man Jongilanga, want Themba Mavi to be the representative of Zone Six? Please raise your hands right now."

As Skade finished talking, it was quiet to the extent that I could hear the heartbeat of a man sitting two rows from me. For a moment I thought everybody had withdrawn when I heard a creak from the other corner. Another old man, who was from the AmaTshawe clan, stood up and supported old man Jongilanga's view and thus qualified me to contest against whoever else was to be nominated.

"All right, now we will need the second candidate. And, remember, we need only one representative and two candidates will be taken to contest for this portfolio."

Several hands went up and I knew right there and then that competition was to be really tough. A young man rose, clutching a red hat with both his hands.

"I nominate you, Mr Chairperson. I need not motivate my decision, because everyone knows your role in the struggle. If it were not for people like you, we wouldn't be here today." He promptly sat down and more hands rose.

"I stand to second the last speaker. It's about time for those who suffered during the struggle to be rewarded."

I could see contentment written across Skade's face. I knew he had lectured those boys before coming to the meeting.

"Now, two names have been suggested. From the two candidates, myself and Themba, you will have to choose which man will be your representative; which man will represent your needs during council meetings; which man will best express the pain and the suffering of the poor people of Zone Six; which man truly knows what it is to be poor," he said, speaking through his clenched teeth and putting emphasis on each word.

I was now determined to contest for the position just to make sure that I did not grant Skade an opportunity to ridicule me and continue with his boasting in the township. The voting began and, to my surprise, I beat Skade by twenty-four votes to sixteen. He could not believe it and asked for a re-count and the results came out reflecting the same margin. He was no longer interested in remaining until the end of the meeting. I

243

was rejuvenated as I watched Skade scurrying away with anger and disappointment. When I had to make the speech I spoke with the vigour of a victorious man. I did so with the purpose of affirming their confidence in me.

* * *

I took the responsibility of being a councillor for Zone Six with mixed feelings. It was an honour for me to be the leader of my people. I also knew that leadership had its challenges. Poverty in the whole of Grahamstown was a real and visible thing. The toilets in many townships, including Sekunjalo, were still the bucket system type. The latrines were cleaned once or twice a week. The sight of a man carrying a bucket overflowing with human excrement was common in the community. It was the norm to walk past buckets placed along the street waiting for the arrival of the sewage truck. I would walk briskly ahead repressing the urge to hold my nose, for people would say I thought better of myself. The majority of the community had no jobs. The few who were lucky enough to find good jobs moved away from the townships to live in the affluent suburbs. I was determined to stay in the township and help lift the scourge of poverty that afflicted the community of Sekunjalo.

Old man Jongilanga made another long speech lecturing me about the morals of leadership.

"Son of Gwebani, you come from the pedigree of a very strong people, the AmaMpandla clan. A house where even a chicken is never defeated; the ones who skinned a live leopard. We gave you the name Themba because we had hope in you. We still carry that hope and we believe that you will bring salvation to this soil of Makana. We chose you because you are a great man. You have read many books. Your power is in your head and not just in your arms. Your weapon is a pen and not a gun. Your mission is to save lives and not to cause casualties.

"Son of the AmaMpandla clan, go the authorities. Speak in the white man's tongue. Tell them that we, the people of Sekunjalo, are very poor. Tell them that we live in the shacks and that we have no jobs; tell them also that we need water to drink. I take a moment to smoke."

I found the demands quite pragmatic and very basic. In summing up the long speeches, I highlighted running water and sanitation as the primary needs that required immediate attention at Sekunjalo. Both issues affected me directly. The sight of buckets full of human excrement lined along the streets was disgusting. Perhaps my parents could have been saved from the fire if there had been running water in the settlement. I was determined to ensure that these basic human rights were granted to the community of Sekunjalo.

* * *

On the next Thursday I attended the meeting of the Makana City Council on behalf of Zone Six. I met Mr Bongani Vabaza, the mayor, for the first time in person. The man could surely not have dreamed of becoming a model. He had froglike eyes and his cheeks seemed as if he was blowing a whistle. He was pygmy-like with massive hands and a protruding belly that threatened to break the braces that held it. I still wonder who had advised him to grow that long grey goatee of his. But the man was popular for his eloquence in speech. BV, as Mr Vabaza was fondly called, was a great philosopher and had a following all over Grahamstown. He was the kind of a man with whom you could be sure of a victory whenever he was on your side. I was one of BV's greatest fans because of his impressive speeches. The years that he spent as a political prisoner on Robben Island taught him a lot. Sitting in a meeting with this honourable man was an overwhelming experience for me.

What was even more striking on the day was seeing Mr Vabaza's secretary. She reminded me of my wife before her beauty got buried in fat. She had a captivating smile, a face of rounded cheekbones, light skin and brown eyes. She was adequately endowed with firm breasts like two neat watermelons. I am a married man, but I can't restrict my eyes from appreciating the beauty of nature when they see it. It's a problem, I know. Maybe it's not my problem. Perhaps it's a gender problem. Manhood problem, that's probably what it is. Any man who says he never gets tempted is a liar. We all do, but most of the time we brush temptation aside.

The beauty that I saw that day was far more deceiving than the snake of Eden. I sat in a strategic position to allow us to assume eye contact. An electric current flashed through my body as our eyes met. She dropped hers momentarily and then looked at me again. I smiled benevolently. She also smiled. I knew I had made an impact. That's my secret weapon. If I look at a girl and smile in a compassionate way and she smiles back, I count that one as mine. I cannot remember the proceedings of the meeting very clearly as my mind was stolen by the sight that was across the room.

Delegates were ordered to submit the memorandums to the secretary so that the mayoral council could view them. I took this as a good chance to introduce myself to her. She told me that her name is Dolly and she came from Uitenhage. I could not miss the opportunity of knowing her better.

"How long have you been working here?" I asked, hoping that she would tell me more about herself.

"It's only my second month. I finished a diploma in Office Administration last year," she said proudly.

"So, how are you getting home, Dolly?" I asked with the hope that she did not own a car.

"I'll take a taxi as I always do," she said smiling.

"Can I offer you a lift?" I said with excitement.

"I don't think we will be going the same direction. I stay in Section F."

"That's not a problem. I can take you there," I said with great confidence.

As we got into the car I was debating in my mind. I was trying to figure out which method I should use to express my feelings for her. It always happens like that. It is easy to tell a girl that I love her when I do not mean it. Words never come easy when I sincerely mean it, not on the first day at least. The silence was interrupted by Dolly.

"So, what do you do?"

"I'm a school principal." After a brief pause I decided to add, "It's a lousy job, I know. But I'm used to it. After a while you enjoy the tricks that teachers and school children play."

There was silence again in the car. The next time Dolly talked was when she told me where to turn.

"So, when can I visit you?" I asked.

"You can't."

"How come, are you staying with a partner?" I asked with the purpose of finding out if she was seeing someone.

"Not exactly, I'm staying with relatives and they are kind of fussy when it comes to male visitors."

"Why don't you move into a flat?"

"I'd like to. It's just that I can't afford it at this stage. Maybe in about two months when I get promoted."

I was stunned to hear that she was expecting a promotion in such a short period of time, especially when she did not have previous working experience to qualify her for a senior position. I was interested in finding out what she had done to deserve promotion, but I could not figure out how to ask without divulging my curiosity.

"Oh, so you are expecting a promotion."

"Yes, the mayor will create me a position of a director in one of the departments in the council," she said, with a smile across her face.

"Okay, if I assist you in paying for a flat now, would you allow me to visit?"

When we got to her house I switched off the engine. She unexpectedly gave me a gentle peck on the cheek and thanked me for driving her home. We both got out of the car and walked towards the house. We embraced and kissed in the doorway. I walked to the car and before opening the door I turned to look back. She waved and walked into the house.

The councillors were to convene the following week to hear the response from the mayoral council. The mayor's response was, to put it bluntly, that the demands of the people were not going to be met. He told me that if people needed running water and proper sanitation, they would have to pay for the rent first.

"How do they expect the services to be delivered if they do not want to pay for those services?" He had asked.

"The council is looking forward to developing Sekunjalo. Preparations to build a park with a swimming pool are underway," he added.

"Mr Mayor, I'm sorry to interfere with your plans." I was deeply annoyed but I tried to keep the required level of respect. "In my view, a park should not be considered as an urgent issue at this juncture..."

"Mr Mavi," the mayor interrupted, "I am disappointed by your shortsightedness. The park is not merely for entertainment as you think. It will help to reduce the rate of crime and disease. One of the major reasons why people commit crime is that they do not have an alternative thing to do. Children from the squatter camp swim in that stinking pool full of maggots across the road. They fill the hospitals because of the diseases that they collect in the dams. The swimming pool will be maintained and kept clean."

I respected the mayor but I could not let him continue mixing up the priorities. "Mr Mayor, I understand your predicament but I also understand that, at this very moment, people in Sekunjalo

247

are living under unhygienic conditions. They don't have proper housing…"

"Mr Mavi, I'm sorry I have to cut you there," I could hear in his voice that he was getting irritated. "It seems to me that you still don't understand the kind of work we are doing here and, unfortunately, I don't have time to explain to you. Just hear me out; it is impossible, for any municipality, to give free housing to every soul that roams its streets. We do not have accurate statistics of the population of Grahamstown because of people that move in and out of town. Two years ago we asked people to register for free houses in Extension Nine. You know what happened?" He looked me straight in eye to show that he expected an answer. It was clear that he had every desire to humiliate me.

"No, no, I don't know, Mr Mayor," I said with a bit of mortification and regret.

"Our people registered for themselves and for their long lost relatives. We have people who live in as far as Cape Town but own houses in Grahamstown. You know what they do with the houses that we gave them for free? They rent them out. The so-called 'homeless people' suddenly became landlords. We cannot allow that to happen again. This squatter camp you are talking about is populated with chance-takers from the former Ciskei and Transkei homelands looking for opportunities to get free houses from the municipality." He took a pause by sipping from his glass with ease.

"As I said, Mr Mavi, I do not have time to give you all this background. It is for you to find out what exactly is happening around here. Now, let us move forward to more urgent issues on our agenda today. What needs immediate attention is the imposition of tax laws on the street hawkers. We must make sure that all unlawful hawkers are removed from our roadside, especially in the areas of tourist attraction."

It was already clear that the mayor and I had differences of opinion. I did not care what he thought of my inquisitiveness. After all anyone could tell that I was not his favourite person in that meeting.

"But, Mr Mayor, the majority of the population in Grahamstown is unemployed. They survive by engaging in small businesses like selling fruit and vegetables. How do we expect them to pay tax under those circumstances?"

I was concerned because I knew what it meant to be a street hawker. As a child I used to sell fruit and vegetables in the streets. The competition was really tough then because each and every woman and her children in the township sold the same things. Our target market were the busses that passed through Grahamstown after midnight when the shops were closed.

"If we allow them not to pay tax, everyone will opt for the so-called 'small business' and thus avoiding to pay tax. We cannot subject the municipality to that kind of a situation. No illegal business should be allowed in this city. Everyone must take the responsibility of paying tax."

His eloquence did not convince me at all but I had to compromise, as I seemed to be the only councillor who found the decisions problematic.

Back in Sekunjalo I had to give a report that was obviously unacceptable. I tried to impress the elders with my oratory skills.

"Elders of the community, fathers and mothers, my brothers and sisters. My fellow residents of Zone Six, I greet you in the name of the struggle. You sent this son of Gwebani to represent you in the city council. I took the responsibility with great pride and enthusiasm conscious of the fact that you entrusted it to me knowing that I am capable and keen to carry it out with great determination." I went on and on, saying all the things that politicians usually say during meetings of that nature. I explained to them the proceedings of the City Council meeting.

A dark cloud of dissatisfaction was cast over the room. Skade was the first person to raise his hand for questioning.

"Thank you Mr Councillor Mavi." I was not prepared to entertain his sarcasm but had to give him the floor because our democracy allows every fool to talk.

"I must say that I am not surprised by the report you just gave us. It's what I expected from you anyway. I am saying this because I know you very well. We grew up together and as far as I can recall, you never took any leadership position. Not even in a soccer team. It is surprising that some people gave you the responsibility of taking vital decisions for the community when you can't even take decisions for yourself..."

"Thank you, Skade, your point is noted." I said with agitation. I knew he had been yearning for my downfall. His remarks did not bother me much though; my obligation was to regain my impeccable reputation in the community. I got even more embarrassed when old man Jongilanga lifted his hand.

"Son of Gwebani, I stand here as a very unhappy man. If I die today, my soul would not go to Heaven. It would not be welcomed in the ancestral world either. Because my age mate, your father, my son, would

249

say I let him down by not putting you in the right path.

"Son of Gwebani, allow me to ask: what kind of people did you hold the meeting with? What kind of people would be keen to give water for swimming but refuse to give it for drinking? Son of the AmaMpandla clan, go back to the authorities. Tell them that all that the people of Sekunjalo want are essential services for survival. Tell them that the people of Sekunjalo are too weak to swim. And tell them also that we are too thirsty to play. Let me take a moment to breathe."

The last time I saw old man Jongilanga with that discontented face was when Skade told him to sit down. Now I had disappointed the very man that had so much faith in me. Skade's face was beaming with satisfaction as I walked out of the building in shame and embarrassment.

* * *

I didn't know where I was going, but my legs took me to Dolly's flat. The sight of a silver-grey BMW in the driveway gave me a surge in my stomach. Dolly was now staying in a flat for which I assisted in paying rent. I knocked at the door with the bravado of a police officer in possession of a warrant of arrest. I heard a delicate clink of cups and saucers and I knew Dolly was entertaining the visitor. I could not wait for her to open the door. I was greeted by a cloud of smoke as I opened the door and I knew whoever the visitor was lacked etiquette. The bravado that had pushed me into the house fizzled away as I found that the visitor that Dolly was entertaining was Mr Vabaza, the mayor, my boss in a sense. The two empty cups and the ashtray filled with cigarette stubs on the coffee table told me that the two had been there for a while. They were sitting on a couch with Dolly's back to the door. I was considering turning and walking away when Mr Vabaza jokingly said: "Hey Mr Mavi, why do you keep following me everywhere? Or, have I forgotten we had an appointment?"

"Mr Mayor, the door was open so I just came in," I said apologetically. "I'm just here to see Dolly."

"You want to see me?" Dolly looked at me as if I was a strange creature that had dropped in from another planet. I nodded. I wanted to say "yes" but apparently I had lost my voice with nervousness.

"Okay, just wait in the kitchen," Dolly said without even looking at my face.

I sat in the kitchen wandering what the urgent matter was that they could not wait until the next working day to discuss in the office. I was growing impatient with waiting, but I had to treat the situation with a bit of adult merriment. I had done it before. Forcing myself to smile even though I carried large lumps of depression in my heart.

"Hah, hah, hah, hah…"

The thunderous roar of laughter came from the mayor. That laughter of his always irritated me. Whenever he laughed he opened his mouth like a braying donkey.

"Huhh, Bongani, heh, heh, heh…"

I grew apprehensive as I heard Dolly addressing the mayor with his first name. As I stood there I felt a lump of bitterness growing inside me. I began to wonder if Dolly had been surreptitiously performing unsavoury acts with the mayor. I tiptoed towards the lounge and as I peeped through the door I saw the old man holding Dolly's hand, the way that a loving husband would do. The sight spurred me into action and my gentlemanly propensities flew out the window. The next thing I remember is that I was in the lounge.

"Dolly, I cannot wait any longer. Can I see you in the kitchen right now?"

"Can I?" she said to the old man gently pulling him by his long goatee.

"Well, seeing that the young man is in such a hurry, why not?"

I unleashed my fury as we entered the kitchen.

"Dolly, what are you doing with this old man?"

"What do you mean what am I doing? Don't you know what lovers do?"

"C'mon Dolly, you can't call that man your lover. He is old enough to be your father!" I had raised my voice.

"I can't believe you've just said that. Have you forgotten that you have a wife to go home to? Themba, please leave and stop bothering me in my house," the tone of her voice revealed annoyance.

"Dolly, you can't treat me like that. I pay half of the rent here."

"Well, who do you think pays the other half, eh?"

"Oh, now I see. This is all about money. You are doing this because this old man has promised you a promotion."

"Themba, I do not have time for this. Just leave!" she said and walked back to the lounge.

251

I was convinced that Dolly did not have feelings for the man, but somehow monetary values thrived over human dignity. She had allowed him to visit her, to touch her and probably sleep with her just for the sake of securing a job. I followed Dolly and found the old man still sitting cozily in the couch resembling a caricature of an old fat chimpanzee. My palms were sweating as I stood in front of him trying to suppress the urge to tear his protruding belly open with the knife that was on the table. The fat that filled his stomach was surely enough to feed the whole of Sekunjalo.

"You," I said pointing at him with my index finger. I bit my lower lip trying to control the projection of the words coming out of my mouth.

"You will cry someday." My voice was a bit shaky, which betrayed the anger that had filled me up to the throat.

"Young man, please don't disrespect me. I will not tolerate your childish remarks," he said in a low relaxed voice as if nothing had happened.

It was clear that I had lost Dolly to him, but I was determined not to lose my temper. Loss of temper leads to abnormal behaviour. A man that behaves abnormally has no dignity. A man with no dignity is not a man.

The man appeared as a winner because he had the authority and the money, but that did not make me a loser. I believe in the premise that a compromise under certain circumstances does not make me a weak man. Compromise is not always a bad thing. It is at times the best thing. Let's put it this way, it is better to compromise a situation than to compromise an idea. For a man and his idea are inseparable. To challenge an idea is to challenge the man. I shall not compromise my ideas.

*

Siphiwo Mahala was born in Grahamstown, Eastern Cape. He studied Literature and Creative Writing at Fort Hare and Rhodes Universities respectively. He subsequently completed a Masters degree in African Literature at the University of the Witwatersrand in 2003. Siphiwo has published several short stories in various literary journals. He is currently working for an NGO based in Pretoria, while at the same time writing a novel.

Jimmy

Eddie Vulani Maluleke

They say that you will never get over it. That once you dance there, once you inhale it, once its music filters into you, you'll probably never be the same again. And if you ever fall in love there then it will never leave you. Yeoville, or at least our Yeoville had an aliveness about it. It was the afternoon basking in the streets and the regularity of a midnight drink at Times Square. It was the mesmerising offerings of reggae from the Rooftop Tandoors, when it was still open. Even Laijah, a seasoned Rastafarian who mingled himself in and out of these streets, could get to you with his chanted recollections of the last rhythmic Thursday night session at Tandoors before he braved the Babylon night to kill his last spliff before the Metro police came out to roost.

I wish you had met Tsoana, who ran a public-phone stand opposite my bedroom window. She always said that sometimes the water towers looked pretty at night but it depended on how you saw them. I try to picture their beauty now and believe me they are not. And the Ponte tower doesn't tattoo the night sky with endless opportunities for entertainment anymore. Maybe when *Coca Cola* still blazed in the sky, maybe. The culture expressed in foreign tongues scattered along Rockey Street doesn't capture what we once were, how we used to dance, and drink and get so high; it was like walking in Rosebank but without the Roses and the Banks.

It had a charm about it, our Yovilla. That's how I could understand why like snakes we got caught in it, mesmerised by the rhythm, the rhythm of our heartbeats caught in an unforgetting embrace.

That's what they say. That's what we all had to say, but we had bruises on our faces, and past the eloquence of our poetry, our singing and our dancing, we knew the eerie silence that envelops you on an empty night filled with memories and regret, and you were the only one in the street hollering at three at night. Hollering like the devil had your soul by the gut and Jesus' last temptation didn't count. And always like fate, like salvation, a fat white Mercedes Benz would slow past you, roll down its window and offer you sweet forget, and if not, a quick fuck for fifty rands.

253

That is our Yeoville now.

I lived there for so long, took so much of it into me. On my bedroom
wall I had a painted mural of Steve Biko. And under my father's hero, I
lay on my bed, legs crawling open in anticipation, waiting for all that
Yeoville fire that Jimmy possessed to enter me. Then in those moments,
hardly stolen, offered to me rolled up in a *Rizla,* were the sweetest
stories, the true stories of Yeoville. In those moments when I inhaled,
Yeoville entered me. I imagined the struggling drummer in the flat above
me stopped sweating himself into a frenzy to catch his breath and I
remembered Tsoana, who was once the most beautiful woman I ever saw
with the most intelligent neckline and yet so tragic because a bullet
shattered her head in broad daylight right outside my window for her
phone. Those moments, I lay under Biko with Jimmy on top of me were
bliss, complete, all I ever craved to just be.

I lived there for so long, hoping to capture a little music that would
fade everything else away. I didn't notice the bruises on my soul past the
façade of singing and dancing and Jimmy until all my passion for Yeoville
had withered to its last strain of regret.

* * *

"Yeoville, Yeoville, Yeoville, Yovilla, Hillbrow, Mountainview
Ngena lapha sesi
Kuya Shesha la!"

It's almost intriguing isn't it, a little itch in the middle of Jo'burg.
You can't help but scratch at it until blood oozes out and the smell of a
freshly opened wound is an invitation to suck. I had a friend who visited
Italy and came back saying that it was like being in a little summer villa
capturing the scent of fresh flowers standing in the sun every morning.
I went to Yeoville instead, hard and crusty like mud when the first stroke
of sunlight catches it by surprise. I first saw him in Braamfontein
though, Jorissen Street. I didn't really look up at him at first glance,
not like you would at the beginning of some fine romance in Italy.
He was actually about my height, and was standing very close to me.
I remembered this clearly: He smelt of Lapidus,[1] musky, very musky.

We were waiting in a line to get into the last taxis to Yeoville. I kept
letting people climb in because I hate getting in the back seat; it's too
condensed, saturated with late-afternoon sweats and laboured breathing.

[1] Very strong musk cologne for men

Jimmy had skin like toasted white bread. I love toasted white bread in the morning with a slip of butter on it, and just delicately brimming with a generous tease of honey. And then his dreadlocks lapped over his face, constantly being caught in a slight flick of his head back to reveal his eyes. The clearest brown eyes I ever saw. They captured so much sun, the colour of varnished pinewood.

Maybe I'm making him seem a bit of a…well he was. He really was. I look ordinary, never attracting any real attention. My only redeeming grace was a crop of very thick curly hair. But plain as I was, he looked back at me. In a rushing Braamfontein road, gushing at its seams with bodies just wanting to get home, he caught my eye.

"Brrrrea, Hillbrow, Yeovilla, Yovilla, Yovilla, Yovilla"

He caught my eye.

I didn't grow up here. My parents were exiled in America. They never talked much about South Africa, maybe not with me anyway. It was a sad disillusion on their part that South Africa might never be our home again and so maybe they were trying to spare me an infertile nostalgia. There would be a tinge in their shoulders when I asked them to tell me about home and so when I was old enough to stop, I just stopped asking.

But sometimes I would sneak behind the sofa, peering my ears to catch the conversations when Nangula, my Meme's friend, came over. It was actually the funniest thing, Meme would announce: "Nangula is coming over for coffee", but they would mix bitter lemonade and gin. Nangula was the most exciting friend my Meme had. She was from Namibia and went home often and that's how she had things to tell. She was always so animated, her delighted body heaving big in excitement, and always spilling a bit of drink onto her lap.

When Meme asked about home, Nangula would pace her time and my Meme and Tata would lower their shoulders and stop breathing altogether to listen. She told them about the stirring in the townships, of shit waiting to happen and be written about, of clenched fists refusing to surrender, of voices defiant to sing, of children refusing to bow out.

Tata would take in enough, start tensely tightening and un-tightening his fist and then he would leave the room. Meme and Nangula would wait to hear the front door close behind him, then they would pour themselves another drink and talk about whom, and why they were

255

caught doing what they were doing in the shebeen and always about what somebody named Themba was all about.

At the end of their afternoons, so flavoured with their spicy laughter swirling around the room, my Meme would wake me up so as to say goodbye to Nangula. Then Meme would sit me on her lap playing with my hair, curling and uncurling it around her fingers, before she had to go and make supper.

My Meme didn't live to see 1990. I regret that she died with that piercing disillusionment that South Africa would never be free. She died with Nangula in a car accident on their way up to Washington. A warm day in November, the phone rang and was quickly picked up. The music was turned down low. Then my Tata's footsteps climbed up the stairs. He came into my room and sat on little chair, his fingers playing with a lock of my hair. His eyes were far away, and a dark unsettling aura shadowed over his frame.

"I think that there was a bright light in their eyes," I remember he said. "And so they couldn't have seen the other car coming. But maybe Nangula pulled off too fast, thinking the other driver would have stopped when the light was amber.

"Tata?" I had asked him, searching for some comfort in his words.

"Your mother is in a coma." He replied instead, his voice already pronouncing the finality of my Meme's life.

We didn't talk about it all the way to the hospital. Tata crushed my little hand in his palm as we walked in. There was understanding in the meeting of stares from other strangers. We passed a man in the corridor, dragging his fingers along the wall. He stopped to look at us.

"She doesn't live here anymore. She doesn't live here anymore." First he whispered and then he started to shout.

"She doesn't live here anymore! She doesn't live here anymore! You won't find her! She doesn't live here anymore!" A nurse with the quickest pace came up from behind and dragged him away.

"Not here! Not here!" He continued to chant, as we steadily walked on. "She doesn't live here anymore."

The doctor came up to meet us. Tata placed me on a big chair and moved to speak to him. I kept trying to make my feet reach the floor. It was grey and grimy. The doctor was nodding his head. My father nodded his head as well. The doctor placed a hand on his shoulder. My father's face turned grey like the floor.

"You should probably go in now," the doctor said.

My father turned to look at me. I managed a little smile for him. The doctor's beeper rang and he turned it off quickly.

"I have to go. I'm sorry." He said and his voice trailed off behind him.

My father came to sit down next to me, his hands clumsily trying to button the top of my jacket.

"Stay right here." He said with a strong smile and walked into the room.

I sat there, hoping that my feet could stretch and stretch and touch the floor but I was afraid to fall off. The nurse walked up to me; knelt down and gave me a little pat on my head, and walked into the room. My father came out, his shoes squeaking off the linoleum floor. He took my hand and led me away. The panic that my mother wasn't coming with us began to overwhelm me.

"Meme!" I cried. "Meme!"

My father crushed my little hand tighter.

"Meme!" I cried, but my father pressed on, my cries bouncing off the walls. Tears began to fall to the grimy floor, choking my plea. The man from the corridor earlier came out of his room. He looked at me and placed a finger on his lips.

"Ssh," He whispered "She doesn't live her anymore. She doesn't live here anymore." I kept quiet, seduced by his words and mesmerised by a sinking lump settling in my stomach. I dragged my fingers along the wall, hoping to ignite something, some cry that would bring my mother back.

* * *

"Berea, Hillbrow, Yeoville, Yeoville, Yeoville, Yeoville"

The taxi marshal, colourfully dressed in a Swazi blanket, was motioning rapidly like a fish caught out of water, for Jimmy and I to climb into the taxi.

"Yeoville?" the taxi marshal asked us. And in that space of silence while the taxi marshal was waiting for a response, Jimmy said hello to me, his face and his voice standing out like a flower caught among weeds.

"Hello," I replied.

A warm, comforting silence grew between us, like warm chocolate chip cookies baking in the oven. I was searching for the right laugh with

him. Not the right words but the right laugh, a soft giggle, a touch of a
whispered indulgence or even a smile. A smile I craved.

"*Ag, Abakhulume. Izi-romance ama-Bold & the Beautiful e ma taxini!
Voetsek!*" The taxi marshal expressed his annoyance with us. "The whole
Bold and the Beautiful eTaxi rank!" Everyone laughed at our expense.

"*Kodwa ama-taxi a Yeoville a Shesha! Hambani!*" The taxi marshal
then scuffed us out of the way to usher more people in.

"It's not really as hot as it should be," Jimmy said to me. "We could
be sweating harder than this." He said flicking back his dreadlocks from
his face. Believe them when they tell you that Jimmy was a charmer.

"It is very hot," I replied.

"I like your accent." He moved closer to me. "American?"

"South African." I shook my head, but it was too late to take back the
stupid explanation.

"*Kutheni uthetha ngathi uvaleke impumlo?*"

"Sorry?"

"Then why the accent?"

"Exile." Like that in itself explained everything.

"*Hillbrow! Berea! Mountainview! Yeovilla! Yeovilla!*" The taxi
marshal started up again. The taxi we ignored was pulling off, fighting
and spluttering for its last breath on these roads.

"I'm having a small thing at my place tonight," I said to him. Dark-
skinned people don't blush, but I felt a flush on my face. "It's also a
party for a friend of mine, who's published himself a short story."

He looked behind me caught by something more interesting.

"Are you okay?" I asked and his rudeness dawned upon him. I tried
to follow his eyes, but he looked back at me before I could discover what
it was that had lured his attention.

"Fine," he said, and scratched behind his ear.

I wanted so badly for the moment to gather and lift me off that
street. I wanted to fall in love with him, the realisation that I had been
painfully unaware that I was looking for 'it' ached in me. I hadn't felt so
needing, so urgent for attention since my Memes' funeral. Our lounge
brimming with strangers' legs draped in black stockings and grey
trousers, strangely there to comfort us. I remember the room smelt like
old flowers that had been left in the sun for too long, and had started to
burn and wither.

"What time?" Jimmy was asking me.

The long legs draped in black stockings and grey pants cleared away and my father's arms were reaching out for me. We sat on the chair where Meme would sit and play with my hair. But my father's hands were nervously straightening my dress. Drawing me close, he whispered,

"Your mother loved the break of dawn when we lived in Meadowlands. She said the dust lifted off our matchbox houses as if our prayers from the night were being elevated up to God's ears. She loved listening to the morning, loved listening to you sleeping." Tata started to play with my hair like Meme used to. "You look like her. Now we'll have to find somewhere where they can sort out your hair." I look like my Meme.

"What time?" Jimmy was asking me.

"People start coming around seven." I replied.

"Yeoville! Yeoville! Yeoville! Berea! Berea! Hillbrow!" the taxi marshal started again and this time we climbed in, joining the taxi for what really should have been its final journey on these old roads.

* * *

That evening he showed up admirably late of course, swaggering in through my front door. He had on his suede hat, tipped. It was an old brown thing he used to cover over his dreads; in fact, the only thing really worthy on it was a little red feather that caught my eye like a robin at a dull gathering. He was smiling, in a myriad of tipsy laughter and tall complaints oozing from people's mouths, he was standing at the door smiling. He caught sight of me in the kitchen where I was barely nursing a glass of wine and, without engaging in any other stare nor entertaining anybody else's smile but mine, he swaggered over to me.

"You came," I said.

"I had nothing else to do." A sour combination of wine and pretzels started running wild in my stomach as a smile spread to both our lips. He took my glass of wine from me and slipped his lips around it. I don't think I've told about his lips, he had juicy fuck-me lips. Juicy fuck-me lips in the morning.

"Overmeer," he said. Returning the glass to me.

I laughed and replied, "It is a party after all." Like he knew anything about good wine.

We moved to the balcony, trying for some intimacy. The night sky was so lit up, Ponte soliciting her bright wares, blazing the night sky crimson red and occasionally flashing across our faces. The Metro police

259

had begun patrolling the area, so the pimps had warned their girls to stay out of sight. When lights from fat luxury cars glossed across the street, all the girls hiding in the shadows were lit up like diamonds, only to disappear. Encroaching sirens bellowing out from the direction of Hillbrow would make the girls retreat even deeper into the crevices like little shy things. If one were high enough, you would think they were falling stars.

Below on the street, Laijah, the last Rastafarian in Yeoville who didn't live in the Rasta village, was engaged in an intelligent conversation with a stop sign.

"Them be closing down Tandoors," he shouted loudly for all in the street to hear. "Them try to take I too into the prison. Them Babylon! Me se me cyan believe it. Him! I se, gimme the strength of the conquering Lion! Comma take me into the prison?" He continued struggling with top of his pants. "Them tell me I cyan light the holy herb no more! They say illegal. I roll up the fattest spliff, and I stand." He held up his chin and placed his arms on his waist, but the last spliff made him sway a bit. "I lit it. Burn down Babylon! More faya unto Babylon, I cry." Laijah finally got his unzipping right and moved on to piss on his companion.

"Mo faya Brother!" Jimmy shouted at him. Laijah turned around, and flashed us a brilliant smile.

"Burn down Babylon!" the Rastafarian retorted, zipping his pants up and with a final salute of a clenched fist over his heart, he left his comrade behind; bellowing out snitches of 'Redemption Song' into the darkness.

"You know Laijah?" I asked Jimmy.

"Only from the night…"

"…when Tandoors closed down."

"You were there?" he asked me pleasantly surprised. "I would have seen you."

"Probably not. I didn't really stay long. I wasn't in the mood." I took a deep breath. "Actually it was the same week that a friend of mine, Ntombi, passed away. I was annoyed that the only thing people were going on about was the fact that she died from…"

"Oh," Jimmy said quickly, cutting me off. "Do you smoke?"

Jimmy prepared a spliff from his little kit. Very few people I knew had such an impressive kit for their herb. He was really gifted. It wasn't even like rolling it up; it was like he was muffing the *Rizla*, teasing it with his tongue. We got very high, caught up in the ringing of laughter around us. Only when the long sunlight peering above the rooftop caught our tired bodies in the act, then did we come into the full realisation of how precious that time had been. And Jimmy didn't just smell like musk, he smelt like a fuck and a smoke afterwards.

There was really no thought involved. No intricate plan or rehearsal in the mind. We kissed. It was so natural, our first kiss, the first sinking of us into each other, hoping that we didn't taste of sour breath after a long breath. That was when we were our best, when we kissed. His lips on mine, my fingers curling into his locks, his hand reaching for my neck, my hip drawing him closer to me and the tiredness of our eyes easing off.

Did we? Yes, and had a smoke afterwards.

Looking back, you never know about some things. Like the prostitutes in the street only until they reveal themselves or are caught out like rabbits, you won't know they are there but you can feel a stirring of spirits. It was the way Jimmy went to sleep. He was uneasy, clutching onto me too tightly, and in the morning he would almost refuse to open his eyes. He would lie on the bed for some time, just listening to his own breathing. Checking that it was all there, and when he was sure, then he opened his eyes.

* * *

In the days, and the weeks that had spun into some months, Jimmy and I had grown closer and a love that could only spin itself into a web around one's heart settled, and our time together was very loving and not needing. We were lying in bed; the midday sun coming from the bedroom window was too comforting to give us any motivation to get up. Outside, Yeoville carried on, the sounds and smells very much alive and intrinsically organic.

"Jimmy, do you love me?" I asked him. I had never asked how he felt about me; I just assumed that what we had came so easy, it had to have been good. He didn't respond to my question. Outside in the street below, a car pulled off, Oliver Mtukudzi blared from its speakers. My neighbour upstairs started drumming, warming up slowly before he fell into his usual seamless rhythm.

"Jimmy? Do you love me?" I asked again. He nodded and looked away.

I remember at my Meme's funeral instead of pleasant coffee being poured, my dad poured everyone a drink of bitter lemonade and gin. Nangula would have appreciated the gesture but my Meme would have blushed a little. Nonetheless, everybody toasted with remorse. Sympathy cards adorned with flowers, crosses and beaming lights from clouds above were stacked high on the table, once read they all sounded the same. I crept to my little corner behind the sofa, hoping not to be caught out so that someone could relish the opportunity to remark: "She looks like her, doesn't she? Poor man." I wanted to listen, hoping that someone would sound like my Meme, laugh like my Meme when she was with Nangula, and come pull me out from behind the sofa like my Meme used to and play with my hair. Instead, the legs clad in black stockings and grey pants moved on to politely comment on how tasteful the décor was. "She had wonderful taste, you know," they said and sounded nothing like my Meme. After what seemed like a long breath being expelled, my father said something. He picked up the framed photo of Meme that had been looming over the room from the fireplace. He stroked her face very gently. I closed my young eyes imagining my Meme's face in the frame, gently shifting the curve of her face to allow my father's hand to stroke her.

"It's a pity," he said and the room turned to look at him. "We ran away from the raids, the police interrogations, and the smell of dying always hanging above us like ripe figs. We came here running, minds clogged with dreams of liberation. Instead, after all that, before we could even catch our breaths…" Tata couldn't finish his words; he placed the picture down and walked away from it. Everyone nodded and looked away.

"I never told you about my mother did I Jimmy?"

"*Hayi*," he said shaking his head.

"She died when I was small. It was a car accident." Jimmy started to tap his hands against the mattress to the drumming upstairs. I could tell that his mind was elsewhere again. "It doesn't really matter anyway. I don't remember much of it," I said.

Jimmy got up from the bed and walked to the window. When he opened it the sounds from the outside rushed in. Our bedroom faced out to the street directly, the outside could never be ignored or shut out. I could hear Sister Tsoana laughing all the way from her phone stand. I got out of bed to join Jimmy at the window. His fingers were tapping on the glass.

I peered over his frame to see what he was looking at. Tsoana was chatting with a female customer. Her arms were crossed over her chest, nodding her head vigorously. I could tell she was biting into the juiciest news of the day because she would at appropriate junctions swing her finger dangerously above her head. She saw us at the window and waved. Two boys walked up to the stand and she stopped momentarily to punch in some units into the phone for them, and went back to her conversation.

"Jimmy." I came up behind him, stretching my hands around his waist, pulling him closer to me. "Do you love me?" I asked. He turned around, allowing me to stroke his back. He leaned down a little to kiss me. I pulled away and lingered to hold onto my arm.

"I'm going to take a bath," I said, and he smiled and looked back at Tsoana below.

Suddenly a shot rang out, and at first I thought it was a car backfiring, but the queasiness of it piercing through the air made me a little dizzy. Another shot rang out, this one faster than the first sending me down to the floor for shelter. I imagined the bullets, sharply opening their eyes out the dark barrel, searching for the smell of fresh blood.

Jimmy stood at the window. His face locked in an awkward way, almost mesmerised. Holding onto his leg, I crawled up to look. Two boys were running off, one tripped and couldn't recover in time before a bystander lunged on him and held him down. The other boy continued running with the phone under his arm, calling for his friend to catch up. Tsoana had fallen to the floor; a thick crimson tide was gathering under her. I tried to pull Jimmy back down with me, but his eyes were fixed.

Finally after short calculated breaths and a soft whimper pressing through my lips, Jimmy crouched down, taking me in his arms. The sirens came closer and closer and more urgent and the screaming grew louder and more hopeless. A voice was calling Tsoana's name but it too dissipated into echoes. My mind acquired the stillness of clarity and silence encroached upon the moment. Jimmy cradled me, nuzzling his face into my hair. My shivering eased. A warm tear crept onto my scalp and rolled down my forehead onto my arm, first one and then another.

"Jimmy?" I tried to look up at him but he was holding me too close.

"Ssh." In the stillness, I heard footsteps running, then suddenly stopping and pacing backward very slowly crunching on the pavement.

"Tsoana?" I desperately wanted to look at him.

"I know." His voice was soft; the only betrayal was the stillness of his breath.

"She's dead?"

"Don't think about it now." He started to rock his body, holding me close, I comforted myself with the sound of his heart perfectly thumping against my ear.

"Do you love me?" I asked and another tear rolled down my forehead, this time I caught it on the tip of my lip.

"*Mamela*," and he swallowed hard. "*Ndine*-AIDS."

Someone was screaming.

The sirens were right outside our window now.
Tires pulling off
Smoke frozen in the air.

He stopped drumming upstairs.
The floor stopped pulsating
And grew cold.

Jimmy took a deep breath.
Like a locked door without a key
He grew cold.

Your mother is in a coma.
My father's voice was saying
So cold
Another tear fell on my face
It grew cold.

The sirens stopped and grew cold.
Tsoana dead in the street
She grew cold.

Jimmy let go of me.
I was a child, and the first drop of menstrual blood
Falling on my Saturday panties at my Meme's funeral
And my legs grew cold.

It all stopped.

Like my mother laughing with Nangula in the car, they stopped
And flew through window.
And they grew cold.

My mother wasn't sitting in the sun, playing with the curls in my
hair.
The room grew cold
Stopped
Cold
And Jimmy had AIDS.

*

Eddie Vulani Maluleke is a young black female writer. She began
as an actress, touring South Africa, London and the Czech Republic
with the play *Umm...Somebody Say Something* and *Venus Hottentot: The
story of Saartjie Baartman* running as double bill performances. She then
went on to write her first play *enuf...when I neither black nor female*
which premiered at the Grahamstown National Festival of the Arts for
Student Drama. She went on to write *Unswept Room* and *Sun City* in
2003. While being involved in the Spoken Word scene in Johannesburg,
Eddie began writing short stories, her first short story *Melodi* won
second place at the Era/Anglo Platinum short story competition in 2003.

Currently she is studying towards a Master of Arts in African
Literature at the University of the Witwatersrand, Johannesburg.

Khaki and Scarlet

Peter Merrington

The Cape Town *sangoma* or traditional healer Malibongwe Ngingingini was far from home and deep in thought. He sat beneath a *kameeldoring* bush at the side of a sandy track, miles from the nearest town. This, moreover, was the tiny settlement of Pella, some ninety kilometres from Pofadder, in the most isolated, most arid region within the broad borders of the Republic.

"Which could it be," he thought to himself, "the valve timing, or the ignition?" He hoped it was the camshaft chain, which he could set quite easily himself. He fiddled at his battered off-road Yamaha, now coated in the fine red dust of the Northern Cape where this remote province followed on the fringes of the trackless Kalahari Desert.

Malibongwe Ngingingini was exhausted – and not only from the heat and dust. He was commissioned by the great-grandchildren of a Canadian soldier, who had died a century ago in the Anglo-Boer War, to find by means of divination the forlorn remains of their forefather. For hours he had struggled with the contending energies of a variety of ancestors – his own, those of local Nama, San and Griquas, of long-gone Takhaar Boers, of Imperial Yeomanry, of Major McBurnie of Strathcona's Horse, late of Montreal in Lower Canada. "*Indaba*, my fathers", he weakly muttered. Who would have thought this desert so thickly populated with the costive Unseen?

He looked up as a rhythmic squeak and jingle came to his ears. It was his apprentice, his *handlanger*, Anna Persens, known to her friends as the Subaltern. Riding in a cart with fat bald tyres, holding the reins to an ambling donkey, she jerked slowly closer to his bush.

"Well done," he called. "Now we can cart the bike to Pofadder for repairs."

Anna, never one for words, flashed her dark eyes at the sauntering donkey's rear. A ten-mile journey had taken nearly an hour. She wondered what she was doing in this sandy waste. Her chariot lurched off the track, dragging her through the thorny branches of Malibongwe's tree as the donkey made for the sparse green leaves. She drank briefly from a flat, round water bottle and tossed this vessel to her master.

"*Hau!*" cried the *sangoma*, "where did you find this then, Anna?"

"A Bushman gave it me."

"Where did you meet this Bushman, Anna? Look at the back of the bottle – what do you see?" The steel surface was engraved with a regimental crest, and the initials A.E.M – Albert Edward McBurnie, of course, the late Major McBurnie of Strathcona's Horse! "And where did you fill it?"

"The Bushman filled it from a Baobab tree."

"Take me to your Bushman if you please."

So they heaved the Yamaha up into the little cart, and squatting awkwardly on the side Anna teased the donkey into motion. Malibongwe paced beside her through the sand, fingering the weathered steel of the army-issue water bottle. His brow was furrowed. It seemed too easy, this chance find, this artefact whipped from nowhere, evidence from beyond…

* * *

A gravel road runs north from Pofadder to the old mission settlement of Pella. In the distance are the low-slung mountains which form the valley of the Orange River, the mighty Gariep. Some way up the road stands an isolated four-square, whitewashed, tin-roofed house. The interior is cool, bare but musty, an old man's home. At the back, among stunted lemon trees, *Oom* Serfaas Vermaak appears to be executing a slow and curious ritual dance. With his battered broad-brimmed felt hat clamped as ever to that bony head, he swings and stands on one leg, then the other, and waves his thin arms in delicate spirals. Two urchins in torn shorts peer through the plumbago hedge, eyes wide, stifling their laughter at the vision of *Oom* Serfaas, '*Kwaai* Serfaas', vendor of vile liquor to the region's poor, miser, dedicated man of meanness and misery, now gyrating slowly beside his water tank, between the scrubby trees. Only last week *Oom* Serfaas was taken in by the new sergeant of police at Pofadder for practices best described as from the Old South Africa. Change came hard for him, if it came at all. Not a profound racist, he was just a *bliksem*, one who liked to take it out on others, specially the meek and humble, which meant the working folk of Pella district, the lightly-built and light-voiced people known as Nama. What then is this tough old serpent doing?

* * *

As dusk tinged the sandstone with a golden glow and the dusty roads became kaleidoscopes of setting light, a donkey cart came into view, two weary comrades resting on the shafts, a battered old motorcycle in the back. Urchins and dogs raced wildly with the energy at sunset only dogs and children muster, laughing and crying out, keeping easy pace with the shambling outfit.

"*Haai! Kyk die motorfiets!* A motorcycle! Vroom, vroom!" the urchins laughed and cheered. "*Kyk die ou toppie!* Just look at the old guy! He's all covered in dust. They've been in the *veld*. Yay, yippee, faster little donkey faster!"

Anna tried to pretend they did not exist. She brushed dust off her Out of Africa oatmeal pants, and concentrated on the thought of a long cold Campari. Malibongwe's temper was less easy. He stood up on the shafts and shouted at the children.

"*Hambane bafana. Kry julle weg, julle snot penkoppe!*" Bugger off you little pests!

They responded with hoots of laughter and wilder leaps and gestures.

Then came a vision that made Anna stiffen and take note. Down the road towards them, drawing the little children to her like *muggies* to a glass of lemonade, a young woman with such perfect poise, such gentle sway of hips, such ease matched with purpose, such red hair and peachy skin as to make Anna bite her lip, in a burgundy crush skirt and close-cropped top, with a voice at once low and sweet, Kitty her name, Kitty Dippenaar, tai chi teacher at a neo-hippie ashram which had risen on a plot outside the town. It was Kitty Dippenaar for whom old Serfaas was gyrating in his *agterwerf*. It was Kitty whom the children clustered round, and left off taunting the morose donkey. It was this newcomer for whom Malibongwe's long face at last softened and broke into a spontaneous smile.

Anna shook the reins and twitched the donkey's rear with a switch of quince. They had yet to find their Bushman. No stopping to bandy with that over-decorated gypsy. Malibongwe'd better behave himself.

On and on they trundled, past the scrappy edgings of the town, on in the growing dusk, heading for a *kopje* in the middle distance from which a clutch of ancient baobabs rose up like tousled heads on thin bodies black against the last glow of light.

A small man in khaki shorts and unbuttoned khaki shirt stood up among the tumbled stones. "That's him", said Anna. "Hello Dawid,

268

here we are again. Can you tell this man – Malibongwe he is called – where you found the water bottle?"

The small man cleared his throat. He had tight close hair, a light and almost oriental face, high cheekbones, and many wrinkles from many years of sun and dust.

"*Haai*," he said, "not an easy thing to say."

Malibongwe sighed, stifling the urge to beat someone up, an urge not uncommon in the Northern Cape and largely due to vexations brought on by heat, thirst, and distance. He took out his wallet and waved a fifty rand note.

"*Haai*, sir, please. I do not mean that." The Bushman bristled with dignity. "I will explain."

And so it turned out that the stainless steel water bottle was borrowed goods. Sidelong looks, gestures of innocence, wild conjecture onto half a dozen others, Leah, Maria, Kleinboy, Jantjie, Dwergie, Siena.

"No my *baas*, I give it to the lady (gesturing at Anna) from my heart (two-handed gesture at the thin, bony breast). She is tired, she is *maar moeg*, she is *dors*. Jesus say give it to the lady. I, Dawie Disselboom, I give her water. Living water, says the *Jurre*."

"You did well", Malibongwe interrupts. "We aren't here to pick fights or to blame anybody. I don't care if the water bottle was stolen, I don't care if it descended from Mars. All I want is to find out where it came from. And it was good of you to rehydrate my apprentice. *Nkos'*. I thank you."

So Dawie Disselboom led the weary pair another mile or two, and pointed out a four-square old house which stood pale in the darkness, alone in the middle distance. Remote bright stars flared silver in the moonless night. On such a night as this, a century ago, the Canadians of Strathcona's Horse engaged in hot battle, bullets and bloodshed with a Boer commando. Vibrations ran through Malibongwe's ears. He heard snatches of shouting, the crack and bark of Lee Metford and of Mauser. He shook his head and again it was the vexing donkey with its long ears silhouetted against the starlight, Anna muttering about cramp, and their wizened guide who seemed reluctant to proceed farther down the track. Malibongwe gazed at the pale square house. The leaves of stunted lemon trees glimmered in the yard behind.

"*Kwaai* Serfaas", whispered Dawie Disselboom, and he melted away into the night.

* * *

Meanwhile Kitty Dippenaar prepares the Pella mission hall for her weekly classes in Tai Chi and Eurythmics. Chairs are stacked against the walls. On a schoolroom table she lays out bundles of sage and wild lavender, and lights a stick of incense.

"From the diaphragm", she orders in her low sweet voice, "In, and hold. Count of eight. And release. Can you feel your diaphragm, Chantelle?"

"Yes, Miss Kitty."

"Slowly, slowly, Cornelius van Deventer. Here, let me hold." The postmaster of Pella blushes as Kitty puts her arms about his thick midriff and presses on the solar plexus. Chantelle van Deventer's face reddens. If only Kitty were less fetching.

Kwaai Serfaas practices diligently in the corner, unaware that he has visitors at home. The slightest word from Kitty, of approval or correction, is more therapy to his withered heart than all the *reiki* or past-life regression within her esoteric repertoire.

"Come, Serfaas, you're doing well. Stretch into the space around you. Gently, Serfaas, gently." Serfaas makes swimming movements in a bath of unaccustomed love.

* * *

Half a mile away, Malibongwe and Anna have their noses pressed against the panes of *Kwaai* Serfaas's living room.

"I know it's here," says the sangoma. "*Isekhaya apha.*"

"What?"

"I'm not sure, but it's hot. We're on track. Major McBurnie lies nearby, I feel it. We've got to get inside."

Anna drew a skeleton key from her shoulder bag and fiddled with the lock.

The floor is part bare wood, part linoleum, worn and faded. In the moonlight emerge sad mementos, the lineaments of frozen desire. A high dado with three items hanging: a faded framed photograph of a stern couple in church-going black; an unremarkable oil painting of a mountain pass; a certificate from the Agricultural Society. A set of souvenir teaspoons with municipal crests on them. Oudtshoorn and Lambert's Bay. The Voortrekker Monument and the *Eeufees* festival. Beside the passage door is a brass-bound elephant's foot, and a tired blesbok trophy is screwed to the wall. A delicate shudder passes through

Anna's modish frame. An oak sideboard, a decanter, and a single glass under a clean cloth – marks of modest bachelorhood. Malibongwe steps quickly to the corner where an antique bandolier and a heavy Mauser rifle lie on a yellowwood kist. He raises them in his hands, and under the silvery moonlight he drinks the musty air.

"Ah. Aha! Vibrations, Anna, vibrations. Terrible, oh terrible, the smoke, the blood, the singing sword. McBurnie, Major McBurnie, Major, are you there?"

Deep silence, save for the ticking of the clock; and then:

A-a-a-arooah! York-york-york, a-waaah!

The donkey is on heat. It bellows. It repeats this every minute for a quarter of an hour. During which time Serfaas returns from Tai Chi practice, suffused with delight, for Kitty Dippenaar is coming in for a glass of Hanepoot Muscadel.

"*Wat de dooie donder!*" shouts *Kwaai* Serfaas. "Whose donkey is that *pronking* in my yard? So help me, I'll get the *bliksems*, they'll rue the day! Where's my gun?"

Kitty shook her head. "Dear Serfaas, so much anger."

"Aa-aa-aa-arooah!"

"*Wat die donder maak julle mense in my werf? In my huis, sowaar!*"

"*Hau!* Anna, this is pandemonium. Hey, wait for me!" But Anna was halfway through the plumbago hedge, her long legs waving an inverted farewell to her master as he ran for the kitchen door.

"Arooh! York-york-york."

"Stand still everyone! And shut up!" It was Kitty's voice. "You too, you silly donkey." She wore about her an unexpected mantle of authority, and Serfaas and Malibongwe fell silent, shamefaced, unused to such exquisite power. Anna slithered from the hedge and joined the group. Over their shoulders the donkey's ears loomed in a large and silvery 'V', his long teeth bared for yet another convulsive but stifled cry.

The anger which spills from Serfaas and scourges the lives of those who live in his neighbourhood runs deep in this withered old man. Like biltong his goodness is all stored up and dried out. It will only be tasted when something softens. His goodness dried out some fifty years ago, or maybe even fifty-five, when his father took a *strop* to him; when his mother became like a washing-up *lappie* which meant either buried in grim tasks, silent in the cement washbasin, or squeezed out on the line to dry, all the charm and colour blanched out, or stingingly used as a means of slapping him on his ears or about his bare legs.

271

Serfaas had learnt to store away his goodness where it might never be seen – except for the advent of Marietjie, when he was seventeen and she was sixteen, and how Marietjie and he would sit for an hour together at sunset when the light was so golden and reflected in her hair, and would walk together in the *veld* to call the sheep, and would pick loquats; and how Marietjie's father who was the dominee in Pofadder said he would not have his daughter spending time with the son of such 'backveld' people, and how he never got the courage to speak the words of his love, and this is now a poisoned well of stagnant waters.

All this Malibongwe discerns, for new vibrations have emerged from dado and mantelpiece, from kist and well-worn sofa, lapping up against him when the deadlocked group re-enter the house. Major McBurnie is forgotten. Kitty too feels something. Against her natural insouciance, so does Anna. She deftly mixes a powder from a twist of paper (something she thought she might try out on Malibongwe) into the tumbler of Hanepoot Muscadel.

This has an unexpected effect on *Kwaai* Serfaas. He wipes his chin and glares at Malibongwe and Anna. He is going to deliver them a thousand words of wrath, but he swallows, chokes, turns red and gasps:

"Marietjie! *Sowaar, o, sowaar!* I buried her in the yard, not her I mean, I mean her ring. She sent me it when she left for the Cape. *Ag, o sowaar, o die vrywende geknaag van my gewete! O vergewe my O God!* Oh me, oh my, the pain."

* * *

Malibongwe has to dig deep. The sand of the yard slips back until he reaches the darker subsoil. Serfaas has to dig deep. Kitty sits beside him on the sofa, holding him round the shoulders. He sobs. He shudders. He looks small and frail, a forlorn remnant among the mementos of a vanished universe. Anna digs deep to keep a measure of sympathy with both Kitty and Serfaas, and a measure of patience with Malibongwe. She needs her sleep. She helps herself from the decanter and flips through old issues of *Farmers' Weekly*.

Finally it comes together. "Marietjie!" cries Serfaas, half-rising from the sofa, the light of conversion suffusing his lined face, "*Ek het jou lief!*"

"Eureka!" cries Malibongwe as he struggles from his pit flourishing a rotted khaki helmet, a tarnished silver ring in his other hand. "Yes!"

cries Anna Persens, emerging from her *Farmer's Weekly*. "Here's the man for me: 'wealthy well-groomed farmer seeks girlfriend for pleasure cruise. Send recent photo, SAE'."

Tumblers and tin mugs are fetched and toasts are drunk in Hanepoot Muscadel. Toasts to love, to courage, to Major McBurnie and Marietjie, and Serfaas's father and his mother. To the crippled shades, to ease them, to set them dancing in the silver moonlight all along the plumbago hedge and among the lemon trees where tiny buds of blossom refract the silver glow. Tai chi for the living and the dead. There is the sound of hoofbeats down the dusty road, but not the beat of cavalry or commando. It is the hoofbeat of a sweet, fat donkey mare, panting from the half-hour gallop in response to those convulsive cries. And from afar, from the *kopje* with its baobabs, sweet singing, light laughter, and the clap of hands to naked dancing feet.

*

Peter Merrington is Associate Professor and Head of the Department of English, University of the Western Cape. He writes in the field of South African and British literary history, and he is working on a series of *sangoma* stories. He plans to establish an Institute of Thaumatography.

Triumph in the Face of Adversity

Kedibone Seku

When my father died, I shed no tears for him, but I cried at my mother's funeral, not because losing her saddened me, but because I felt sorry for her after the empty life she had led. Like us, her children, she was a victim, a victim of the man who saw her as an object to be controlled and used as a punching bag depending on the mood he was in. My mother never fought back. Instead she gave up hope, forgot to live her life, and forgot to live for her own children. This affected us badly, especially my young brother and sister who at the time still needed to be loved and nurtured. I as the older sister had to step in and take control.

As I watched her coffin go down, I mourned for the waste of life. Standing there by her grave brought back a lot of grim memories; memories that I swore would never ever resurface in my life, memories that belonged where they had been for the past twelve years.

I was very young when we moved from my grandmother's place to live in Phambili Squatter Camp. The move was rather abrupt, because my grandmother made my mother's life so unbearable that she could not take it anymore.

My grandmother, MaDlamini was an old-fashioned woman who had grown up in the rural areas of Natal. She believed that the location we lived in did not have a woman who would make a perfect wife for her only son. That is why she was not happy when my father announced that he was not going to look for a bride from her homeland.

"Jabulani, *amantobazana ase goli* do not know anything about respect, culture and most of all they are very lazy," she had said to my father in an attempt to discourage him.

"Mother, this girl and I have a child together; do you expect me to abandon her?" my father had asked her.

"All you have to do is pay *inhlawulo*, for the child. Thulisile can come and live with us while we find you a suitable bride. I can help you raise her. *Awuboni ukuthi lentombazana* is trying to trap you!"

MaDlamini's pleas fell into deaf ears. My parents got married.

When my mother, Thembekile, came to assume her duties as *umakoti*, rules were awaiting her. She had wanted to continue with her

274

studies and become an actress, but she was told to bury the dream and concentrate on being a good wife. In addition to the rules, she was not supposed to wear trousers or mini skirts. Nobody was supposed to see her legs. She had to keep her head covered all the time as a sign of respect. House duties started at five in the morning. She had to sweep the yard, cook, wash and iron the clothes of the entire household.

Although my mother did as she was told, MaDlamini was never satisfied; she always found something to complain about. She never let my mother have time to herself.

"*Makoti, makoti!*" was all we could hear her say morning, noon and night.

"*Yebo Ma,*" my mother would say, annoyed and very irritated.

"*Letha amanzi,*" she would say even when she was standing next to the tap.

My mother made a mistake of trying to negotiate with MaDlamini about giving her time to herself.

"I told Jabulani that he was making a mistake marrying you, you are useless to have you around. Our *lobola* has really gone down the drain," MaDlamini said.

My mother was very angry and she felt insulted; she demanded that my father do something right away.

"I will try to speak to her," he had said but she did not believe him.

It seemed the only solution was for us to leave MaDlamini and find our own home. Our stay at Phambili Squatter Camp was a temporary measure until my father could afford to buy us a proper home. That never happened. In fact things got worse; he lost his job not long after we had moved to Phambili.

Phambili Squatter Camp, like most camps, consisted of tin shanties, built out of flammable materials such as chipboard. The shacks were built so close together that it would have been impossible to prevent a fire from spreading to another shack. Pools of water blocked the narrow passages that divided the shacks. The toilets provided were used by a number of people, and because they were placed at the end of the block it was not safe to use them during the night. There was no electricity and no garbage removal. The smell in the air was that of stale urine and excrement, as most people never got as far as the toilets during the night. It was impossible to get up in the morning and breathe fresh air.

There were two communal taps and they were always in use. The schools were very far and the route was not safe for young children. Yet this was home to a lot of people and to some a beautiful place.

The place was never without incidents. One night the sound of people screaming woke us up. When we went out, some of the shacks not very far from us were on fire. We ran to safety. The following day we learnt that my friend Ntombi had been burned in the shack. Although she had survived, it was said that she had sustained severe injuries; even plastic surgery could not help. I never went to see her, I was too afraid. Days later I heard that some family had offered to take care of her. I wished the opportunity had come to her when she could enjoy it. Somehow I envied her, I wished it was our shack that had burnt down; probably we would have had a chance to live a better life as well.

I also witnessed a man being stoned to death after he had raped a little girl. It turned out that the man had been HIV positive and somehow believed that sleeping with a virgin would cure his status. A belief that cost him his life. There were many strange things happening in that place but not as strange as witnessing my father slowly evolving into something despicable and my mother turn into a hopeless soul.

My father's search for a job yielded no results and his frustrations made him aggressive towards us. Every day my mother would try to comfort and console him, but that never worked.

"Jabulani, please be patient. Something will come up," she would say.

"Thembekile, when?" he would say.

I knew that our lives would never be the same again the day he came home late and very drunk. My mother had waited for him but when he didn't arrive on time she decided to lock up. He was very angry when he found that the door was locked. He banged on the door with his fists.

"Open, open up!" he said at the top of his voice.

"There is no need to wake up the neighbours," my mother said opening the door.

"I am still the man in my house, the fact that I am not working does not give you the right to tell me what to do," he said, angry and bitter.

"But Jabulani…" she said, but before she could not finish what she had to say he slapped her across the face. She went sprawling to the floor. He continued to beat up her even though he could see that she was defenseless. No amount of screaming from me made him stop. It was the first time he ever laid his hand on her, but it certainly was not the last. That is the day my mother changed. Her beautiful smile was replaced by fear.

When my brother Bongani and sister Zanele were born my father was a complete monster. They were constantly beaten, for no reason. My mother knew better than to try and stop him, because she knew that she would be next on his list. I could not understand why we had to continue to stay with him. My mother's parents were alive and they begged her over and over again to come back home, but she refused. Ultimately we stopped visiting my grandparents because my mother said she could not stand the way they looked at her. She said the sadness in their eyes tormented her.

Food was hard to come by and we had to depend on the generosity of our neighbours. My friend Nthabiseng always brought enough lunch to school for the both of us, but I never ate because I saved it for my brother and sister. We were trapped in poverty and constant abuse and we could not do anything about it – I blamed my mother. Hopelessness and helplessness became the order of the day. My performance at school was dropping dramatically.

One day, one of my teachers called me to the staff room. He was very concerned and angry with me because I had failed my class test again and he knew that I had lots of potential to do better.

"Thulisile, you really can't continue like this! What is going on? Have you forgotten that getting an education is the most important thing in life?" the teacher said

"Sir I...I..." I said sheepishly.

"Don't give me that, I want to know what is going on and I want to know now," he said

So I told him, I expected him to feel sorry for me and offer his help but instead he said:

"You cannot allow your home situation to control you. You have to control your situation." I was very angry. How could he say that? It was so easy for him to judge me when he lived in a nice house, drove a nice car and didn't worry about where his next meal was going to come from.

"But how?" was all I could manage to say to him.

"Focus," he said, and that drove me up the wall.

"Sir I really think that I should leave now; it is one thing to act concerned but making a mockery of me is more that I am willing to take," I said and walked towards the door.

"Thulisile wait..." he said, but I kept on walking.

The following day I did not go to school, and I told myself that I was never going back. I knew that Mr Nkwane would tell everybody about my situation and the last thing I wanted from them was their pity, because it was not going to feed me, put clothes on my back or even help me in getting my school work on track. Besides the fact that I was poor didn't mean that I didn't have pride.

I had to swallow my pride when my brother and sister came back from school later that day. They were upset to find that the usual bread that they got was not there.

"Thuli I am very hungry," my younger sister Zanele said.

"I know, but don't worry, I will make a plan."

"Where are you going?" my brother Bongani asked as I walked towards the door.

"Don't worry I will be back in a little while," I said reassuringly.

A little while turned to hours as I went from house to house asking people if they didn't want me to do anything for them in exchange of bread. People were not very helpful because they did not want strangers in their homes. The place was crime ridden and nobody knew whether I was really in need of help or whether I just wanted to look at their houses and then alert my criminal friends about what was inside. I finally found help at the far end of the location. The owner of the house, Mme Sadike was an old lady who lived in a very neat house. Everything in the house was in perfect order. I was even afraid to enter the house thinking that I would dirty it. She was very gracious and let me in. She even allowed me to sit on her very expensive couches. I was uncomfortable but she made me feel at ease. She told me who she was and asked for my name.

"Thulisile, but my friends call me Thuli," I said

"That is a very beautiful name. So what should I call you?" she asked.

"Thuli," I said almost whispering.

"Where do you stay?" she asked, and I told her that I was from the nearby squatter camp.

"Are you in school?" she asked.

"Yes, but I did not attend today because I was too embarrassed."

"Embarrassed by what?" I broke down and told her the whole story. She held me in her arms. For the first time I let it all out, the anger, the pain, the frustration, everything.

"There is no need for you to feel that way, many people go through that in life, you just have to make sure that you rise above the odds," she said after I had calmed down.

"That is exactly what my teacher said to me but I really do not know how am I going to be able to do that."

"There are a lot of options; you can either go to a social worker or the police and tell them your story."

"Will they be able to assist me?"

"Of course they will, but it will help if you take your mother along," she said.

When I left her house I had a loaf of bread and a lot of hope.

When I got home I told my mother about either consulting the social workers or the police but she refused and told me that she did not want anybody knowing our business. I was even admonished for talking about our life with a stranger. It was clear that our home life embarrassed her; she thought her silence would remedy it but it made it worse. Although I was very disappointed by my mother's reaction, my determination for a better life was not shaken. I spent the whole night thinking. I knew that I could not allow things to continue the same way, something had to be done and soon. I had to stop being a charity case. The following morning I had a plan. I went to visit my grandparents' house on my mother's side. My grandmother was slightly worried to see me that early in the morning.

"Is everything okay, why aren't you at school? Where is your mom?" That was my grandmother's question before I could sit down.

"Everything is okay and mom is at home. I need a little favour from you," I said, trying to stop her from asking me a lot of questions about our home life. Talking about it would have spoiled my plans completely.

"What do you need my child? You know I will do anything for you," she said.

"Granny I need to borrow some money, I promise I will pay you back, but you can never tell mom," I said.

'You don't have to pay me back. As for your mother she doesn't come here and she has stopped us from having any contact with you, so when will I tell her? So how much do you need?" I could hear a tint of sadness in her voice.

"Thirty rand." I said hesitant.

"What can you possibly do with thirty rand?" she asked, amazed.

"A lot, I am not going to tell you now, but I need you to trust me," I said excitedly.

"I trust you, and I will loan you the money, but I need some assurance that you are not going to do something illegal."

My grandmother was right, there was no way she could just give me the money without asking questions, so I relented and told her. When she gave me the money I could not stop myself from smiling, it was the first time that I had ever held so much money in my hands.

My business of selling sweets to the students was doing really well. I managed to pay my grandmother back. She was very delighted, although she did not want to take the money.

I decided to expand my business at home. That was a bad idea. One day I came back from school, my money was missing and my mother didn't know a thing about it. It became clear where my money had went when my father came home stone drunk. He got very angry when I asked him whether he had seen the money.

"Are you accusing me of stealing?" he said

"I want to know what happened to my money," I said.

"I don't know, perhaps you better start taking care of where you put your money because I won't be questioned by you in my house."

"I want my money," I said choking on my tears. I never forgave him. How could he have shattered my dreams like that? It's hard to say what I felt about my mother at that time; she just sat there and did nothing. Yes my father beat her up, but she could have reported him to the police. Having him locked up would have done us a lot of good. The reasons that kept her in the relationship were beyond me. It couldn't have been love. I could swear I saw hate in her eyes whenever she looked at him; however, she stayed and we suffered.

I was afraid to go back to my grandmother to ask for help. Instead, I went to look for a job at the nearby fish & chips shop. At first the owner, Mr Rathebe, was very reluctant to employ a fifteen-year-old girl, but after I told him my story he agreed. I ended up with a job as a cleaner after school and over the weekends. The job did not pay much, but it was enough to look after Bongani, Zanele and me. My parents also benefited in some ways, but that was only because we stayed in the same house, otherwise they wouldn't have mattered. The other thing that was good was that Mr Rathebe allowed me to take leftovers home. At last we did not have to worry about where food was coming from and for the first time I was able to help some of our neighbours. Mr Nkwane helped me to open up a post bank account, because I could not imagine the possibility of having my money stolen ever again.

My dream of having my own business had not died. After a while I started my business again and things went really well. My father would constantly be scratching in the shack for money but there was none to be found. Desperation got the better of him. He went to Mr Rathebe and told him that I said he could get money from my wage as we had an emergency at home. I did not find out about this until the end of the month.

"Mr Rathebe don't you think you have short-paid me this month?" I asked.

He reminded me that I had sent my father to him.

"Oh, how stupid of me to forget," I said forcing a smile and wishing that I could disappear.

I was very disturbed because it seemed my father was unstoppable. I was sick and tired of fighting a battle where I was the loser all the time. I felt I was stuck in my situation forever. I stopped talking to him. I told my mother what happened and she told me to forget it.

"You really don't want to upset your father," she said, and it was clear that she did not want any discussions about.

"Upset him! What about me? What about how I feel?" My questions were never answered.

There I was, trying to save my family but my efforts were not appreciated. The path ahead seemed very bleak. I hated feeling like a victim. That night I cried but in the morning I had calmed down.

My friend Nthabiseng showed me an advert in the paper during lunch break.

"I don't understand, what has this got to do with me?" I said.

"Do I have to spell it out? You should try out, it will be perfect!"

"I do not think so, besides..." I said and grimaced.

"Besides what?"

"I don't have anything to wear."

"Phone them and make an appointment," she said

"I don't have a telephone number, how will they get to me?"

"Excuses and more excuses, you are getting to be really boring.
The contact number can be anybody's number we will give them my home number and when they phone I will give you the message."

"I don't think that is going to work," I said, but Nthabiseng went ahead and made the appointment.

The local TV station was looking for presenters for their new kids programme and my good friend thought of me. I was called in for an audition, it went well and I got the job. That was a life-changing moment. I was swept from the life of poverty to the glamorous world of television.

* * *

When I managed to find a *proper house* that I wanted to buy in the nearby location my father was not at all impressed. I needed him or my mother sign for me as I was not allowed to purchase property at my age. He told my mother that they were not going to sign anything.

"Just because you are now a hot shot TV star, it does not mean that you can come and tell us what to do," he said.

"Mom, what do you think?" I asked hoping that she would see reason.

As usual she said nothing and I was very frustrated. I threatened to move out and go live with my grandparents on my mother's side. I was told that I could go but Bongani and Zanele were remaining behind. I couldn't stand the thought of leaving them alone so I stayed until I was old enough to sign on my own.

When I finally got the house my father told my mother that they were not going to move in with me. This time I refused to leave without Bongani and Zanele; lucky for me he didn't give me much of a fight.

"Mom, can't you see this is our chance to live in a house that we've always dreamt of?" I said desperately.

"I have to stay with your father," she said

"But, why?"

"He is my husband," she said. I guess there was nothing I could really do or say; she had after all pledged to stick with him for better for worse.

At the time of his death my father and I treated each other like strangers. I would go home to give them groceries but my mother was the only person that I spoke to. Every time I would beg and plead with her to come with me and she refused. The only time she came to stay with us was after his funeral. She was very sick and fragile; no amount of care and doctor's visits made her better. It was clear that she was not even attempting to fight back. Before we had a chance to make amends she died. Instead of feeling my grief I let anger get in the way. It was at her funeral that I realised that she was also an injured party. The man who had made endless promises to her of a happy life had in fact let her down, and instead of getting herself out of the situation she decided to stay, because she did not want to appear a failure. That was a costly mistake, an error that nearly scarred us for life.

As I poured soil into her grave I decided it was time to heal, bury the past and open a door to the future. It is true that I had a difficult life but I survived and came out the stronger woman that I am today. I am also thankful that I came across people who had faith in me and gave me the strength to rise above the odds. The future looks bright; a dark cloud of uncertainty that has been hanging around us has disappeared. What remains is endless possibilities.

* * *

I am now living my mother's dream of fame and this has made it possible for me to pursue my business aspirations. It is too bad that the only exposure she got is a snippet of her picture in the local paper indicating when she was going to be buried.

Glossary

Amantombazana ase goli - Johannesburg girls
Makoti - Daughter in law
Yebo - Yes
Awuboni ukuthi - Can't you see that
Lentombazana - This girl
Inhlawulo - Money paid by the boy to the family of the girl for making her pregnant outside wedlock
Letha amanzi - Bring the water
Lobola - Bride price

*

Sophie Kedibone Elaine Seku was born on 11 May 1974 in Pimville, Soweto. She matriculated at Immaculata High School, a Roman Catholic School in Diepkloof and graduated from Unisa with a Higher Diploma in Adult Basic Education and Training. She is an Abet Specialist and has done a number of short courses to complement work that she is currently doing as a Mandatory Grants Coordinator. She is currently studying towards a Business Management Diploma.

283

The Itch

Bernard Tabaire

The palm of my left hand itched. I knew I was going to get money. That is if I did not scratch it. Scratching it would send away the good luck. I learnt that from my grandmother when I was growing up in her household. She always said that when her left palm itched, she would get money. It came mostly from her children – my numerous uncles and aunts – who were scattered working in different parts of the country. I also learnt something else from my grandmother. Whenever the lower eyelid of her left eye twitched, she knew trouble was coming, something like a death in the family.

The lower eyelid of my left eye twitched as I walked to the rendezvous. I should have cancelled the appointment. I didn't. Maybe because, at 28 and with a master's degree in journalism, I dismissed reading anything into itching palms and eyelid tics as plain gobbledegook.

I was going to interview a hot new politician about some of his business dealings for a story I was working on for my newspaper. The meeting was partly my idea. Now I wasn't sure whether to go ahead with it. I felt my neck stiffen, my whole body warm up as if it were erupting in a big sweat. The weather had little to do with it. It was seven p.m. and lukewarm – nothing to make me sweat in ordinary circumstances. I was lost in my thoughts as I crossed Nile Avenue, one of Kampala's chic streets with its blue-chip companies and exclusive bars and cafes. Two steps later, I was screaming for mama's help. *Mama!* A green Subaru Legacy had barely missed running over me. The driver's last-second swerve to her right had saved my life. I stood in the middle of the road, hands on my ears for something like two seconds, just enough to recover my composure and cross. The trendy babe at the wheel sped away.

The Majestic Nile Hotel was just across the street. Inside the lobby, I climbed the stairs to the wood-panelled coffee bar on the first floor terrace. Being a weekday, not many people were hanging out unless they were up to some deal-cutting.

The Hon. J.J. Kibira, the newly named junior minister in the vice president's office, was seated in the middle of the coffee bar, clad in a grey pinstripe suit and matching tie. He stood up and pumped my hand as though we were old buddies who played tennis at the swanky Kampala Club. He appeared a couple of inches taller than me. That would put him at 5 feet, 11 inches. He looked like one who uses the dressing mirror with a purpose. Spotless face, well-kept moustache, short hair thinning a little bit, and short, manicured nails. With his lean frame, he would easily pass for a man 10 years younger than his age of 45. I sat down opposite him. I ordered a Guinness and a Coke. He was drinking Smirnoff Ice.

"Young man, this story you are doing about me, where will it take you?" the Hon. J.J., as he was popularly called, said in a tone that did not really demand an answer.

I kept quiet.

"You journalists are also human beings with needs; I see no reason why you should be going after other human beings working hard to live reasonable lives."

I said nothing, trying to figure him out. I like doing that with people I am meeting for the first time. I let them do more of the talking as I examine their words and body language. In that way I can tell with some certainty the person's character. Besides, I find it a nice little game. Because then the other person starts to wonder whether he or she is making sense at all.

The Hon. J.J. reached into his breast pocket for a pack of Sportsman cigarettes and a lighter. "Will you say something?" he said turning his head with the face up to blow the smoke into the roof of the terrace.

"Well," I said, and then my mouth sort of dried up.

That surprised me because even when I interviewed the president, the minister's boss, a year earlier, my mouth kept moist. I didn't reach for a glass of water even once. This time, however, I took a swig of my Coke laced with Guinness. The drink tasted immensely nice. Over the years, that concoction has always glided across my tongue and down my throat, despite sneers from some. "Either you drink a Guinness or a Coke, period," a Nigerian friend chided me once. Obviously, I ignored him.

"Well," I tried again, "I'm just doing my work."

"Oh, I see, just doing your work," the minister said with deliberate slowness. "Tell me, how did you land on this non-existent story?"

"Through a tip."

"What does that mean?"

285

"It means someone tells you there is something that might be interesting to look at and write about because it could serve the public interest," I said trying to put him off getting into the business of having me reveal my sources.

"Serving the public interest; I used to hear a lot of that when I lived in America years ago," he said. "That's all fine, but it cannot be at my expense because I'm an innocent, hardworking man. Anyway, who exactly gave you the tip, my friend?"

"I can't tell you because journalistic ethics demand that I protect the identity of my sources."

We looked at each other for several seconds, saying nothing. I thought he was thinking that I was a misguided little journalist full of self-importance, and shit too. Whatever he thought of me, I actually had a story that if published would very likely damage his political career. But maybe not.

Take the Hon. W. Kalungi. Parliament censured him because as the minister of culture and community development, he had eaten billions of shillings meant for building and equipping public libraries in all of Uganda's 56 districts. He lost his position in the cabinet. But three years later he bounced back as the minister of national planning, a powerful portfolio given that the country was embarking on a massive economic recovery programme. The public indignation the appointment raised did nothing to change the mind of the appointing authority. Let alone the Hon. Kalungi's own mind.

As for the Hon. J.J., he had simply refused to pay taxes worth 200 million shillings on his car import business since he became a minister two years earlier. He had connived with some tax people to defraud the government. After all he was a minister, and no longer a mere businessman. In fact, even when he was just a businessman, the Hon. J.J. used to evade and avoid tax through such practices as under-declaration of goods. Even when he was investigated, nothing would be done to punish him and recover the money government had lost. He had godfathers high up in government, people to whose political campaigns he had donated sackfuls of cash. Now that he was both businessman and politician, the Hon. J.J. knew he had indeed arrived, as they say in the lingo here. Besides, his party, the ruling party, considered him quite a catch. He had great organisational skills, which were strengthened by occasional flashes of fine oratory. In his campaign for parliament three years ago, all of his skills, and a tidy sum of cash, were on display as he marched on to trounce a senior opposition politician to wrest the seat his opponent had held for 25 years. He now felt untouchable or *unbwoggable* as they say in Kenya.

I had an entire dossier, and this one was neither dodgy nor sexed-up, from a police detective who had helped investigate the matter for a special anti-corruption unit based at the presidential palace. The dossier was six months old but nothing had been done to punish the Hon. J.J.

I had talked to several people based on my understanding of the contents of the dossier. But then I needed to interview the honourable minister in person, to give him a chance to state his side of the story. We had a couple of conversations on the telephone. He denied it all saying it was his political opponents going after him. Sounded familiar. Most politicians in Kampala will say political opponents are behind their troubles, even when those troubles are domestic. Even if there were one scheming politician in the picture, the one who feels wronged will talk of opponents. They prefer the plural opponents to the singular because that creates a sense that there are so many bad people lurking about who do not wish them well.

"Which political opponents?" I had asked during those phone interviews.

"I don't want to make matters worse by naming them."

Excuse me! I almost shot back from my end of the line.

He eyeballed me. Not unlike my grandmother when I was about five and had done something decidedly annoying such as asking a visitor when he would leave.

"I am suggesting that you drop the story, young man."

There was something more than the junior minister's paternalistic tone that unsettled me. I looked down at my glass. I put it up to my mouth but could not drink anything. I then looked in the distance, across Nile Avenue. My eye rested on a rather chunky woman of the night. She looked particularly light-skinned. It could have been because of the effect of the streetlight under which she stood soliciting. She sported a black micro-mini dress. I felt like leaving my table, going over and picking her up for some steamy sex. I am told the women of the night can blow a man's mind. It was a strange feeling under the circumstances. I wasn't sure what to do with this new itch.

"Why should I drop the story, sir?" I said. "Just give me your side of the story, and because you say you are innocent, there should be no problem publishing."

"Spare me that journalistic bullshit. I will make you a deal, but your choice, as a responsible journalist and citizen, should be pretty obvious."

My left palm itched. I refused to notice. But I noticed something else. The phrase 'responsible journalist and citizen'. It was ironic, as I would discover in a moment.

My tablemate reached under his jacket and pulled out an envelope. He put it on the table. It was a thick white envelope. He pushed it to my side of the table.

"There, take that fifteen million shillings and leave me alone." He spoke so calmly that I was as disgusted as I was impressed by his cockiness.

Just before I told him to sprint to hell, he said: "It's the money or your life."

I took another needful swig of my drink. My mind came alive. If I took the money and was caught, what would all those people who know me say? What would my colleagues say? What would my younger aunt, who thinks I am still the little, innocent boy she baby-sat, say? I was sure my American journalism professor would die a bit if he heard that I was practising what he called cash-box journalism. In any case, taking the money to kill a story is as cardinal a sin in journalism as is making up quotes.

But I had responsibilities from which I could not simply walk away. I was paying fees for two nieces in secondary school. Their parents had died of AIDS within a year of each other. Their mother was my big sister, my only sibling. The girls were excelling. So I had to try hard to find the money to keep them in school. Then there was the string of relatives wanting cash for this and that all the time. Plus my girlfriend. Shakila, a final-year food science student at Makerere University, was stunning and demanding. She dreamt of fine gifts, movies and restaurants almost all the time. I tried to make her dreams come true within the limits of my journalist's cartoon paycheque. I just never had the courage to say, hey baby, slow down, slow down. I felt I needed to impress her all the time lest she walked out. I could not imagine her in another man's long, hairy arms. She was my own Cleopatra who quoted Okot p'Bitek and Jack Mapanje and Chris Okigbo and Emily Dickinson for the heck of it. Edward Said, Frantz Fanon or Stephen Hawking were common fare. Her company always juiced up my intellect. I was even thinking of marriage a year after she finished school. By that time we would have dated for four years.

288

But marriage comes with some strings attached. For instance one needs a nice house in which to start and raise a family. After six years in journalism, I was under immense pressure from relatives and friends to leave my one-bedroom flat and move into a three or four-bedroom bungalow, preferably one that I built, just like several of the people with whom I went to university were doing. It did not matter the job one had. You just had to drive an expensive European car. Japanese cars were way too many on Kampala streets to be status symbols anymore. You also had to be living in the right neighbourhood. Mbuya, Lake View in Luzira or Ntinda Minister's Village. One lawyer friend was first deregistered by the Law Council and then jailed for defrauding a number of his clients of tens of millions of shillings. He used the money to buy a Lake View house on the shores of Lake Victoria. The house was sold to recover the money. As for me, I had recently bought a plot of land outside the city that needed to be developed. But I was stuck. I did not have the money to start construction. I was servicing a car loan of eighteen million shillings. I had bought a Mitsubishi Pajero – short chassis. It was a Japanese car, but I did not mind much for now. With all of that going on, I realised I had to choose. I took the money.

No sooner had I pocketed it than I felt a tap on my right shoulder. I turned my head, and then stood. Behind me were two men, both towering over my 5-foot, 9-inch frame and both broad-shouldered. Their identical attire of tight white T-shirts, tight blue jeans trousers and black military boots made the men look all the more terrifying.

"You are under arrest," the shorter one, the same one who had tapped my shoulder, announced in a flat voice.

I looked the Hon. J.J. in the face. He appeared unbothered, pulling at his cigarette and now enjoying a double-shot of Black Label whisky. I held back tears.

"Son of a bitch," I muttered under my breath.

The men identified themselves. They were from the presidential anti-graft squad. They asked me to give them the money, which I handed over without a word of protest. They have powers to arrest. Sting operation, I told myself as the men led me away. They took me to the Central Police Station cells. My cell was so small that the walls were an arm's length away from the middle. That is how come when they pushed me inside the pitch-dark room, I landed on someone in the corner as a dull stench hit me back. The inmate grunted on impact. And then yelled in a high-pitched voice, "Why do you hit me?

Why do you hit me?" He kept quiet, and it seemed as if he quickly fell asleep.

I retreated to a corner and huddled myself up for warmth and thought. But I was too dazed to think clearly. The yelling and banging of metal somewhere near my cell suddenly cleared my mind.

I notice my inmate is snoring. I hate snores. But I ignore that. Reality is dawning on me. For all I know, my ambition of being the number one investigative journalist in the country is dead. *Kaput! Kabisa!* There is no way my career will survive after the story of my arrest is told.

"Aha, you see, they are also corrupt even though they like writing about other people's shortcomings," I can hear a concerned member of the public say.

"It's as if they are not human," another one says.

"They like posturing, taking holier-than-thou positions, now they have been caught in the act," yet another concerned citizen chimes in. "*Bano temuli!*"

"Yeah, I told you these journalists also eat bribes," the first speaker adds. "In fact everybody in Uganda is corrupt. We all eat bribes when chance allows."

"We do," another reaffirms. "I don't even understand why that guy is in. *Gayi bamutte.* Anyway, they are going to release him on police bond and he will be a free man tomorrow."

"A corrupt free man," another jumps in laughing at his own little phrase. "But these journalists. They also overestimate themselves. You can't tackle J.J. and think you will survive. He will pull out your nails. He is a smooth operator. It is even said that he killed a business rival in broad daylight and nothing happened to him."

Huddled inside my cell imagining that conversation on a city street corner caused me real pain. As I raised my hand to feel my aching neck, my eyelid twitched. I smiled despite myself. It reminded me of my grandmother. My 85-year-old grandmother. If I had paid heed to the old woman's interpretation of twitching eyelids, I would have cancelled that appointment. Now I would be sleeping at home in my queen-size bed, possibly dreaming of how to use journalism to change the world for the better. I had paid heed to the itching left palm. The promise of trouble and the promise of money. I went for the money. Now I hated even thinking what that old woman would say when she heard that I was in the cells for bad behaviour. She spent a lot of her time taking me to church every Sunday morning hoping I would turn out just fine. I had been her responsibility, helped on by my aunt, since my parents died in a car crash when I was two. When I grew up and came to the city, my grandmother always told me, I should remain honest and humble and when the time came, I would have to go back to the village to pick a bride. She was willing to help in this vital matter, by way of identifying a good, marriageable girl for me. She told me city girls were not to be trusted. They were jumpy and they would give me *silimu* – her word for AIDS. Now here I was buried in the basement of the Central Police Station, alone and frightened as Philly Bongoley Lutaya sung.

My thoughts were interrupted when I heard someone opening the door to my cell – inserting the key into a padlock. I had not heard any approaching footsteps. Were they wearing rubber boots, I wondered. When the huge steel door was flung open, some light from down the corridor revealed four figures – four men. I saw them from a tight angle as I sat crouching, stuck to the cold wall in my corner. I sighed and braced myself. I feared that they had come for me. I visualised myself being taken to some of the torture chambers dotting the city. Safe houses, they euphemistically called them. Stories abounded about people who had been picked up in the middle of the night, blindfolded and taken from cell to cell around the city, ending up in safe houses run by military intelligence. I know a guy, a doctor, who was taken to a safe house after torture stints in three different cells in the same night. He was tortured for four straight nights in a safe house and then released without a charge. He was immediately hospitalised. Some said he had been collaborating with rebels. Others said he had shagged one of the mistresses of a senior military intelligence official, who was now getting back at him. The doctor has never said a thing about the circumstances leading up to his detention and torture. So I didn't know what to believe. All the same I was sure it was my turn to suffer a broken nose or drink weeks' old urine or both and worse. The punishments varied, I'm told, depending on the mood of the punishing officer.

A heavy kick to my right shoulder brought me back to earth. I turned and was met with a blinding torchlight. I blinked. Both the upper and lower eyelids of my left eye twitched rapidly. I felt twitches and muscle spasms all over my cold body. I was literally vibrating.

"Hey, little journalist," a voice that was unmistakably the Hon. J.J.'s announced. "Get up."

I stood and was shoved out of the cell. I stumbled at the doorway but steadied myself fast enough. My cellmate remained behind. They locked up the place. In the dimly-lit corridor, I noticed that the men who had arrested me and a uniformed policeman had accompanied the junior minister.

"You are free," the Hon. J.J. announced as we entered the reception area of the police station. "I hope you've learnt something; idiot."

I walked on. I tried to look at my watch. It was gone. My cell phone too. And I had neither the big story nor the big money. The twitch had triumphed over the itch. I didn't much care. I still had my wallet. Down at Constitution Square, the city clock read three a.m. I jumped into a taxi and sped home.

*

Bernard Tabaire is a journalist working for the *Monitor* newspaper in Kampala. He attended school in Uganda and the United States. He hopes the Caine Prize administrators will invite him to every African Writers' Workshop to do more of the eating and drinking while writing on the side. But he is concerned that his hopes may be dashed.

The Lie

Veronique Tadjo

The mother was locked up in her lie, a lie so big it engulfed her, it kept her captive in a cell so narrow she could hardly move. She constantly had to shift her weight, think of other ways to keep up the pretence. She made sure she never looked back but always fixed her eyes on the present, not on the future because it was too far, too uncertain. She felt trapped yet she couldn't free herself, caught in her own words, her back to the wall. She was scared that she might find herself naked, vulnerable, her mask removed abruptly and her lie exposed for everybody to see. She was eaten from inside, weighted down by her secret. She had done it herself and could not blame anybody else for the fact that she had lost her daughter. Eve was gone out of her life. Forever. A wall had been erected between them and there was no means to pull it down.

In the early years, when Eve was still a toddler, she had grabbed her love, secured it firmly in her hand, determined never to let go of it. She thought she had succeeded so well, there was little left for anybody else to take. Just crumbs. She felt it was her prerogative as a mother, her natural right to take over her child's life. Yet she had always known deep inside that it would not work forever. It was untenable, really, even though she remained bent on making it last as long as possible. She had invested so much in Eve, given her so much of her attention, she could only be the centre of her life.

But as the years went on, she realised that she had weaved a web so tight, only rebellion could free the girl from her embrace. She often wondered how long she would be able to continue like that, how long she would be able to prevent Eve from leaving her.

Then, on her thirteenth birthday, Eve got up in the morning, washed her face, combed her hair, walked down the stairs to her mother and demanded her liberty. She said she was ready to cut off the umbilical cord once and for all. She was ready to do anything to free herself. And she added with a threatening tone in her voice:

"I am your daughter and I look like you, but I don't want to be one with you. I don't want you anymore."

293

The mother was so shocked when she heard those words that she went on a rampage. She started destroying everything around her. She became mad with pain, drunk with bitterness. She broke the mirror of their former life together, shattered it to pieces. And in another show of anger, she yelled at her daughter, fist raised in the air:

"Why are you doing this to me?"

Eve never gave her an answer. She had found a path out of her home and there was no turning back. She wanted to run through the fields. She wanted to learn about life on her own, discover its many facets for herself.

The mother became more and more resentful as the years went on. Her daughter was growing too fast. She was turning into a young woman, a stranger. She did not know how to take this new person.

So, when the time came to prove her love for her daughter, when Eve really needed her help, when she asked for it, the mother was simply not there. She refused to do anything to comfort the young girl.

She found Eve in tears, miserable and distraught, clearly in distress, but did nothing. She just said coldly, insisting on each word:

"Let nobody know what happened, do you understand? Your father must never learn about this."

It was to become an unspeakable truth, a revelation not to be made. In exchange, she would leave her daughter alone and she would work at avoiding any scandal. There was no question of calling it 'rape'. That just didn't happen. Not to her daughter. Not in her own house. Not with that cousin of hers. What was she supposed to do? Call a family meeting and break the news that cousin George forced himself on Eve? How did that make her look like as a mother? Wasn't she at home when it happened? Didn't she notice anything? Hear anything? She could imagine the questions firing at her.

She just told her daughter to get a grip on herself.

After that, they never talked about it again.

From then on, the mother had to live with the lie. She had to pretend there was nothing wrong. She believed that if her daughter had remained close to her, none of this would have taken place.

She watched Eve for signs. For which signs? She was not sure.

Eve was the shadow of her old self. She barely uttered a word any more. She was withdrawn, so far removed, she had become invisible. Not so much invisible as absent. Totally absent.

Eve thought of all the stories she had read in the newspaper, day after day, too often. Young girls being raped on the way to school, women being kidnapped, babies being...babies? Her mind caved in.

Her face had acquired an infinite sadness. Lost in the semi-darkness of her universe, her eyes were like little sunken stars. Her full lips looked as if they were ready to suck on life, yet they remained tightly closed. Her skin was like black velvet, yet it was not appealing. Beauty had touched her and then, had evaded her.

Eve was afraid for her own life.

She kept saying to herself:

"I shall fly away from my mind, go to a place where time is irrelevant. I'll find peace in a sacred forest peopled by protective ancestors and kind spirits. I do not want to inhabit this world any more."

Eve did not let anybody approach her. She simply hated herself too much. She was dirty. She was worthless. Her body was a mass of flesh filled with blood. It was cumbersome, grounding her in ugliness. She much preferred being in the wind, listening to the clouds humming their songs. She was much more at ease under water, floating among seaweeds and anemones. She was much more satisfied, swallowing water and slowly drifting down to the bottom of the sea.

She wanted to stay there forever, but they came to fish her out as if she couldn't choose for herself. It was so beautiful, the light breaking through the water. It was a perfect resting place. Instead, she was forcibly retrieved from the water and a man gave her mouth-to-mouth resuscitation. She had ended up in the hospital, lying on a bed in a bare and cold room. She would stare at the ceiling, not knowing what to do with herself. This man who prevented her from killing herself, was he now going to help her salvage her life? What good was it to be alive?

She much preferred walking alone through the city, hiding in overcrowded areas, spending time among strangers, anonymous to all. Somebody with no name, no identity, just walking in this big place. Yes, what good was it to be alive when she had already left all of them anyway?

It was not so much about the rape. She had shut herself off during the whole process. In fact, she had felt almost nothing, just the weight of her cousin crushing her and his heavy breath blowing in her face. It was about destruction, about shattering the self. She had no other dream to replace the one she had lost that day. Someone had taken her body away from her. There was no point holding on to it. It was damaged, broken, soiled. She did not care for it anymore.

Eve vaguely remembered a time when love surrounded her. She would look up at a face smiling at her, a face that had always been there, from the moment she took her first breath. She remembered a bond so strong it carried her through life. She was going to be protected, taken by the hand to cross bridges and walk along the difficult paths. She was going to be all right.

Now, she decided she would have to try something else: tablets, chemicals, petrol, anything, it did not really matter, it was all the same for her. Of course, she would prefer to avoid any suffering but if there was no other way, then let it be. She would think about it all the time. The choice she could still make, the only thing that she still owned: her death. It was just a question of logistics. She would do it one day and, this time, nobody would be able to stop her.

On a bright afternoon at the park, he came to her. She did not notice him at first until he was standing next to her, casting a shadow on the grass. It was his voice that woke her up from her reverie although it seemed to originate from far away, filtering through the many sounds of the garden where she had sought some respite: birds singing, children sending peals of laughter, dogs barking and the soft lullaby of a fountain. It compelled her to look up at him. And when she laid her eyes on him, she immediately recognised herself. He was exactly like her. Exactly like she had thought he would be.

She asked: "Who are you?"

And he replied: "I am what you are looking for."

"How could that be?" she continued.

"I can give you what you want. I believe in the sun even when it is not shining. I believe in its light even when it has disappeared."

She nodded her head, smiled at him and got up. Then they walked away hand in hand. The book she had been reading a while ago lay open on the grass, disregarded. They looked at everything along the road, talked about almost everything and still they wanted to say more. He told her how he liked living in the city because of its vastness, its many possibilities. He felt at ease in it. It seemed to care for him. She was afraid of the city, she confessed. Too much evil lurking under the surface. Too much anger in the streets that seemed to propagate fear. It bothered her that the city was still bearing the marks of the past. She saw the dilapidated buildings, the dirt, the noise and the crime as proof that cities were unnatural spaces. But she was ready to think differently, she added. She was ready to overcome her dislike. If he showed her another side to it, she would try to like it too.

They went to his room perched on a hill and lay down on his narrow bed. He had lit some incense. The strong perfume went to her head, filling her with a sense of tranquility and happiness as they held on to each other. They rolled on the covers, played childish games with each other, inspected their bodies:

"And what is this dark spot on your shoulder?" she asked.

"Oh that's just a birth mark," he replied.

"And you, why do you have this scar on your chin?" he inquired.

"I got it when I was a child. I was on a seesaw swing with somebody far heavier than me. My friend landed too hard on the ground. I lunged forward and hit my chin on the handle. I bled a lot. I had five stitches."

He looked more closely at the scar. "It must have hurt," he said softly.

Then they did not speak for a while.

"Can I stay with you, here?" she ventured. "Would you like me to? I promise I won't take too much space."

But the silence continued. Embarrassment was now creeping up on her. Had she been too straightforward? She looked at him again and was surprised to find out that he was crying quietly. He was holding her tightly as he cried. He whispered:

"I am sorry. I cannot give you all that you want. My body doesn't belong to me any more. It has been taken away by sickness."

Then she understood why she had come to him so readily, why she had felt so unconditionally close to him. He was a man deprived of his wholeness, a man whose body had been snatched up by a force bigger than him, a force that had taken over his life and left little room for him. He was not able to stop this devastation. It left him weak, deprived of strength until gradually, one day, nothing would remain of him.

But she said:

"Come, I do not fear your sickness. We can still be together. We can still find a way to call on life."

So, they left the confines of his bachelor flat and went to the biggest hospital in the largest township of this most populated city: Baragwanath hospital towering over Soweto.

An eclectic group of people was guarding its entrance. There were beggars, layabout characters, snotty-nosed kids, street sellers and sick-looking men and women, all mingling as if in a market place. A taxi rank exhibited a long queue of cars. Passengers got off the vehicles while others boarded them. It seemed as if the whole of humanity was waiting at its door.

Somebody showed them the way to the elevator. It was old and rusty, some of the buttons missing. The clinic was on the last floor. The last floor...Maybe the young man would be taken on. Maybe they would be told how to live with this thing. Maybe the drugs would be there, waiting for him. The right tablets, the right cocktail, given at the right time. All that had been out of reach for so long. He was dying, he knew it but up until now, up until Eve, he had thought that it was just his fate: to be singled out in the crowd, touched at random by the hand of death. Oh, he wasn't worse than anybody else, he was convinced of that. He wasn't a better person either. He was just himself and nothing more. Why him, then? He could not find an answer and he suspected there was none.

They sat on a bench, in a corridor full of patients who were waiting for their turn. Some looked really sick, others healthy and out of place in these surroundings. The paint was peeling off the walls. A strong smell of surgical spirit overpowered their senses.

Eve was holding his hand. She did not dare leave his side for fear he would be taken away from her. When the time came, they went into the consulting room together. Eve could feel their future was contained in that one space. The doctor was a short man, wearing the usual white hospital overcoat. Was he God, was he the devil? She asked herself. He had the power to save lives, the power to reverse destinies.

"The drugs have not been tested on human beings yet. This will be the first mass trial. Are you sure you want to take part in this experiment?" asked the doctor. "The risks are high."

The young man looked at Eve for a few seconds before saying yes. "And you, what do you want to do?" the doctor inquired turning to Eve. "Do you know your status?"

"No, but I want to know it. I was...I could have been contaminated."

She gave him her blood. He collected it carefully in a little crystal-clear flask that was to go to the lab. It was thick and of a rich deep-red colour. She wondered what scent it had. While she was watching her blood pouring into the small container, a sentence kept turning round and round in her mind: "Fear leads to the dark side. The dark side leads to suffering."

But she was determined not to let fear overtake her.

Now that they had both entered the same sphere, now that they groped in the same obscurity, she felt a closeness towards him that was stronger than anything else she had known before. They were entering another layer of life, sharing a knowledge foreign to most people. They were conversing with death, negotiating a truce that may or may not be granted to them.

A week after, a letter came from the hospital. A simple white letter. They were having breakfast sitting on the edge of the bed while listening to the news on the radio. A war had erupted in one more corner of the globe. He said:

"We talk of progress all the time, but is it really true? People still kill, maim, torture and commit massacres like in the old days. Tell me, Eve, what has changed? What is so much better in our lives? I just can't see it." Then, he had switched off the radio and gone to the front door to get the mail.

She opened the envelope with remarkably steady hands.

The results were positive.

Was it what she had expected all along? Was it what she had wanted?

She handed the piece of paper to him. He read in silence, then simply folded it and put it away.

She said:

"I have always wished to share this with you. I have always wanted to stay by your side. It is my gift to you. I have nothing and I want everything. We can turn this thing round, turn the pain on its head and defeat the odds."

That very same day, she went back home.

When she entered the courtyard of her family house, she saw that the garden was looking good. The trees were all bearing fruit and the bougainvillea had now completely covered the front wall.

She climbed the stairs and knocked on the door. Her mother was still there. She had grown frail. Her hair had turned grey.

"You can let go of your lie, now." she said to the old woman.

*

Veronique Tadjo is a writer and painter from Ivory Coast. Born in Paris, she grew up in Abidjan where she attended local schools and subsequently became a lecturer at the National University until 1993 when she took up writing full time. She has lived in several countries and is now currently based in Johannesburg. Her latest book, *The Shadow of Imana*, is on the subject of Rwanda and the genocide. She also writes for the youth.

Rules of the Caine Prize

The Prize is awarded annually to a short story by an African writer published in English, whether in Africa or elsewhere. (Indicative length, between 3 000 and 15 000 words.)

'An African writer' is normally taken to mean someone who was born in Africa, or who is a national of an African country, or whose parents are African, and whose work has reflected African sensibilities.

There is a cash prize of $15,000 for the winning author and a travel award for each of the short-listed candidates (up to five in all).

For practical reasons, unpublished work and work in other languages is not eligible. Works translated into English from other languages are not excluded, provided they have been published in translation, and should such a work win, a proportion of the prize would be awarded to the translator.

The award is made in July each year, the deadline for submissions being 31 January. The short-list is selected from work published in the 5 years preceding the submissions deadline and not previously considered for a Caine Prize. Submissions should be made by publishers and will need to be accompanied by twelve original published copies of the work for consideration, sent to the address below. There is no application form.

Every effort is made to publicise the work of the short-listed authors through the broadcast as well as the printed media.

Winning and short-listed authors will be invited to participate in writers' workshops in Africa and elsewhere as resources permit.

The above rules were designed essentially to launch the Caine Prize and may be modified in the light of experience. Their objective is to establish the Caine Prize as a benchmark for excellence in African writing.

For further information, please contact Nick Elam at The Caine Prize for African Writing, 2 Drayson Mews, London W8 4LY.
Telephone +44 (0) 20 7376 0440; Fax +44 (0) 20 7938 3728
e–mail: caineprize@jftaylor.com

Did you enjoy this book?

See a complete list of Jacana titles at
www.jacana.co.za

marketing@jacana.co.za

Jacana Media
PO Box 2004
Houghton
2041